FANN CLUB: BATMAN SQUAD

FANN CLUB: BATMAN SQUAD

BY JIM BENTON

BATMAN created by BOB KANE with BILL FINGER
FANN CLUB created by JIM BENTON

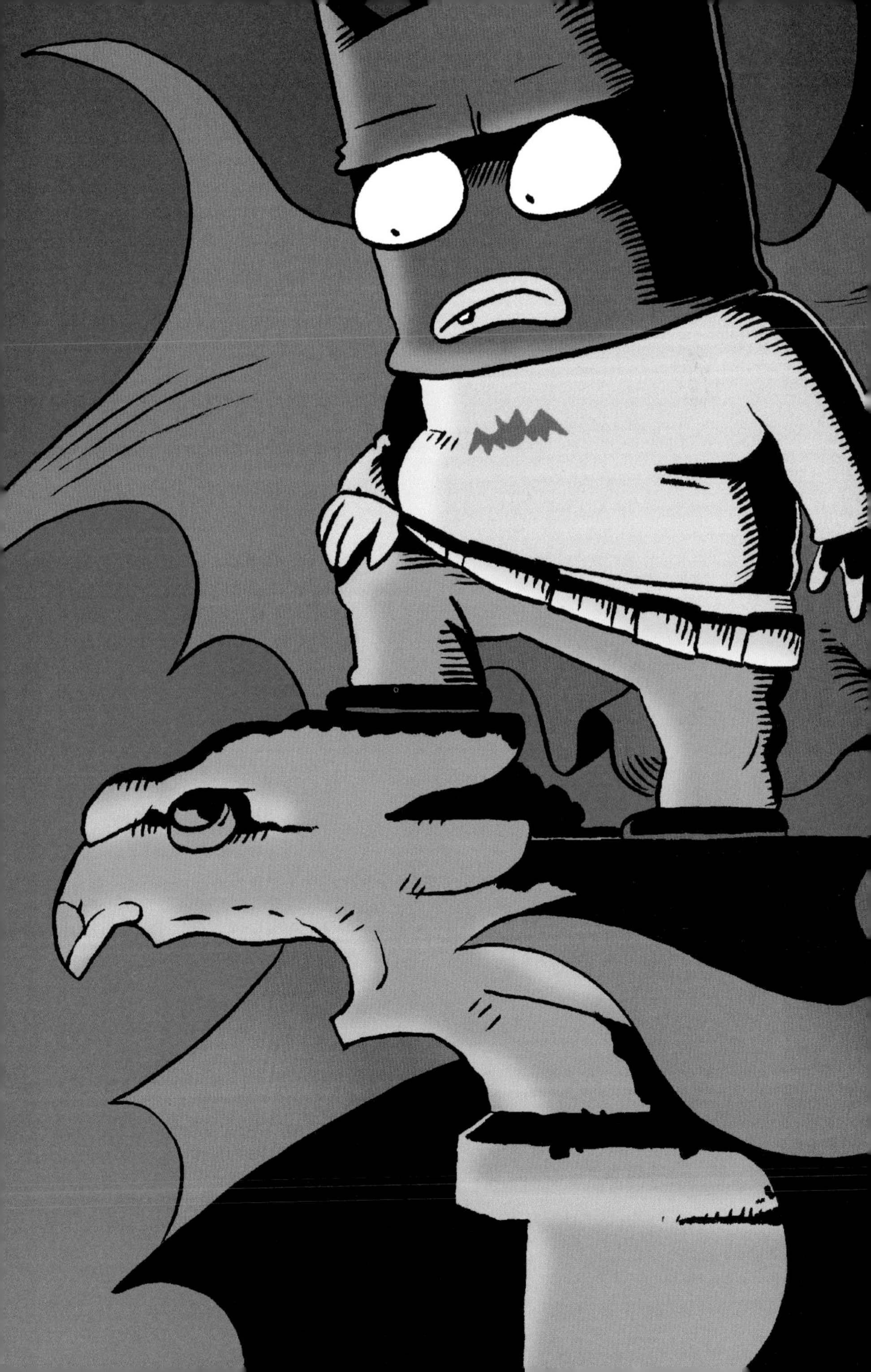

Jim Chadwick Editor
Courtney Jordan Associate Editor
Steve Cook Design Director - Books
Amie Brockway-Metcalf Publication Design
Danielle Ramondelli Publication Production

Marie Javins Editor-in-Chief, DC Comics

Anne DePies Senior VP - General Manager
Jim Lee Publisher & Chief Creative Officer
Don Falletti VP - Manufacturing Operations & Workflow Management
Lawrence Ganem VP - Talent Services
Alison Gill Senior VP - Manufacturing & Operations
Jeffrey Kaufman VP - Editorial Strategy & Programming
Nick J. Napolitano VP - Manufacturing Administration & Design
Nancy Spears VP - Revenue

FANN CLUB: BATMAN SQUAD

DC Comics, 4000 Warner Blvd., Bldg. 700, 2nd Floor, Burbank, CA 91522
Printed by Worzalla, Stevens Point, WI, USA. 4/21/23.
First Printing.
ISBN: 978-1-77950-889-8

Library of Congress Cataloging-in-Publication Data

Names: Benton, Jim, author, illustrator.
Title: Fann club: Batman squad / by Jim Benton.
Description: Burbank, CA : DC Comics, 2023. | Audience: Ages 8-12. | Audience: Grades 4-6. | Summary: Batman fan Ernest Fann takes on the secret persona Gerbilwing and sets up a crime fighting unit with his friends and dog, but things become a little too real when Ernest and his friends visit a bank in the middle of a robbery.
Identifiers: LCCN 2022061485 | ISBN 9781779508898 (trade paperback)
Subjects: CVAC: Graphic novels. | Superheroes--Fiction. | Friendship--Fiction. | LCGFT: Superhero comics. | Graphic novels.
sification: LCC PZ7.7.B453 Fan 2023 | DDC 741.5/973--dc23/eng/20230203
LC record available at https://lccn.loc.gov/2022061485

MIX
Paper from responsible sources
FSC® C002589

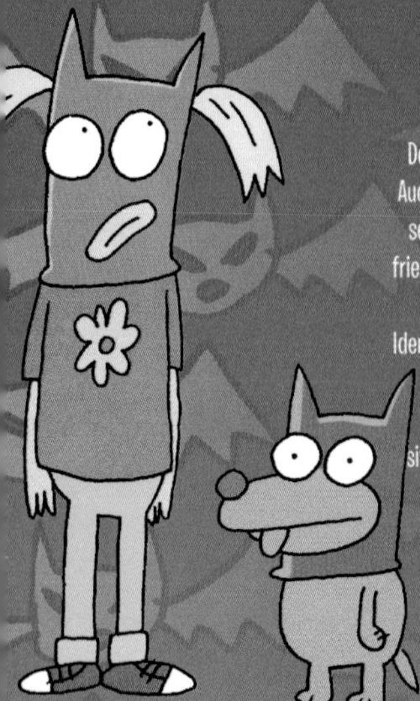

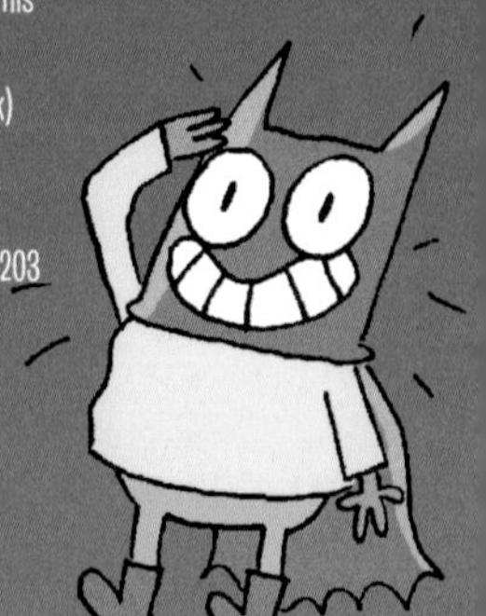

Thanks to Kristen LeClerc.
I couldn't do it without you.
—Jim

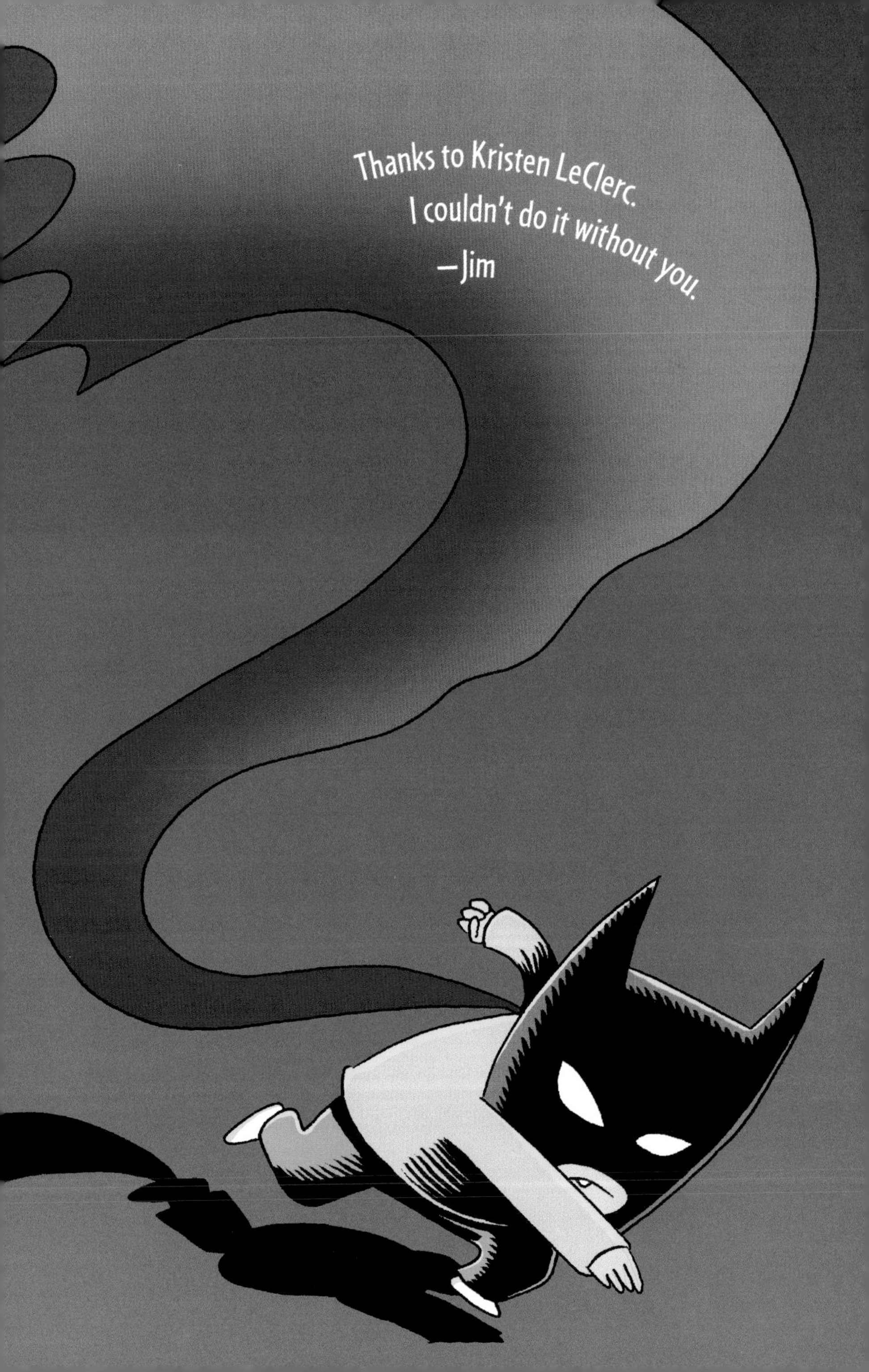

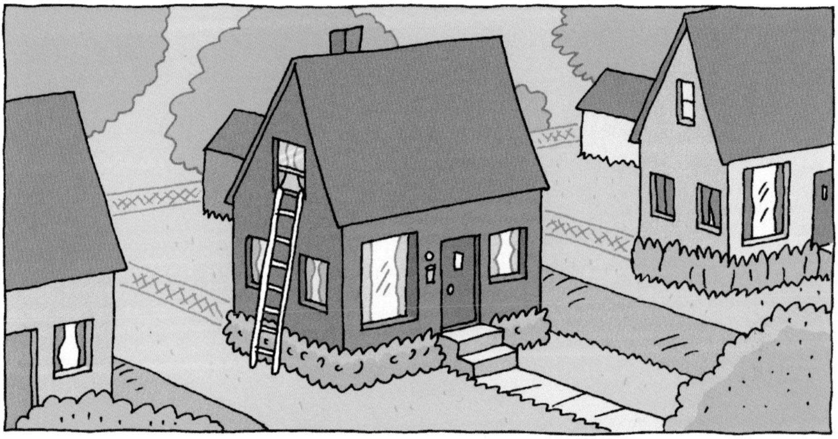

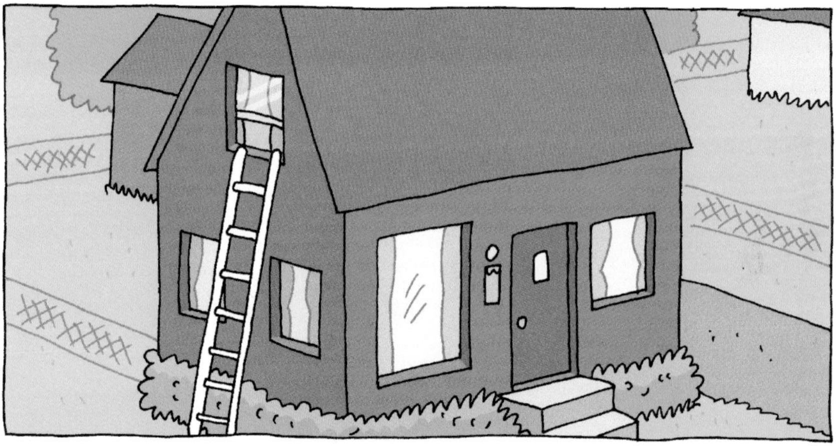

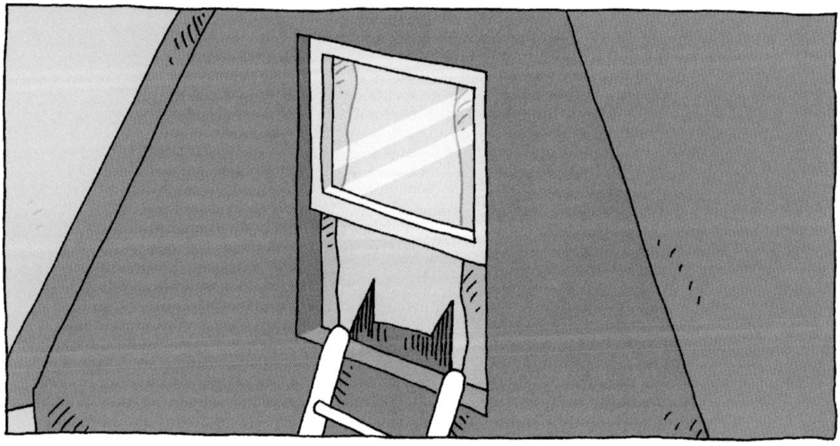

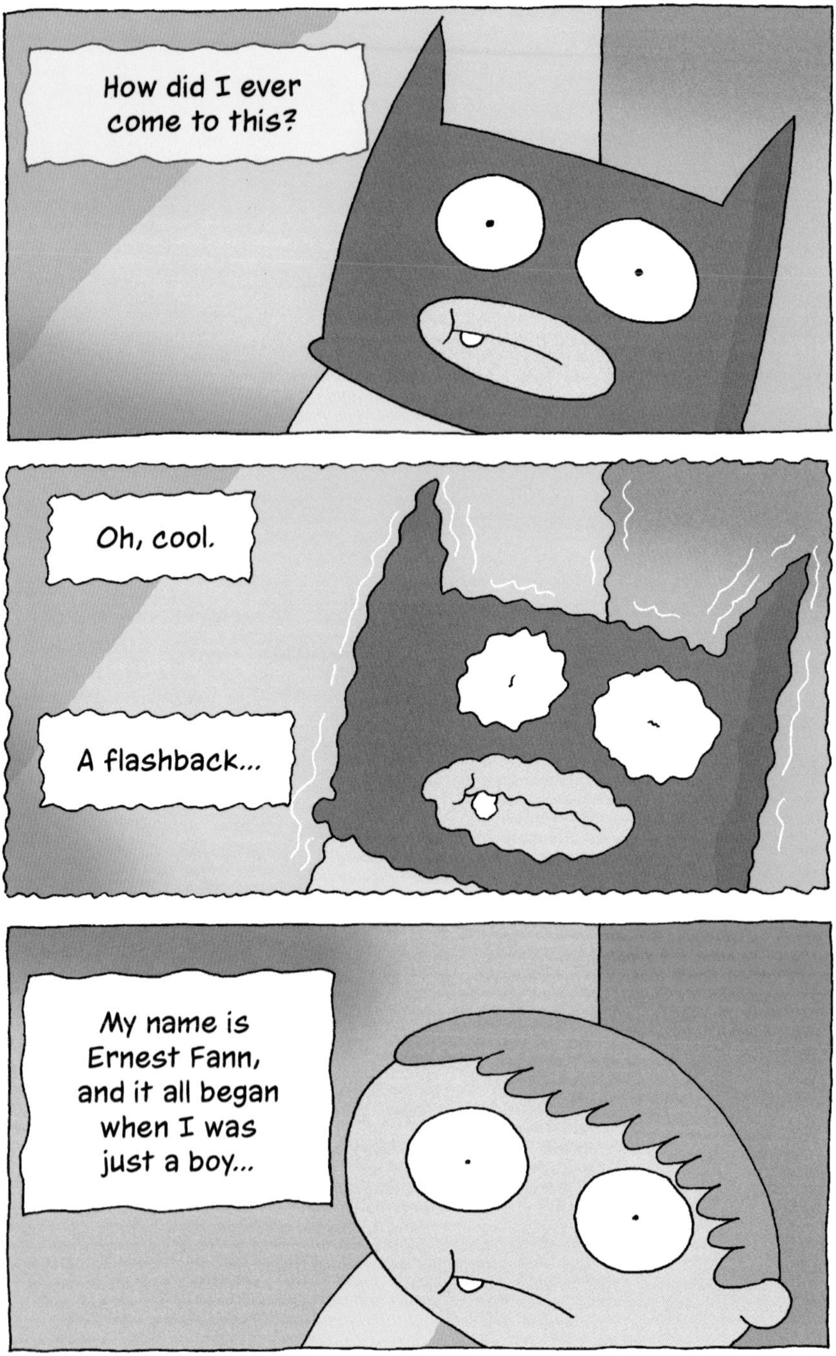
How did I ever come to this?
Oh, cool.
A flashback...
My name is Ernest Fann, and it all began when I was just a boy...

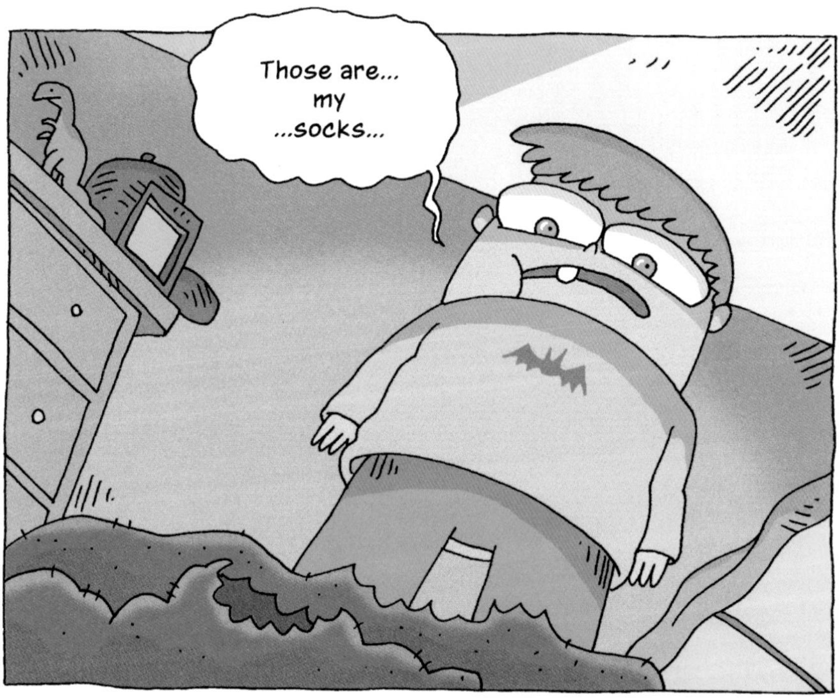
Those are... my ...socks...

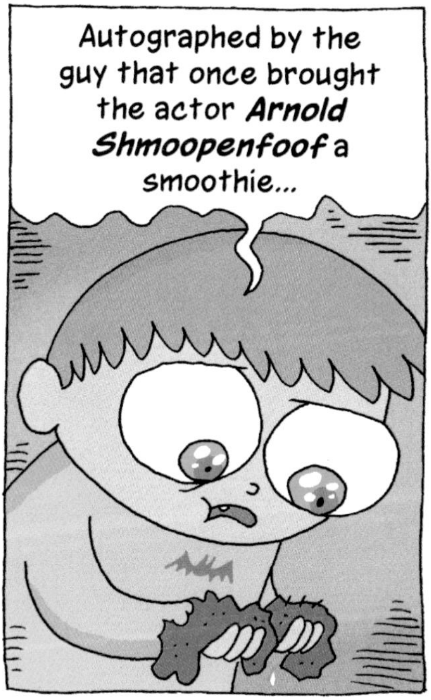
Autographed by the guy that once brought the actor ***Arnold Shmoopenfoof*** a smoothie...

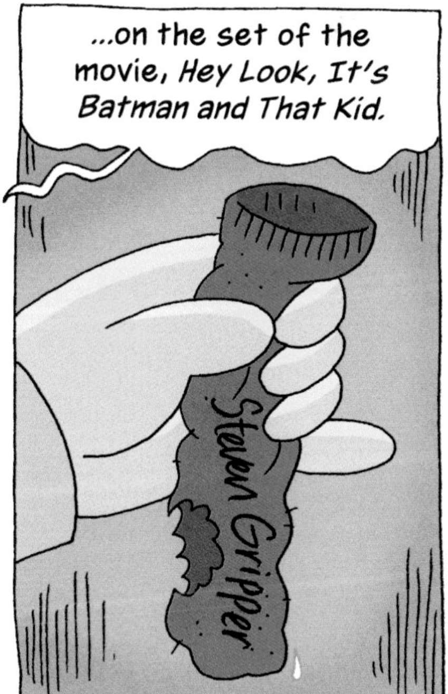
...on the set of the movie, *Hey Look, It's Batman and That Kid.*
Steven Gripper

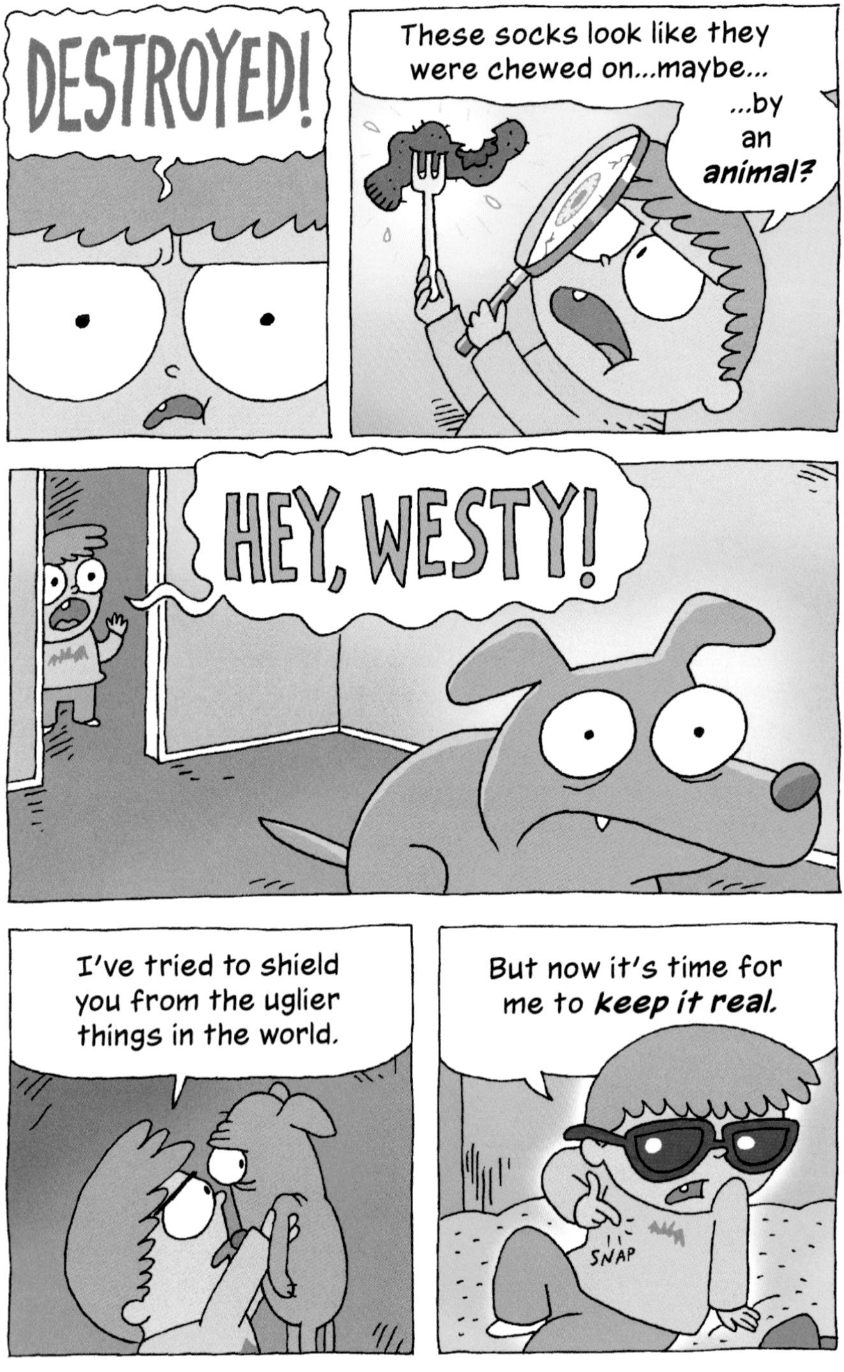
DESTROYED!
These socks look like they were chewed on...maybe...
...by an animal?
HEY, WESTY!
I've tried to shield you from the uglier things in the world.
But now it's time for me to keep it real.
SNAP

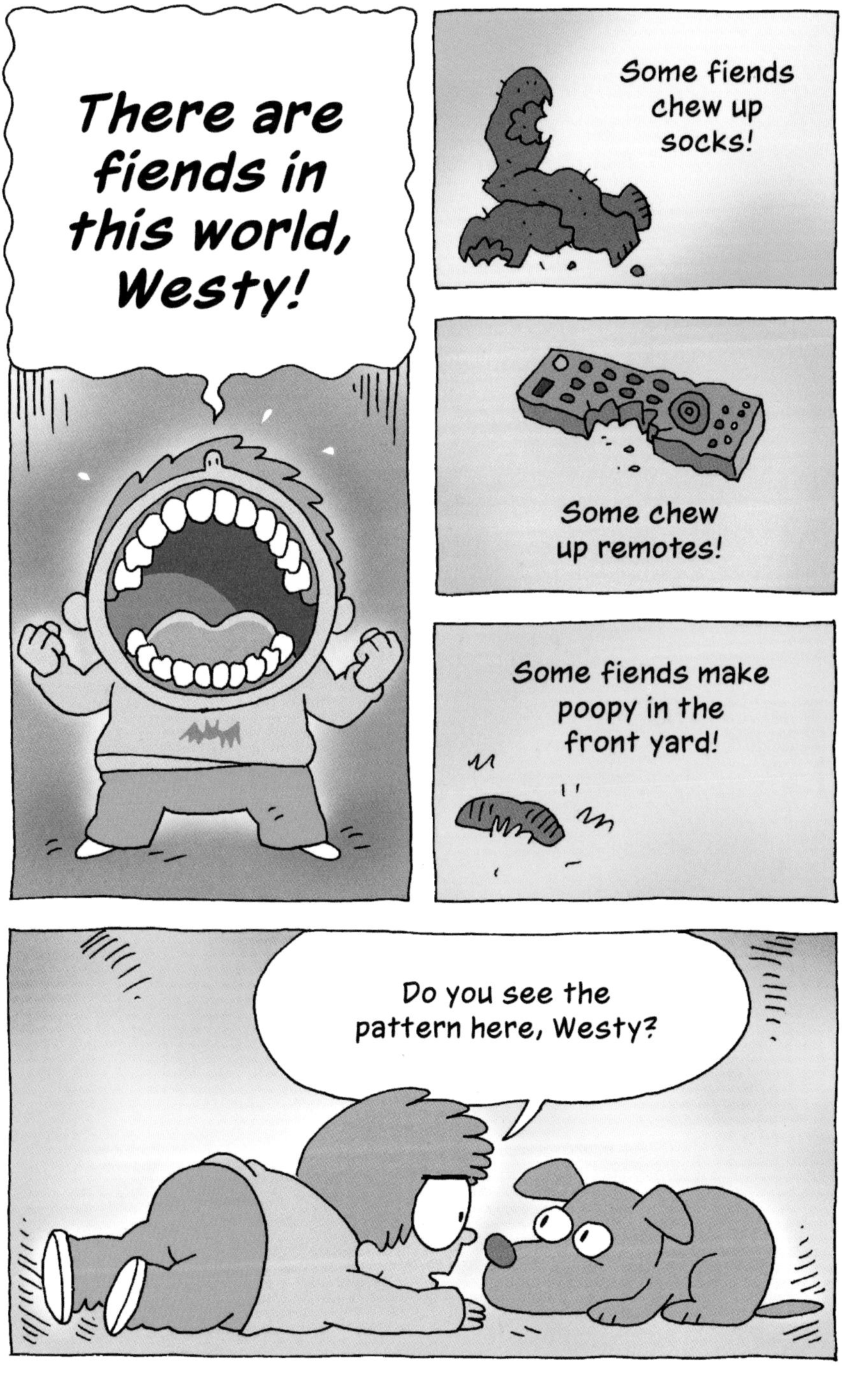
There are fiends in this world, Westy!
Some fiends chew up socks!
Some chew up remotes!
Some fiends make poopy in the front yard!
Do you see the pattern here, Westy?

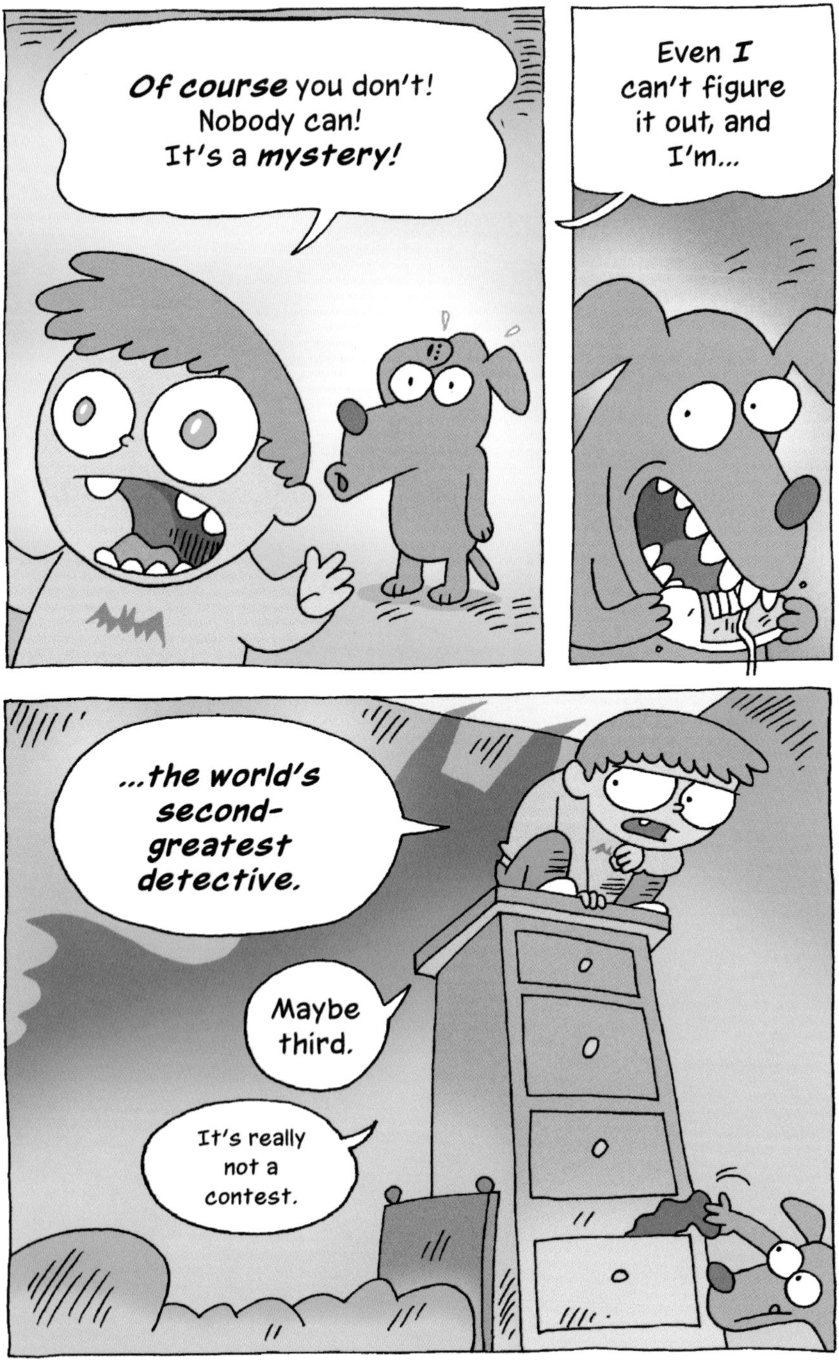

Of course you don't! Nobody can! It's a mystery!
Even I can't figure it out, and I'm...
...the world's second-greatest detective.
Maybe third.
It's really not a contest.

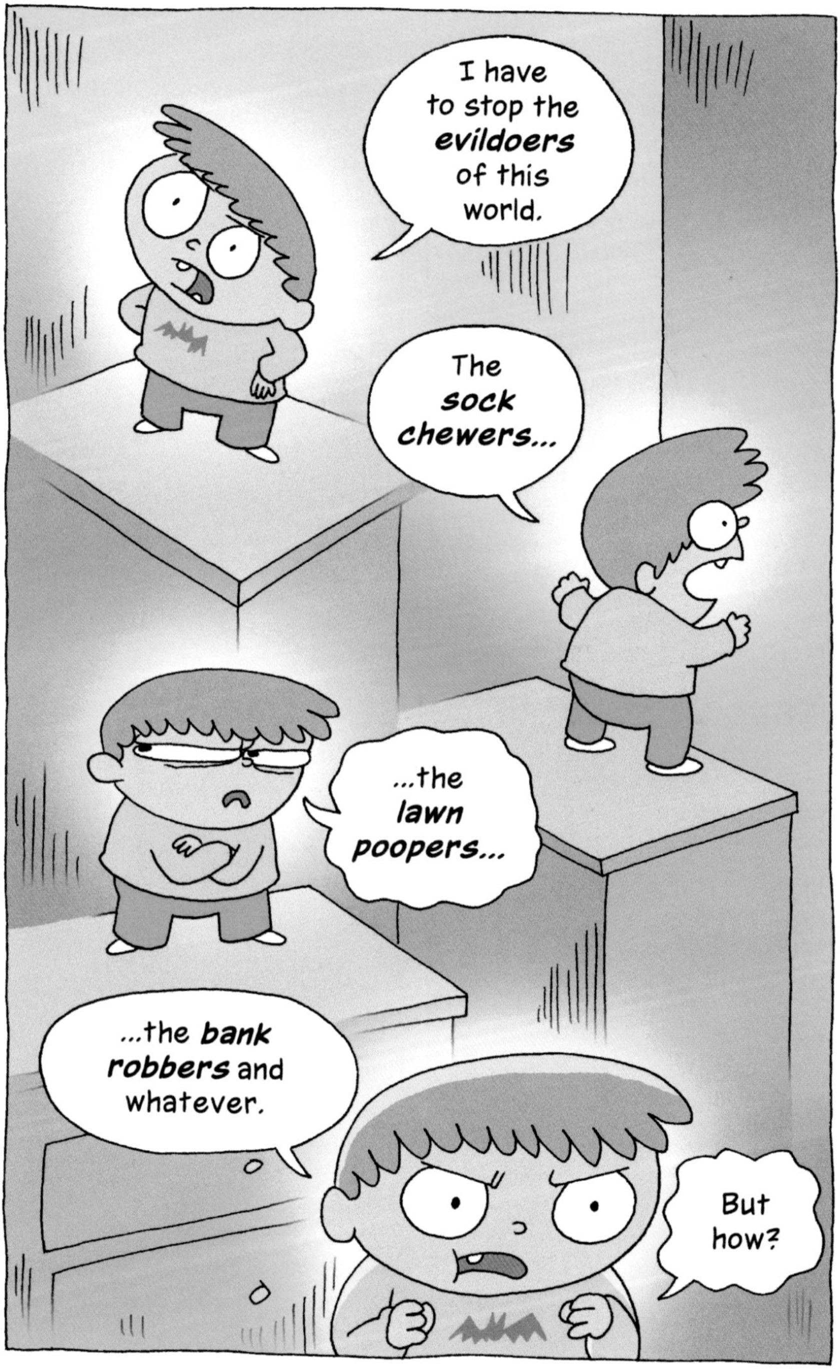
I have to stop the evildoers of this world.
The sock chewers...
...the lawn poopers...
...the bank robbers and whatever.
But how?

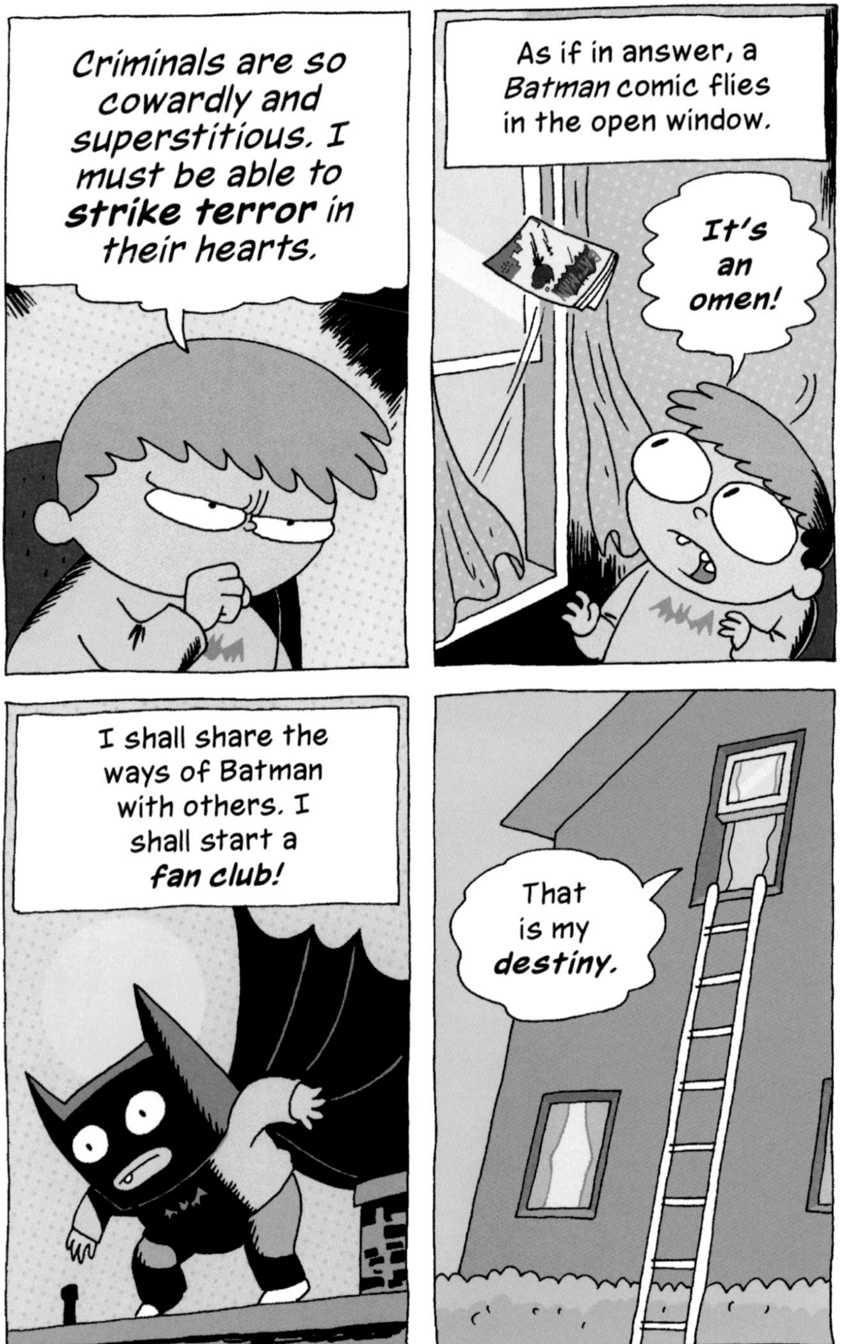
Criminals are so cowardly and superstitious. I must be able to **strike terror** in their hearts.
As if in answer, a *Batman* comic flies in the open window.
It's an omen!
I shall share the ways of Batman with others. I shall start a *fan club!*
That is my *destiny.*

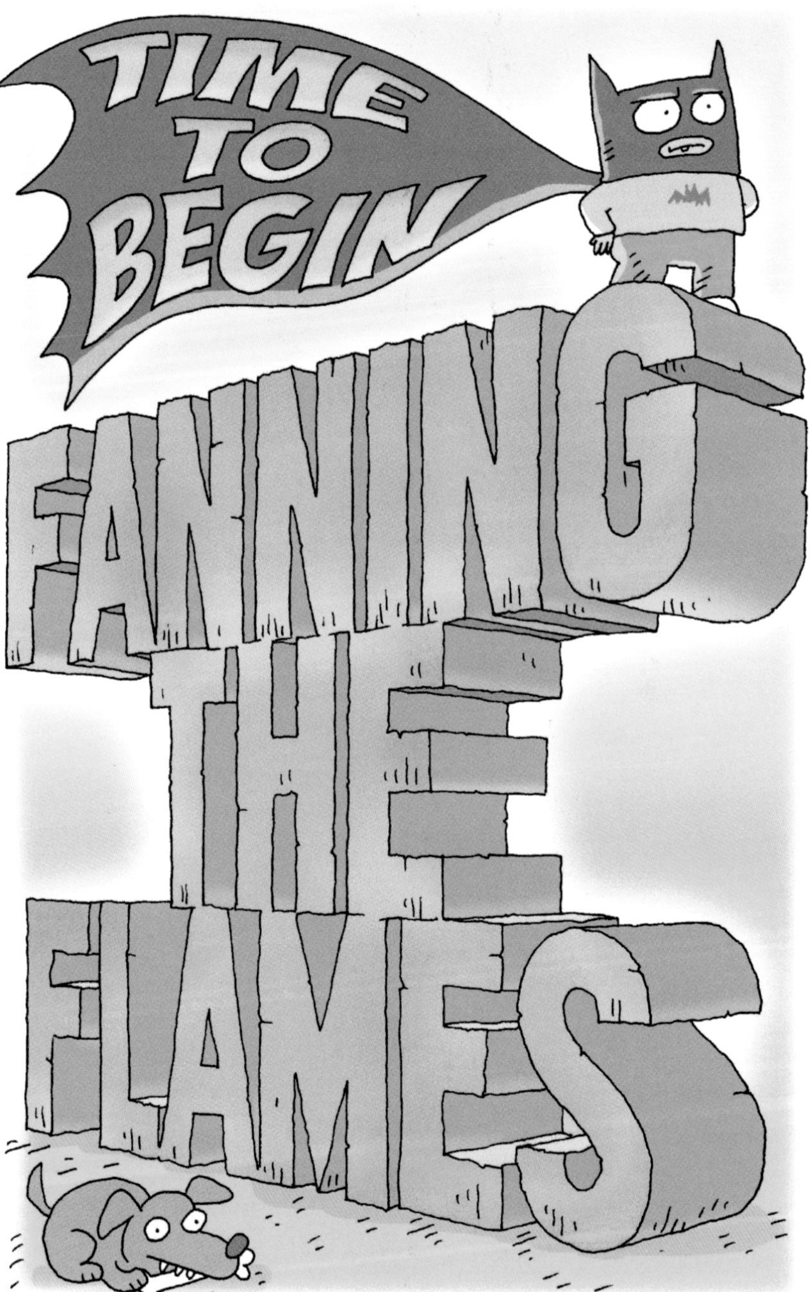
TIME TO BEGIN
FANNING THE FLAMES

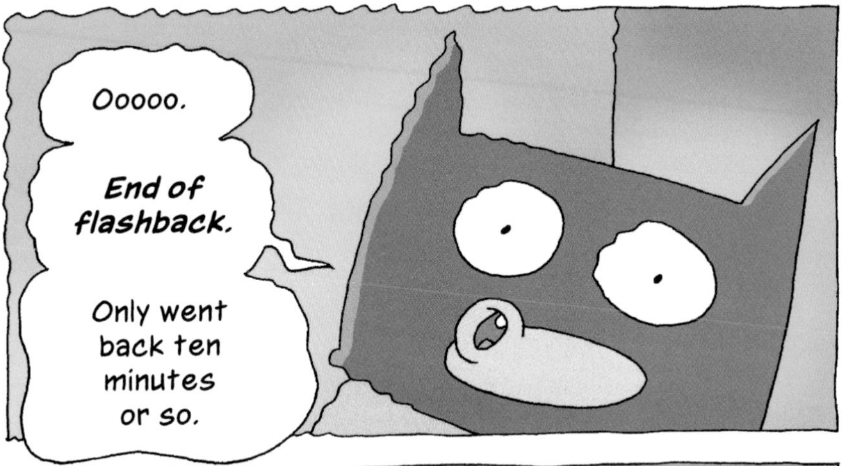
Ooooo.
End of flashback.
Only went back ten minutes or so.

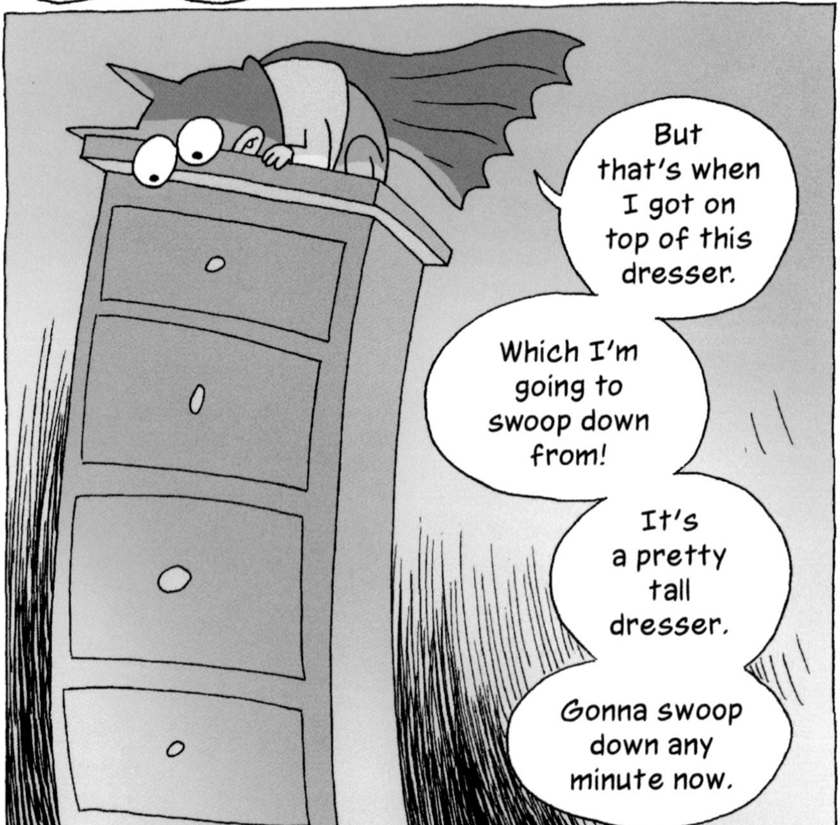
But that's when I got on top of this dresser.
Which I'm going to swoop down from!
It's a pretty tall dresser.
Gonna swoop down any minute now.

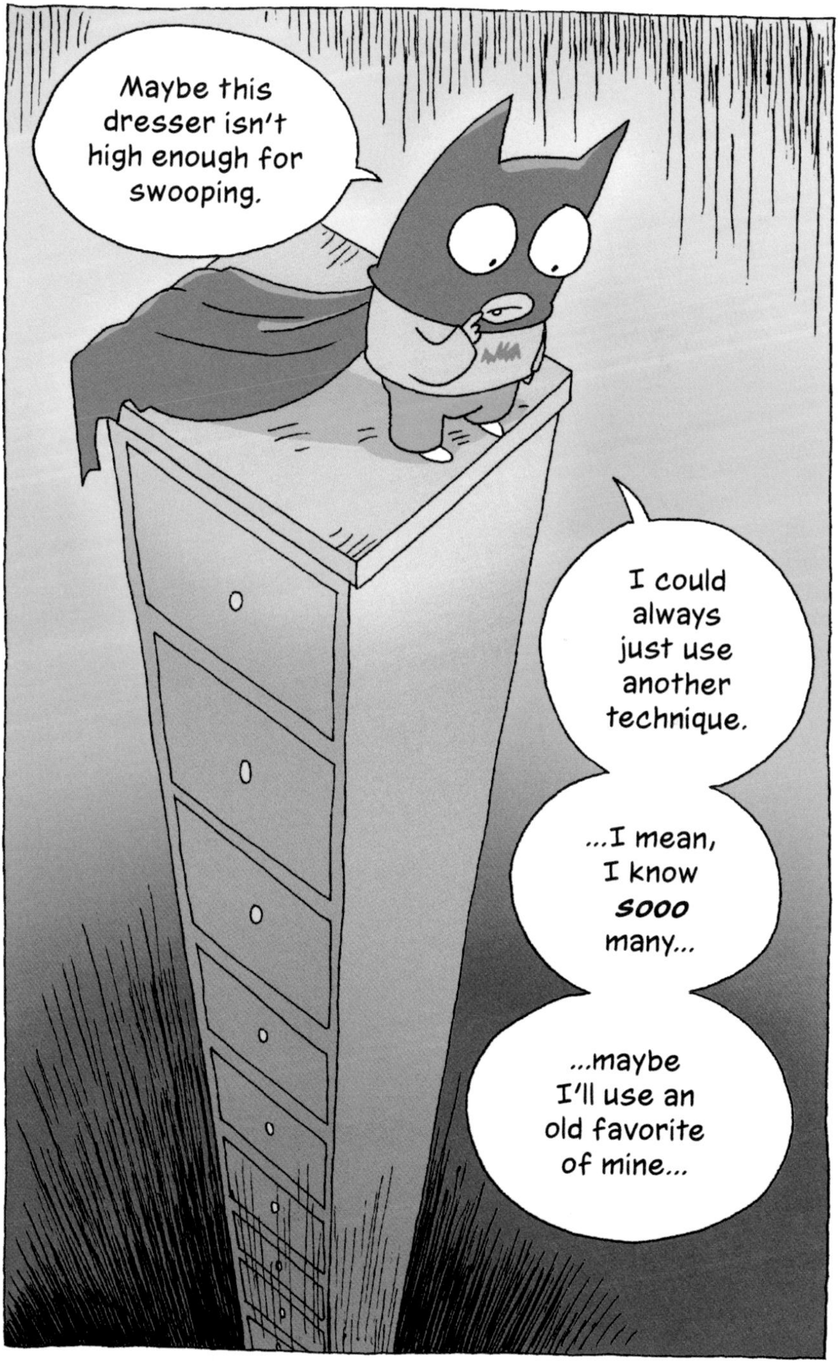
Maybe this dresser isn't high enough for swooping.
I could always just use another technique.
...I mean, I know *sooo* many...
...maybe I'll use an old favorite of mine...

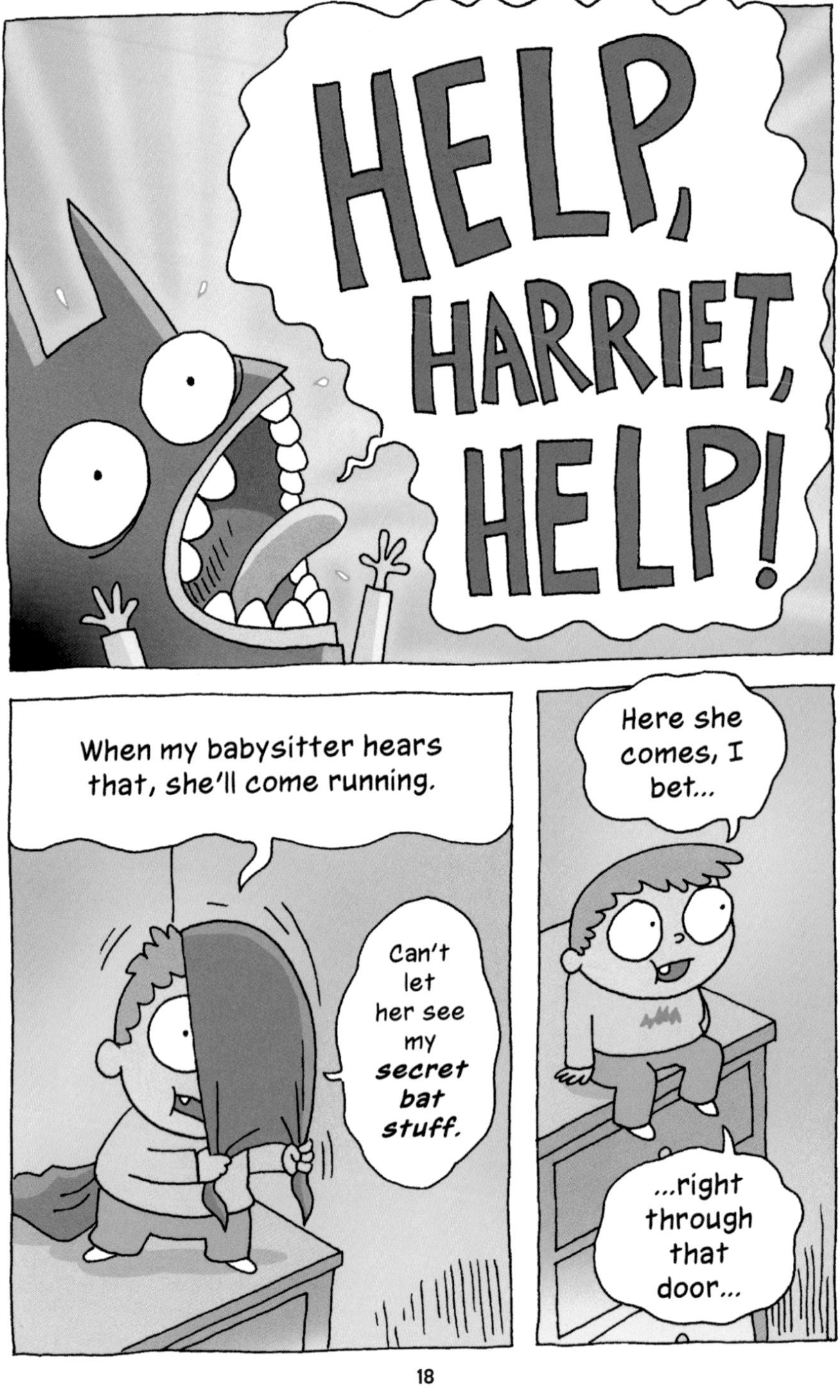
HELP, HARRIET, HELP!
When my babysitter hears that, she'll come running.
Can't let her see my *secret bat stuff.*
Here she comes, I bet...
...right through that door...

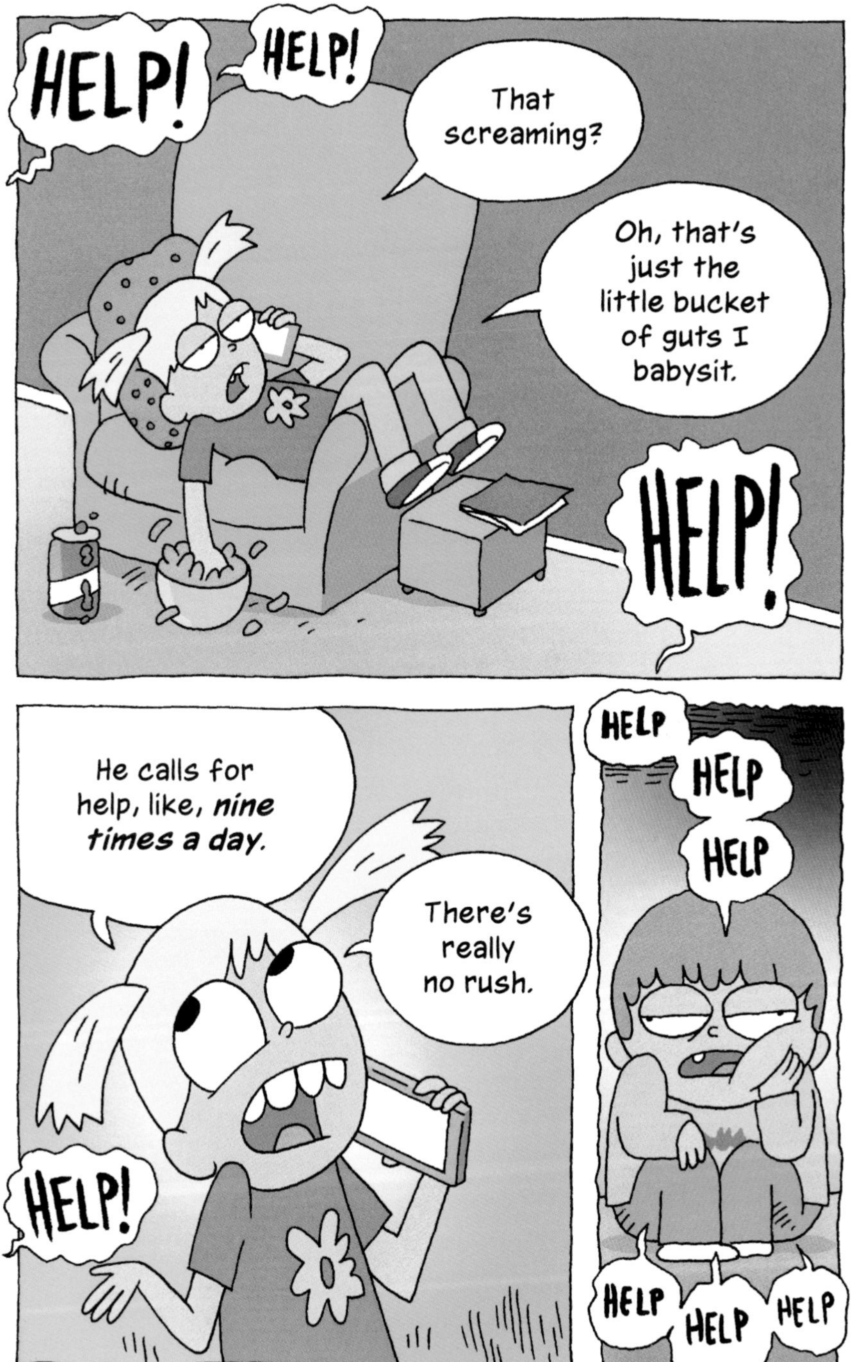
HELP!
HELP!
That screaming?
Oh, that's just the little bucket of guts I babysit.
HELP!
He calls for help, like, ***nine times a day.***
There's really no rush.
HELP!
HELP
HELP
HELP
HELP
HELP
HELP

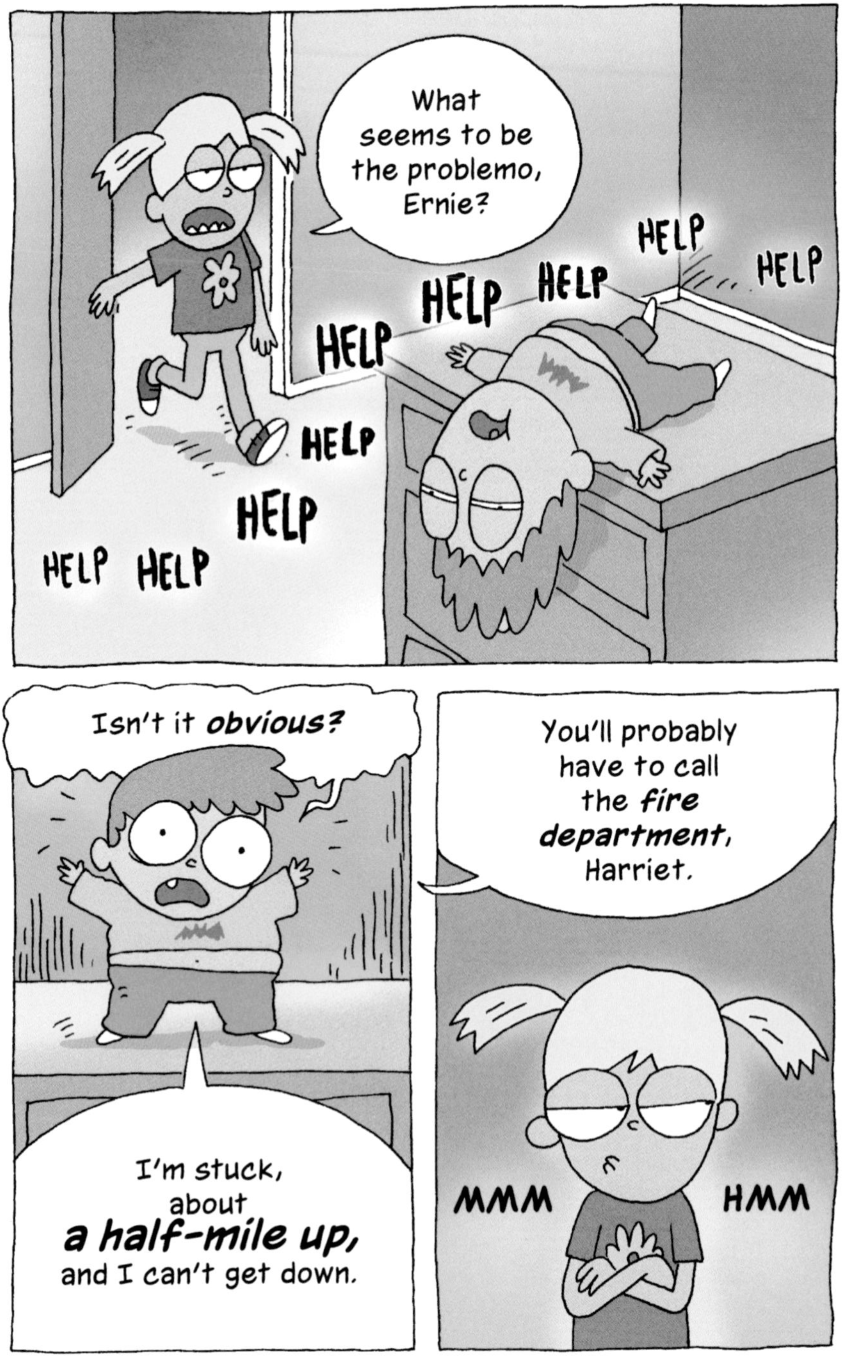
What seems to be the problemo, Ernie?
HELP HELP HELP HELP HELP
HELP HELP HELP HELP
Isn't it obvious?
I'm stuck, about a half-mile up, and I can't get down.
You'll probably have to call the fire department, Harriet.
MMM HMM

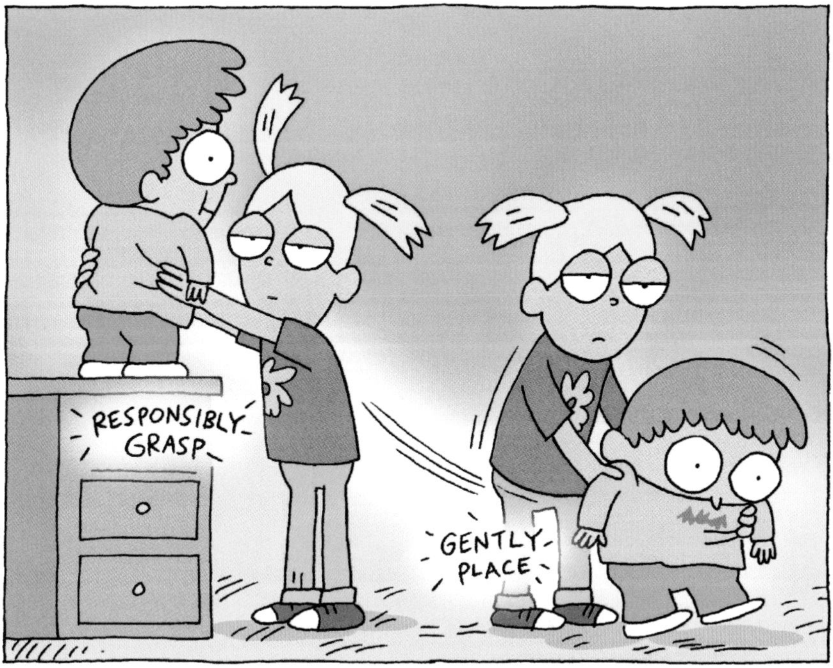
RESPONSIBLY GRASP
GENTLY PLACE

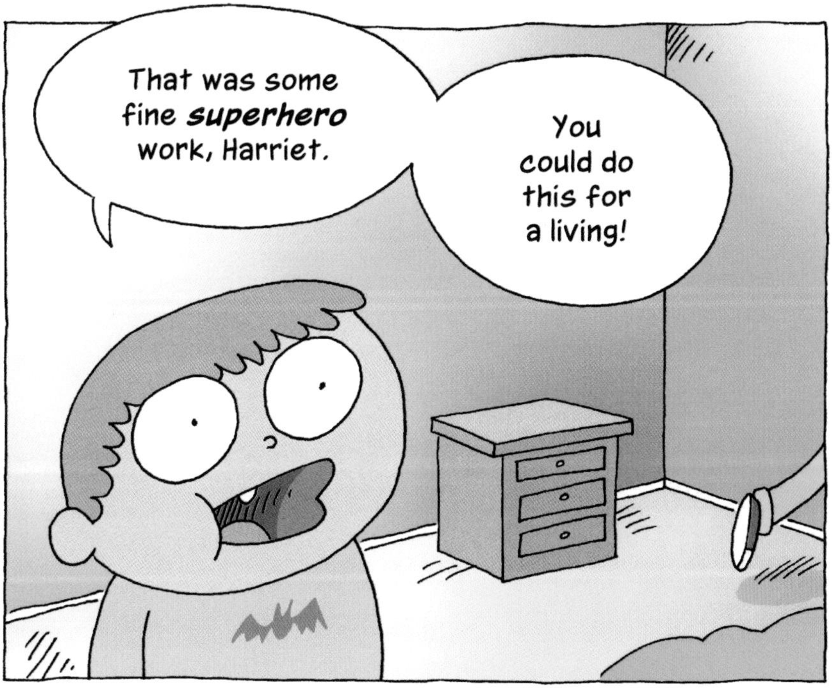
That was some fine **superhero** work, Harriet.
You could do this for a living!

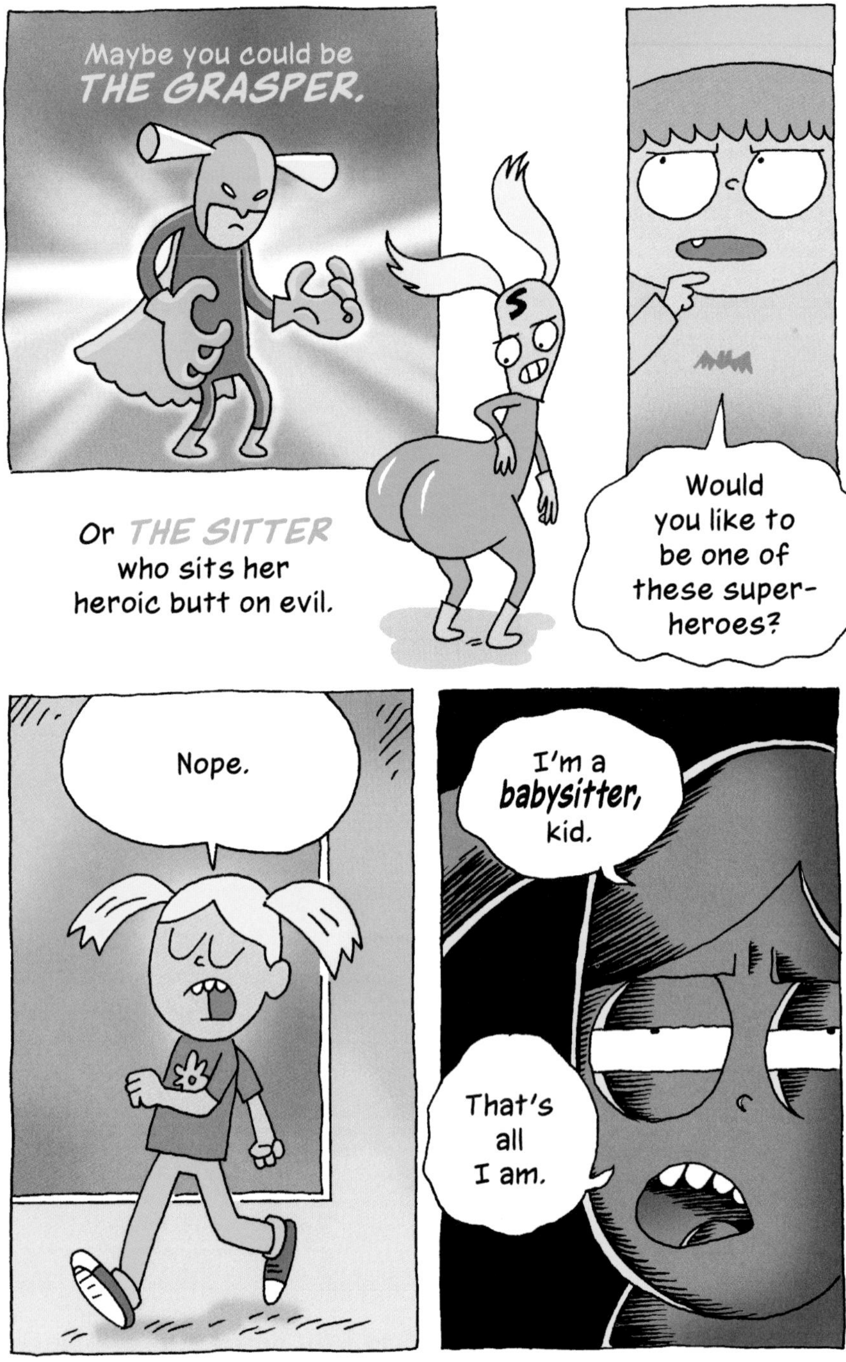
Maybe you could be THE GRASPER.
Or THE SITTER who sits her heroic butt on evil.
Would you like to be one of these super-heroes?
Nope.
I'm a babysitter, kid.
That's all I am.

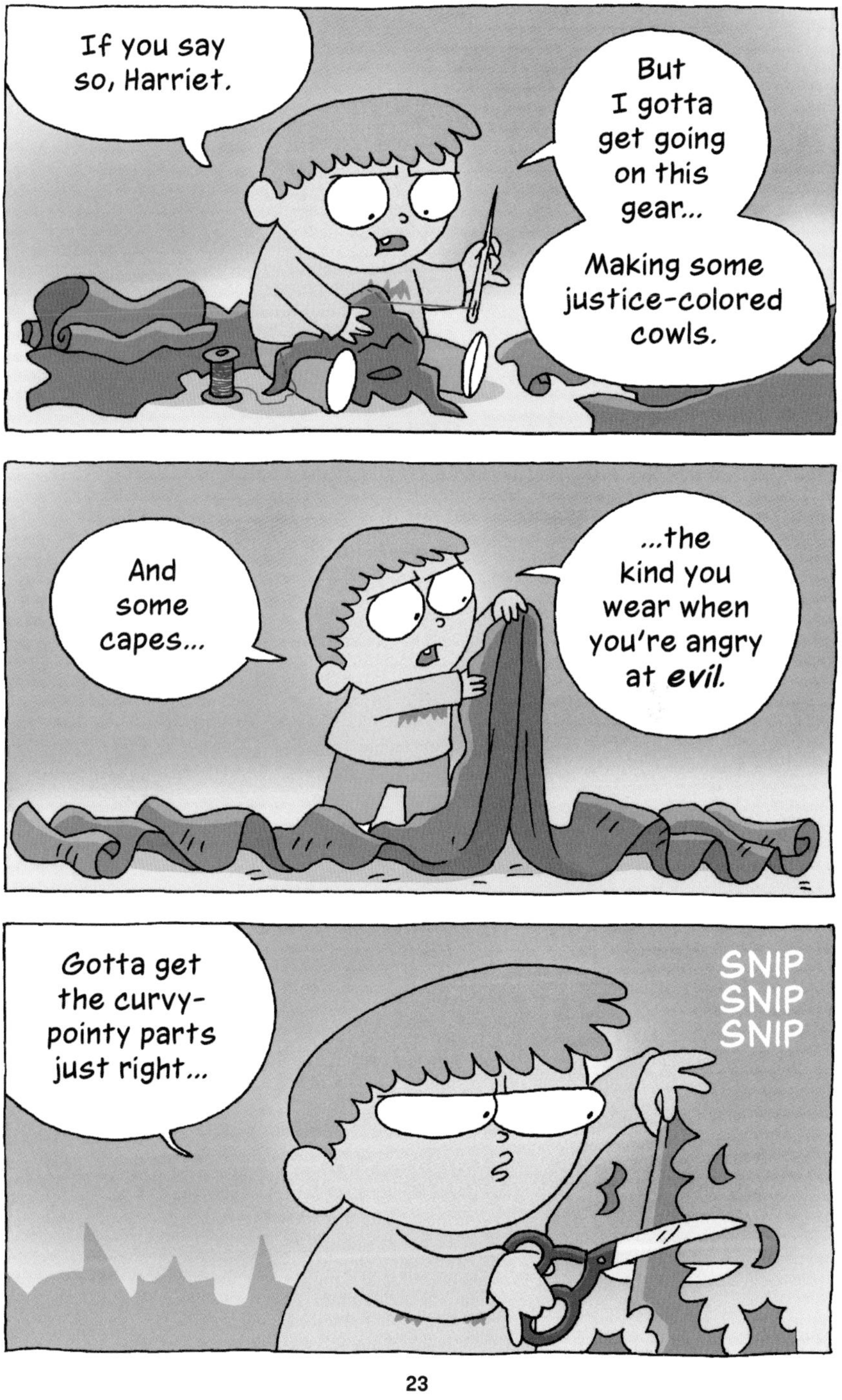
If you say so, Harriet.
But I gotta get going on this gear...
Making some justice-colored cowls.
And some capes...
...the kind you wear when you're angry at *evil.*
Gotta get the curvy-pointy parts just right...
SNIP SNIP SNIP

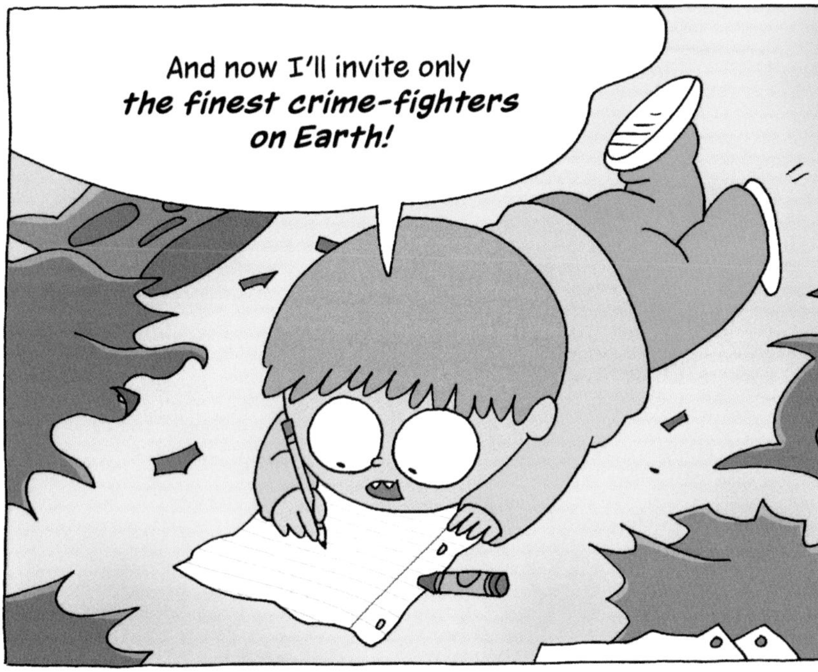
And now I'll invite only *the finest crime-fighters on Earth!*

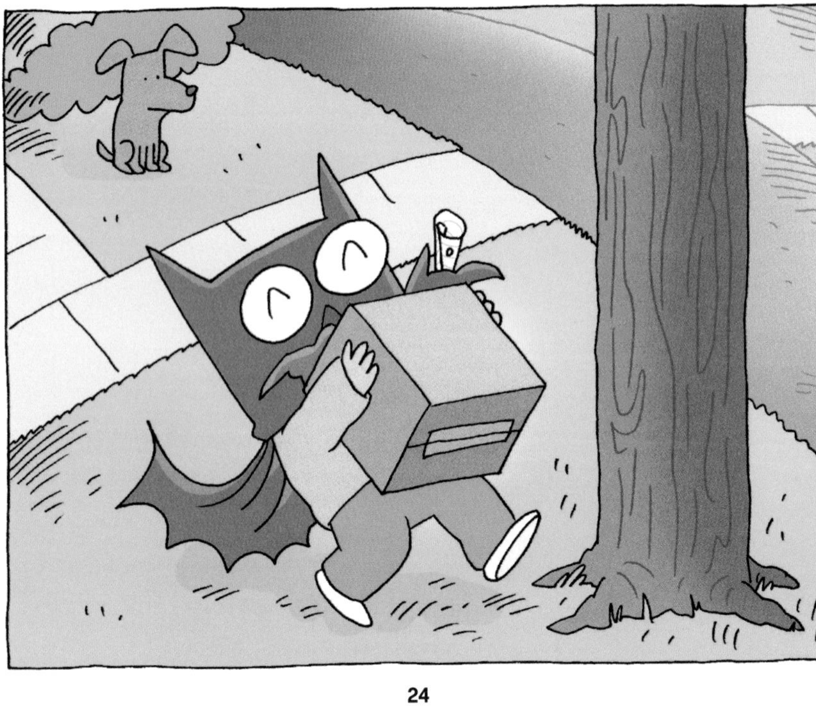

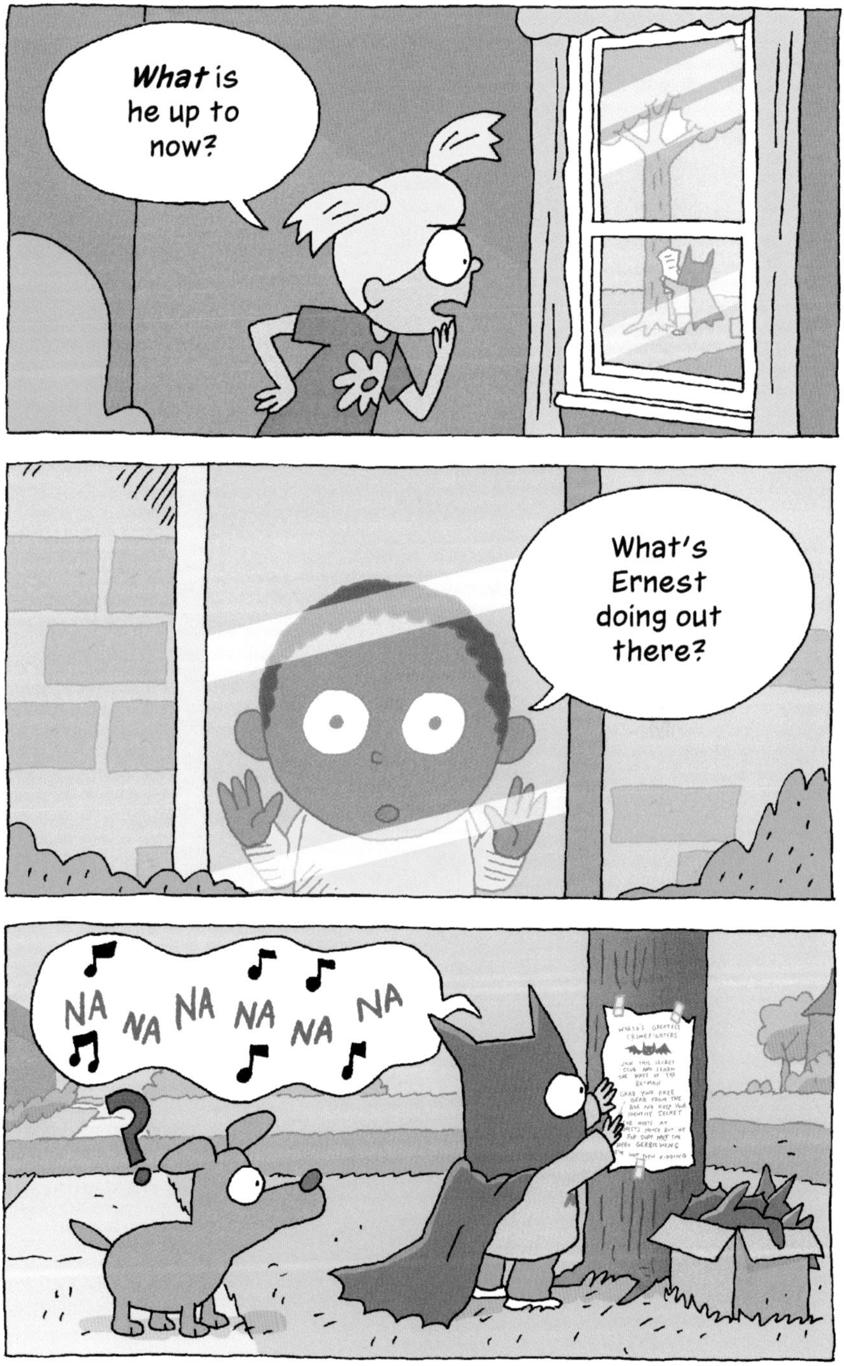
What is he up to now?
What's Ernest doing out there?
NA NA NA NA NA NA

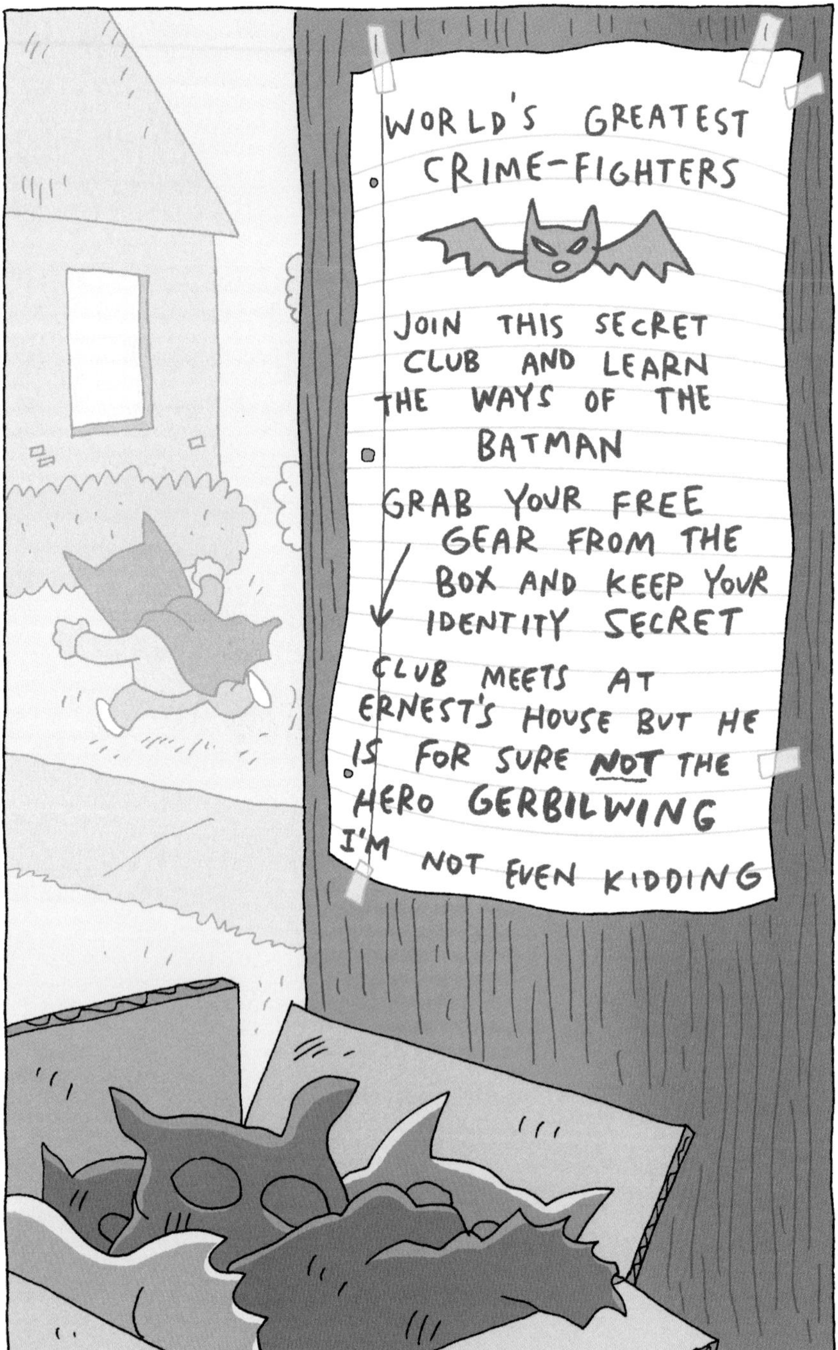
WORLD'S GREATEST CRIME-FIGHTERS
JOIN THIS SECRET CLUB AND LEARN THE WAYS OF THE BATMAN
GRAB YOUR FREE GEAR FROM THE BOX AND KEEP YOUR IDENTITY SECRET
CLUB MEETS AT ERNEST'S HOUSE BUT HE IS FOR SURE NOT THE HERO GERBILWING
I'M NOT EVEN KIDDING

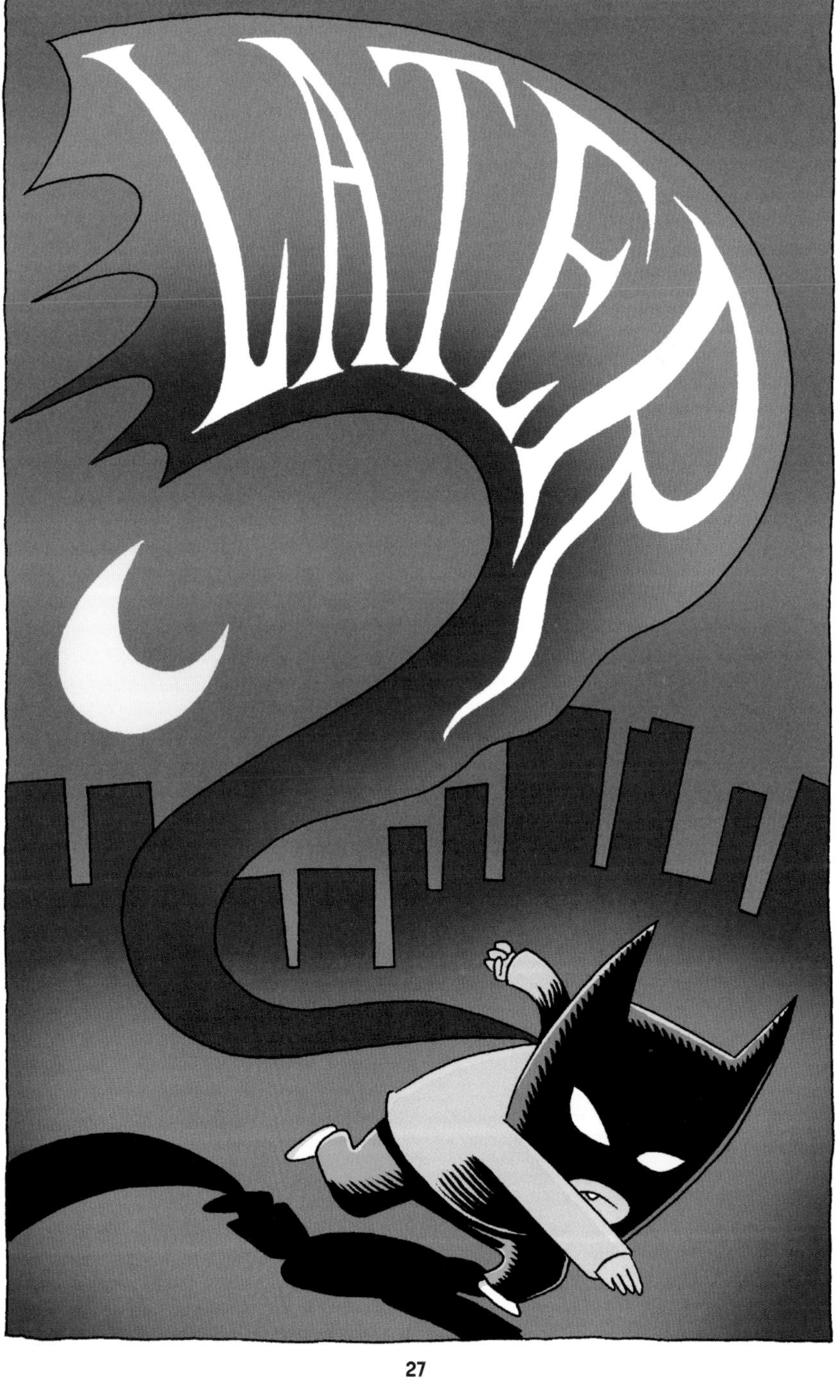
LATER

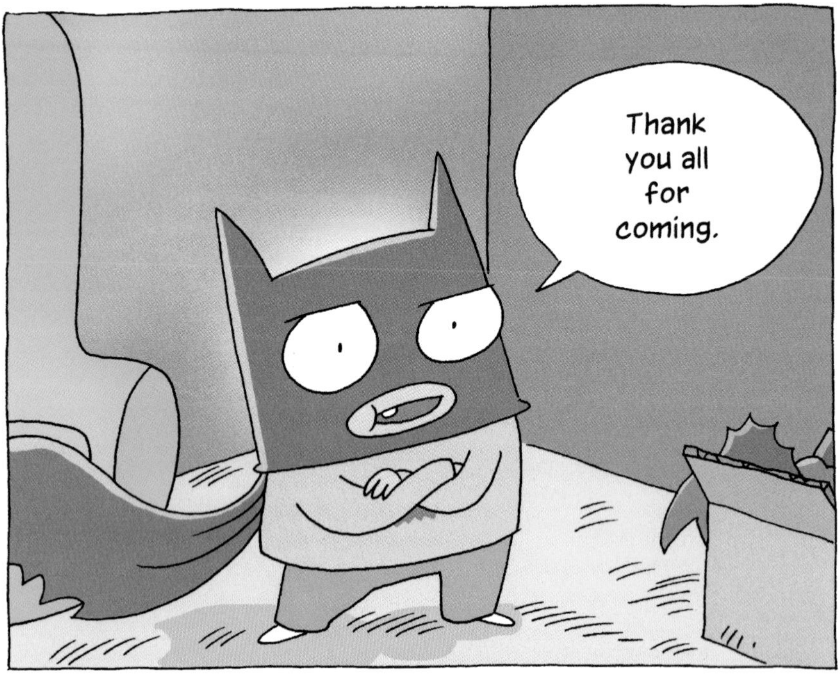
Thank you all for coming.

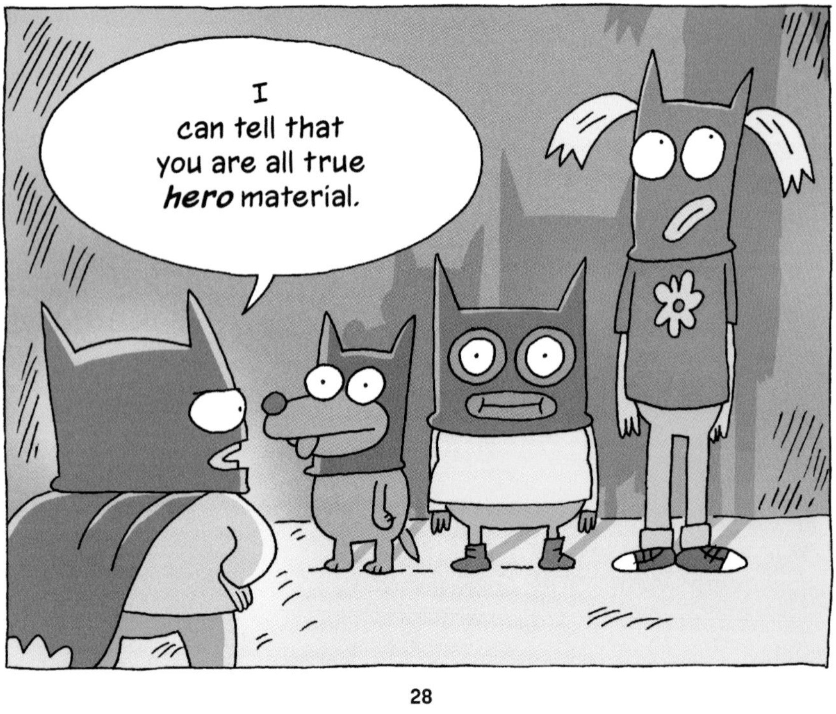
I can tell that you are all true ***hero*** material.

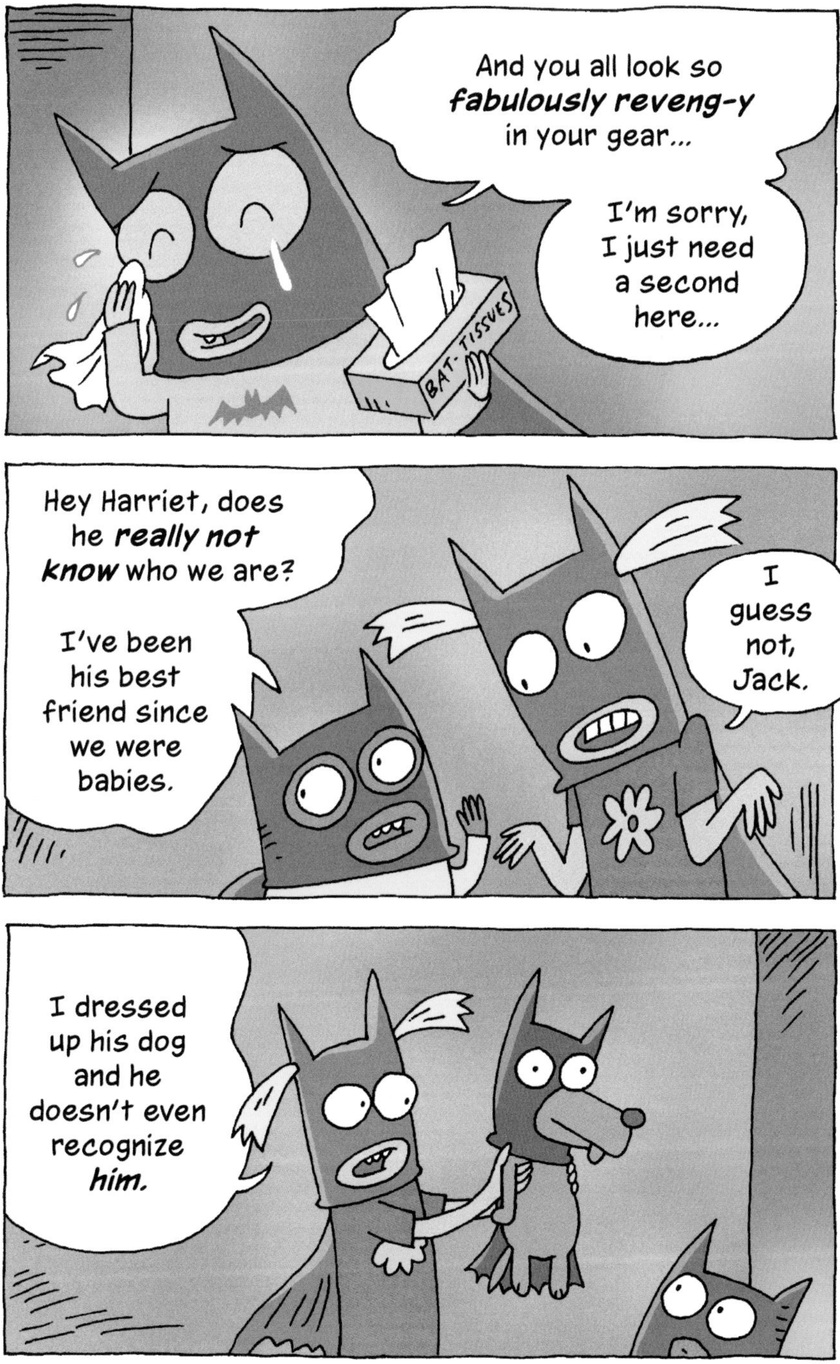
And you all look so ***fabulously reveng-y*** in your gear...
I'm sorry, I just need a second here...
BAT-TISSUES
Hey Harriet, does he ***really not know*** who we are?
I've been his best friend since we were babies.
I guess not, Jack.
I dressed up his dog and he doesn't even recognize ***him.***

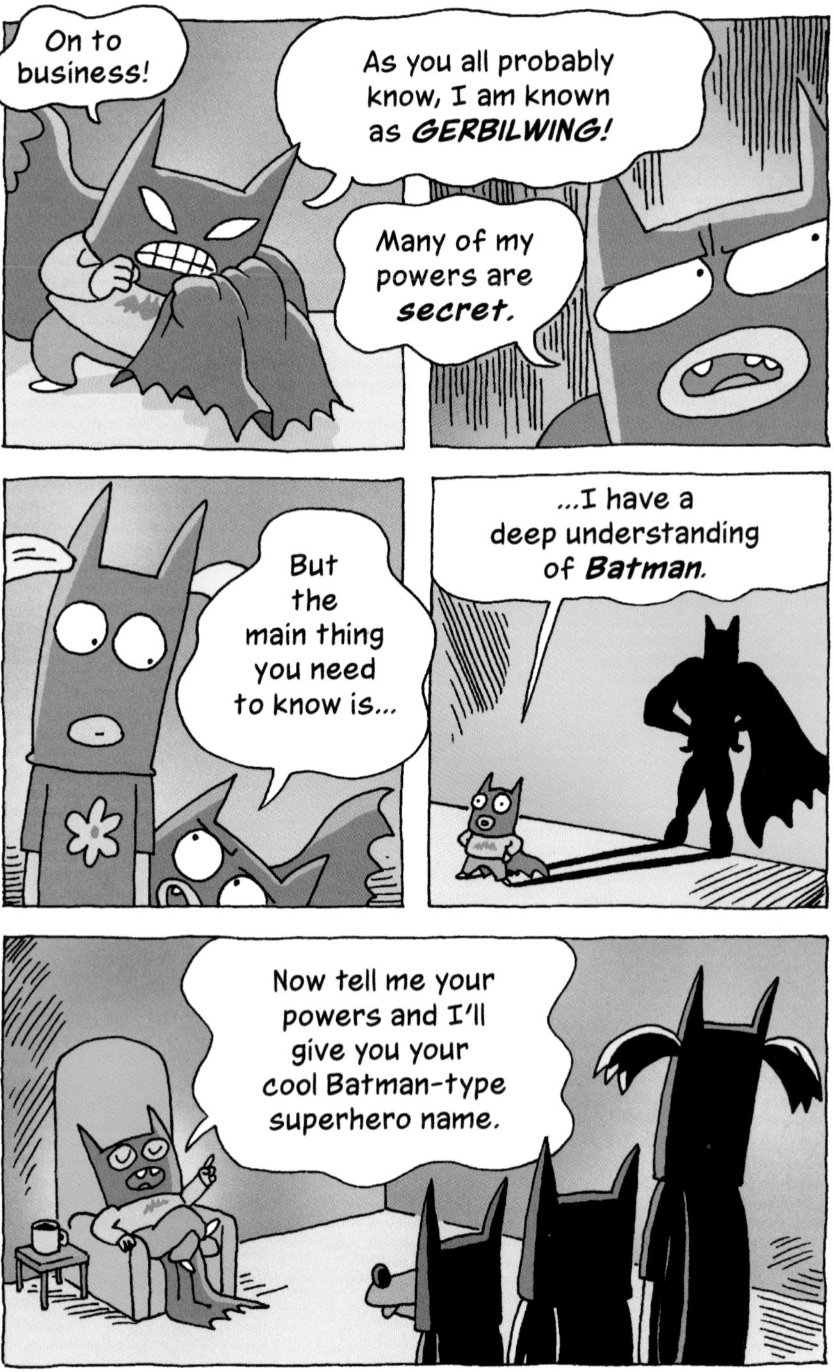
On to business!
As you all probably know, I am known as GERBILWING!
Many of my powers are secret.
But the main thing you need to know is...
...I have a deep understanding of Batman.
Now tell me your powers and I'll give you your cool Batman-type superhero name.

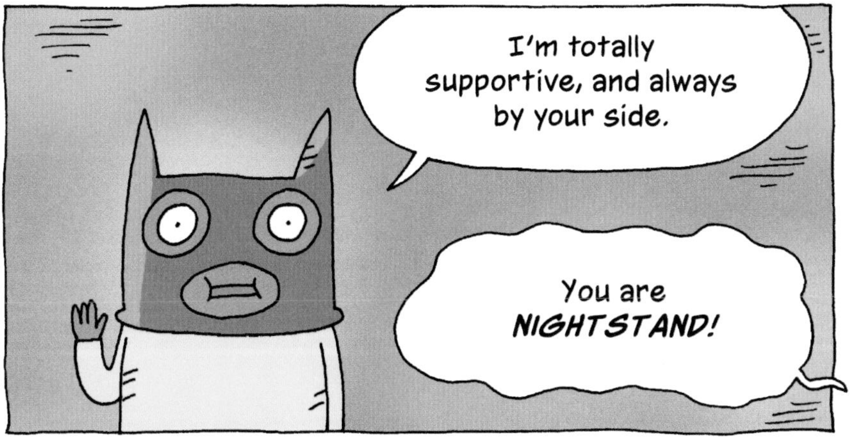
I'm totally supportive, and always by your side.
You are NIGHTSTAND!

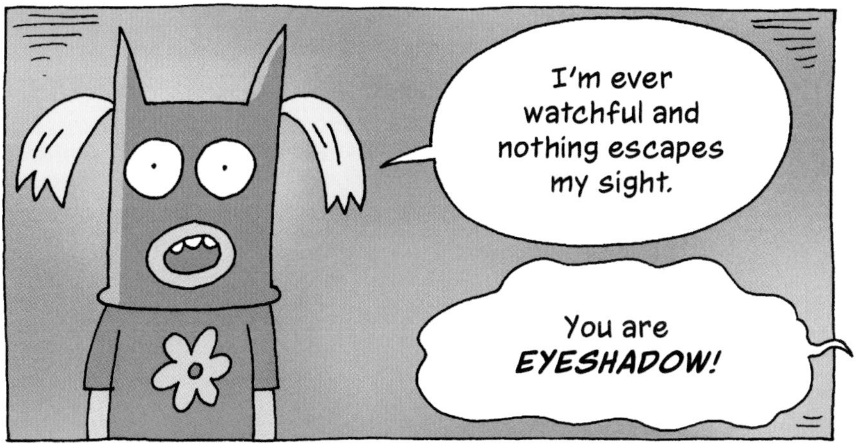
I'm ever watchful and nothing escapes my sight.
You are EYESHADOW!

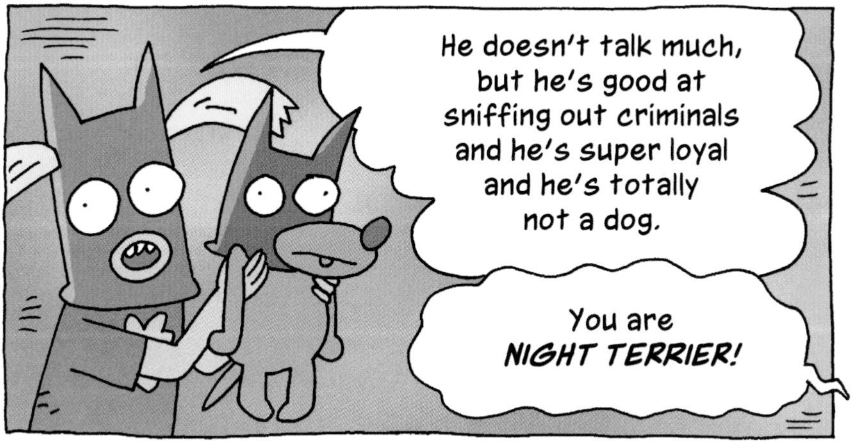
He doesn't talk much, but he's good at sniffing out criminals and he's super loyal and he's totally not a dog.
You are NIGHT TERRIER!

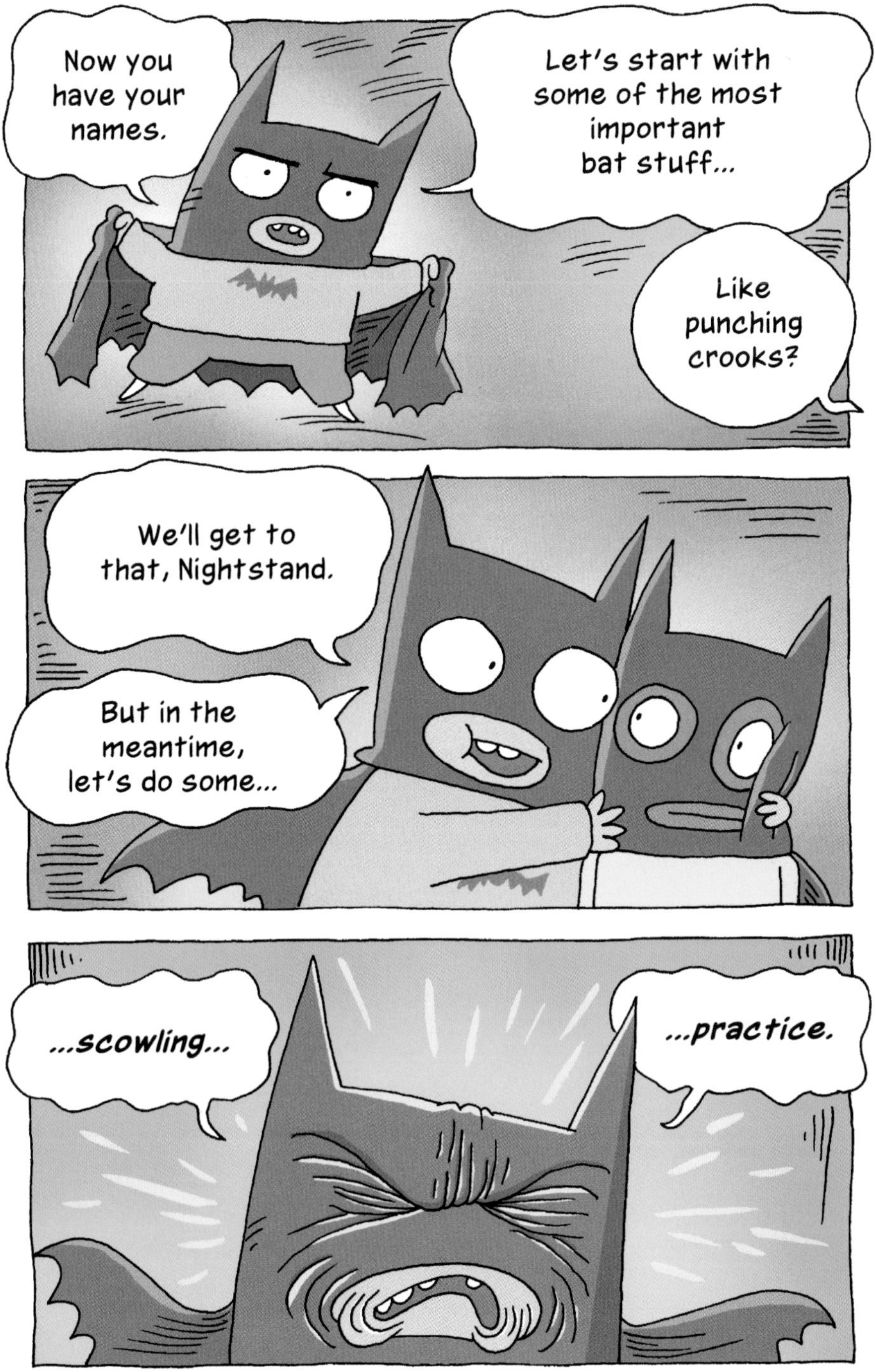
Now you have your names.
Let's start with some of the most important bat stuff...
Like punching crooks?
We'll get to that, Nightstand.
But in the meantime, let's do some...
...scowling...
...practice.

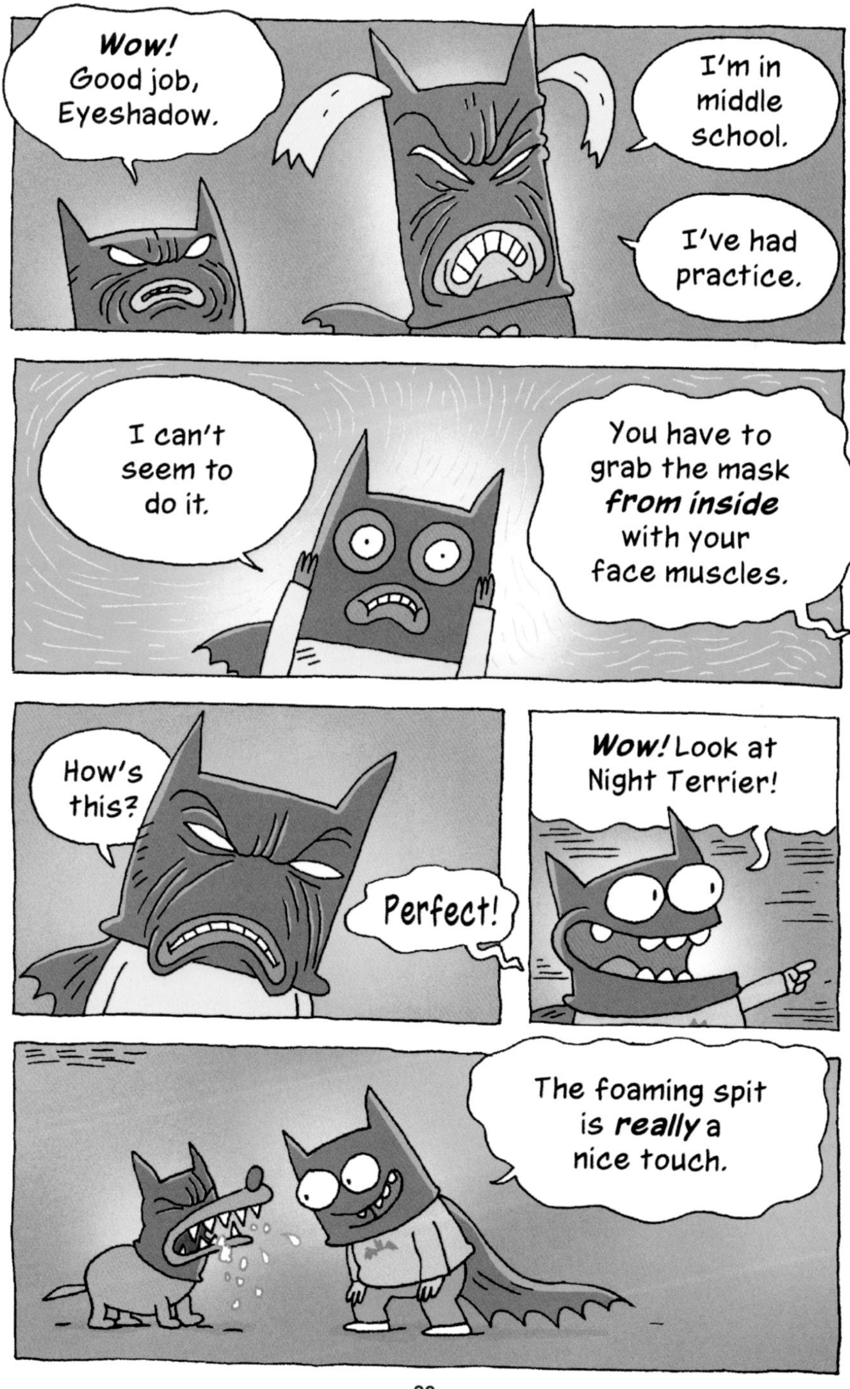
Wow! Good job, Eyeshadow.
I'm in middle school.
I've had practice.
I can't seem to do it.
You have to grab the mask from inside with your face muscles.
How's this?
Perfect!
Wow! Look at Night Terrier!
The foaming spit is really a nice touch.

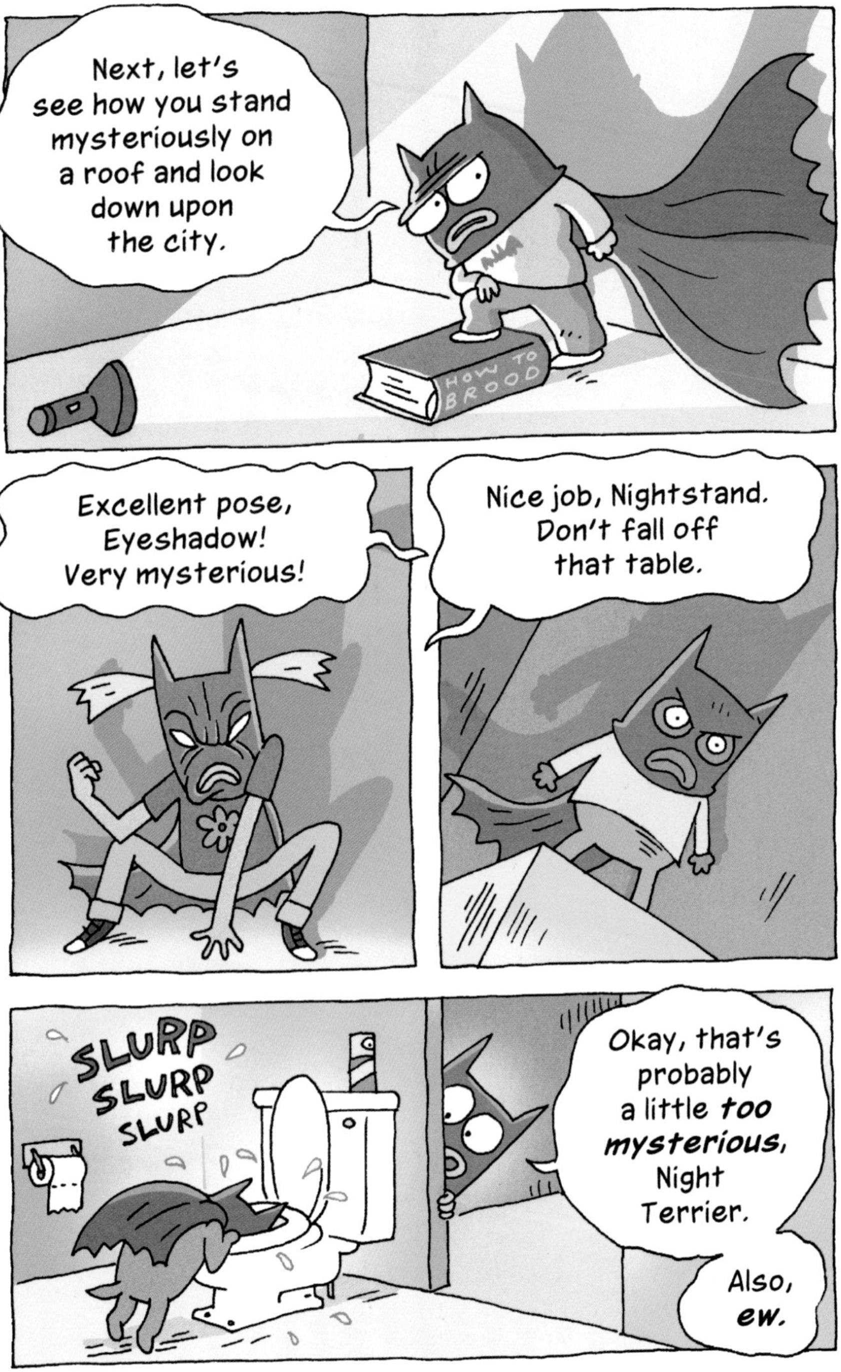
Next, let's see how you stand mysteriously on a roof and look down upon the city.
HOW TO BROOD
Excellent pose, Eyeshadow! Very mysterious!
Nice job, Nightstand. Don't fall off that table.
SLURP SLURP SLURP
Okay, that's probably a little ***too mysterious,*** Night Terrier.
Also, ***ew.***

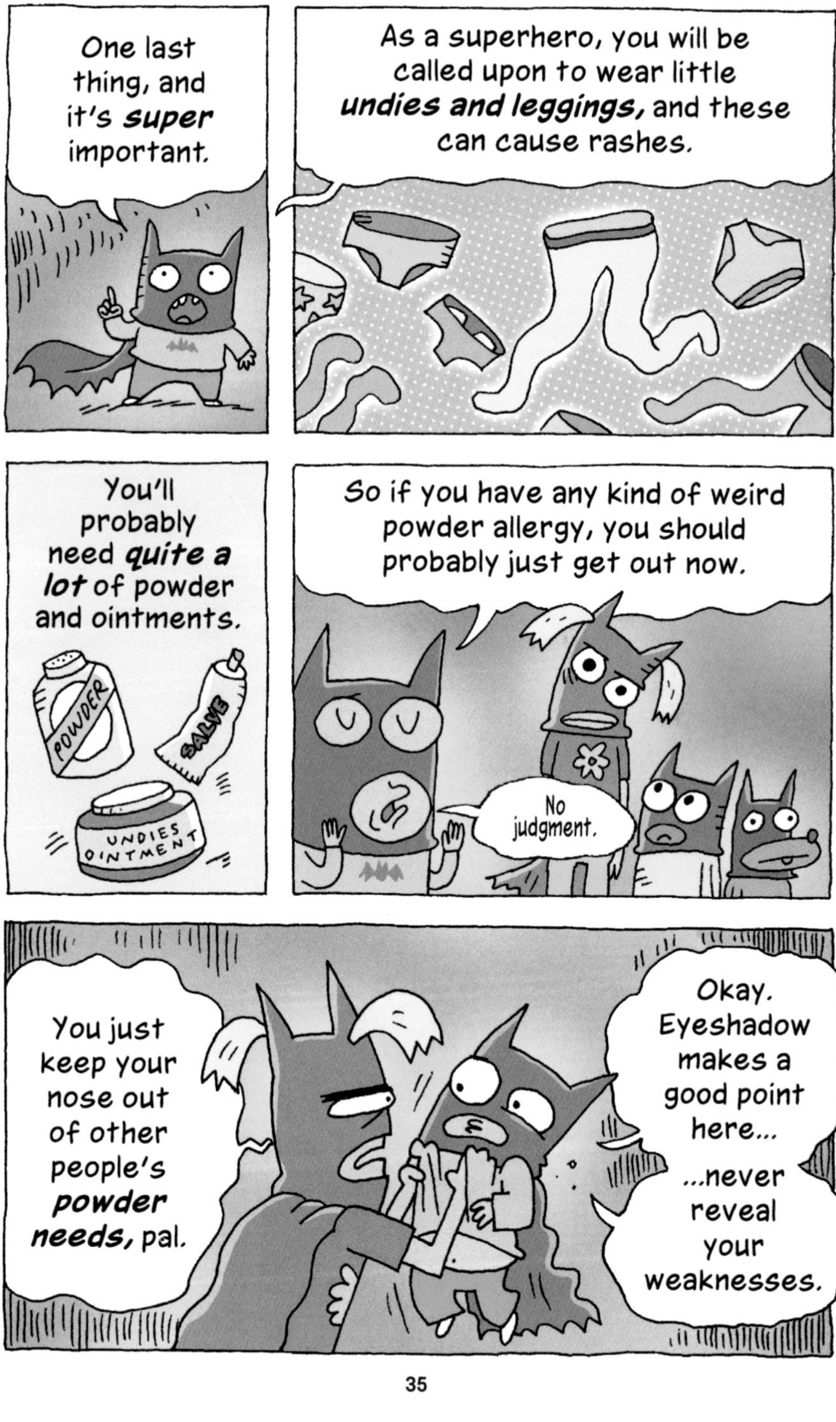
One last thing, and it's **super** important.
As a superhero, you will be called upon to wear little **undies and leggings,** and these can cause rashes.
You'll probably need **quite a lot** of powder and ointments.
POWDER
SALVE
UNDIES OINTMENT
So if you have any kind of weird powder allergy, you should probably just get out now.
No judgment.
You just keep your nose out of other people's **powder needs,** pal.
Okay. Eyeshadow makes a good point here...
...never reveal your weaknesses.

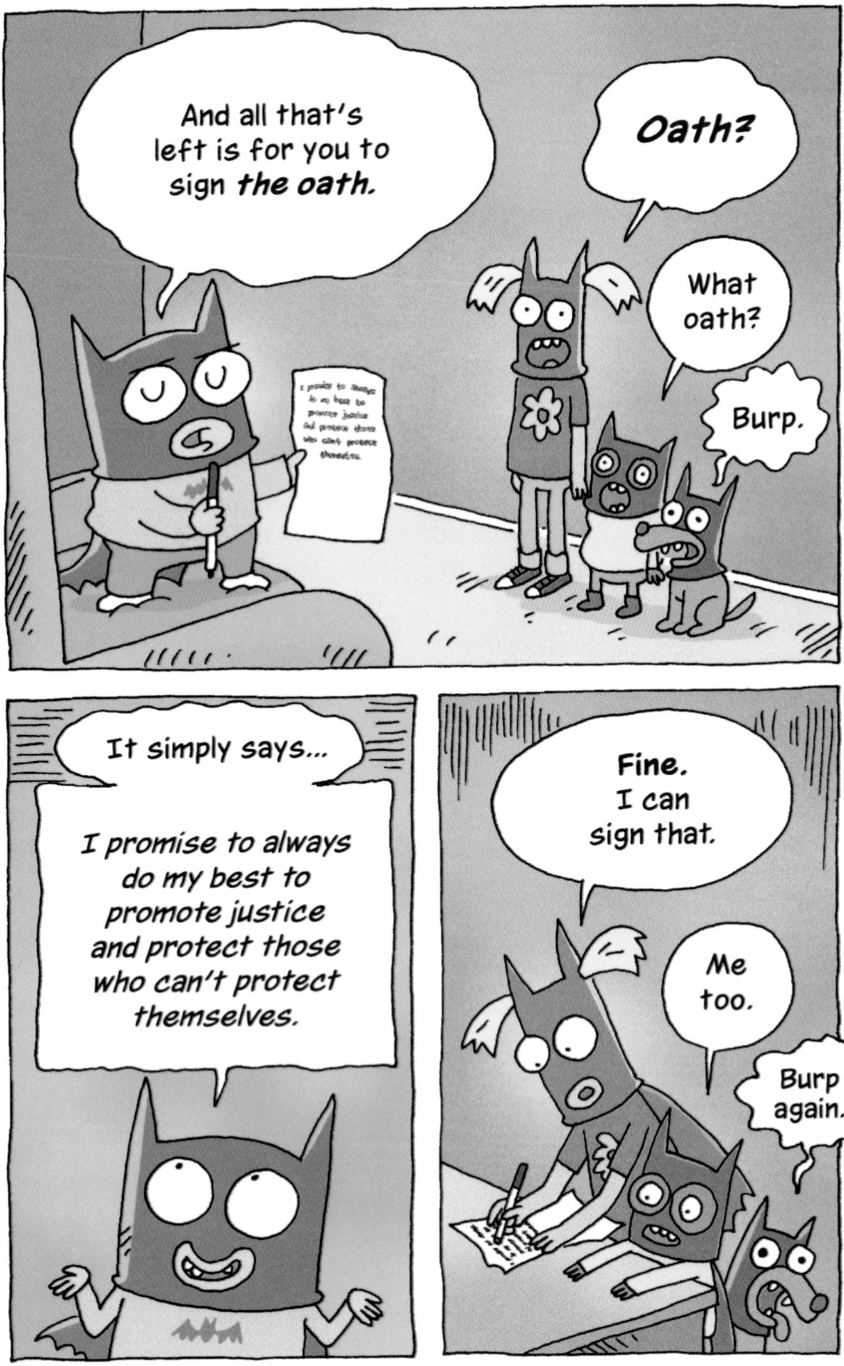
And all that's left is for you to sign *the oath.*
Oath?
What oath?
Burp.
It simply says...
I promise to always do my best to promote justice and protect those who can't protect themselves.
Fine. I can sign that.
Me too.
Burp again.

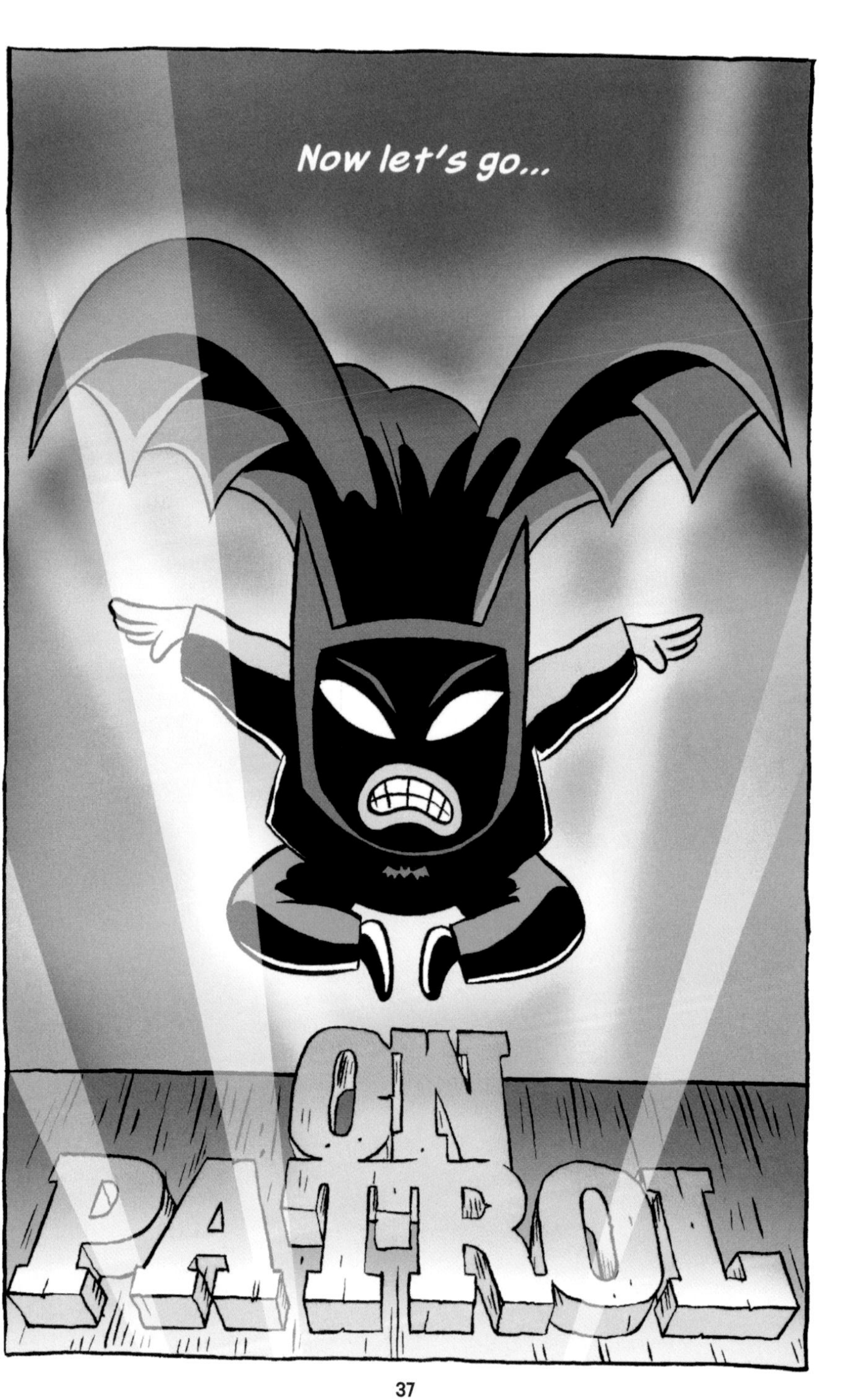
Now let's go...
ON PATROL

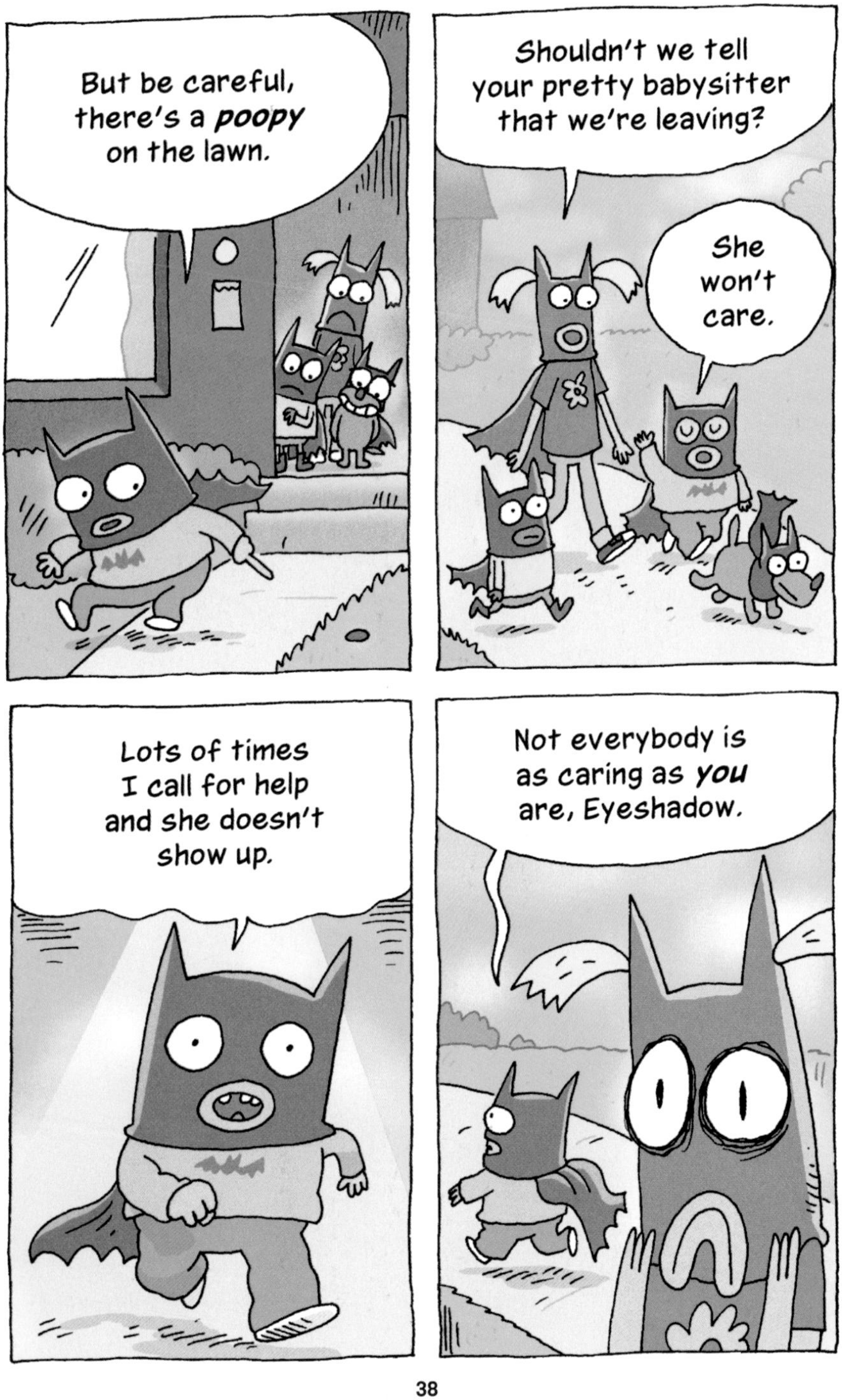
But be careful, there's a *poopy* on the lawn.
Shouldn't we tell your pretty babysitter that we're leaving?
She won't care.
Lots of times I call for help and she doesn't show up.
Not everybody is as caring as *you* are, Eyeshadow.

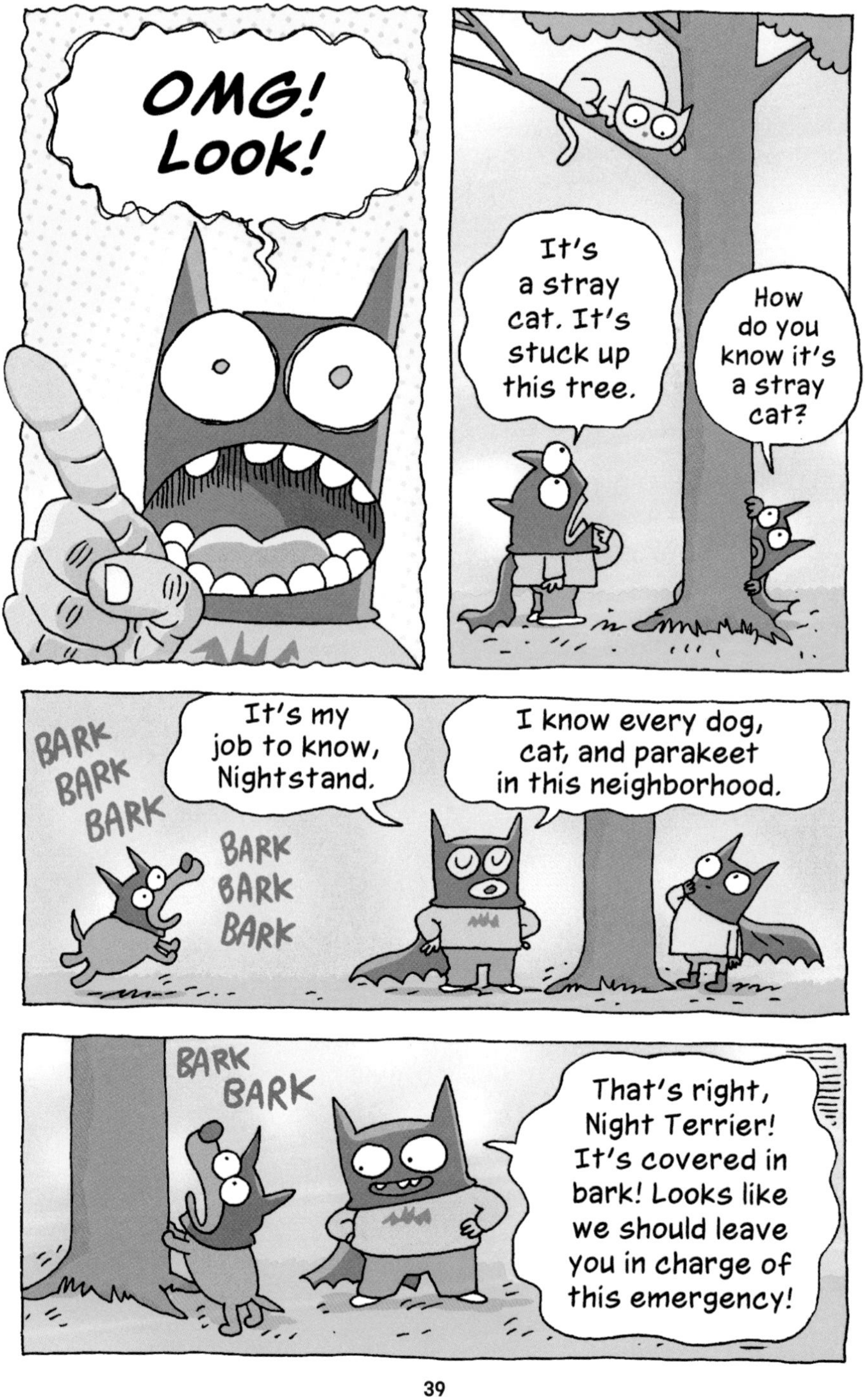
OMG! Look!
It's a stray cat. It's stuck up this tree.
How do you know it's a stray cat?
BARK BARK BARK
It's my job to know, Nightstand.
BARK BARK BARK
I know every dog, cat, and parakeet in this neighborhood.
BARK BARK
That's right, Night Terrier! It's covered in bark! Looks like we should leave you in charge of this emergency!

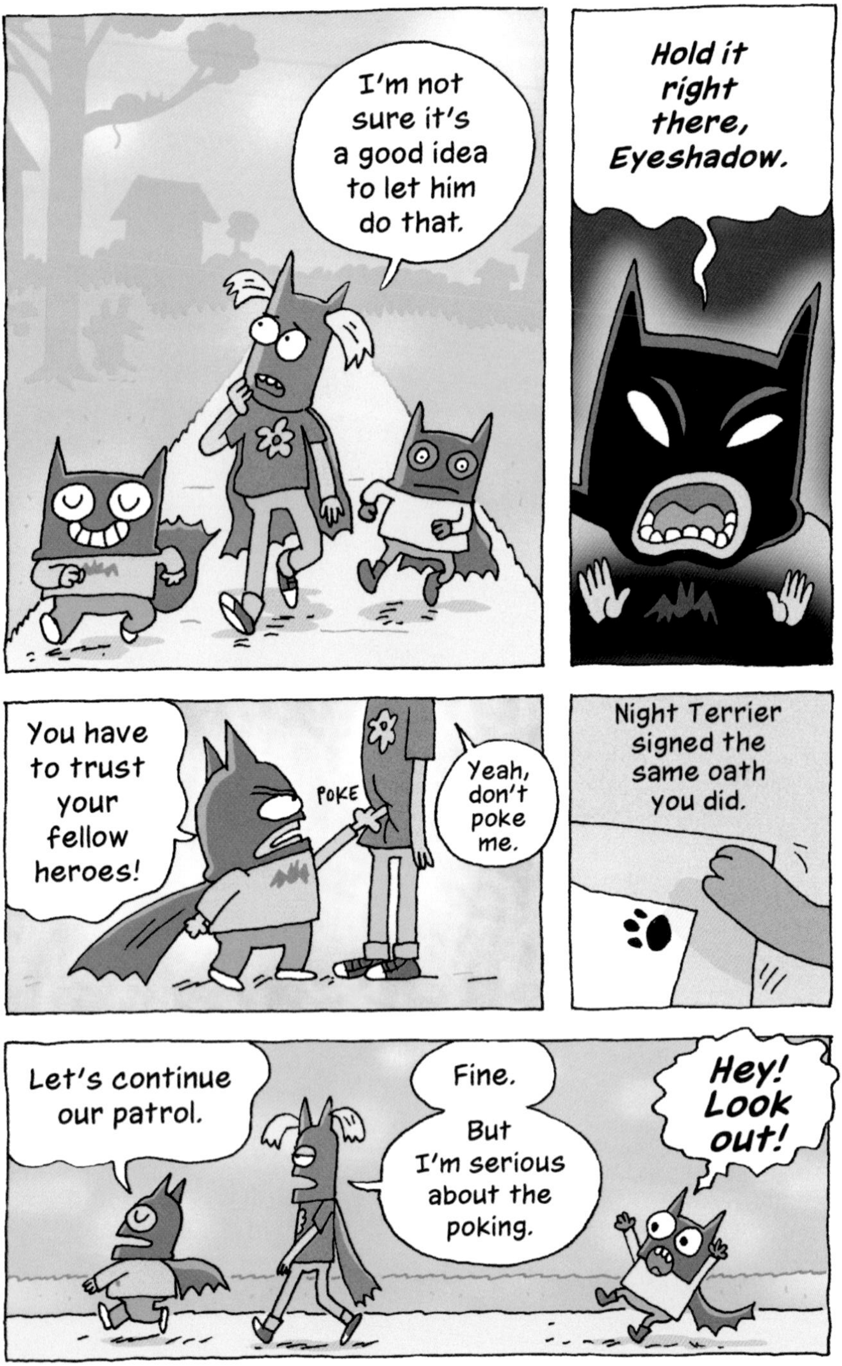
I'm not sure it's a good idea to let him do that.
Hold it right there, Eyeshadow.
You have to trust your fellow heroes!
POKE
Yeah, don't poke me.
Night Terrier signed the same oath you did.
Let's continue our patrol.
Fine.
But I'm serious about the poking.
Hey! Look out!

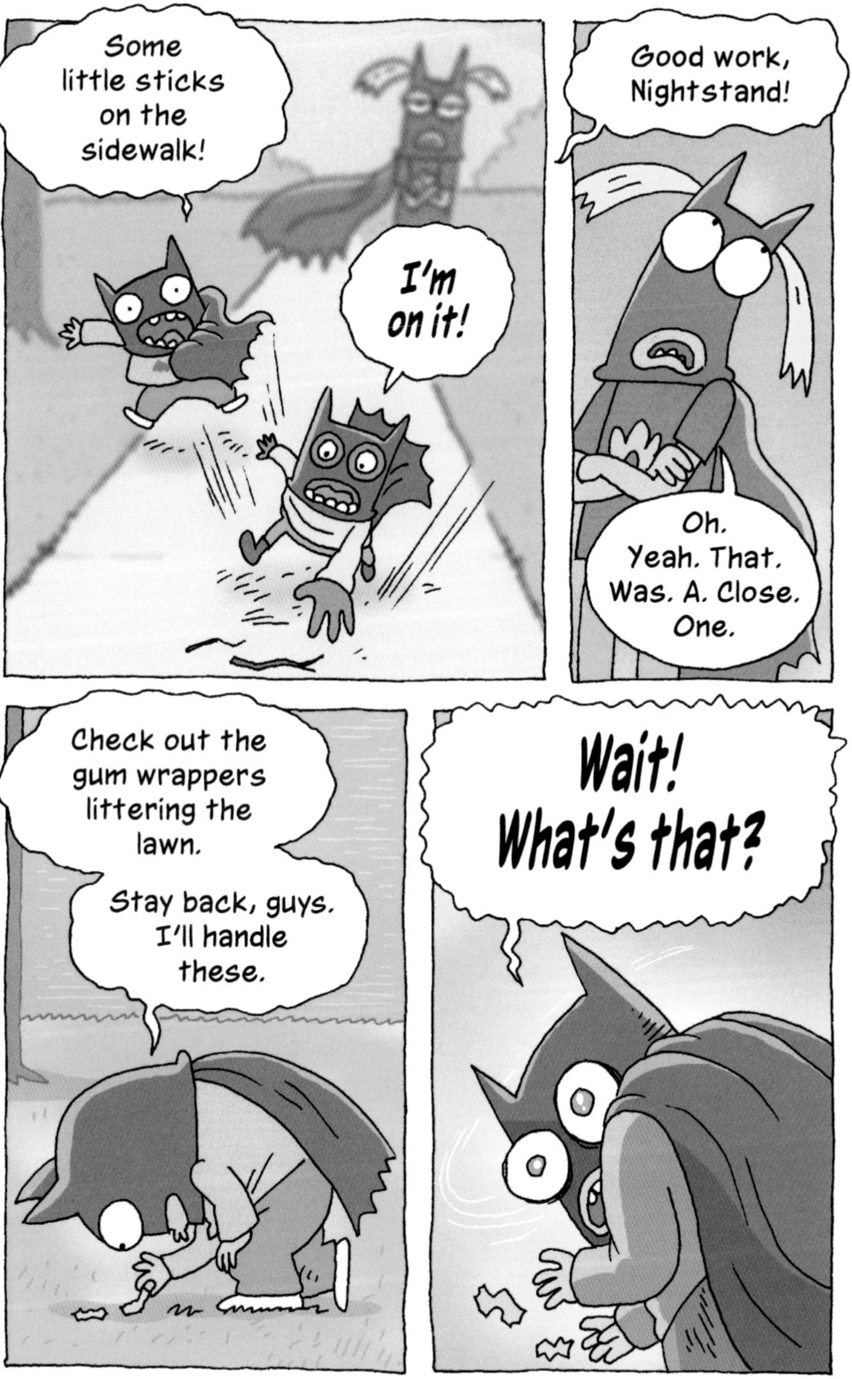
Some little sticks on the sidewalk!
I'm on it!
Good work, Nightstand!
Oh. Yeah. That. Was. A. Close. One.
Check out the gum wrappers littering the lawn.
Stay back, guys. I'll handle these.
Wait! What's that?

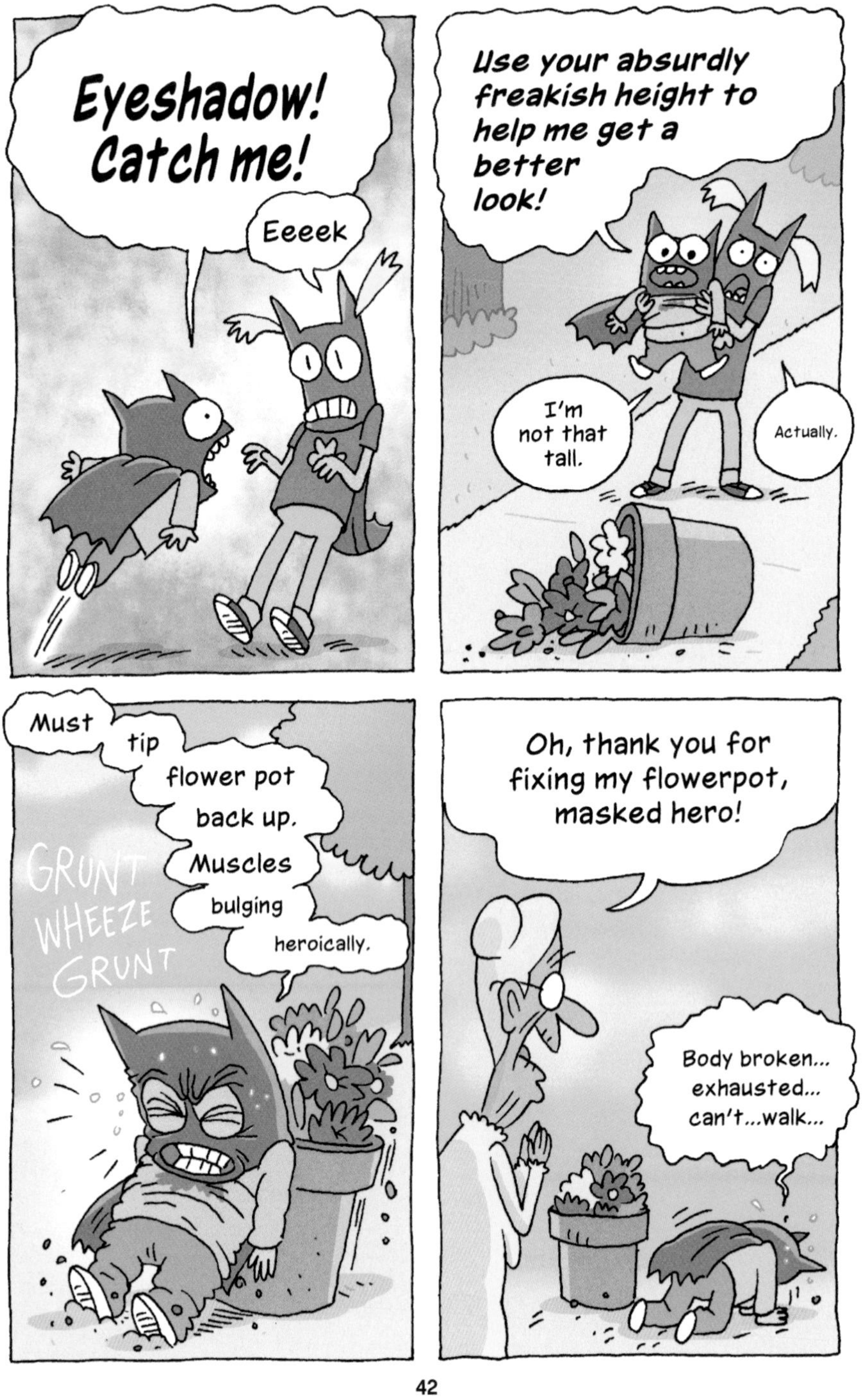

Eyeshadow! Catch me!
Eeeek
Use your absurdly freakish height to help me get a better look!
I'm not that tall.
Actually.
Must
tip
flower pot
back up.
Muscles
bulging
heroically.
GRUNT
WHEEZE
GRUNT
Oh, thank you for fixing my flowerpot, masked hero!
Body broken... exhausted... can't...walk...

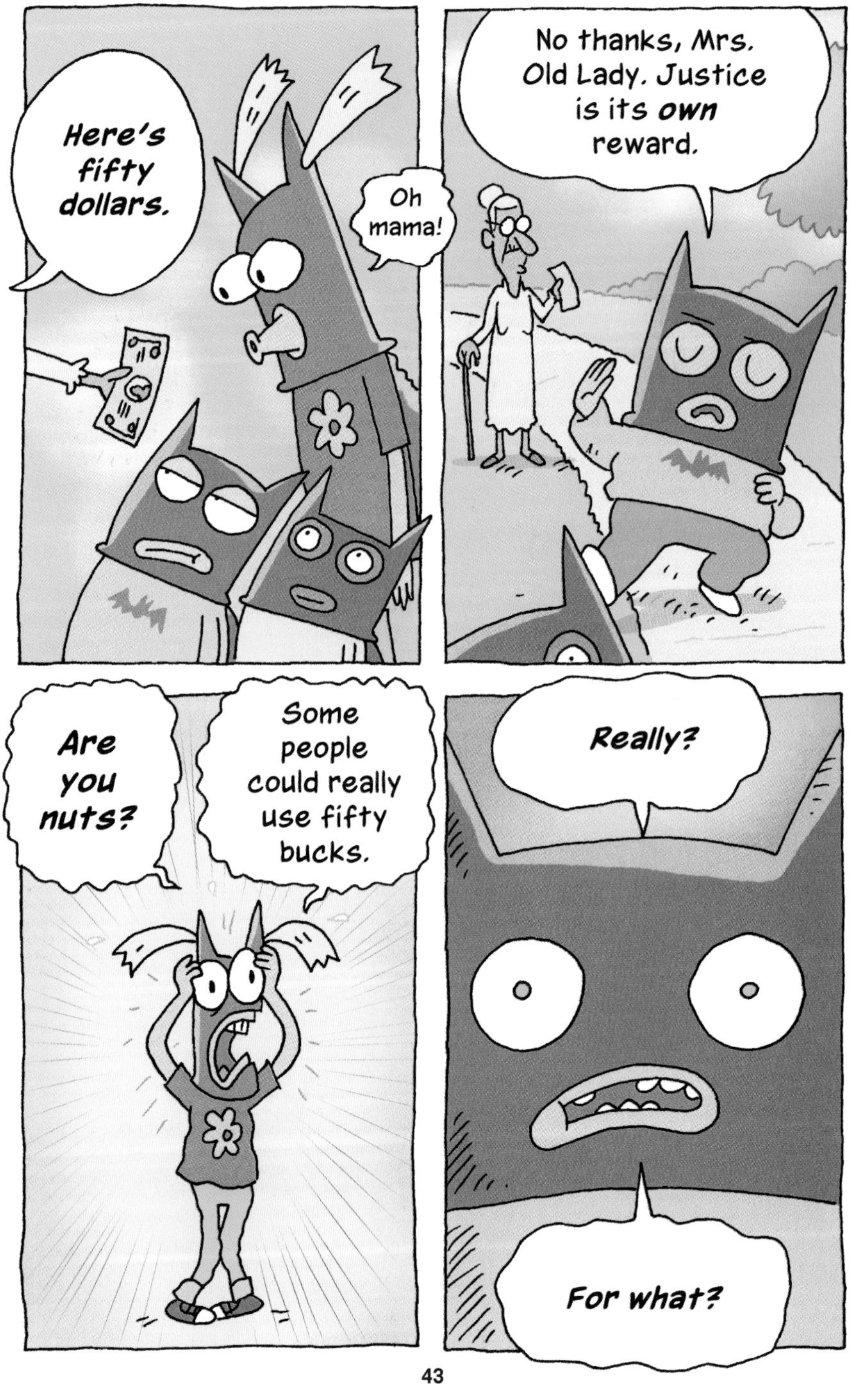
Here's fifty dollars.
Oh mama!
No thanks, Mrs. Old Lady. Justice is its own reward.
Are you nuts?
Some people could really use fifty bucks.
Really?
For what?

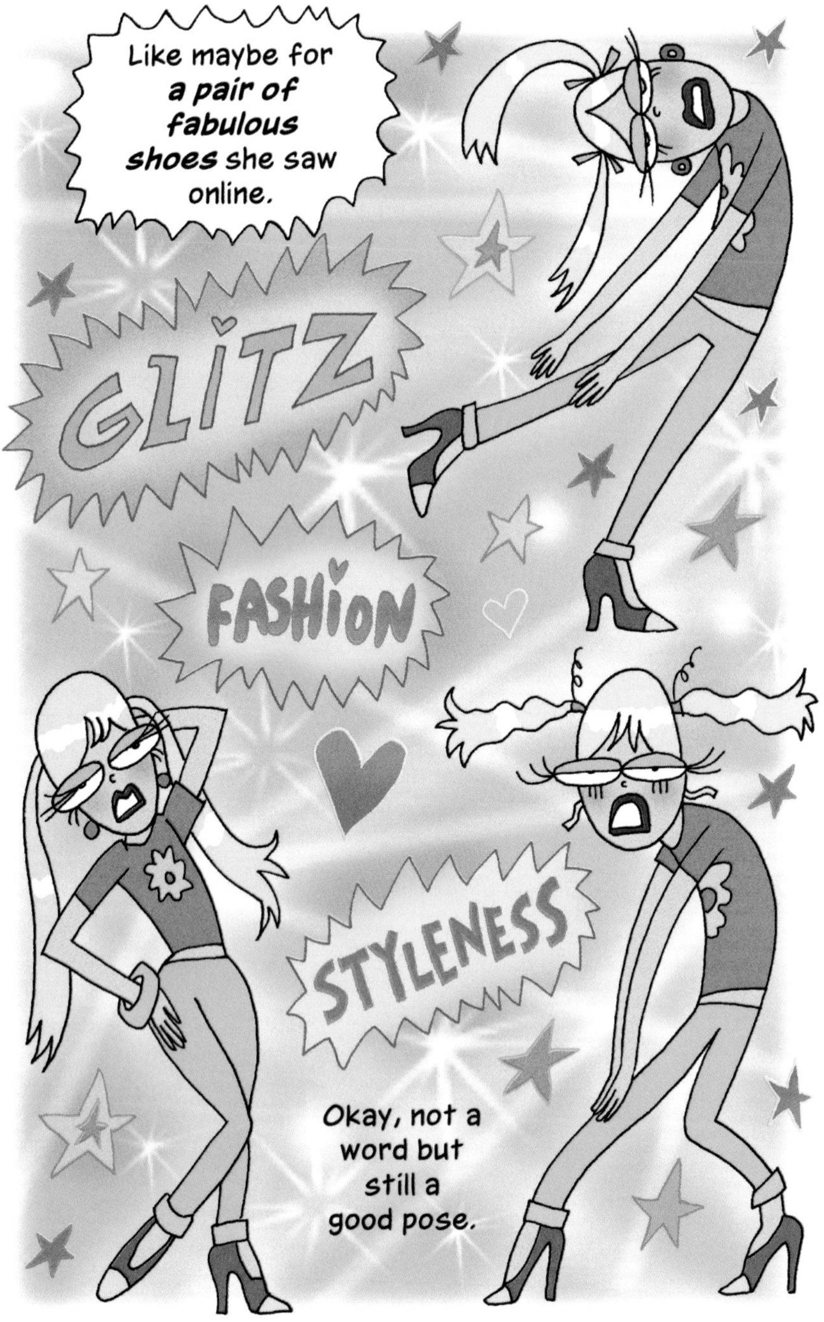
Like maybe for ***a pair of fabulous shoes*** she saw online.
GLITZ
FASHION
STYLENESS
Okay, not a word but still a good pose.

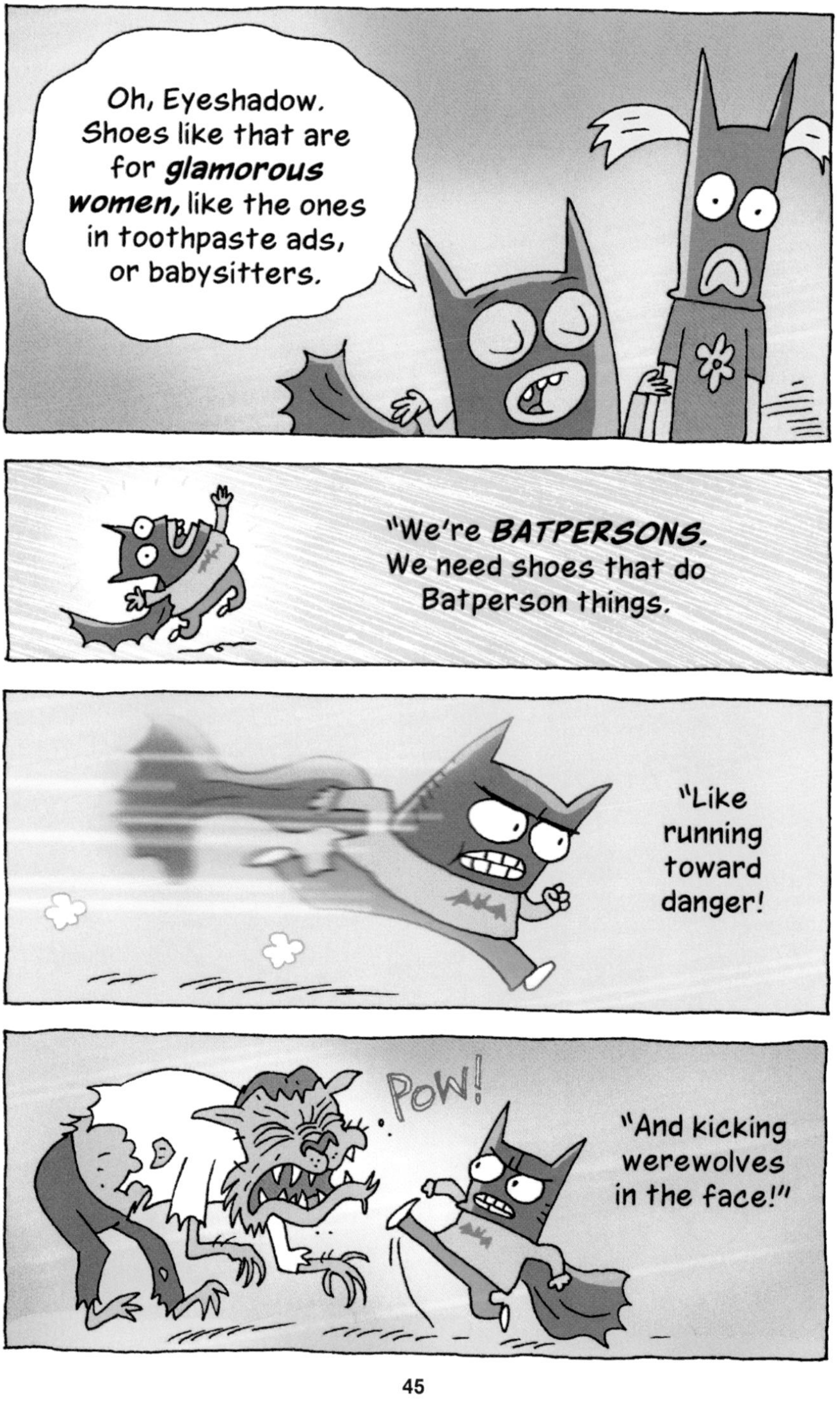
Oh, Eyeshadow. Shoes like that are for *glamorous women,* like the ones in toothpaste ads, or babysitters.
"We're **BATPERSONS.** We need shoes that do Batperson things.
"Like running toward danger!
POW!
"And kicking werewolves in the face!"

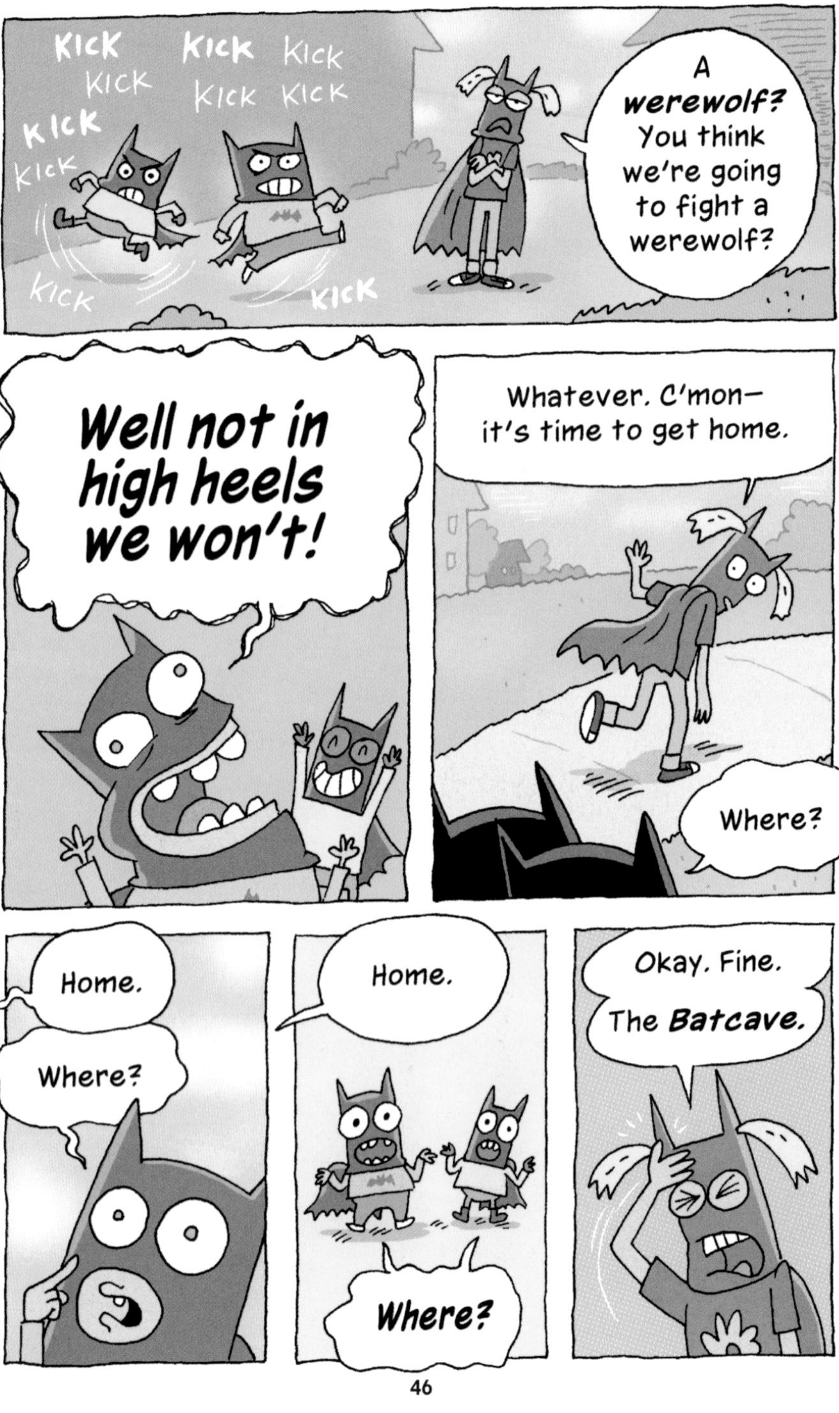
KICK KICK KICK KICK KICK KICK KICK KICK KICK KICK
A *werewolf?* You think we're going to fight a werewolf?
Well not in high heels we won't!
Whatever. C'mon— it's time to get home.
Where?
Home.
Where?
Home.
Where?
Okay. Fine.
The *Batcave.*

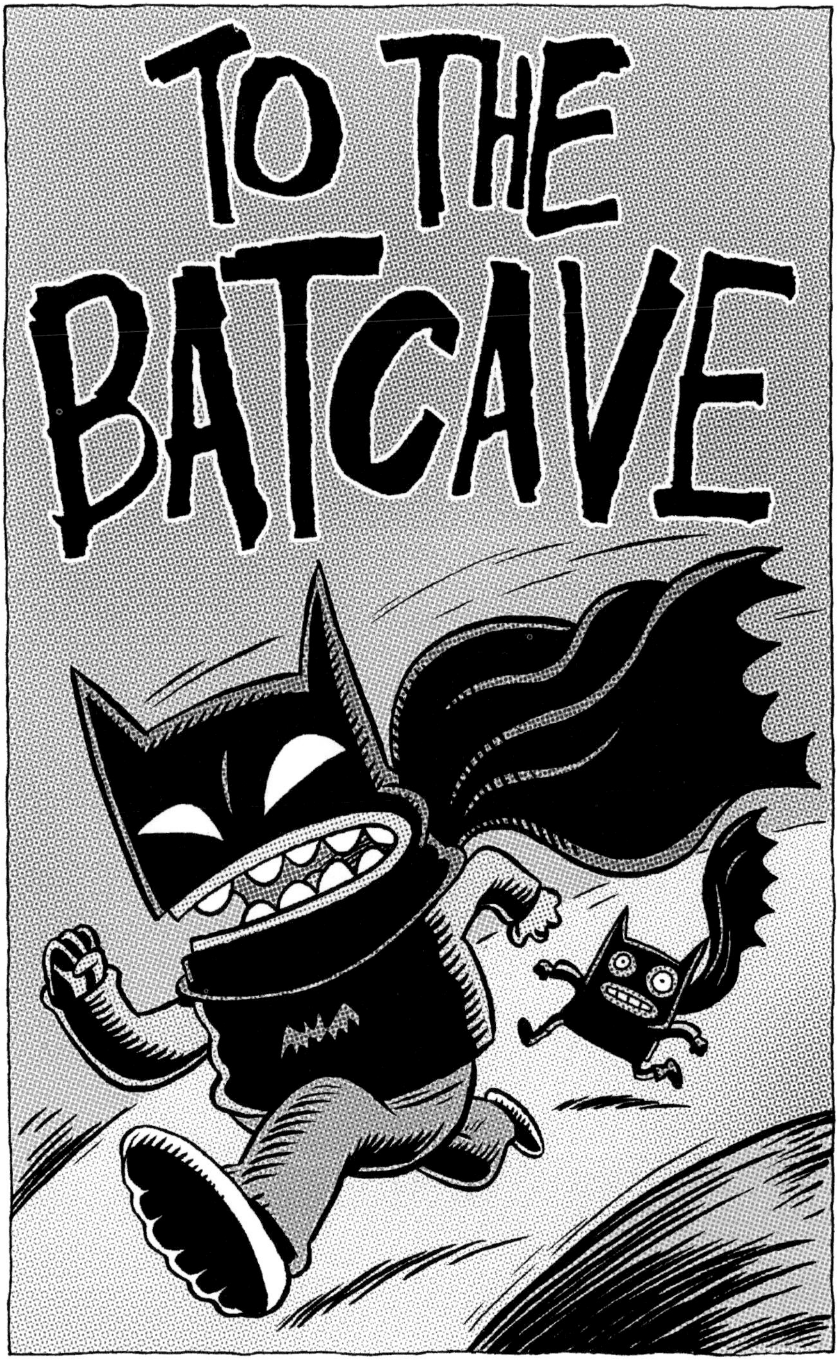
TO THE
BATCAVE

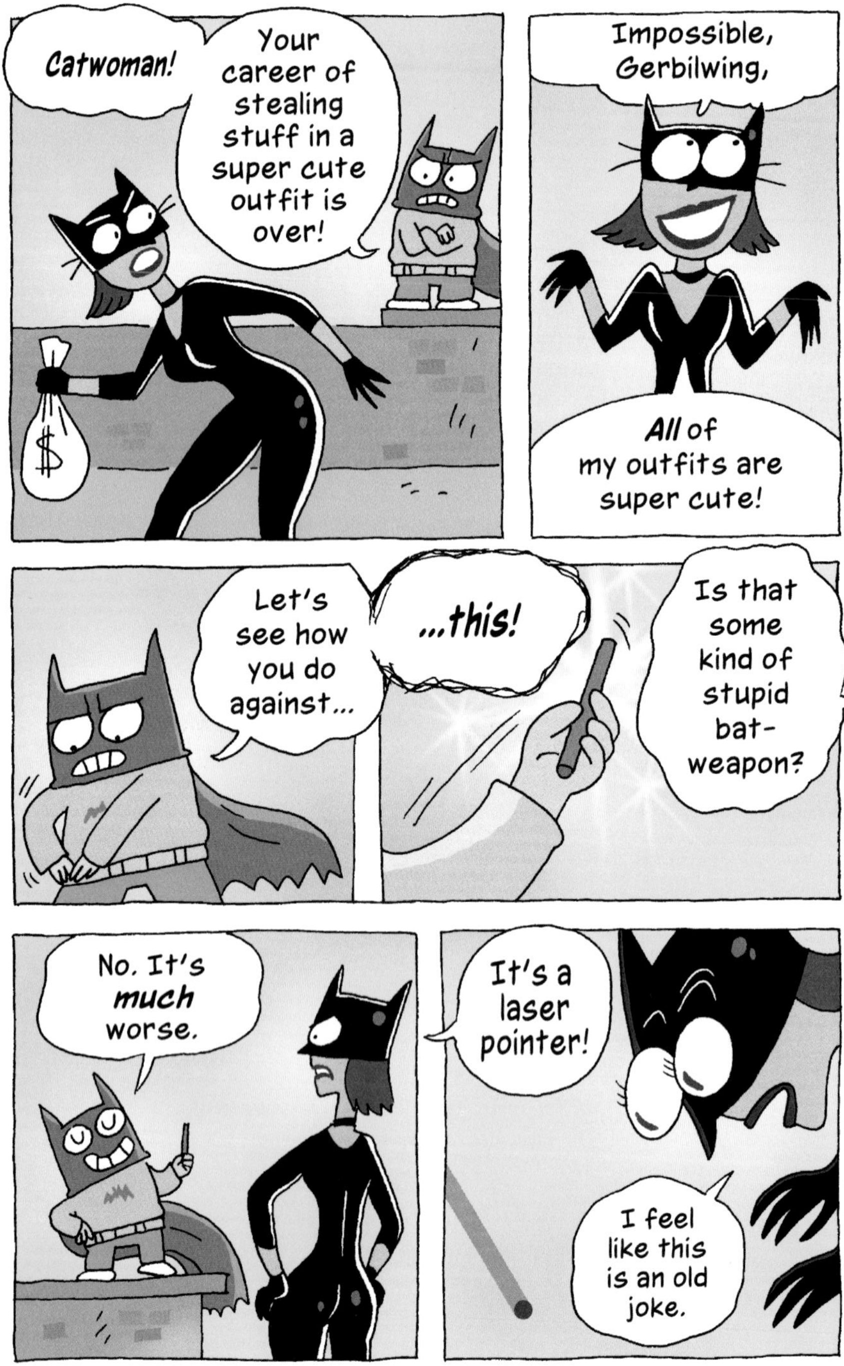
Catwoman!
Your career of stealing stuff in a super cute outfit is over!
Impossible, Gerbilwing,
All of my outfits are super cute!
Let's see how you do against...
...this!
Is that some kind of stupid bat-weapon?
No. It's much worse.
It's a laser pointer!
I feel like this is an old joke.

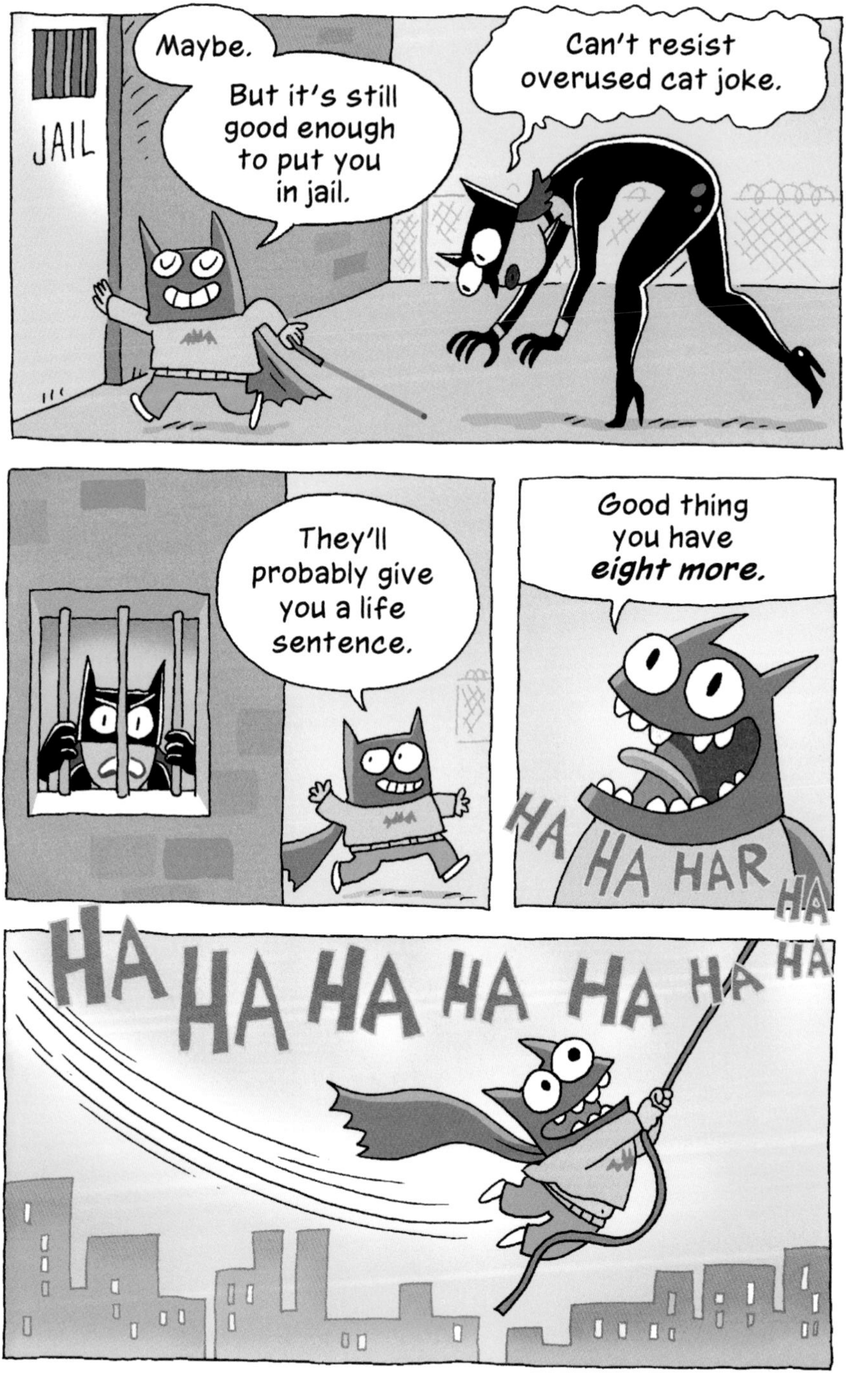
JAIL
Maybe.
But it's still good enough to put you in jail.
Can't resist overused cat joke.
They'll probably give you a life sentence.
Good thing you have *eight more.*
HA HA HAR HA
HA HA HA HA HA HA HA HA HA

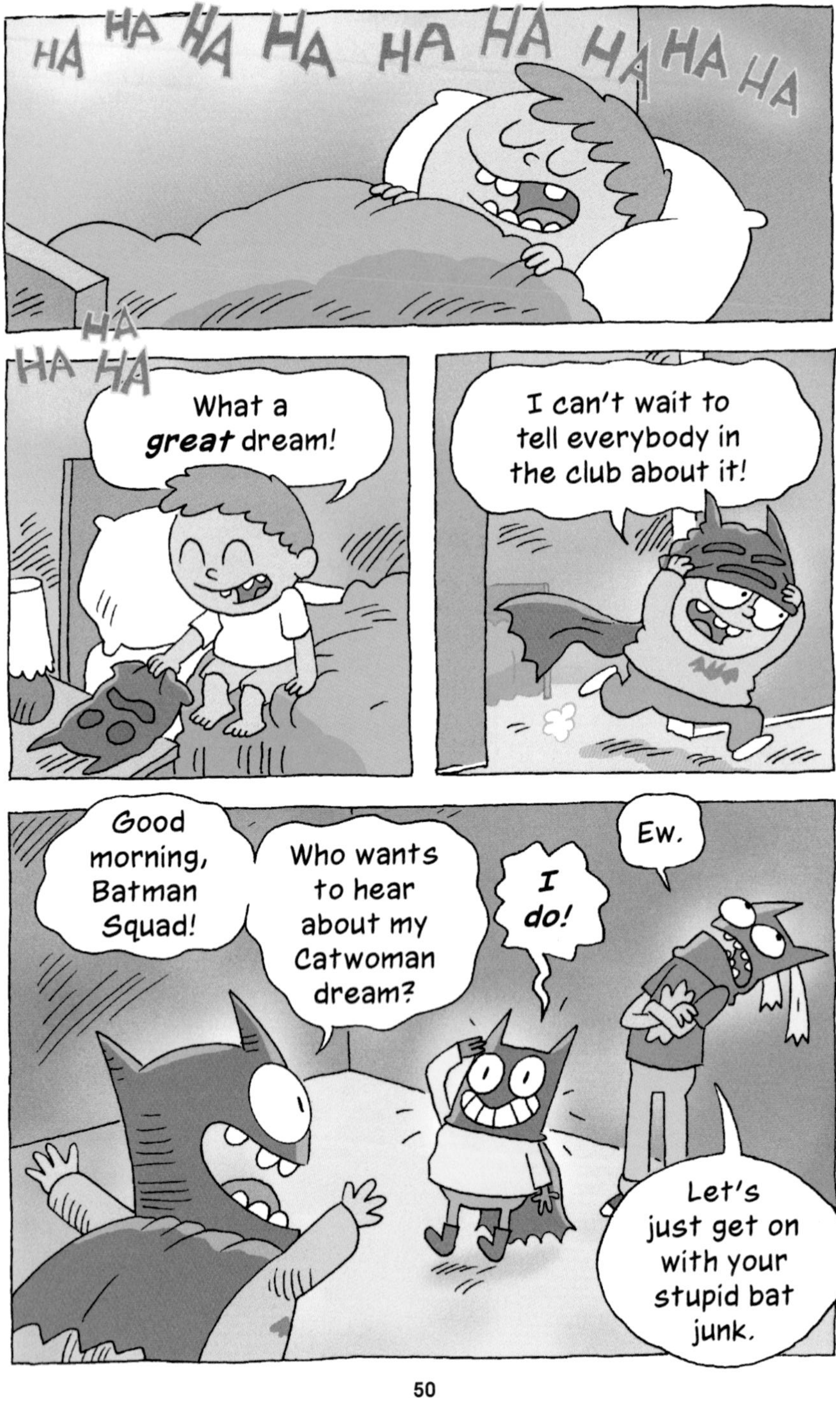
HA HA HA HA HA HA HA HA HA
HA HA HA
What a *great* dream!
I can't wait to tell everybody in the club about it!
Good morning, Batman Squad!
Who wants to hear about my Catwoman dream?
I do!
Ew.
Let's just get on with your stupid bat junk.

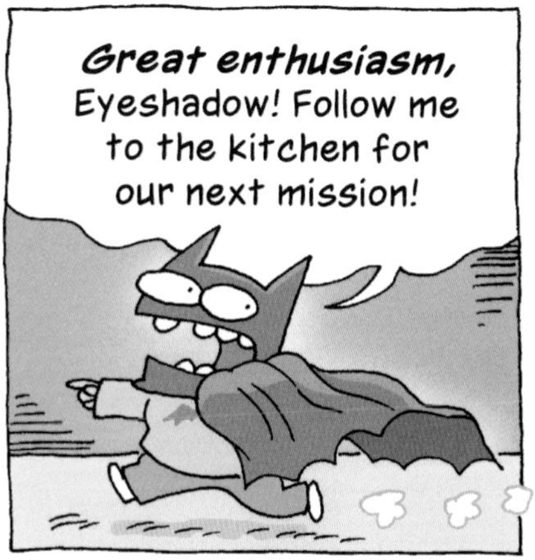
Great enthusiasm, Eyeshadow! Follow me to the kitchen for our next mission!

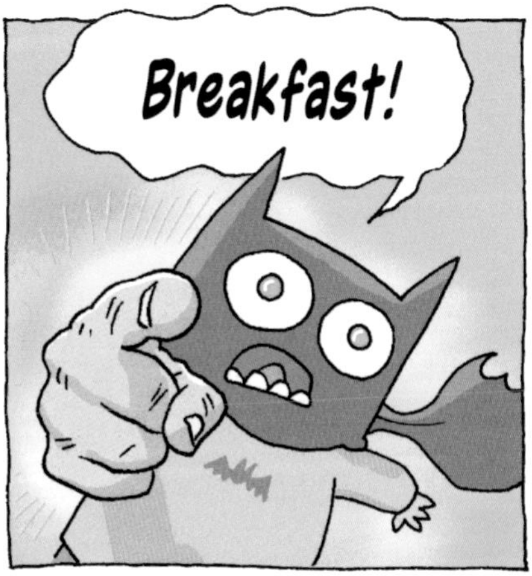
Breakfast!

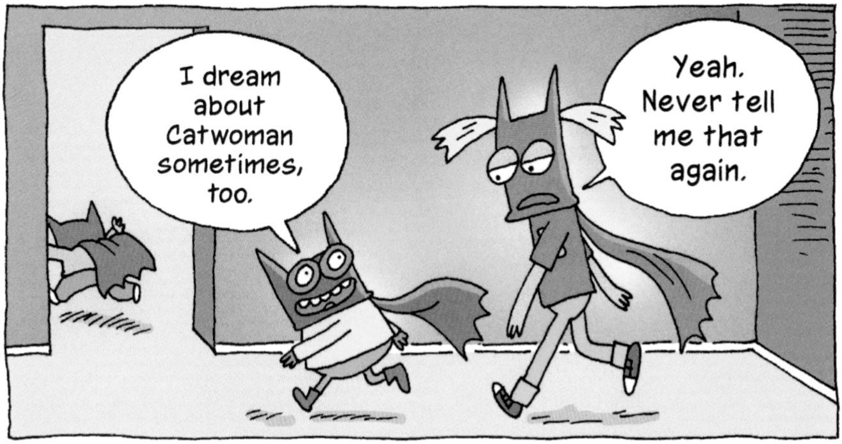
I dream about Catwoman sometimes, too.
Yeah. Never tell me that again.

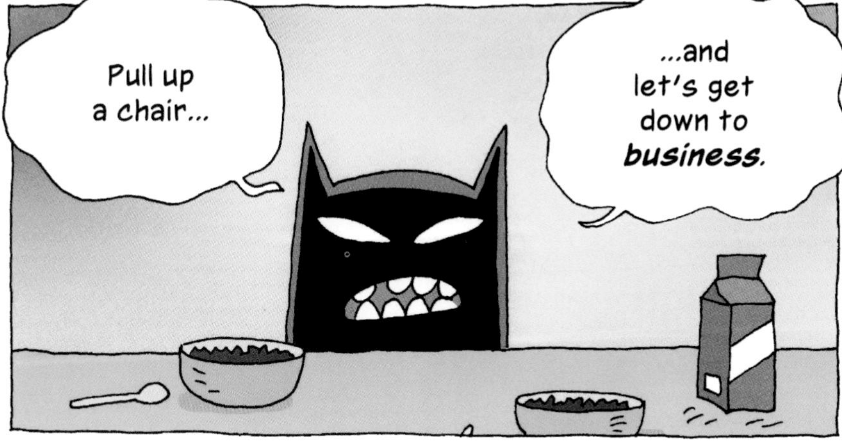
Pull up a chair...
...and let's get down to ***business***.

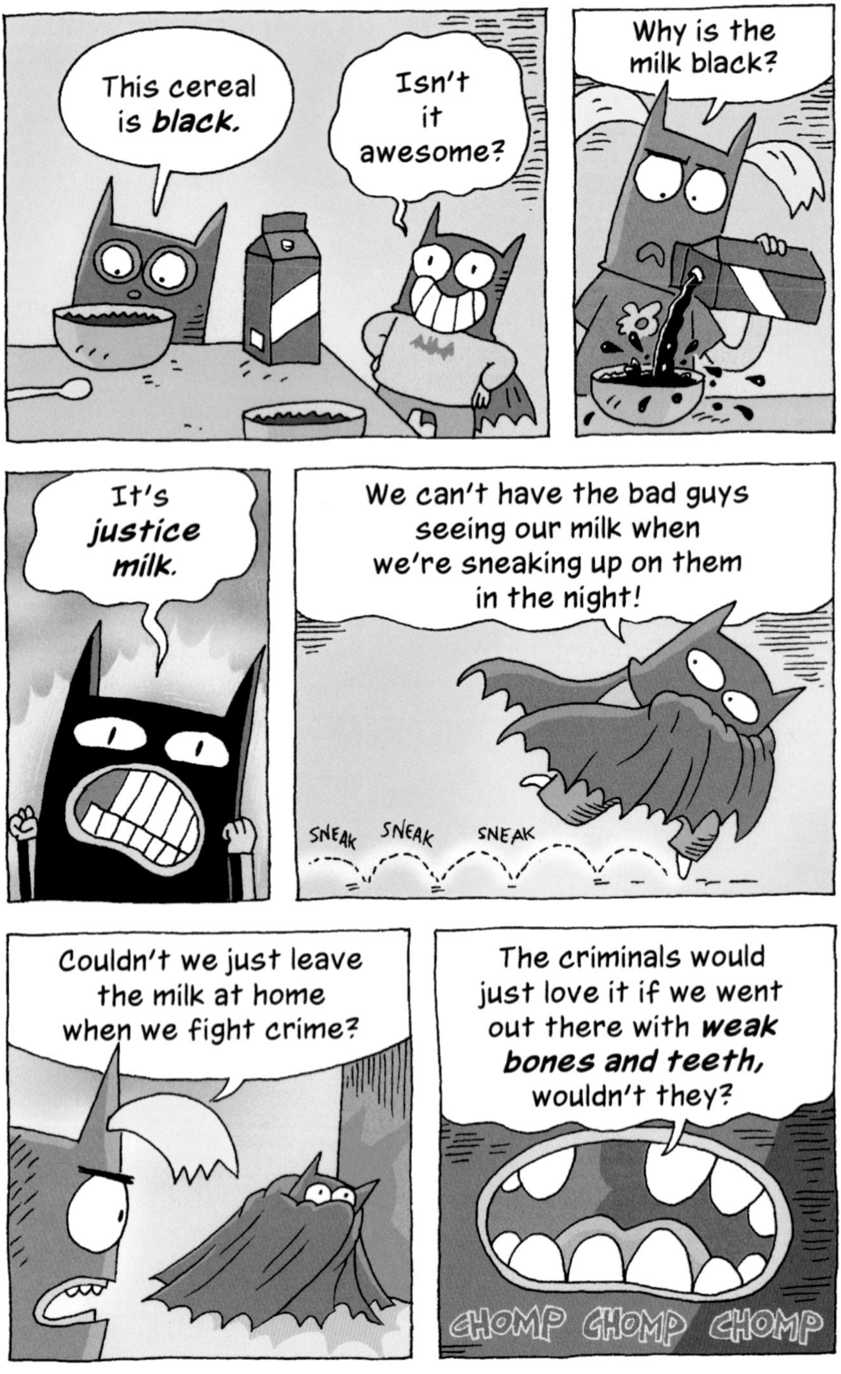
This cereal is *black.*
Isn't it awesome?
Why is the milk black?
It's *justice milk.*
We can't have the bad guys seeing our milk when we're sneaking up on them in the night!
SNEAK SNEAK SNEAK
Couldn't we just leave the milk at home when we fight crime?
The criminals would just love it if we went out there with ***weak bones and teeth,*** wouldn't they?
CHOMP CHOMP CHOMP

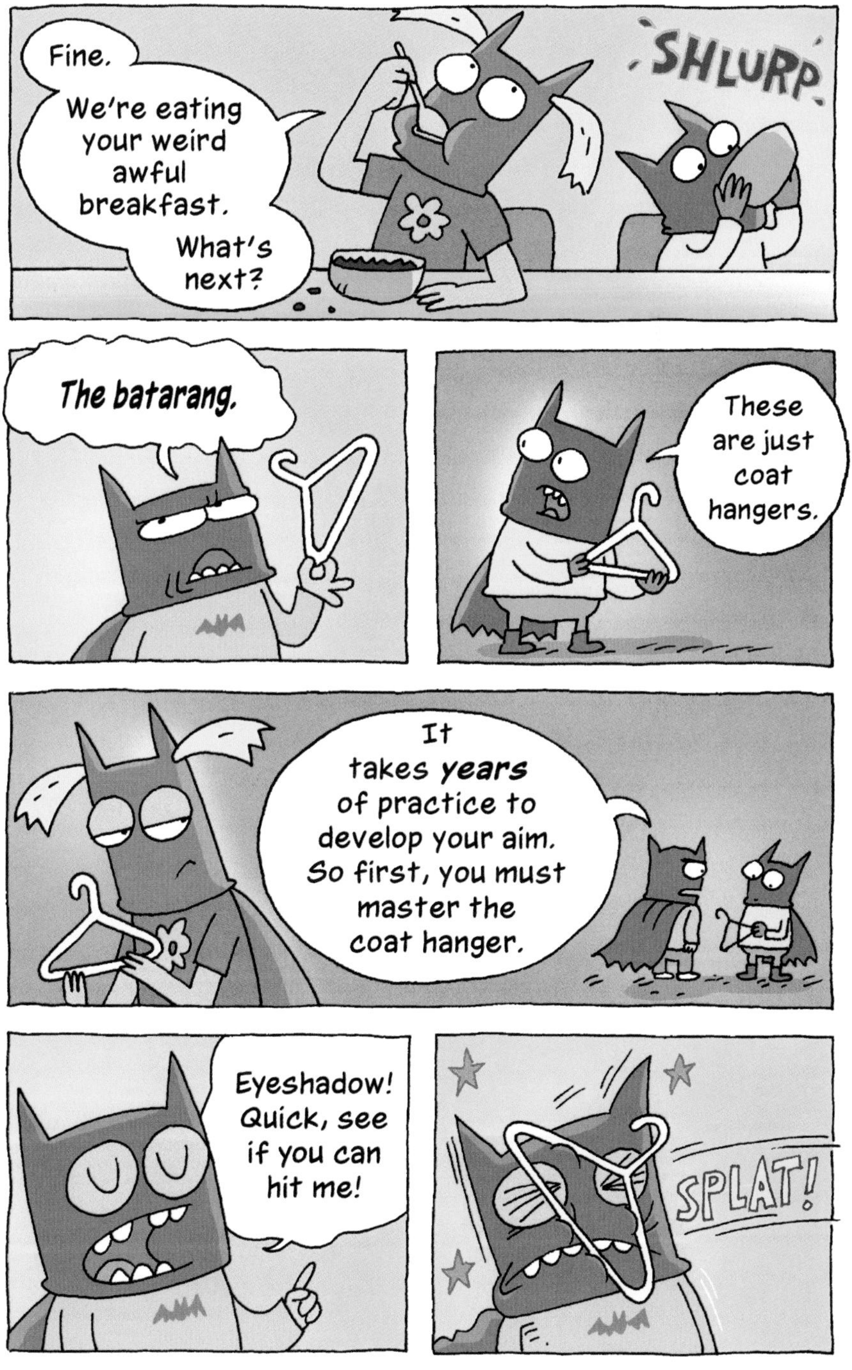
Fine.
We're eating your weird awful breakfast.
What's next?
SHLURP
The batarang.
These are just coat hangers.
It takes *years* of practice to develop your aim. So first, you must master the coat hanger.
Eyeshadow! Quick, see if you can hit me!
SPLAT!

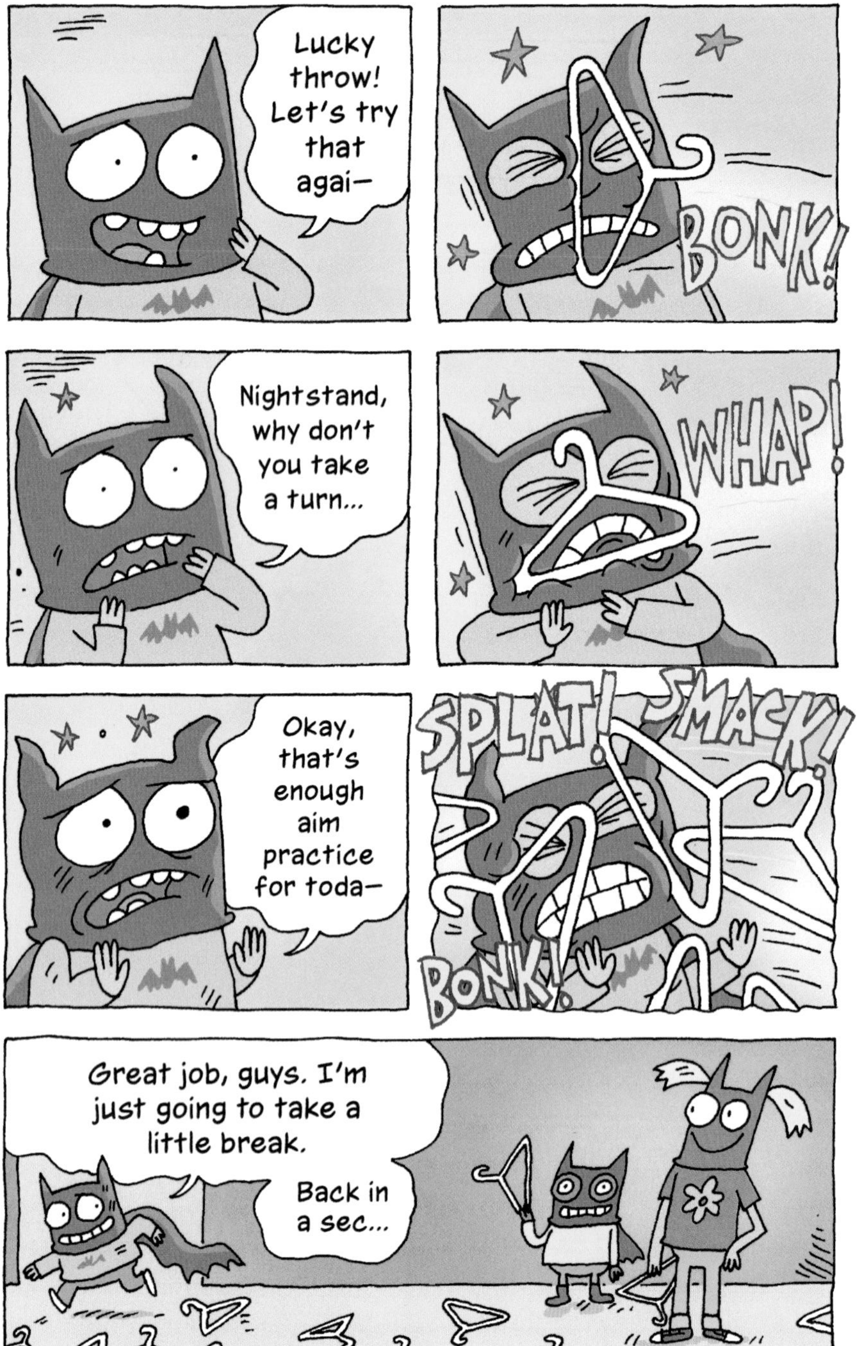
Lucky throw! Let's try that agai–
BONK!
Nightstand, why don't you take a turn...
WHAP!
Okay, that's enough aim practice for toda–
SPLAT!
SMACK!
BONK!
Great job, guys. I'm just going to take a little break.
Back in a sec...

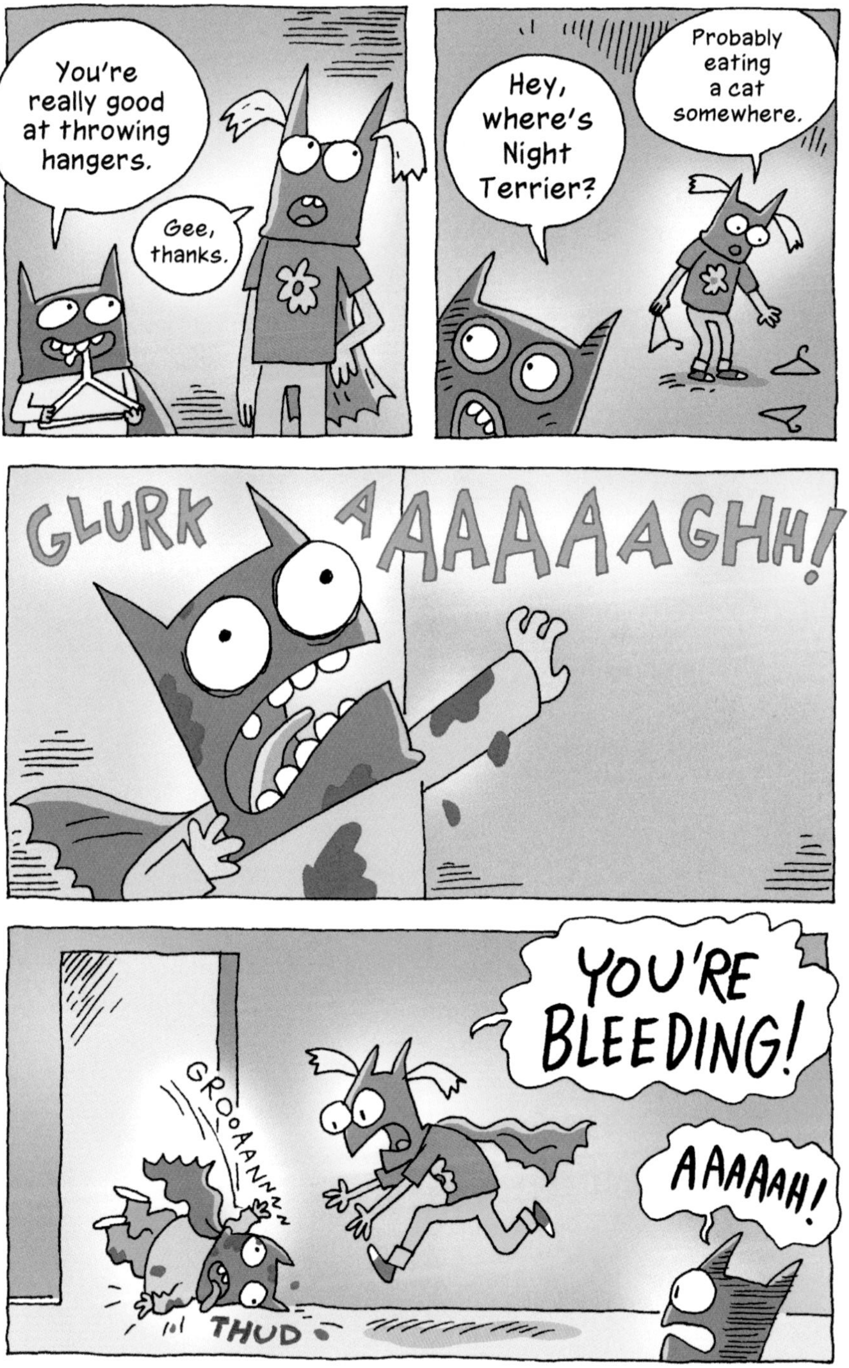

You're really good at throwing hangers.
Gee, thanks.
Hey, where's Night Terrier?
Probably eating a cat somewhere.
GLURK
AAAAAAGHH!
YOU'RE BLEEDING!
GROOAANNZZ
AAAAAH!
THUD

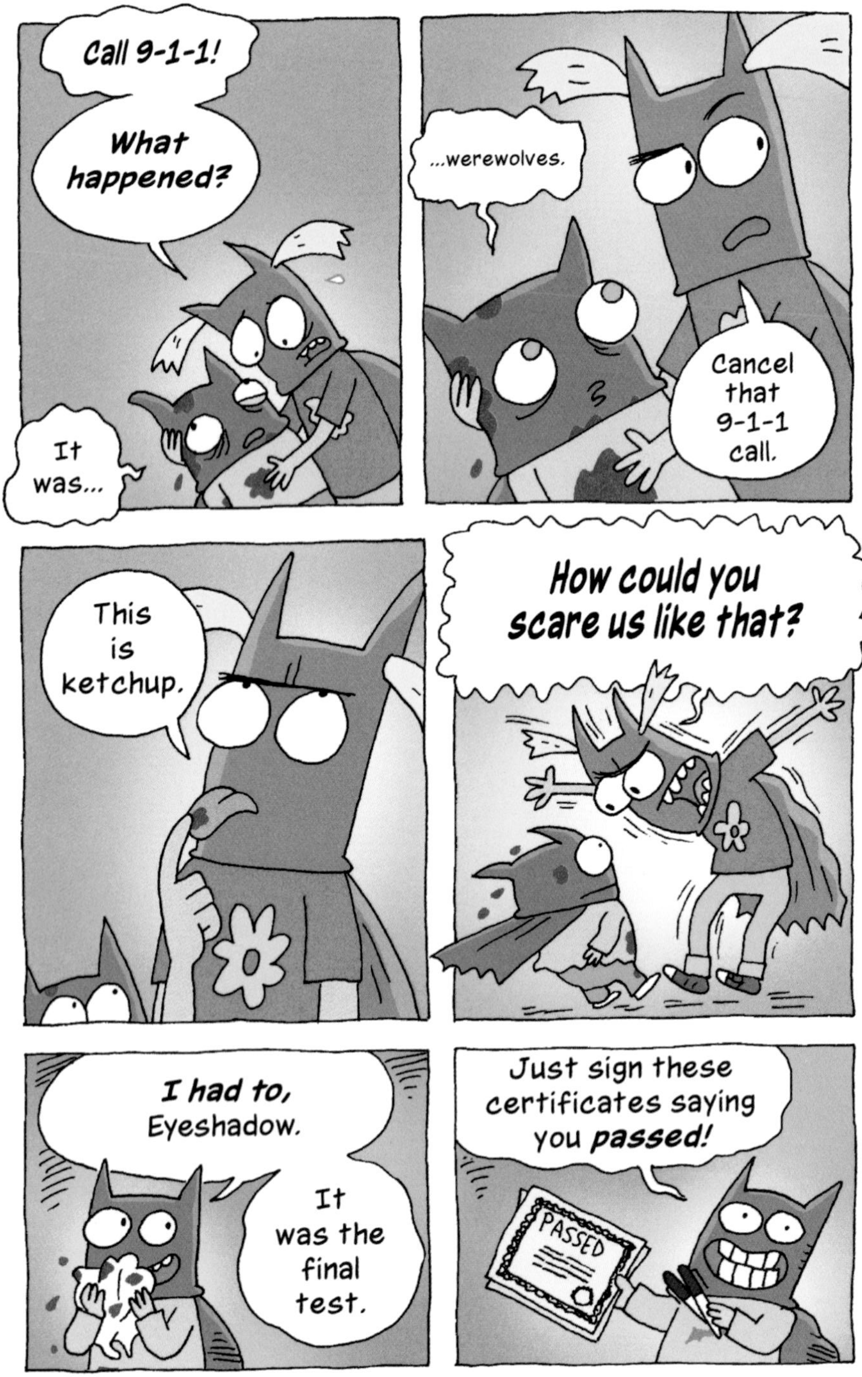

Call 9-1-1!
What happened?
It was...
...werewolves.
Cancel that 9-1-1 call.
This is ketchup.
How could you scare us like that?
I had to, Eyeshadow.
It was the final test.
Just sign these certificates saying you passed!
PASSED

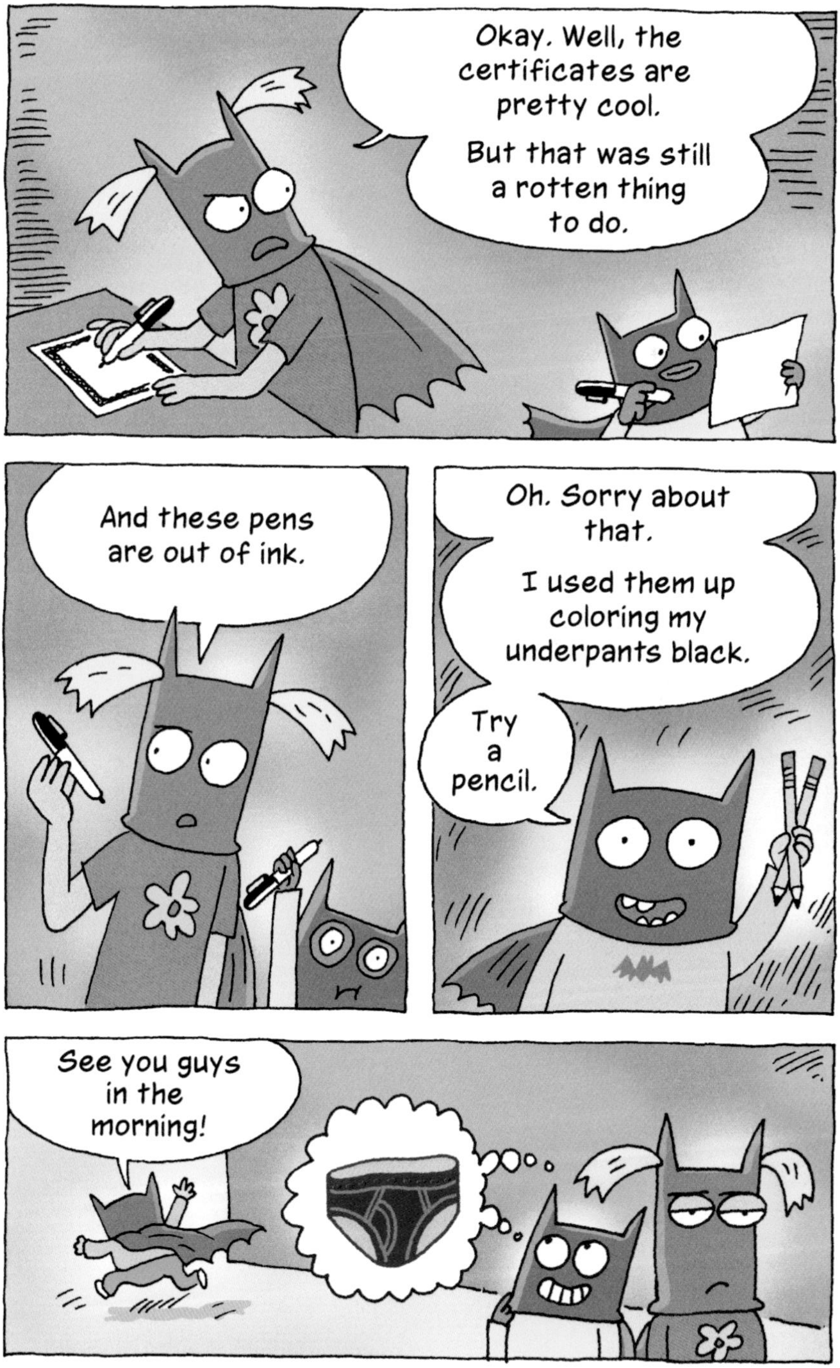
Okay. Well, the certificates are pretty cool.
But that was still a rotten thing to do.
And these pens are out of ink.
Oh. Sorry about that.
I used them up coloring my underpants black.
Try a pencil.
See you guys in the morning!

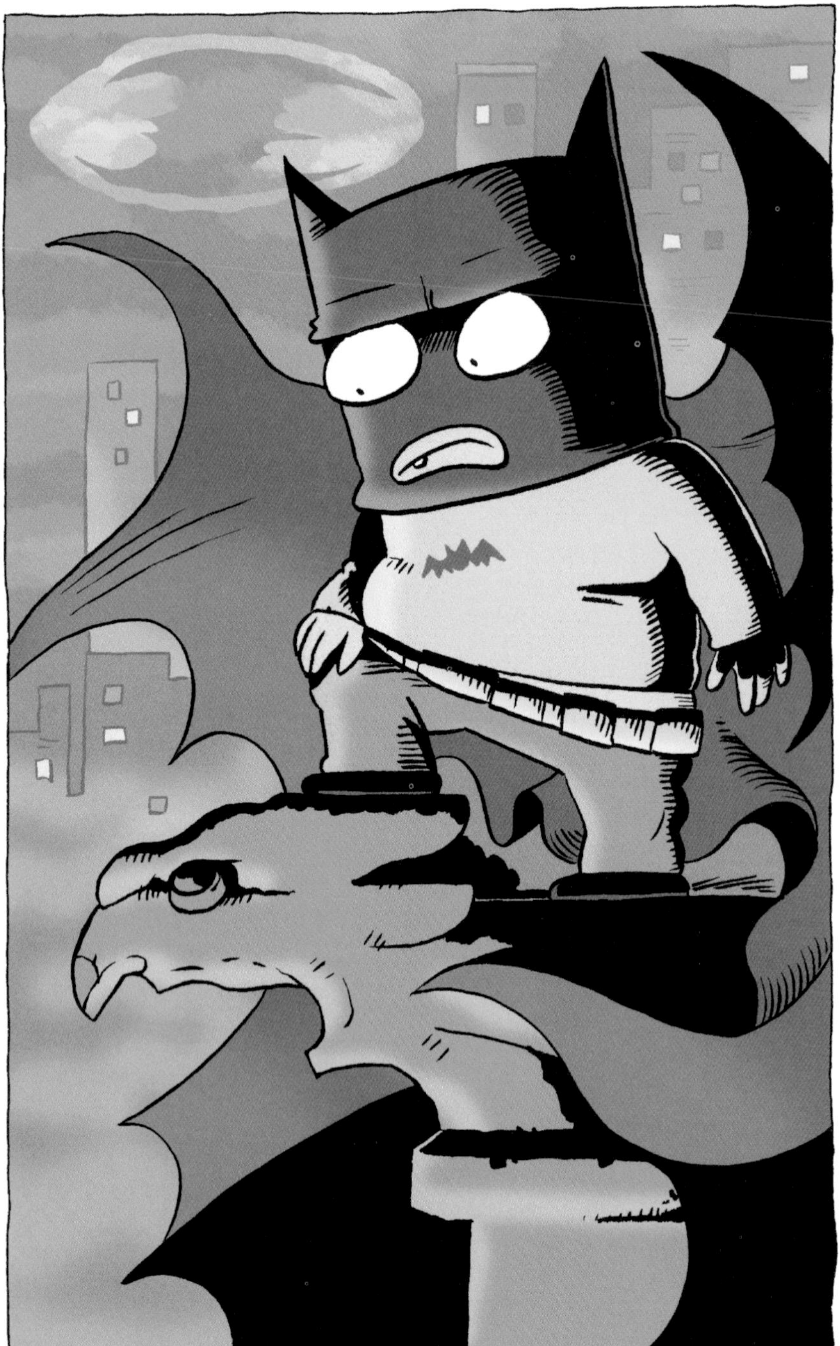

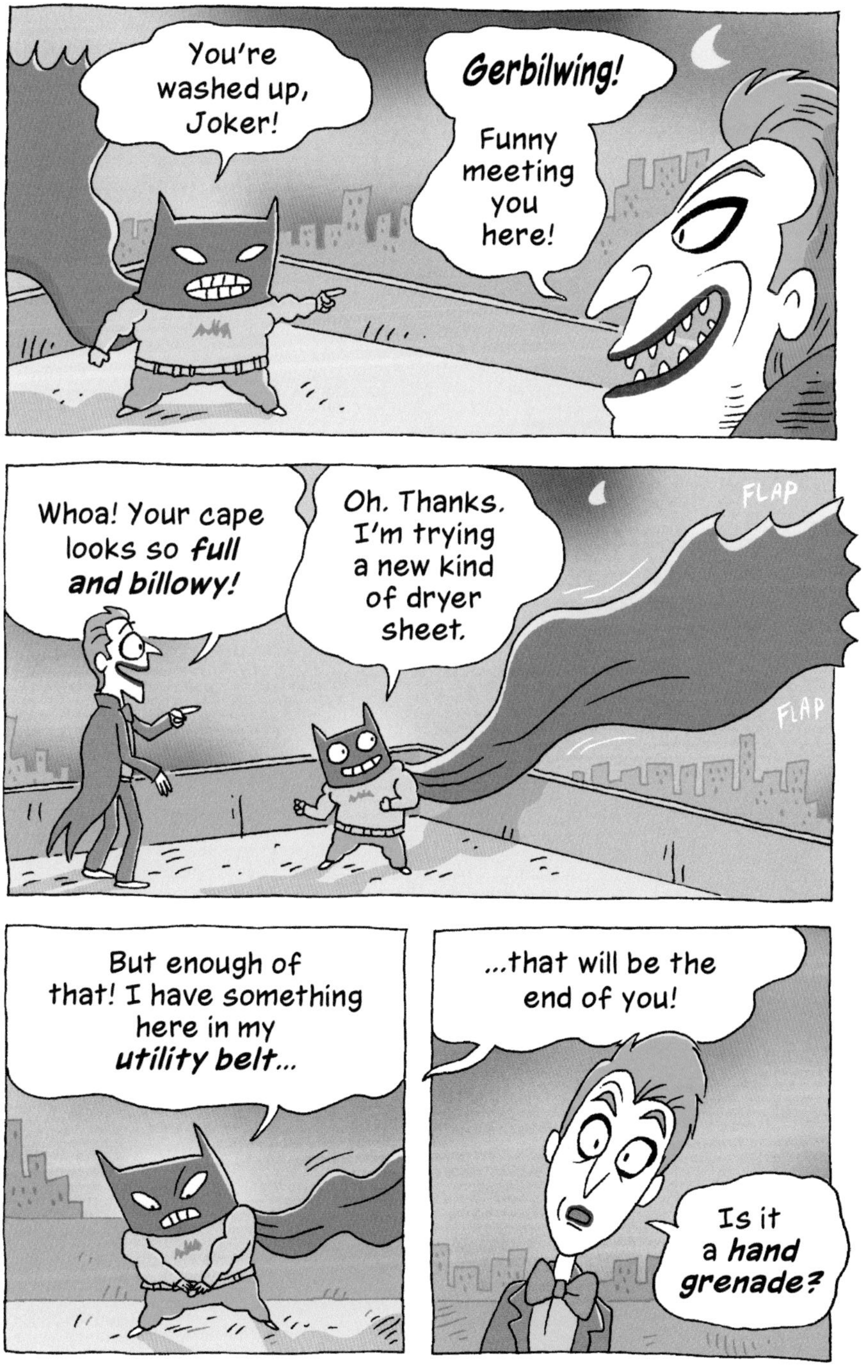
You're washed up, Joker!
Gerbilwing!
Funny meeting you here!
Whoa! Your cape looks so full and billowy!
Oh. Thanks. I'm trying a new kind of dryer sheet.
FLAP
FLAP
But enough of that! I have something here in my utility belt...
...that will be the end of you!
Is it a hand grenade?

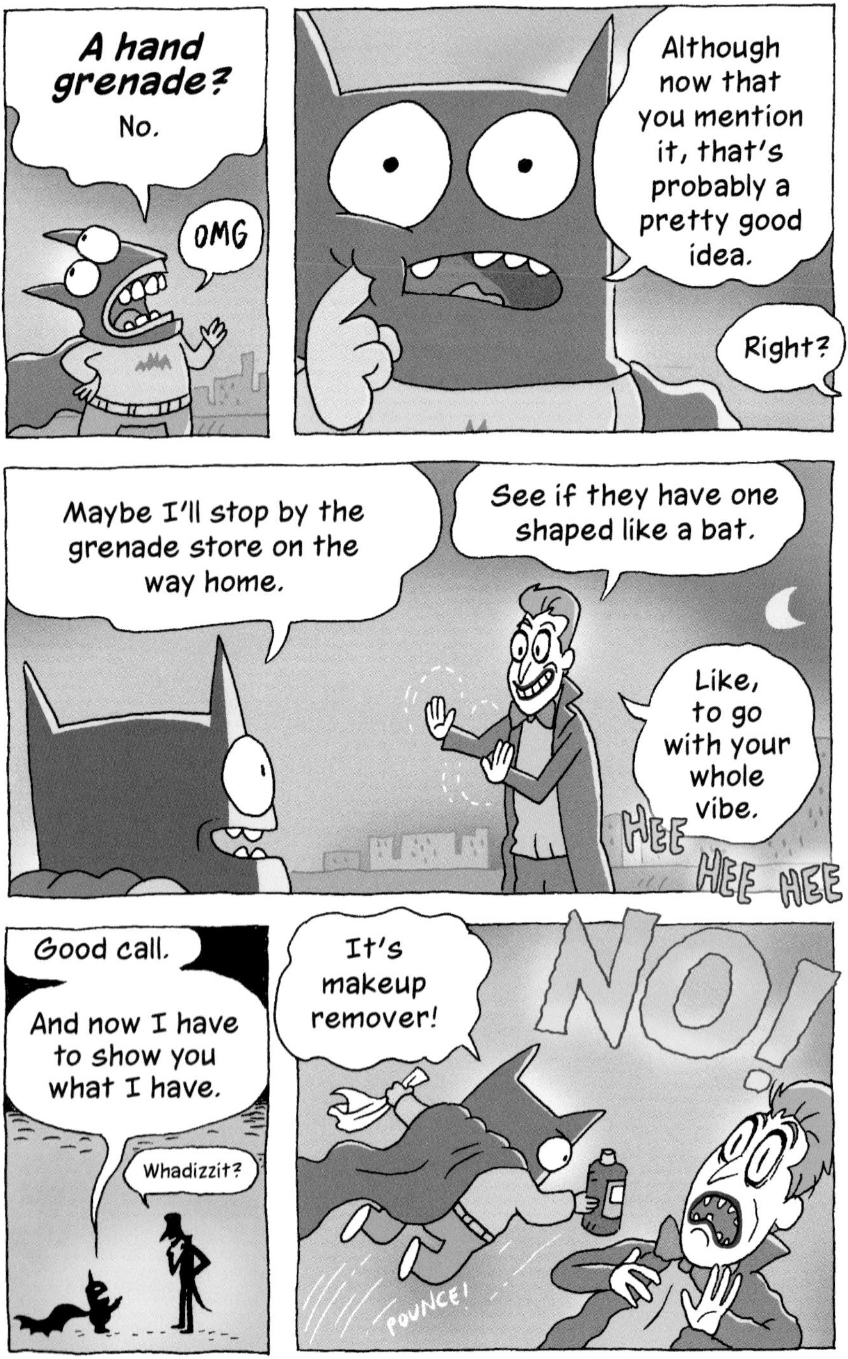
A hand grenade? No.
OMG
Although now that you mention it, that's probably a pretty good idea.
Right?
Maybe I'll stop by the grenade store on the way home.
See if they have one shaped like a bat.
Like, to go with your whole vibe.
HEE HEE HEE
Good call.
And now I have to show you what I have.
Whadizzit?
It's makeup remover!
NO!
POUNCE!

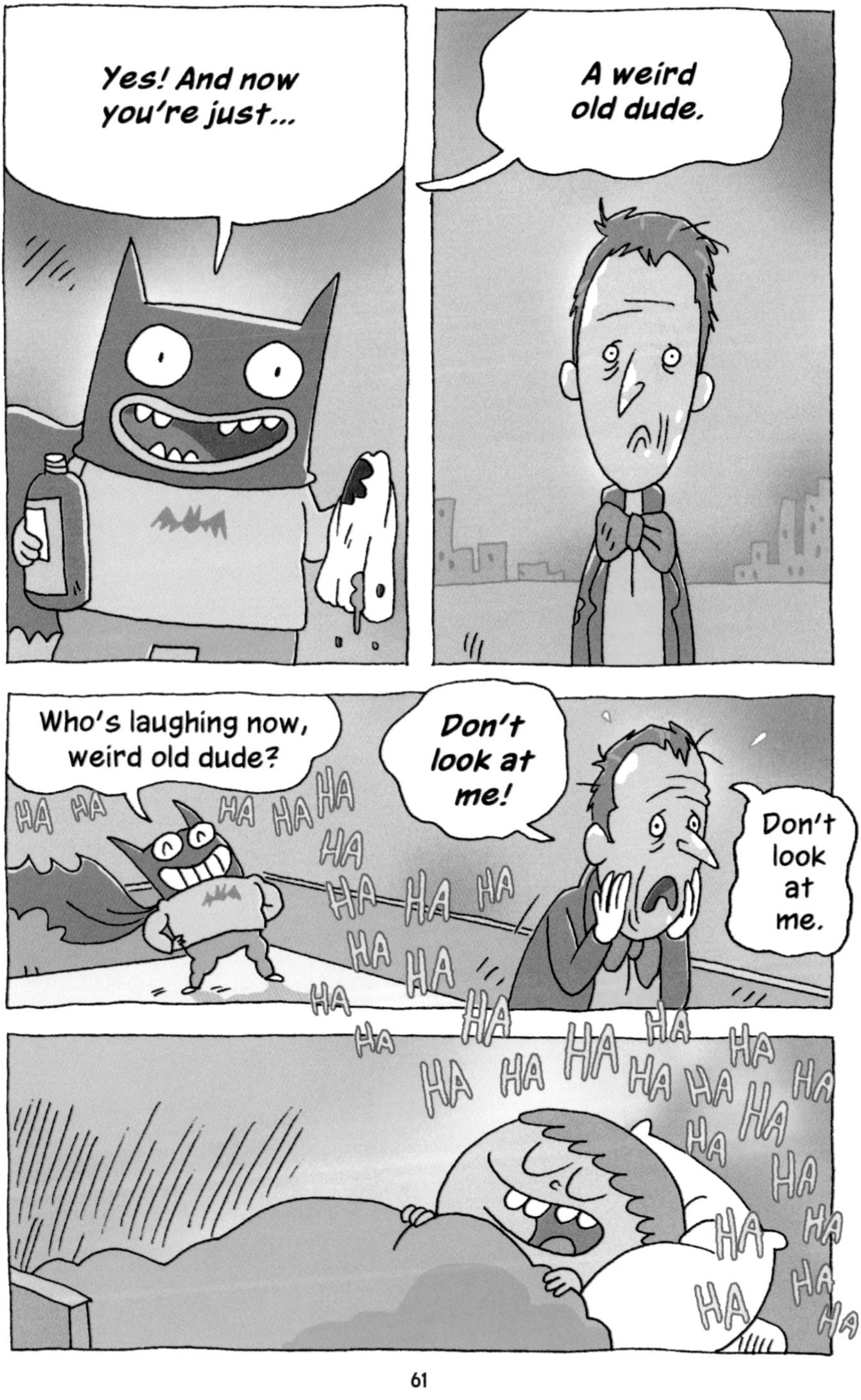

Yes! And now you're just...
A weird old dude.
Who's laughing now, weird old dude?
Don't look at me!
Don't look at me.
HA HA HA HA HA HA HA HA HA HA HA HA HA HA HA HA HA HA HA HA HA HA HA HA HA HA HA HA HA HA HA HA HA

What a *great* dream!

I can't wait to tell everybody in the club about—

—it.

Nightstand! Where is everybody?

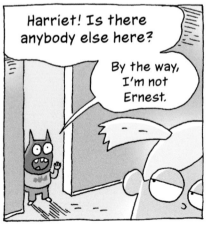

Harriet! Is there anybody else here?

By the way, I'm not Ernest.

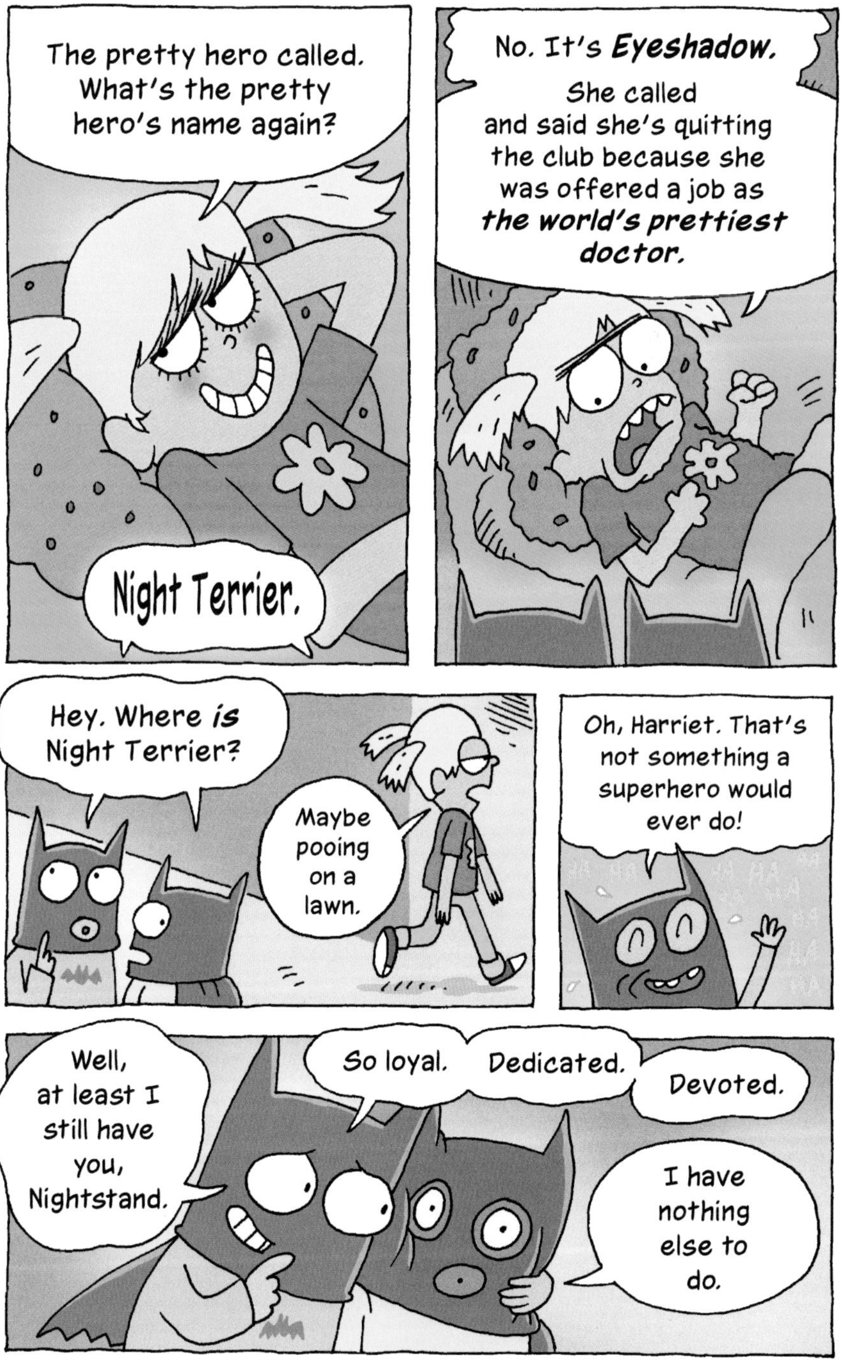
The pretty hero called. What's the pretty hero's name again?
Night Terrier.
No. It's Eyeshadow.
She called and said she's quitting the club because she was offered a job as the world's prettiest doctor.
Hey. Where is Night Terrier?
Maybe pooing on a lawn.
Oh, Harriet. That's not something a superhero would ever do!
Well, at least I still have you, Nightstand.
So loyal.
Dedicated.
Devoted.
I have nothing else to do.

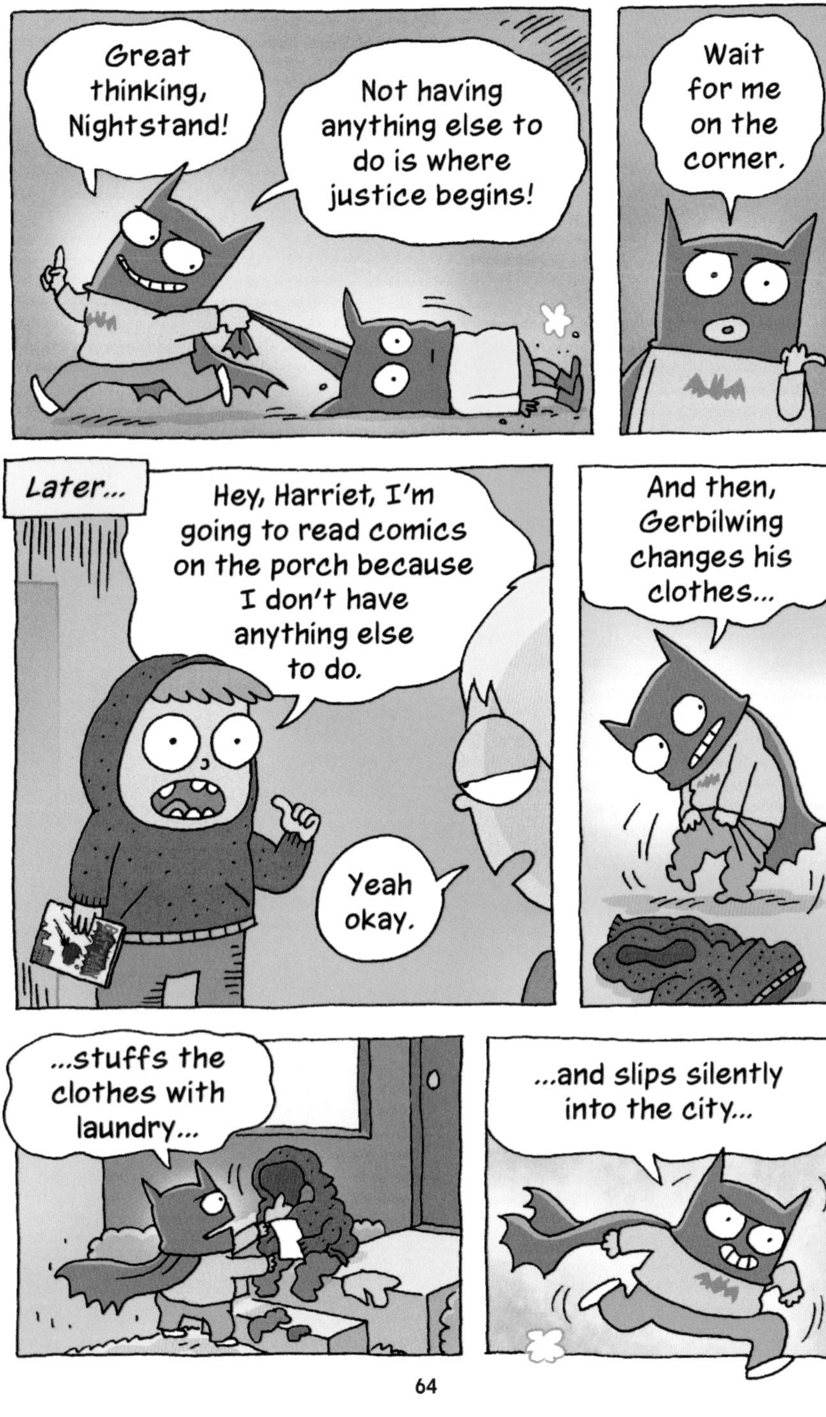
Great thinking, Nightstand!
Not having anything else to do is where justice begins!
Wait for me on the corner.
Later...
Hey, Harriet, I'm going to read comics on the porch because I don't have anything else to do.
Yeah okay.
And then, Gerbilwing changes his clothes...
...stuffs the clothes with laundry...
...and slips silently into the city...

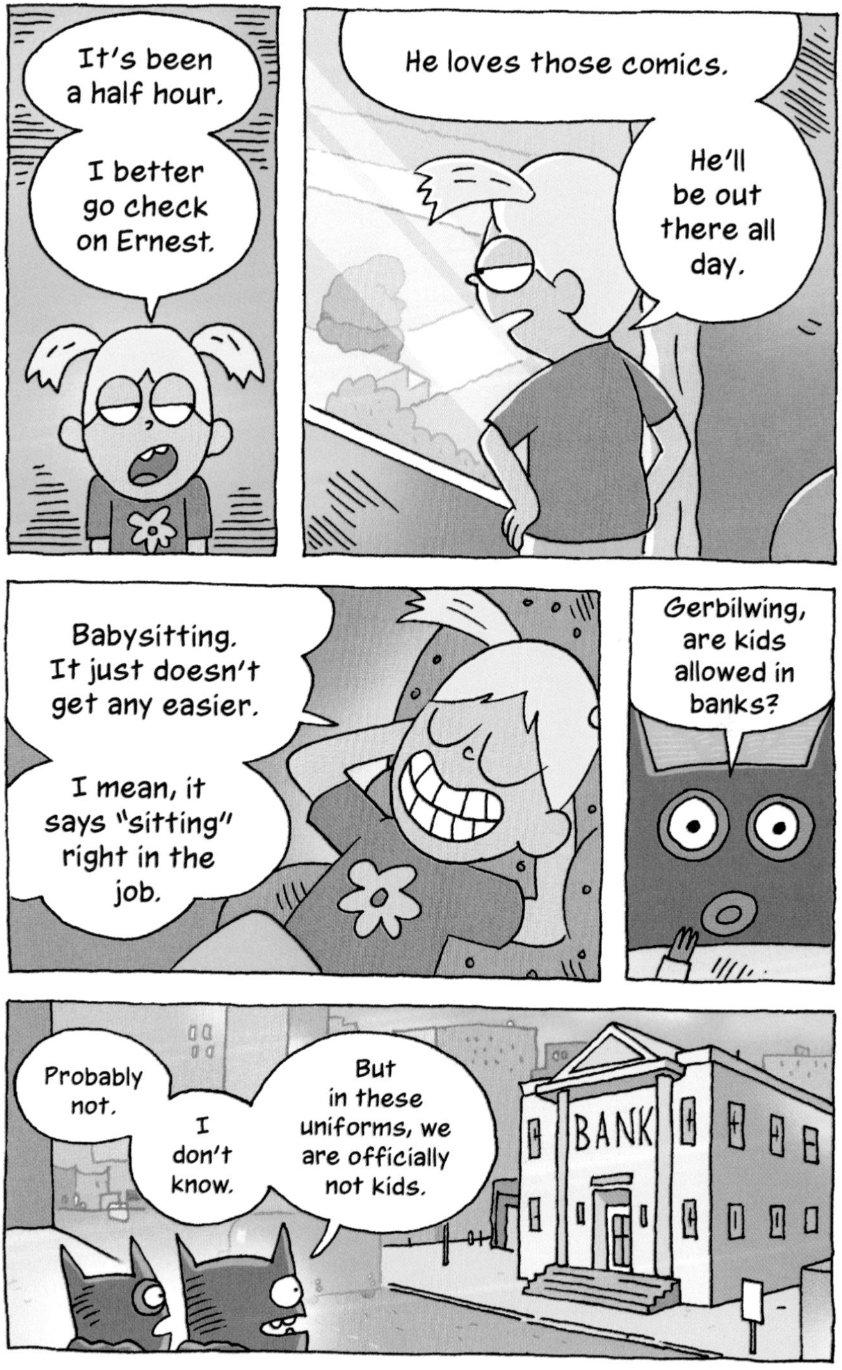

It's been a half hour.
I better go check on Ernest.
He loves those comics.
He'll be out there all day.
Babysitting. It just doesn't get any easier.
I mean, it says "sitting" right in the job.
Gerbilwing, are kids allowed in banks?
Probably not.
I don't know.
But in these uniforms, we are officially not kids.
BANK

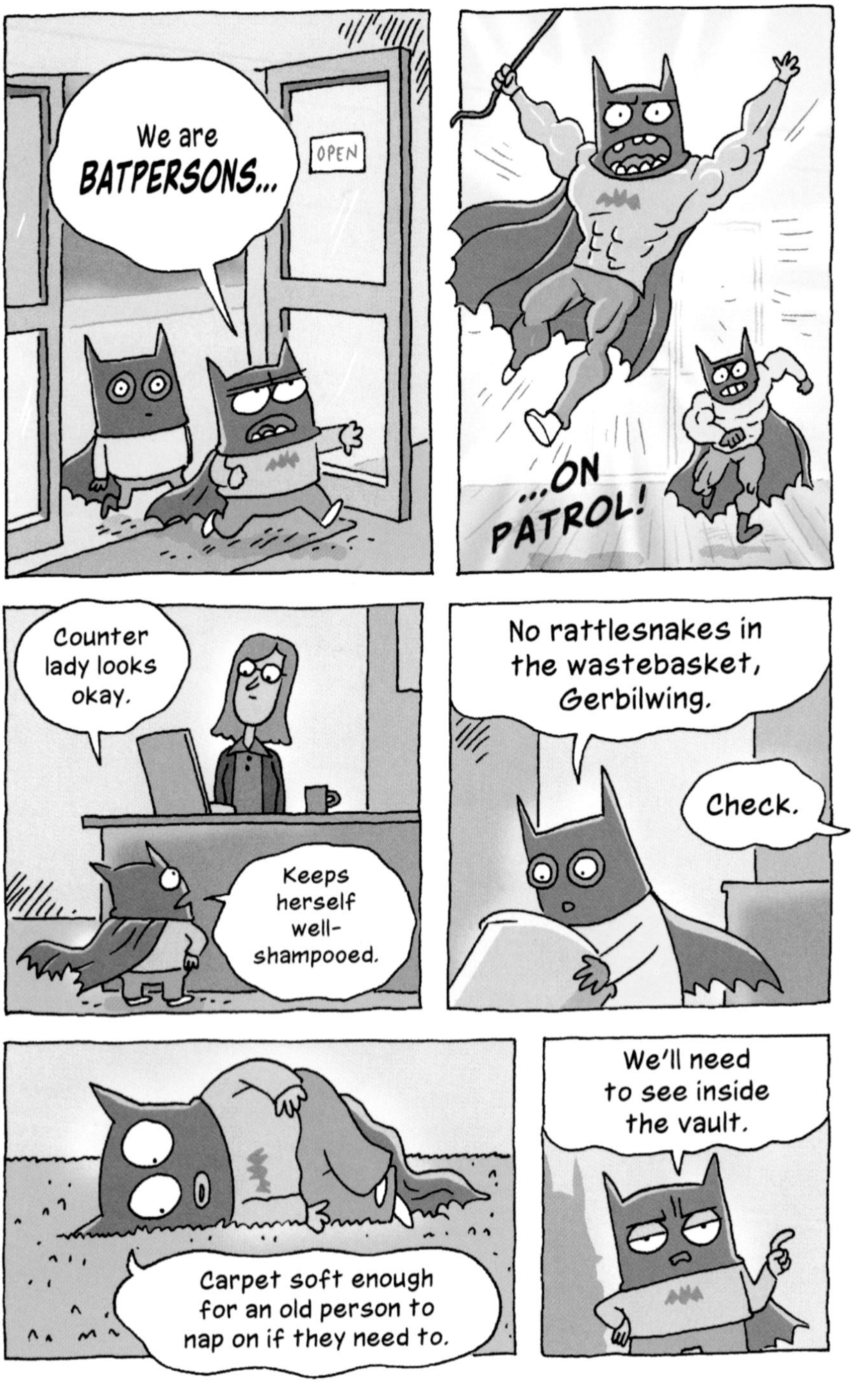
We are BATPERSONS...
OPEN
...ON PATROL!
Counter lady looks okay.
Keeps herself well-shampooed.
No rattlesnakes in the wastebasket, Gerbilwing.
Check.
Carpet soft enough for an old person to nap on if they need to.
We'll need to see inside the vault.

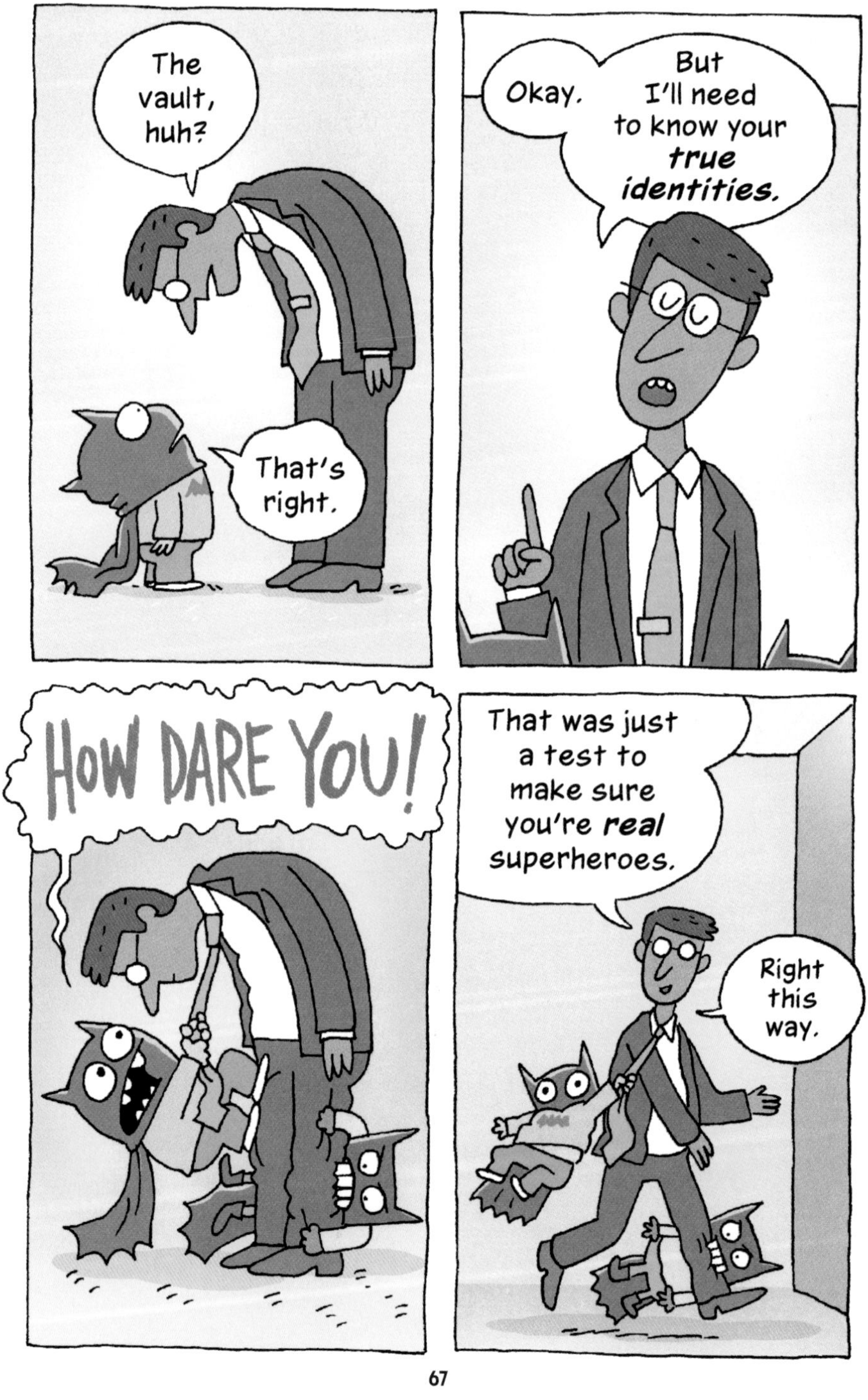
The vault, huh?
That's right.
Okay.
But I'll need to know your *true identities.*
HOW DARE YOU!
That was just a test to make sure you're *real* superheroes.
Right this way.

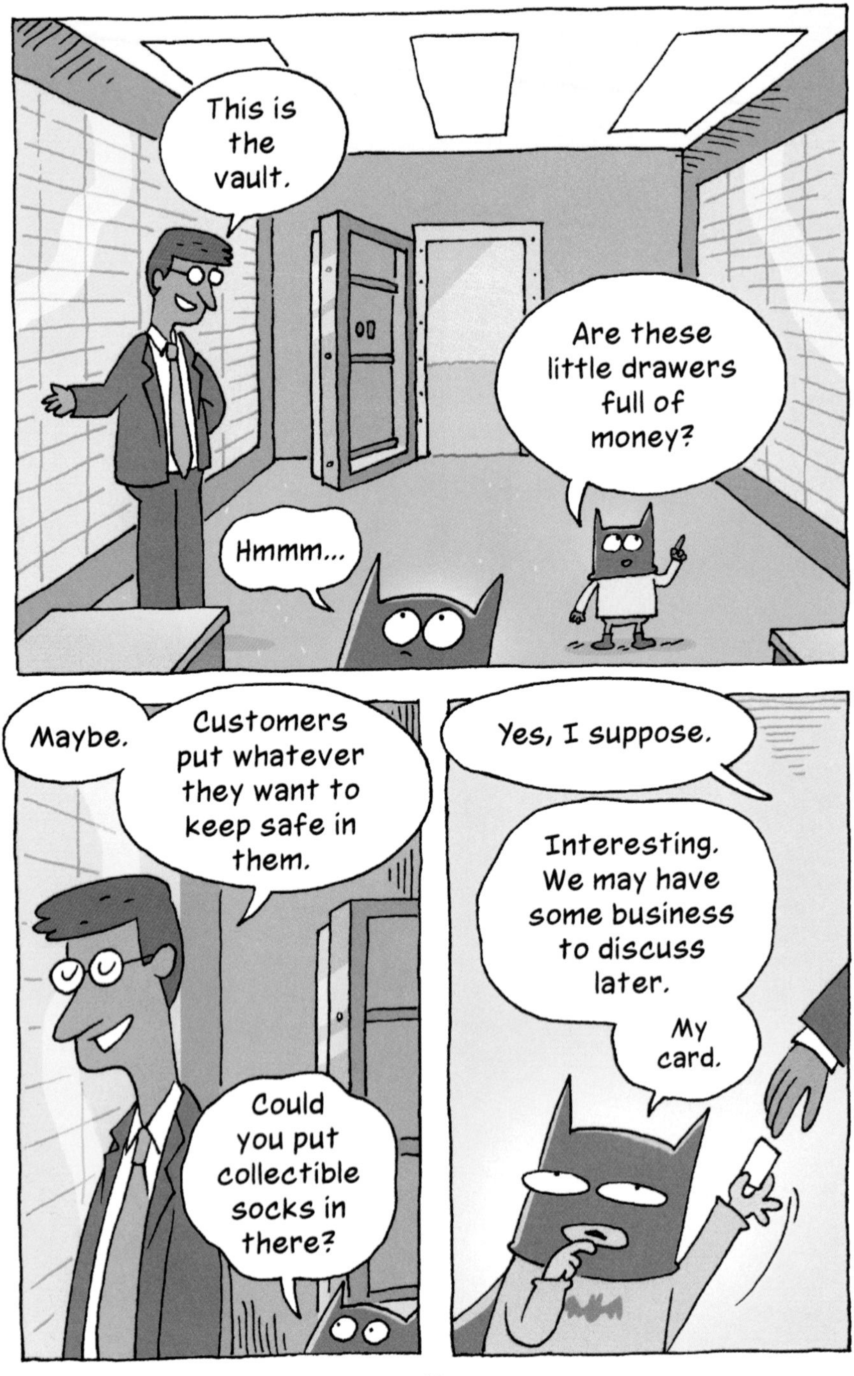
This is the vault.
Are these little drawers full of money?
Hmmm...
Maybe.
Customers put whatever they want to keep safe in them.
Could you put collectible socks in there?
Yes, I suppose.
Interesting. We may have some business to discuss later.
My card.

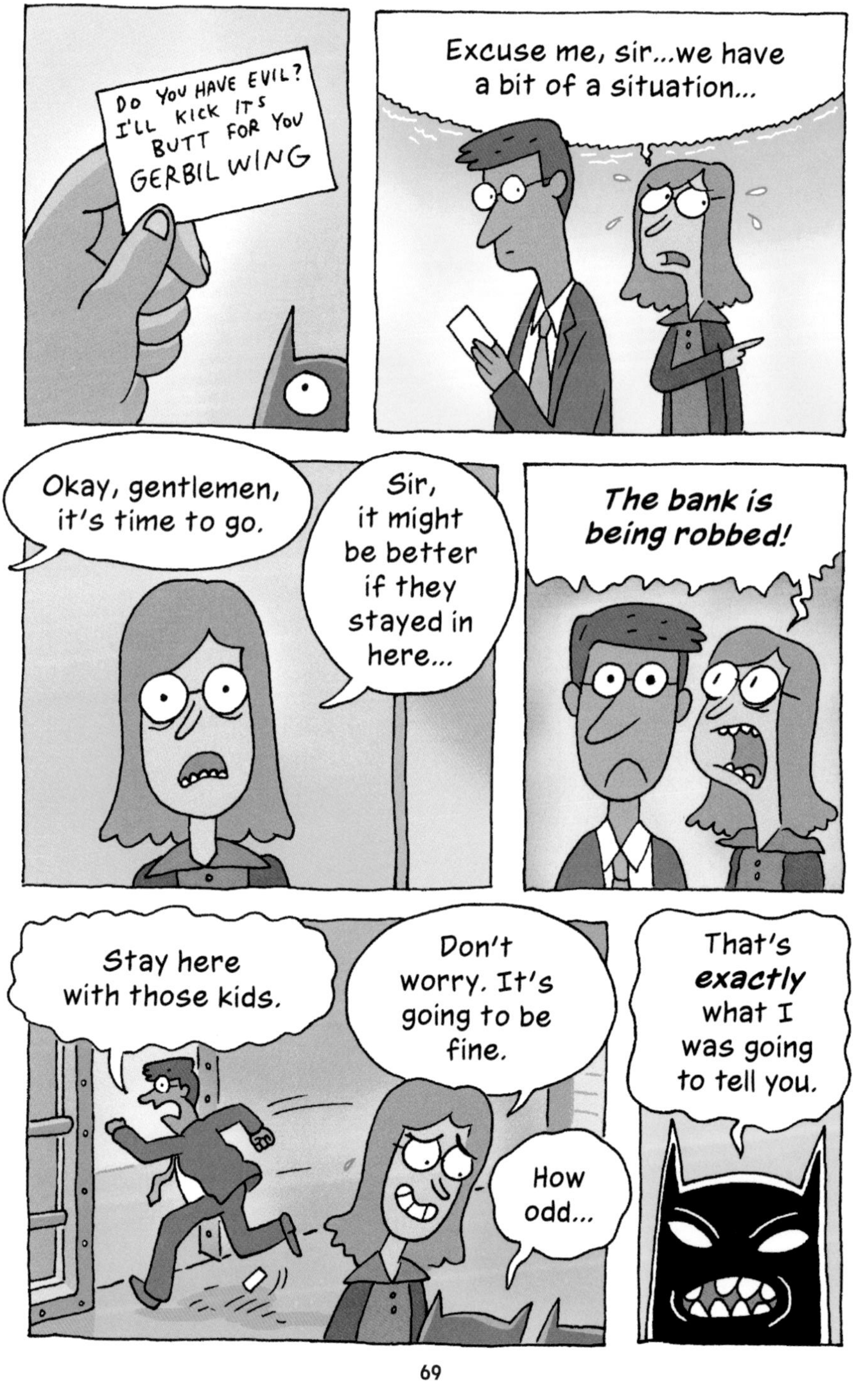
DO YOU HAVE EVIL? I'LL KICK IT'S BUTT FOR YOU GERBIL WING
Excuse me, sir...we have a bit of a situation...
Okay, gentlemen, it's time to go.
Sir, it might be better if they stayed in here...
The bank is being robbed!
Stay here with those kids.
Don't worry. It's going to be fine.
How odd...
That's exactly what I was going to tell you.

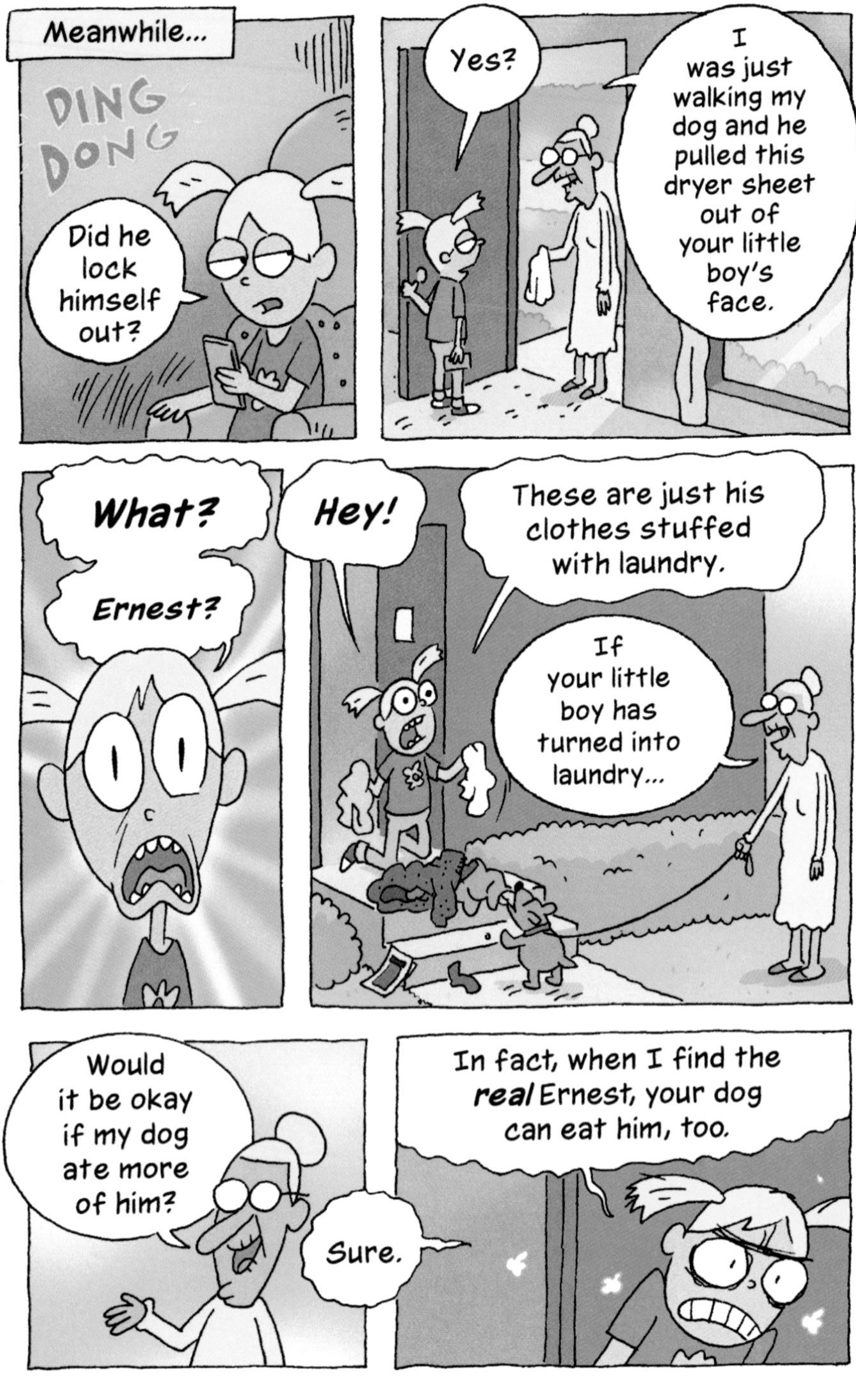
Meanwhile...
DING DONG
Did he lock himself out?
Yes?
I was just walking my dog and he pulled this dryer sheet out of your little boy's face.
What?
Ernest?
Hey!
These are just his clothes stuffed with laundry.
If your little boy has turned into laundry...
Would it be okay if my dog ate more of him?
Sure.
In fact, when I find the *real* Ernest, your dog can eat him, too.

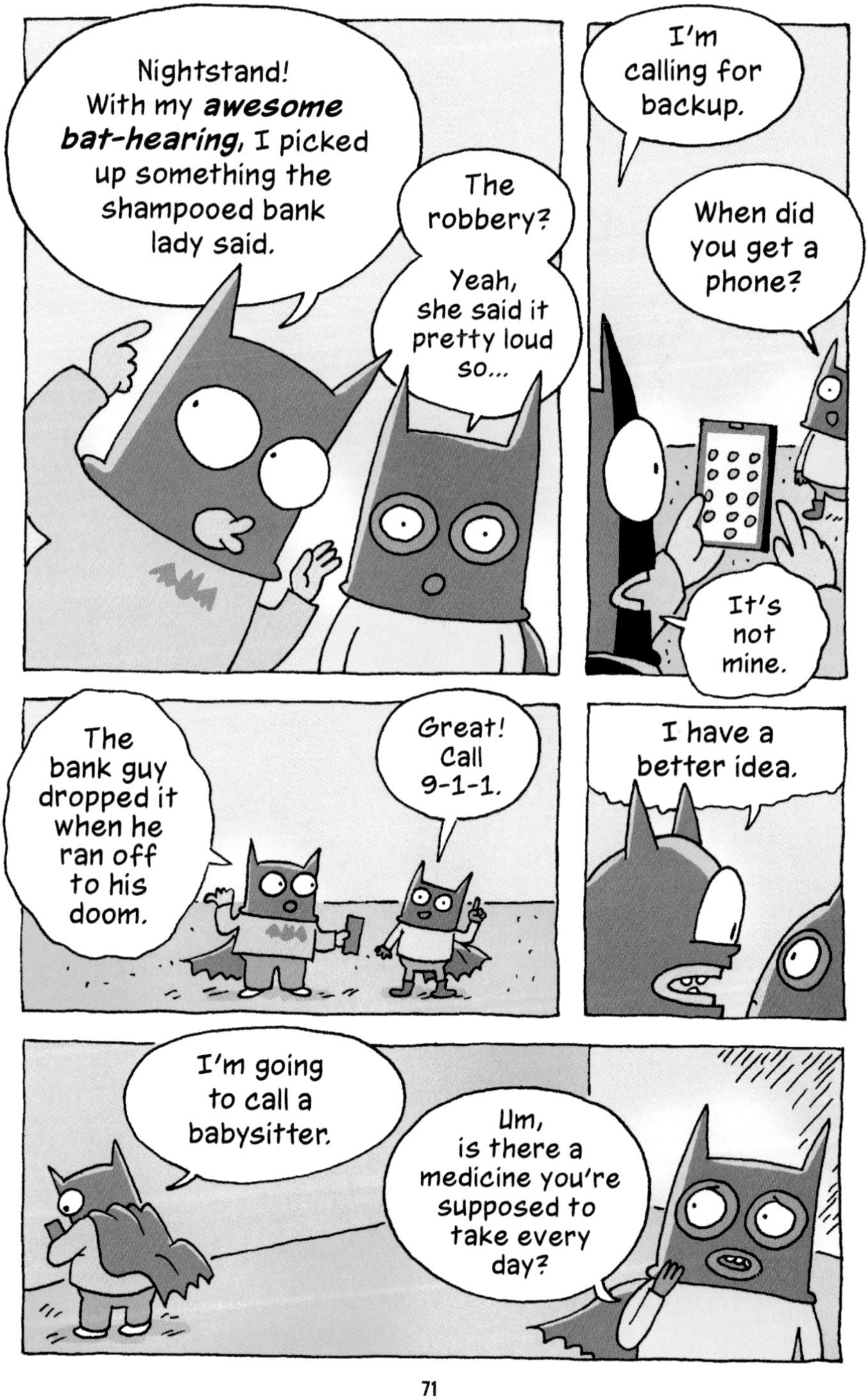
Nightstand! With my ***awesome bat-hearing***, I picked up something the shampooed bank lady said.
The robbery?
Yeah, she said it pretty loud so...
I'm calling for backup.
When did you get a phone?
It's not mine.
The bank guy dropped it when he ran off to his doom.
Great! Call 9-1-1.
I have a better idea.
I'm going to call a babysitter.
Um, is there a medicine you're supposed to take every day?

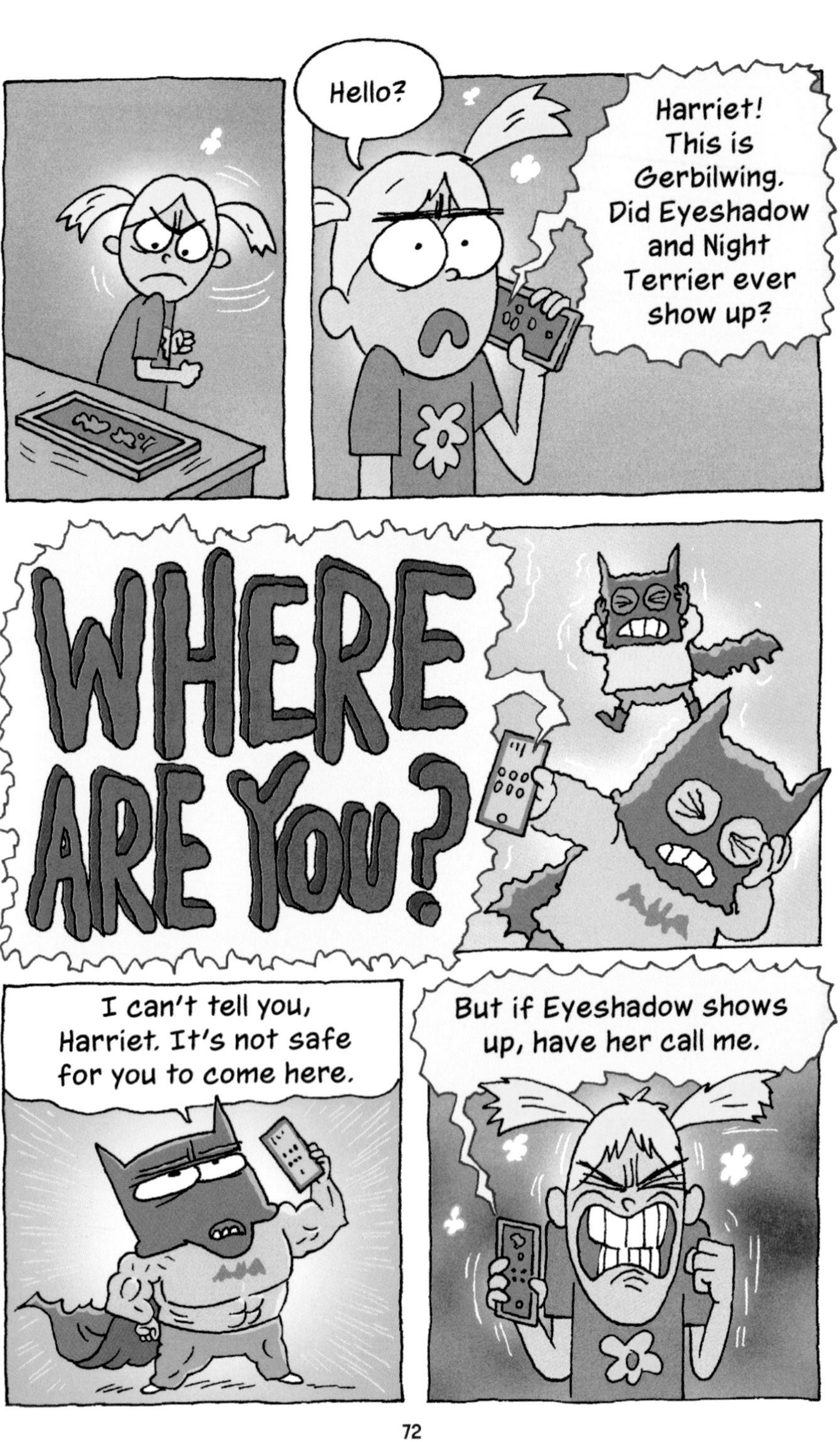
Hello?
Harriet! This is Gerbilwing. Did Eyeshadow and Night Terrier ever show up?
WHERE ARE YOU?
I can't tell you, Harriet. It's not safe for you to come here.
But if Eyeshadow shows up, have her call me.

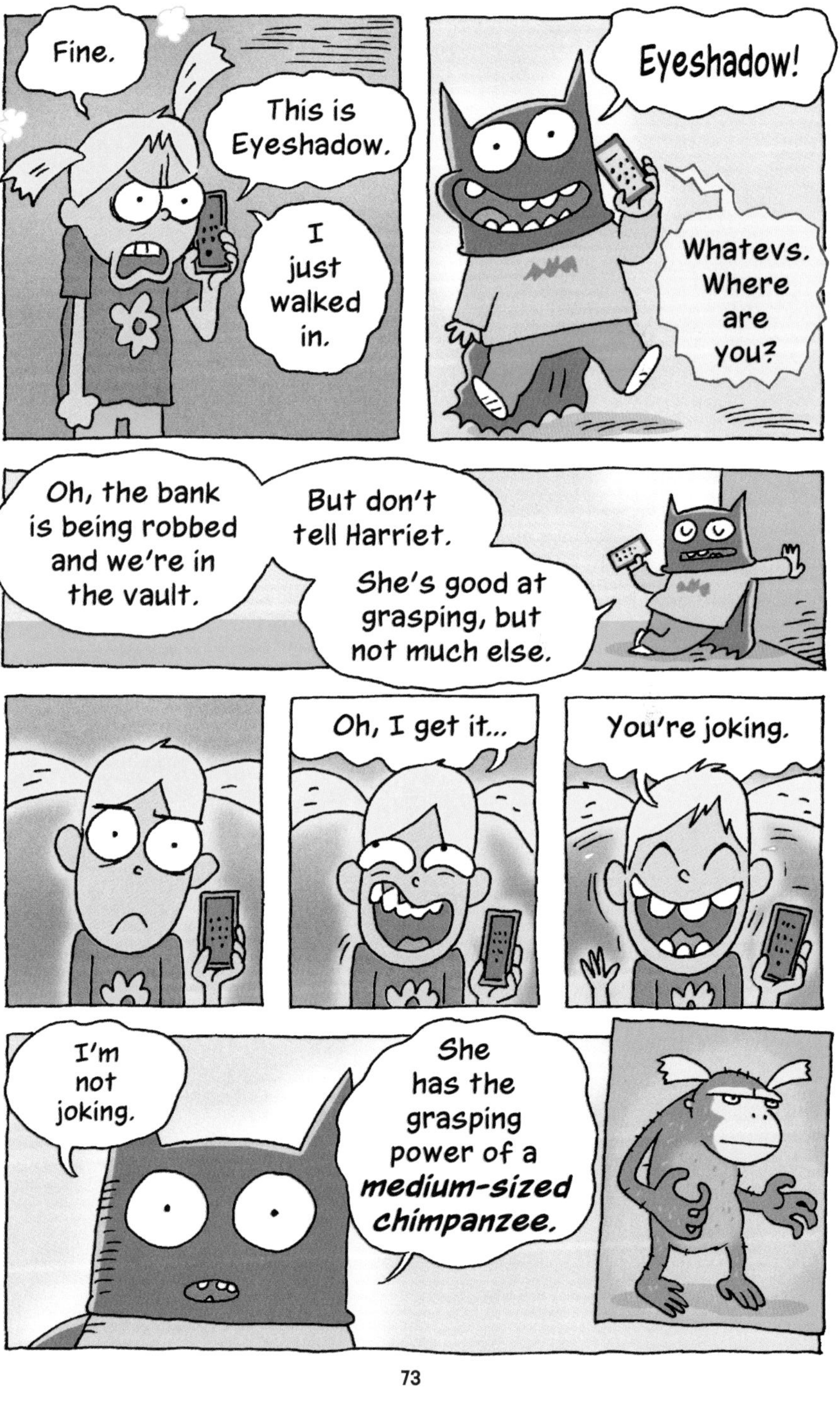

Fine.
This is Eyeshadow.
I just walked in.
Eyeshadow!
Whatevs. Where are you?
Oh, the bank is being robbed and we're in the vault.
But don't tell Harriet.
She's good at grasping, but not much else.
Oh, I get it...
You're joking.
I'm not joking.
She has the grasping power of a *medium-sized chimpanzee.*

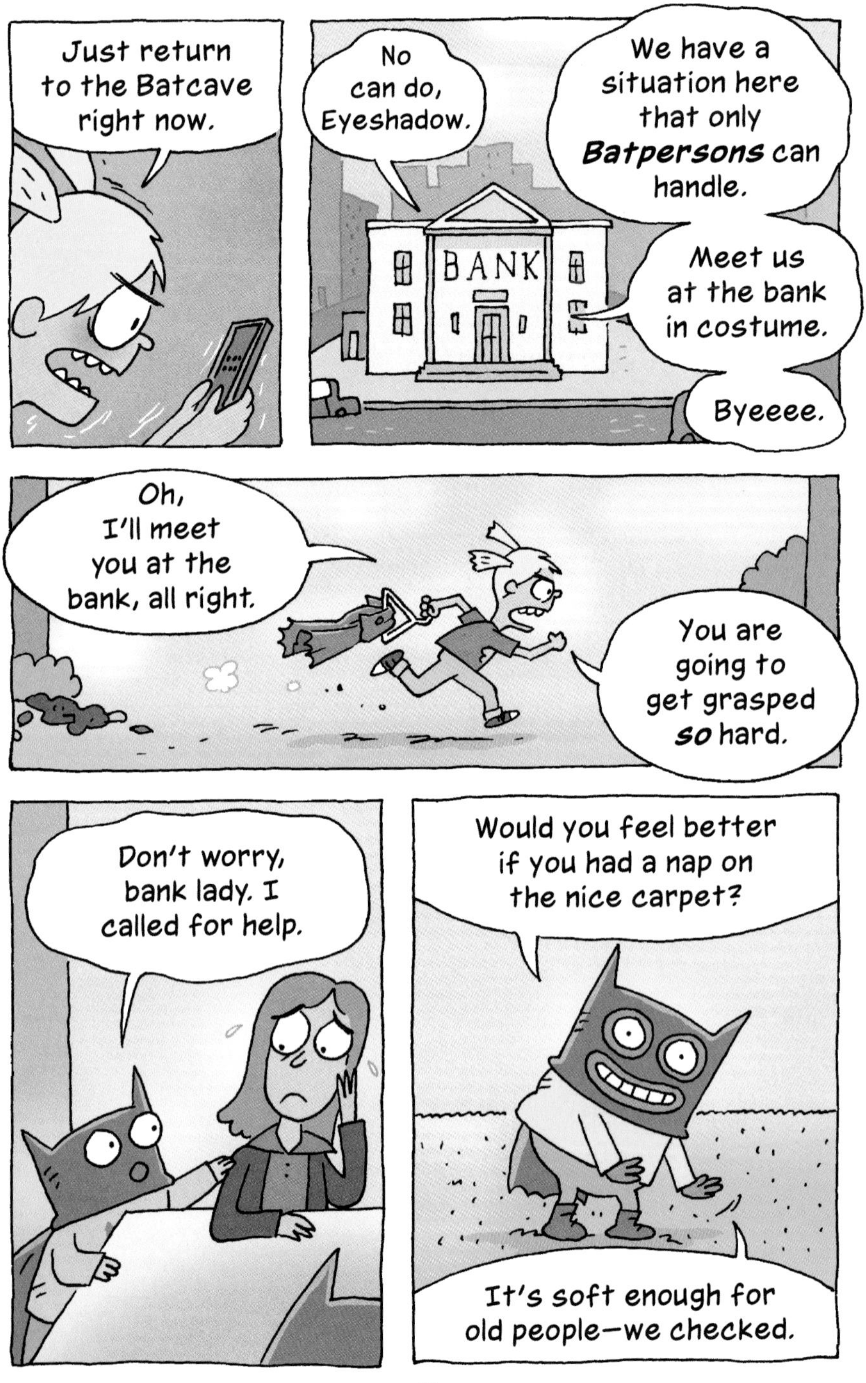
Just return to the Batcave right now.
No can do, Eyeshadow.
We have a situation here that only *Batpersons* can handle.
BANK
Meet us at the bank in costume.
Byeeee.
Oh, I'll meet you at the bank, all right.
You are going to get grasped *so* hard.
Don't worry, bank lady. I called for help.
Would you feel better if you had a nap on the nice carpet?
It's soft enough for old people—we checked.

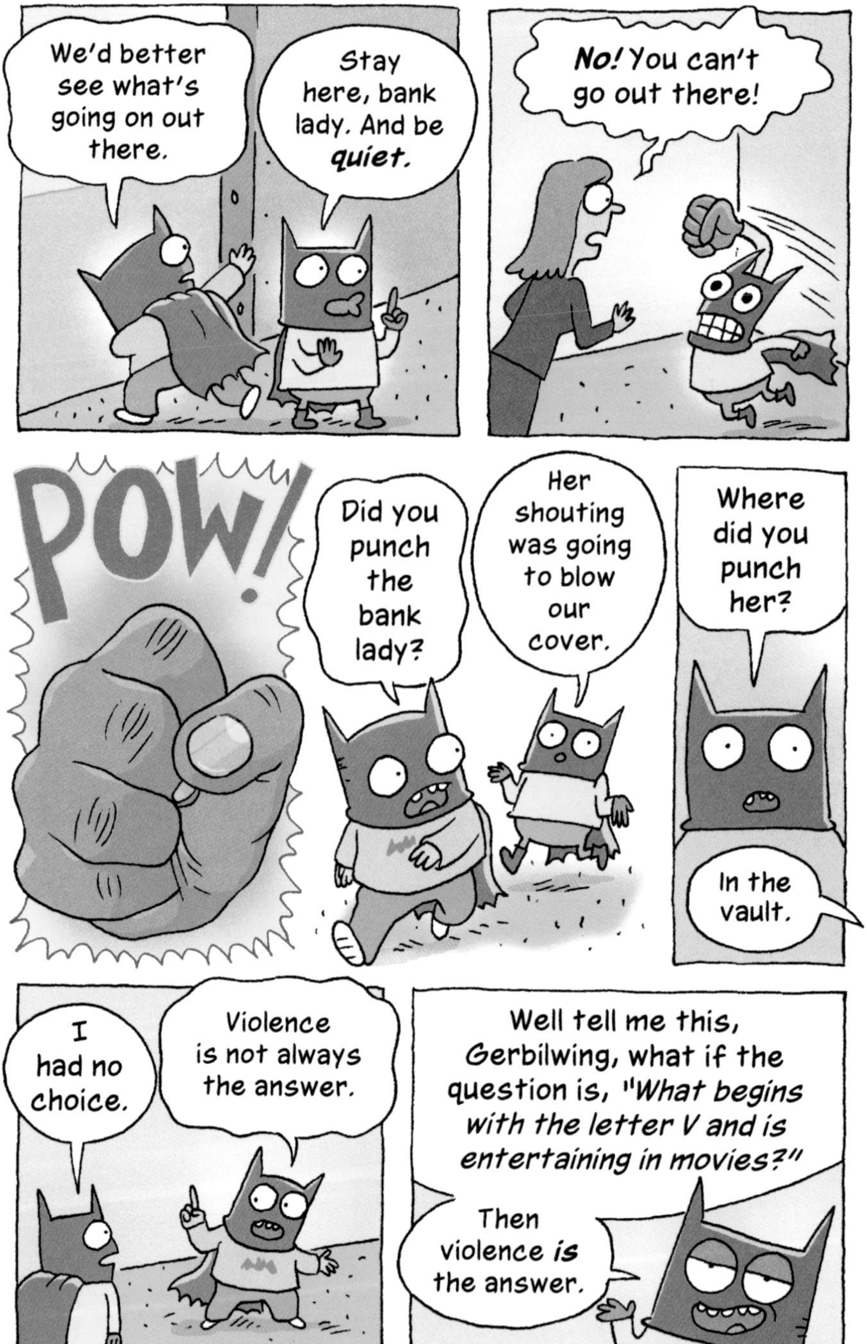

We'd better see what's going on out there.
Stay here, bank lady. And be *quiet.*
No! You can't go out there!
POW!
Did you punch the bank lady?
Her shouting was going to blow our cover.
Where did you punch her?
In the vault.
I had no choice.
Violence is not always the answer.
Well tell me this, Gerbilwing, what if the question is, "*What begins with the letter V and is entertaining in movies?*"
Then violence ***is*** the answer.

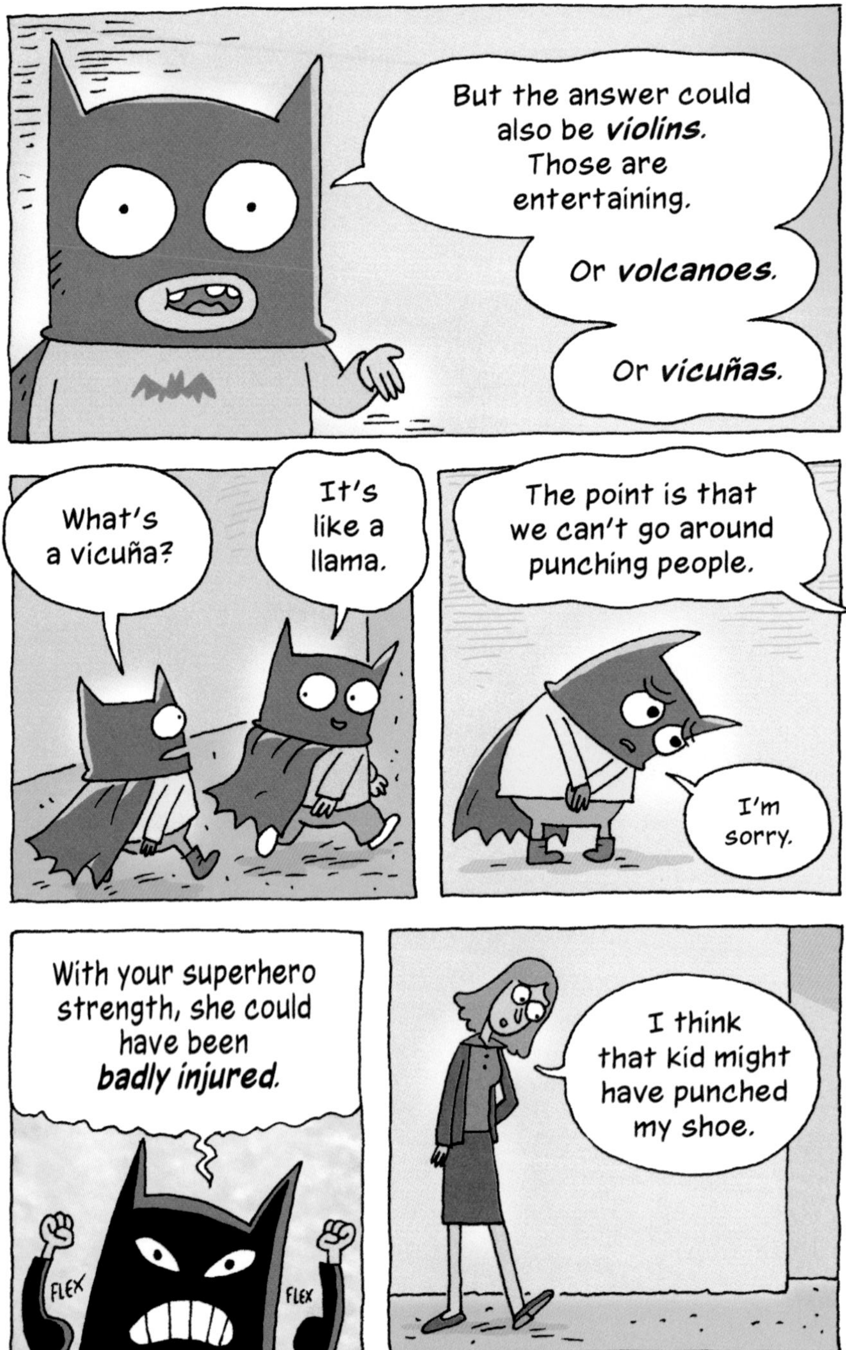
But the answer could also be *violins*. Those are entertaining.
Or *volcanoes*.
Or *vicuñas*.
What's a vicuña?
It's like a llama.
The point is that we can't go around punching people.
I'm sorry.
With your superhero strength, she could have been *badly injured*.
FLEX
FLEX
I think that kid might have punched my shoe.

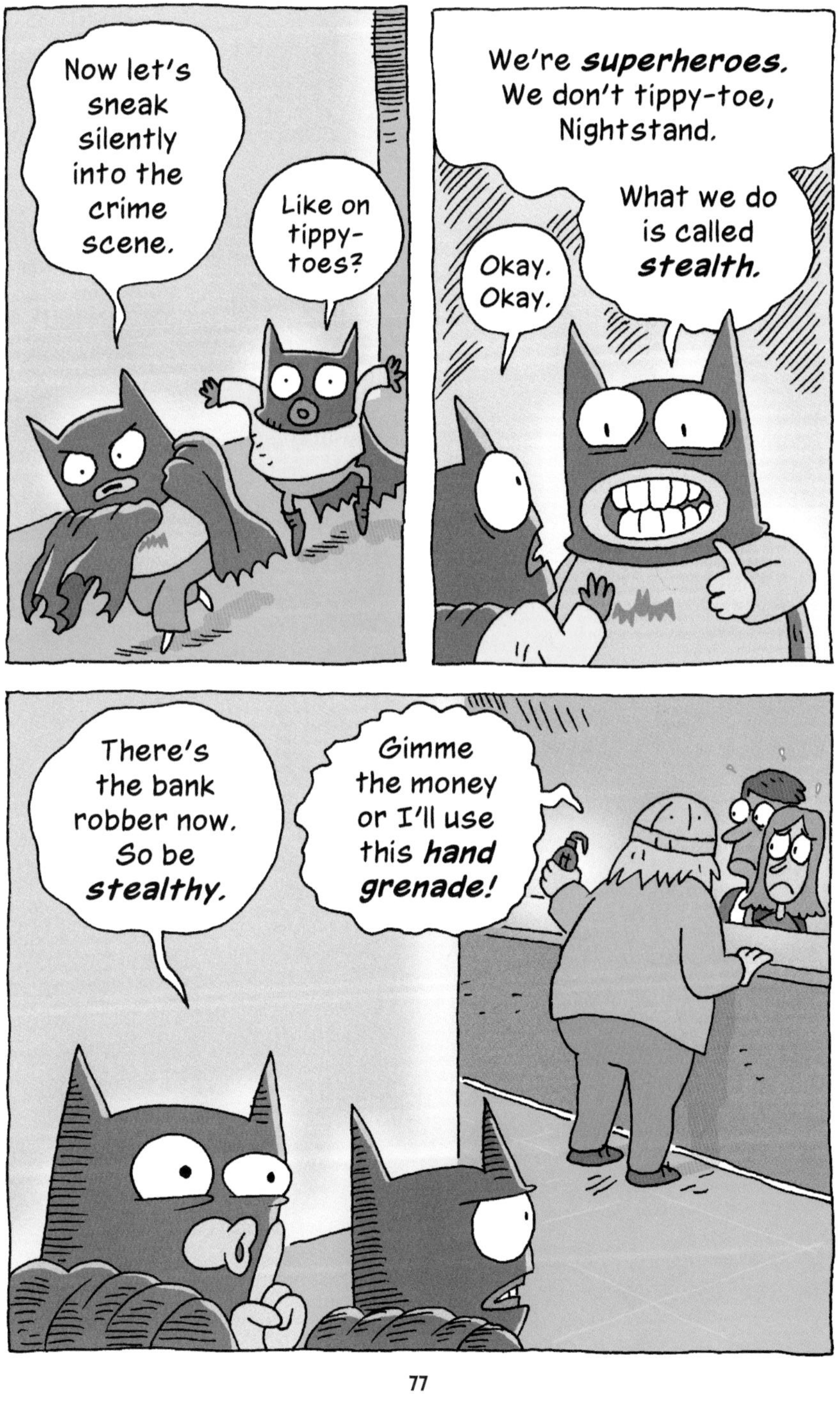
Now let's sneak silently into the crime scene.
Like on tippy-toes?
We're **superheroes.** We don't tippy-toe, Nightstand.
What we do is called **stealth.**
Okay. Okay.
There's the bank robber now. So be **stealthy.**
Gimme the money or I'll use this **hand grenade!**

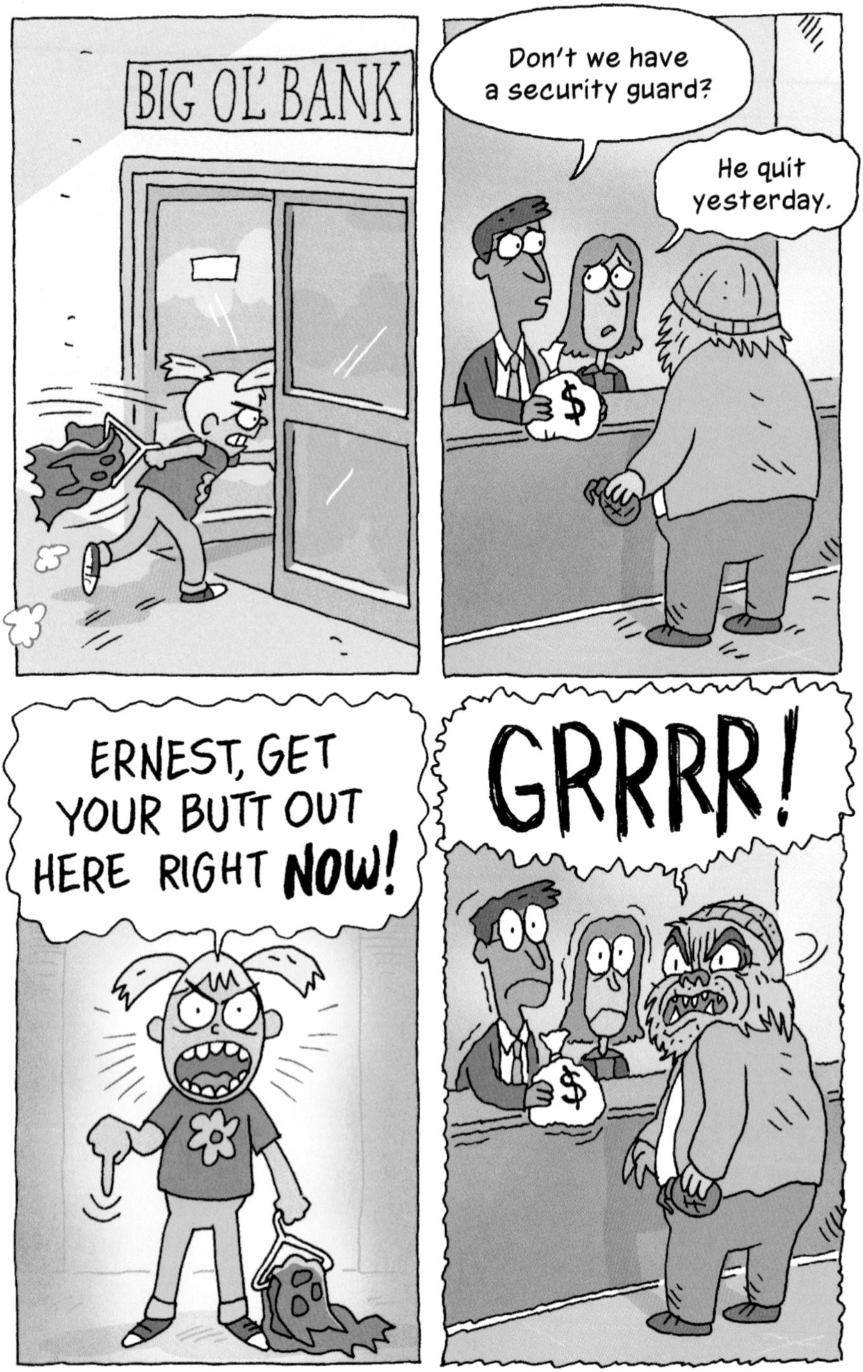
BIG OL' BANK
Don't we have a security guard?
He quit yesterday.
ERNEST, GET YOUR BUTT OUT HERE RIGHT NOW!
GRRRR!

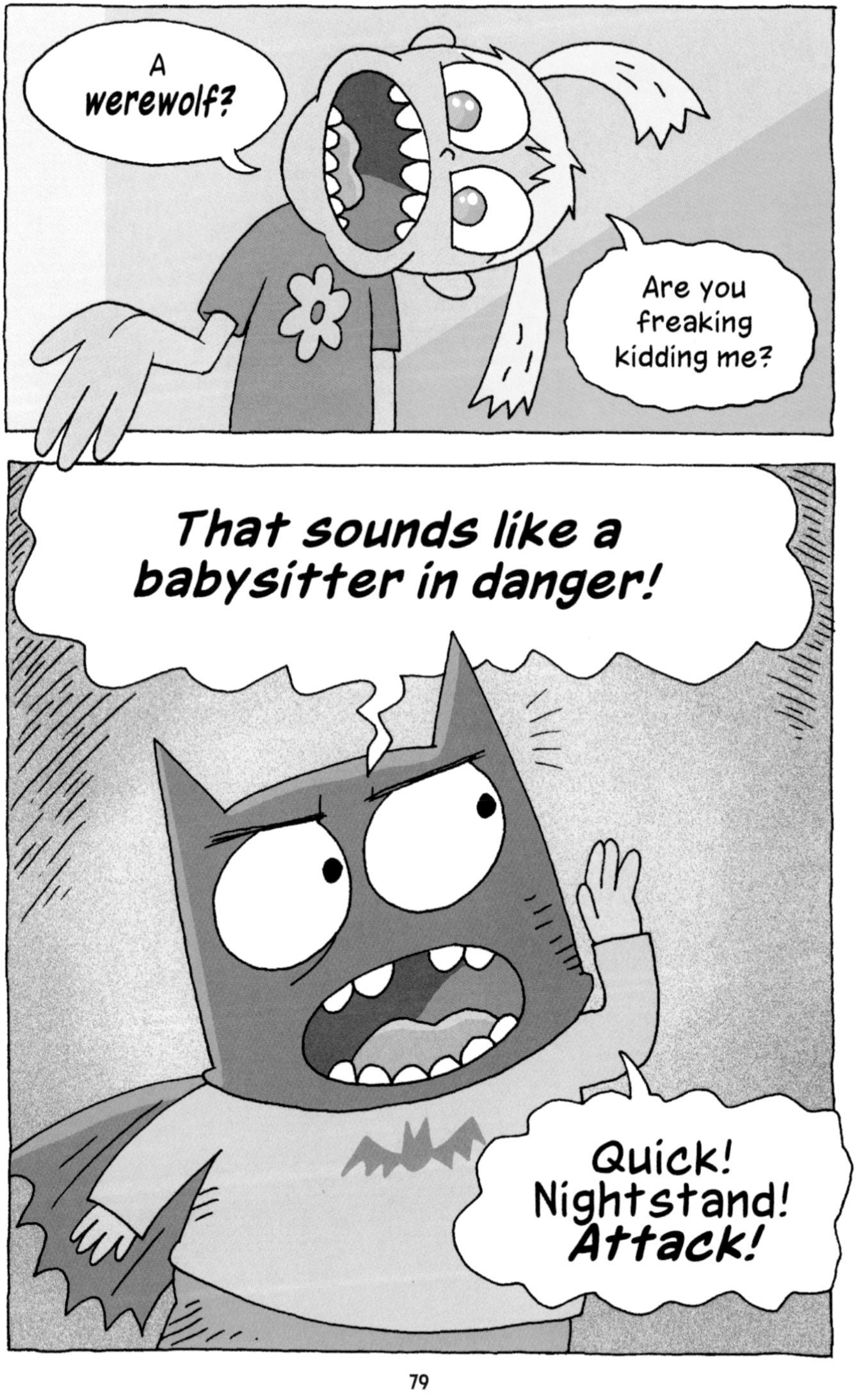
A werewolf?
Are you freaking kidding me?
That sounds like a babysitter in danger!
Quick! Nightstand! Attack!

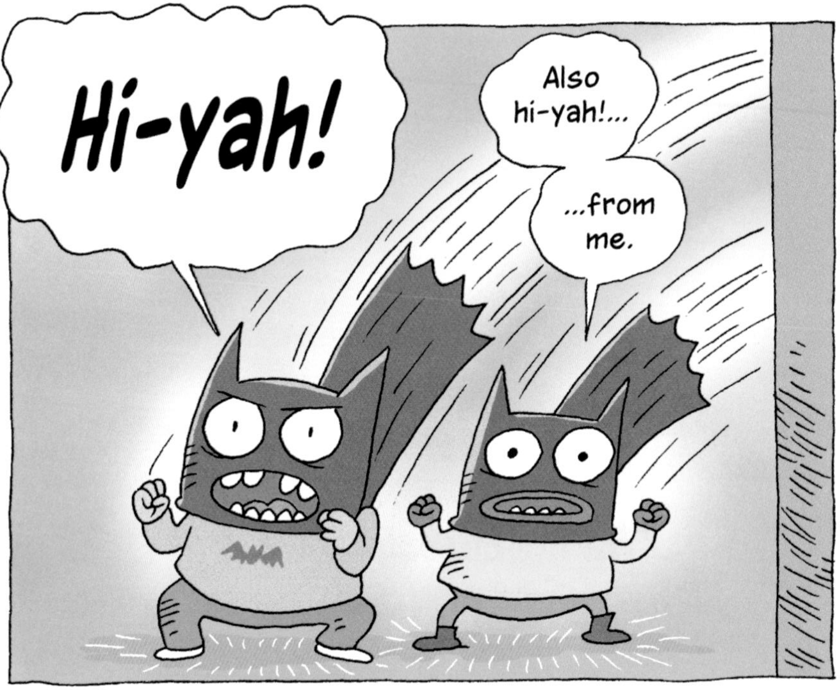
Hi-yah!
Also hi-yah!...
...from me.

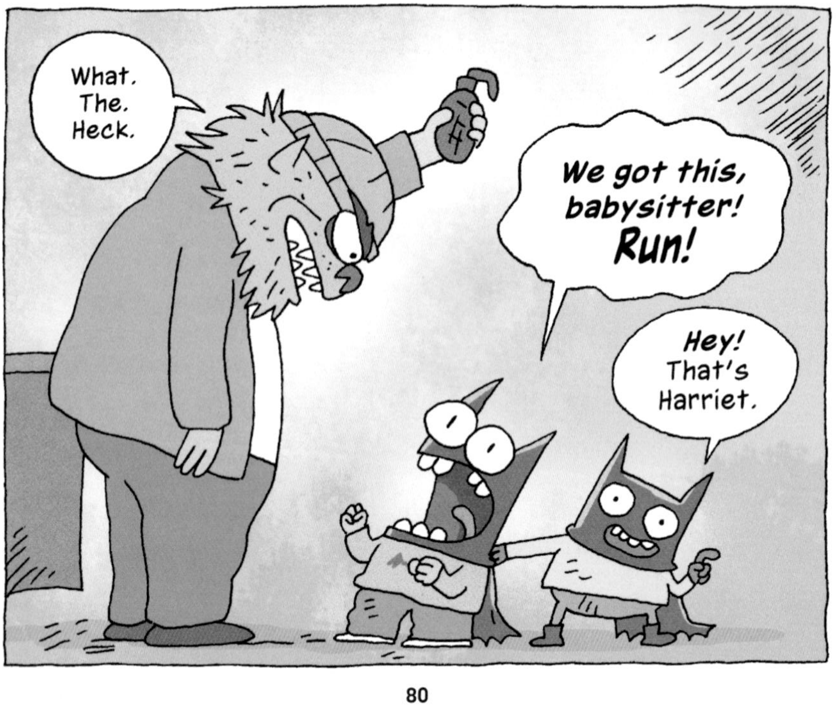
What. The. Heck.
We got this, babysitter! Run!
Hey! That's Harriet.

I think you're right.

Hi Harriet!

I wish Eyeshadow had come instead.

Yeah, but...

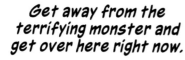

Get away from the terrifying monster and get over here right now.

As a babysitter, you can't understand this, but we're doing *justice* over here.

We aren't leaving until Eyeshadow gets here.

Yeah, but...

SLAP!

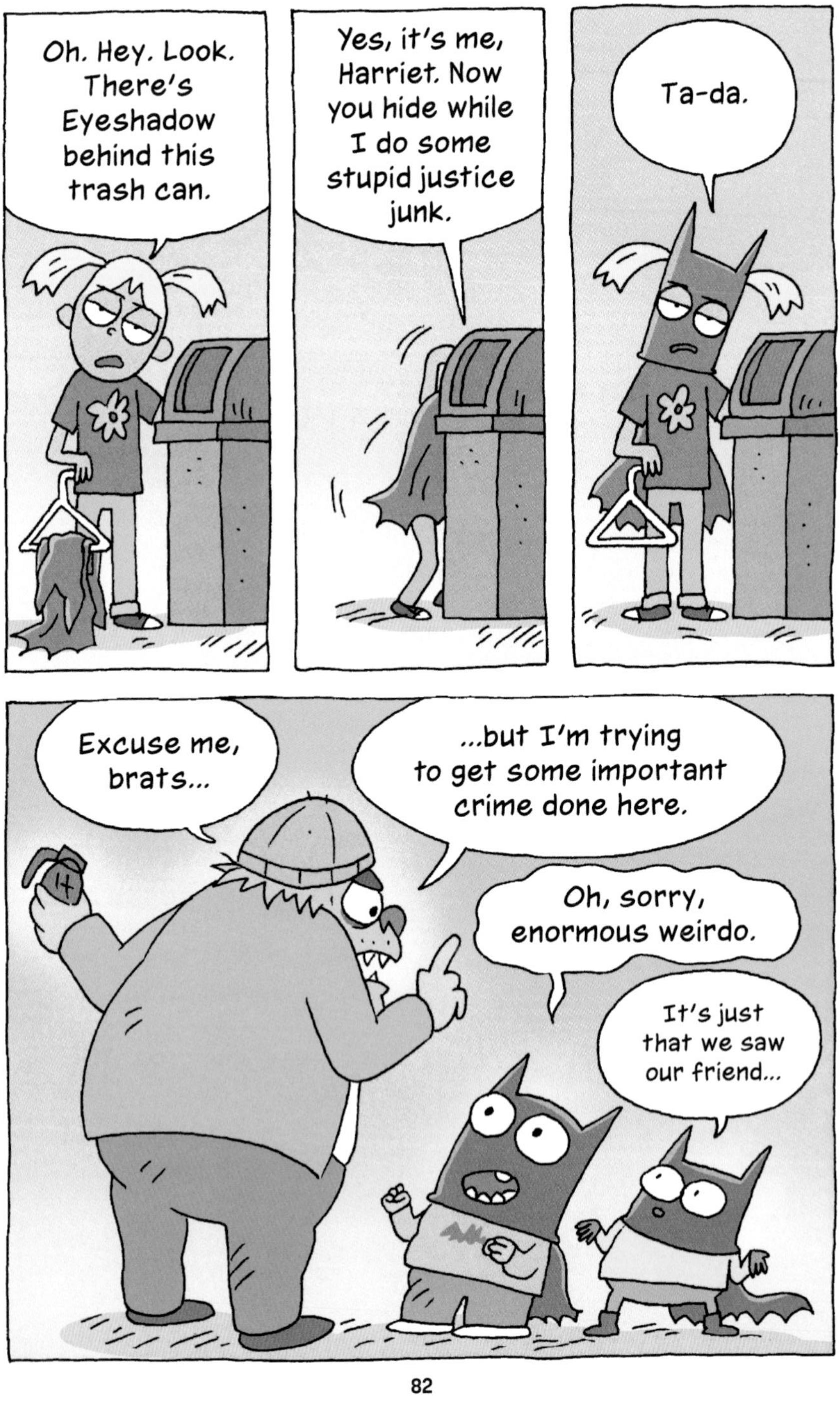
Oh. Hey. Look. There's Eyeshadow behind this trash can.
Yes, it's me, Harriet. Now you hide while I do some stupid justice junk.
Ta-da.
Excuse me, brats...
...but I'm trying to get some important crime done here.
Oh, sorry, enormous weirdo.
It's just that we saw our friend...

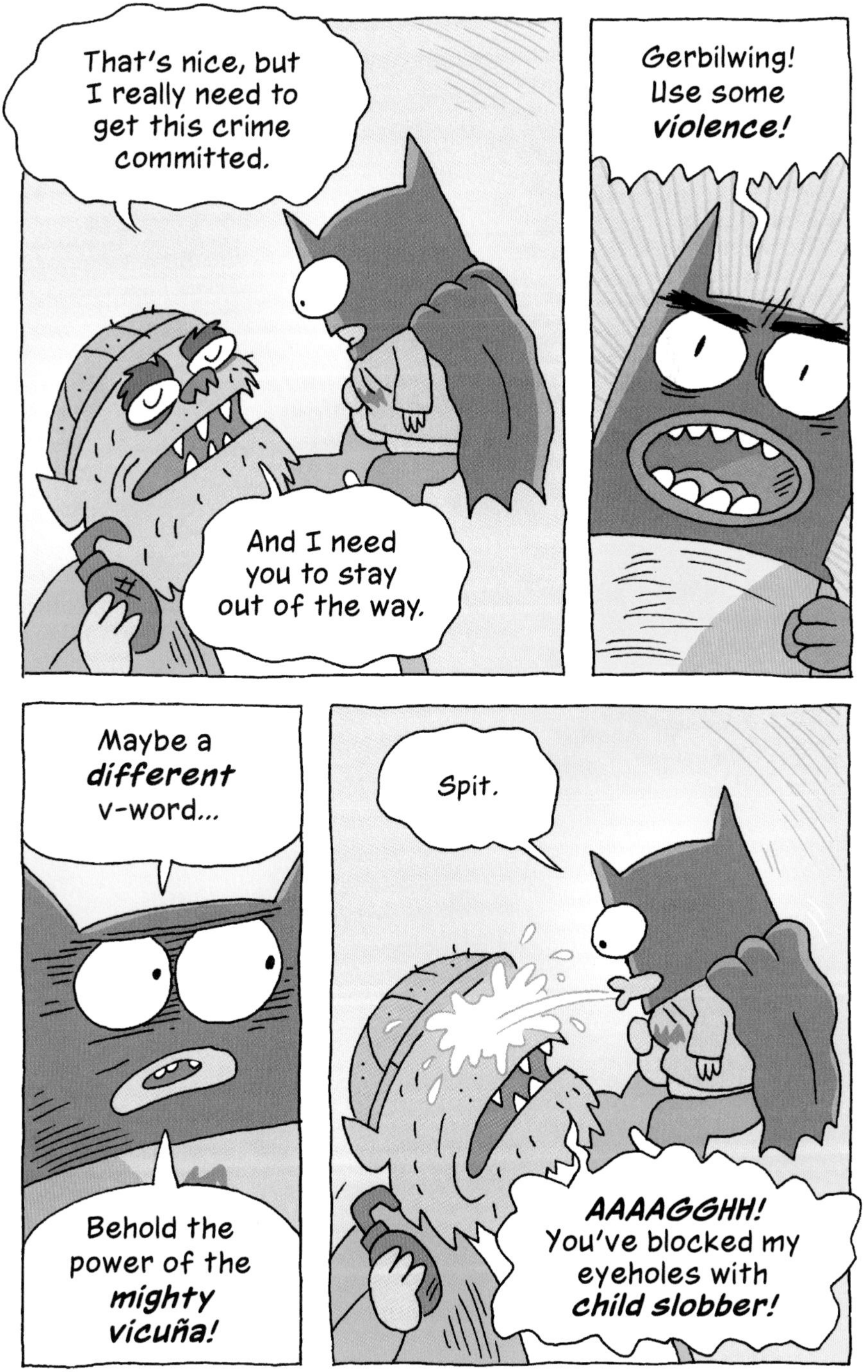
That's nice, but I really need to get this crime committed.
And I need you to stay out of the way.
Gerbilwing! Use some *violence!*
Maybe a *different* v-word...
Behold the power of the *mighty vicuña!*
Spit.
AAAAGGHH! You've blocked my eyeholes with *child slobber!*

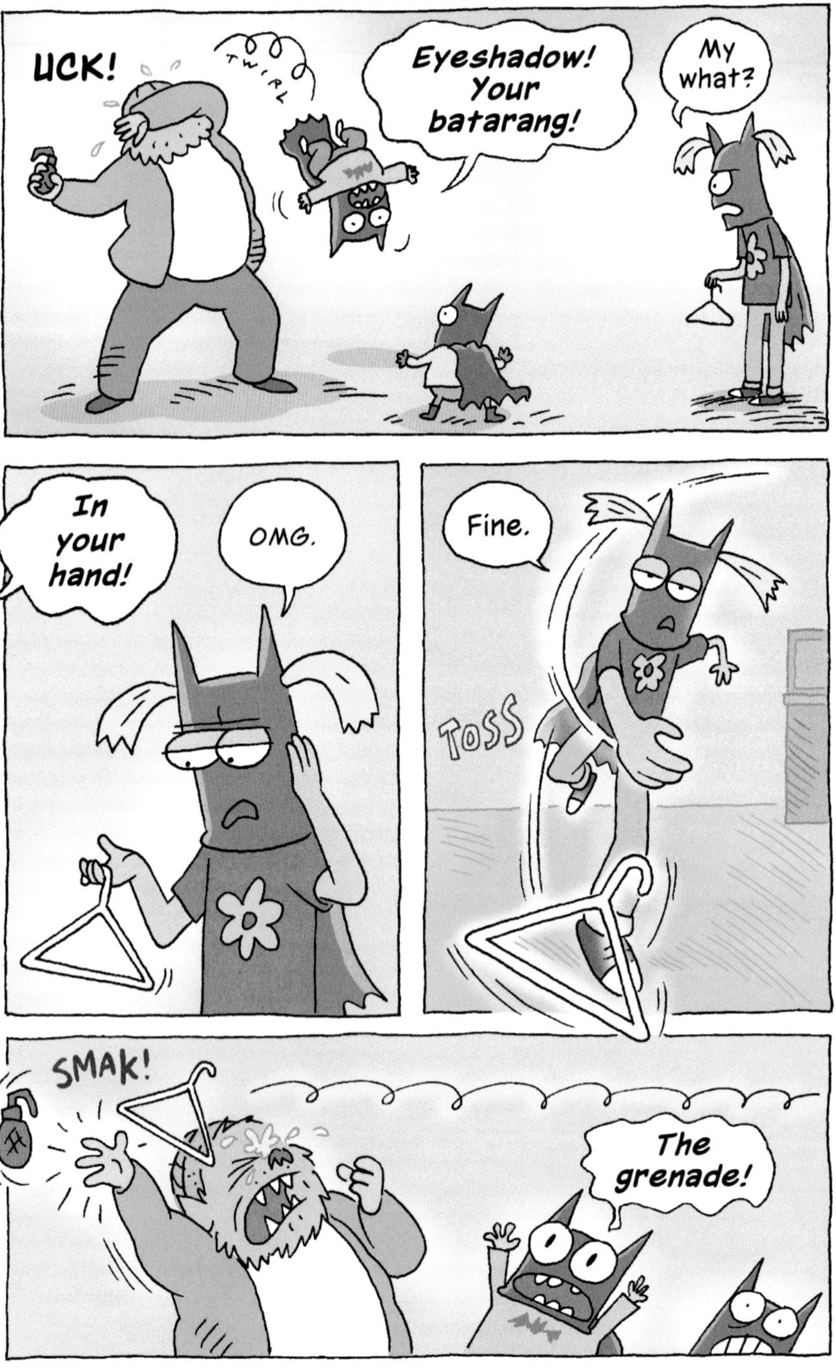
UCK!
TWIRL
Eyeshadow! Your batarang!
My what?
In your hand!
OMG.
Fine.
TOSS
SMAK!
The grenade!

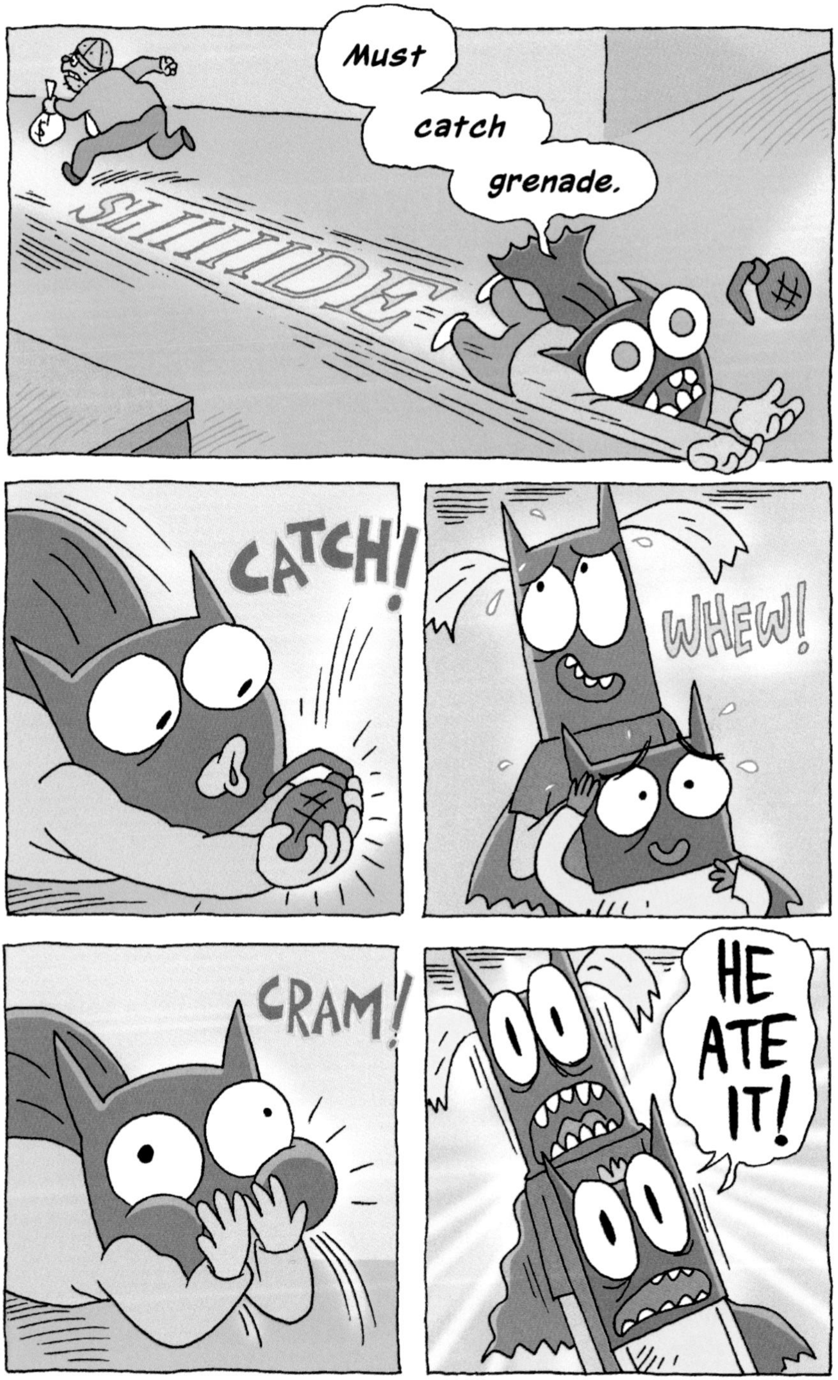
Must
catch
grenade.
SLIIIDE
CATCH!
WHEW!
CRAM!
HE ATE IT!

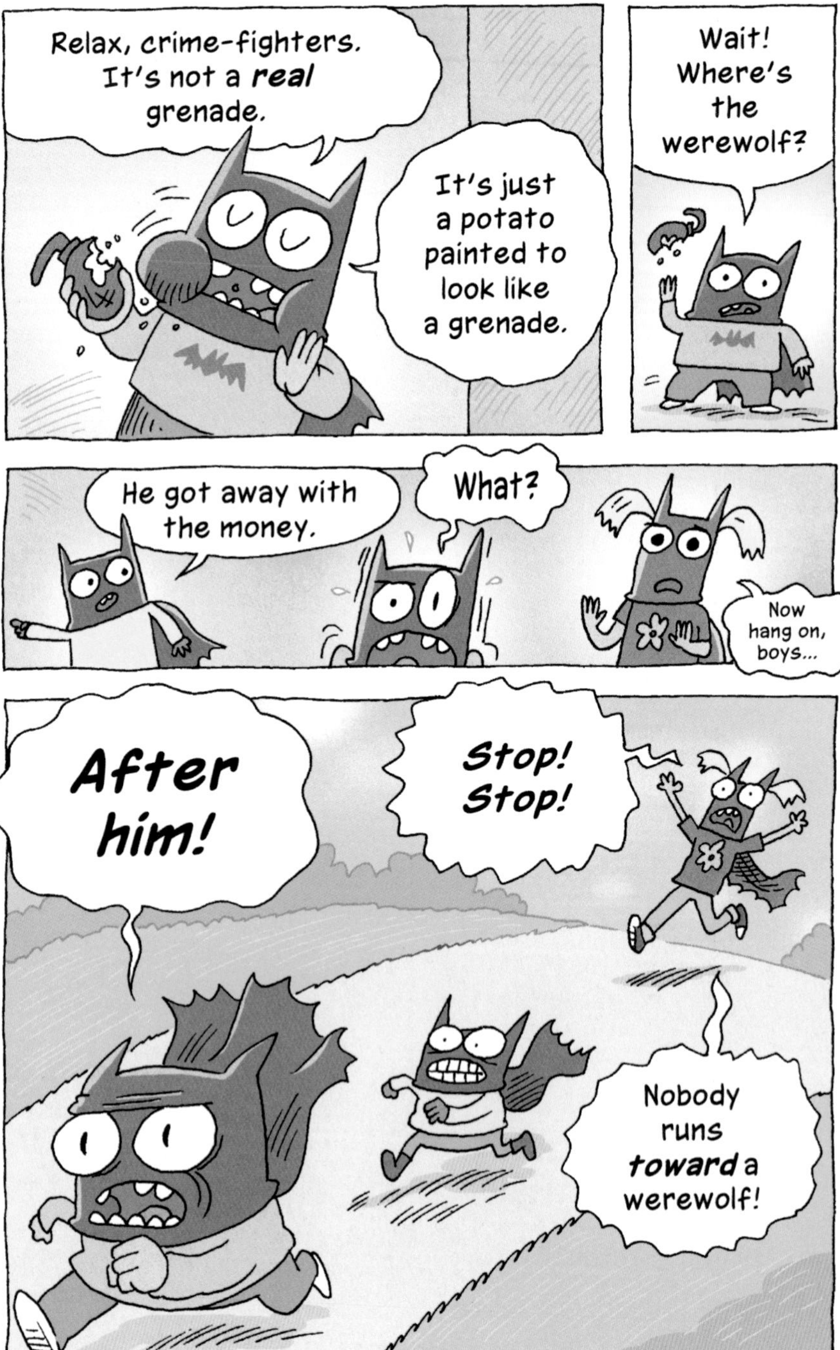

Relax, crime-fighters. It's not a *real* grenade.
It's just a potato painted to look like a grenade.
Wait! Where's the werewolf?
He got away with the money.
What?
Now hang on, boys...
After him!
Stop! Stop!
Nobody runs *toward* a werewolf!

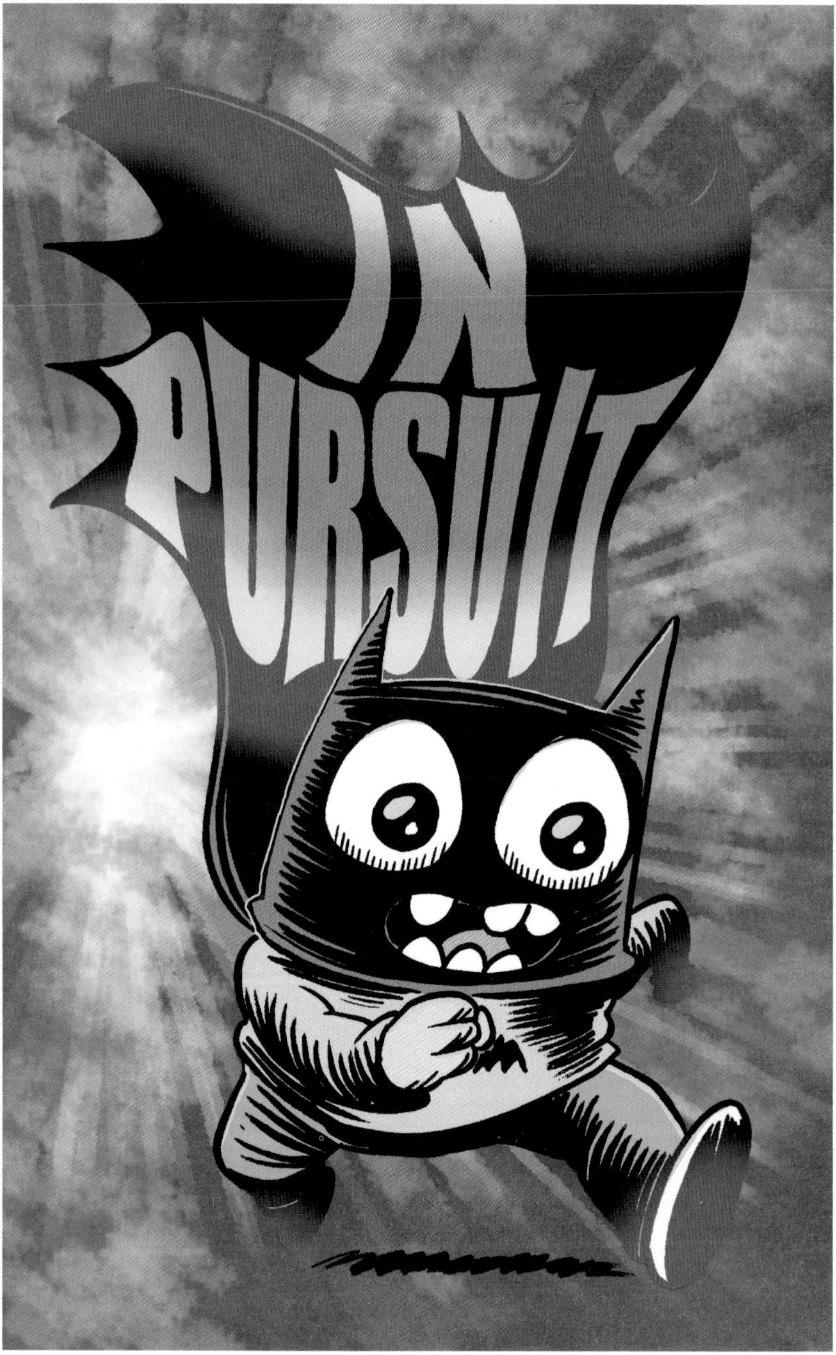
IN
PURSUIT

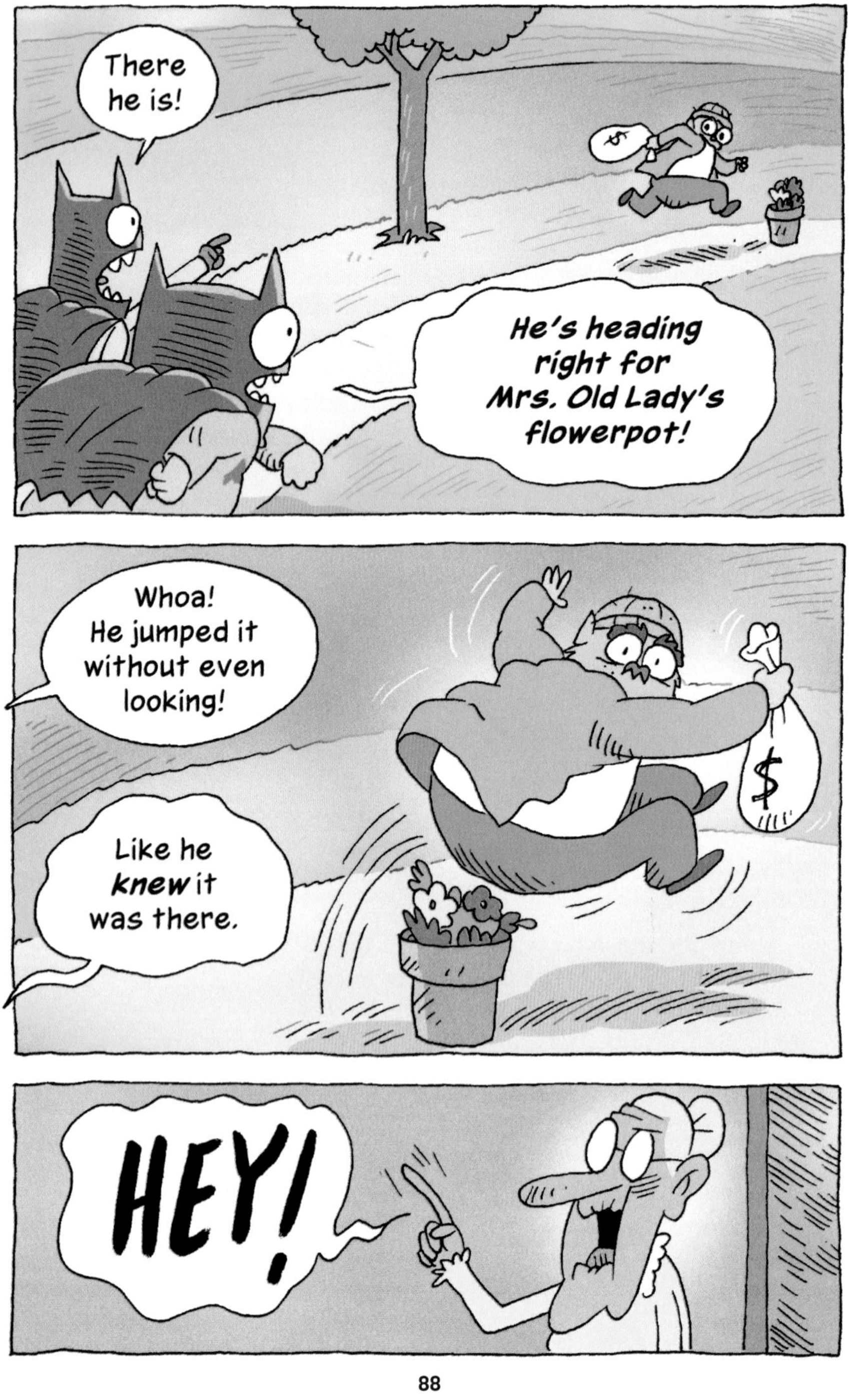
There he is!
He's heading right for Mrs. Old Lady's flowerpot!
Whoa! He jumped it without even looking!
Like he **knew** it was there.
HEY!

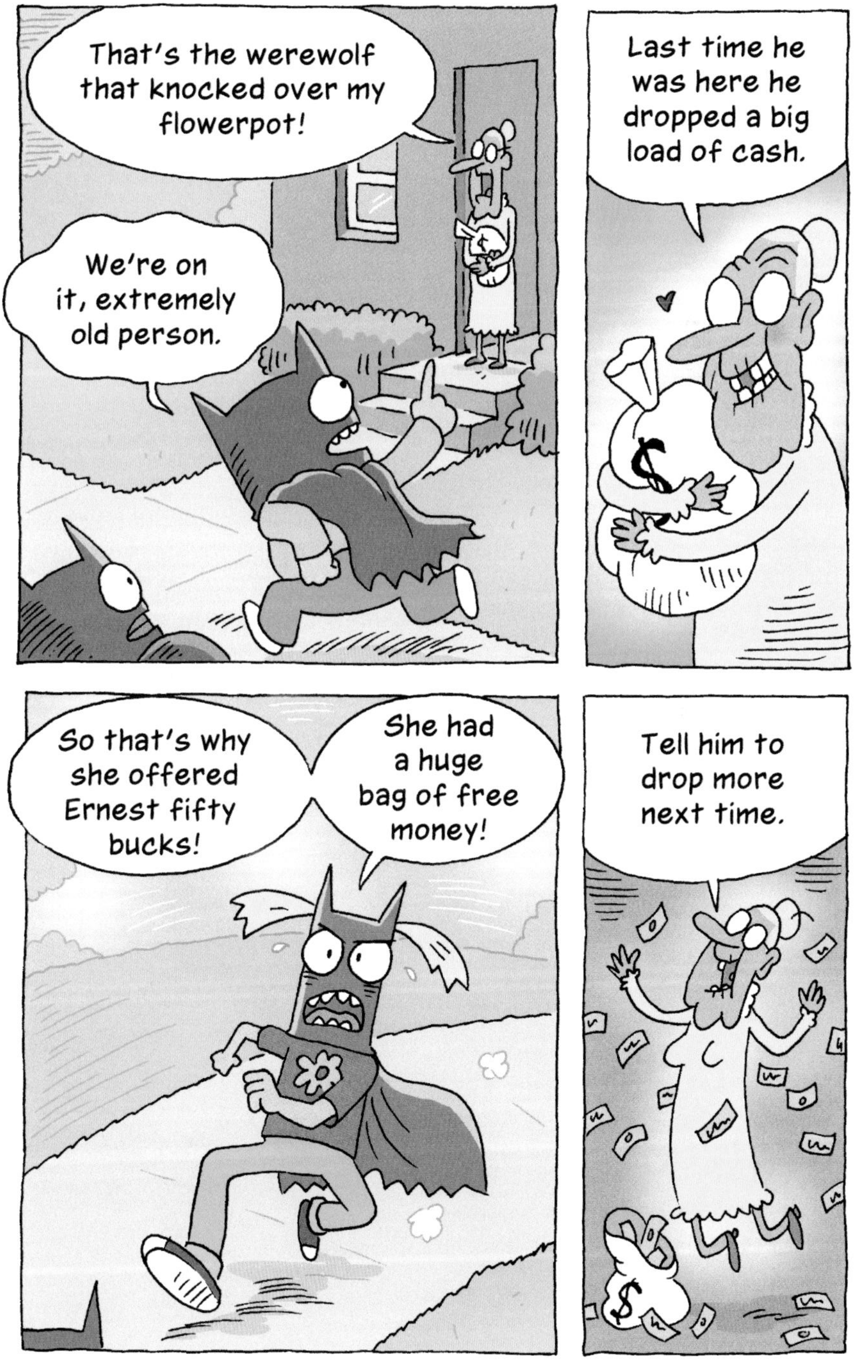
That's the werewolf that knocked over my flowerpot!
We're on it, extremely old person.
Last time he was here he dropped a big load of cash.
So that's why she offered Ernest fifty bucks!
She had a huge bag of free money!
Tell him to drop more next time.

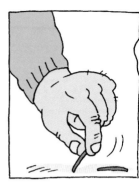

He's stopping to pick up those little sticks!

Why would he do that?

Maybe he needs to pick his teeth after he eats kids.

Wait! Why is he heading down this street?

It's like he's going straight to...

Ernest's house!

GUYS, STOP!

STOP!

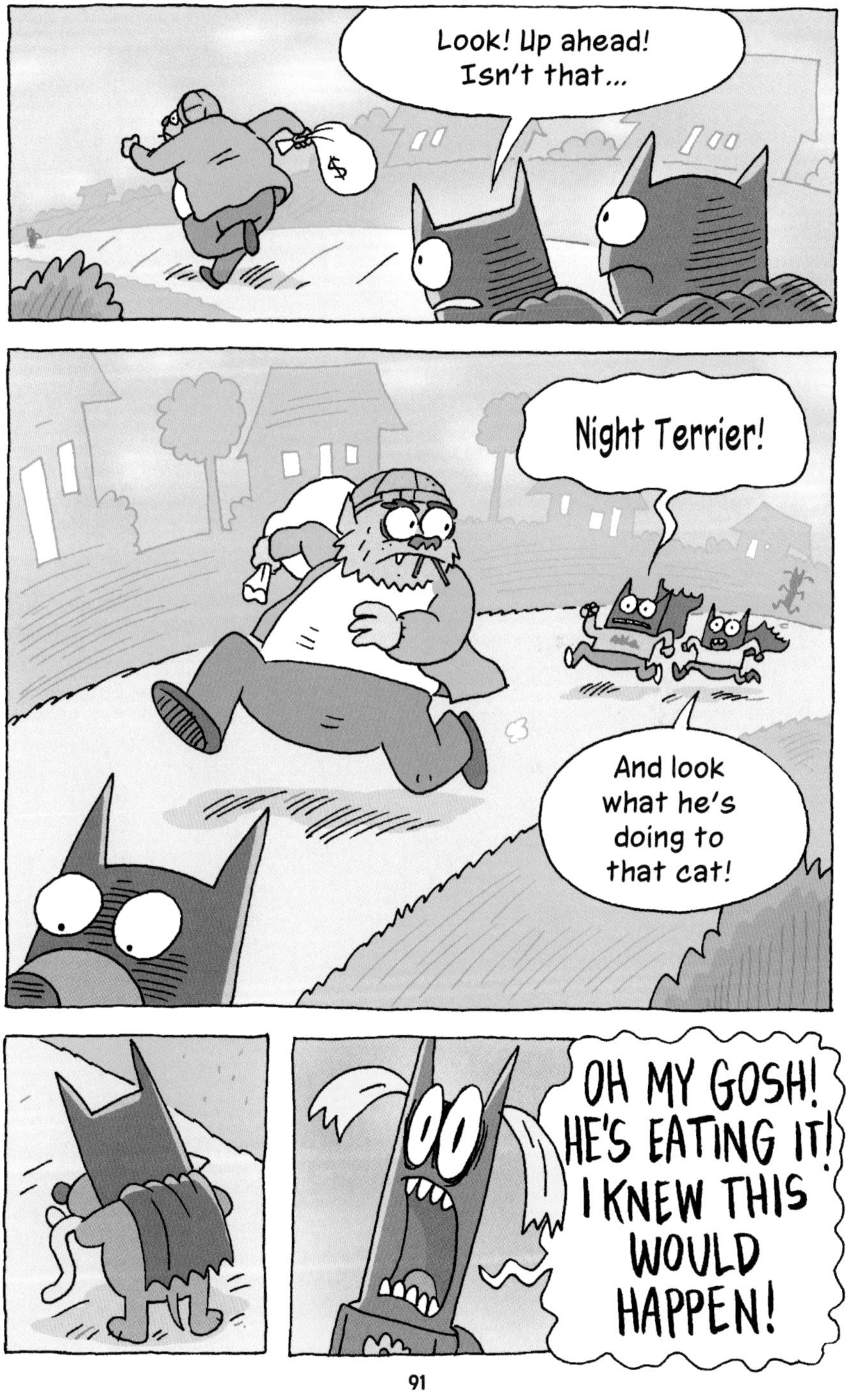
Look! Up ahead! Isn't that...
Night Terrier!
And look what he's doing to that cat!
OH MY GOSH! HE'S EATING IT! I KNEW THIS WOULD HAPPEN!

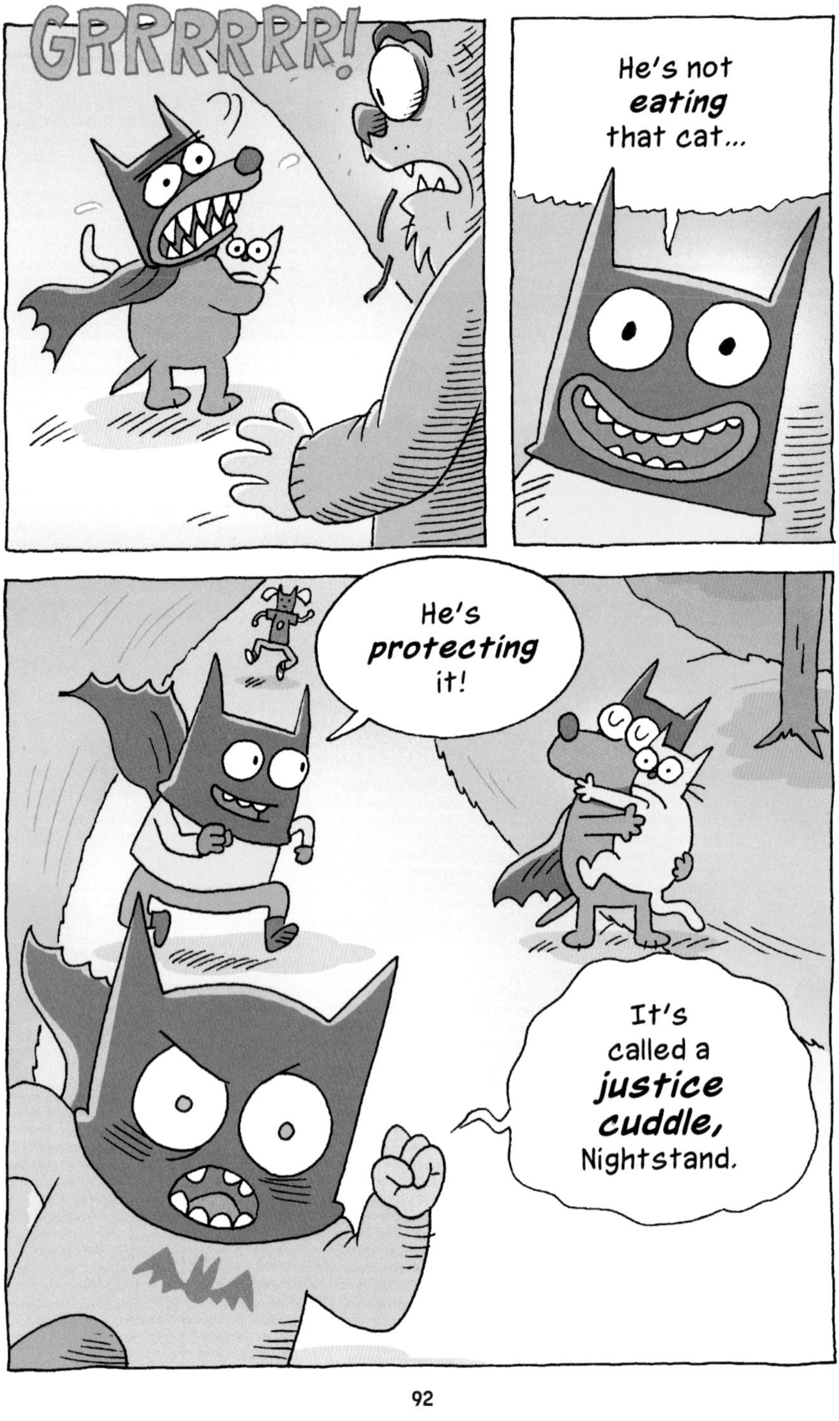
GRRRRRR!
He's not *eating* that cat...
He's *protecting* it!
It's called a *justice cuddle,* Nightstand.

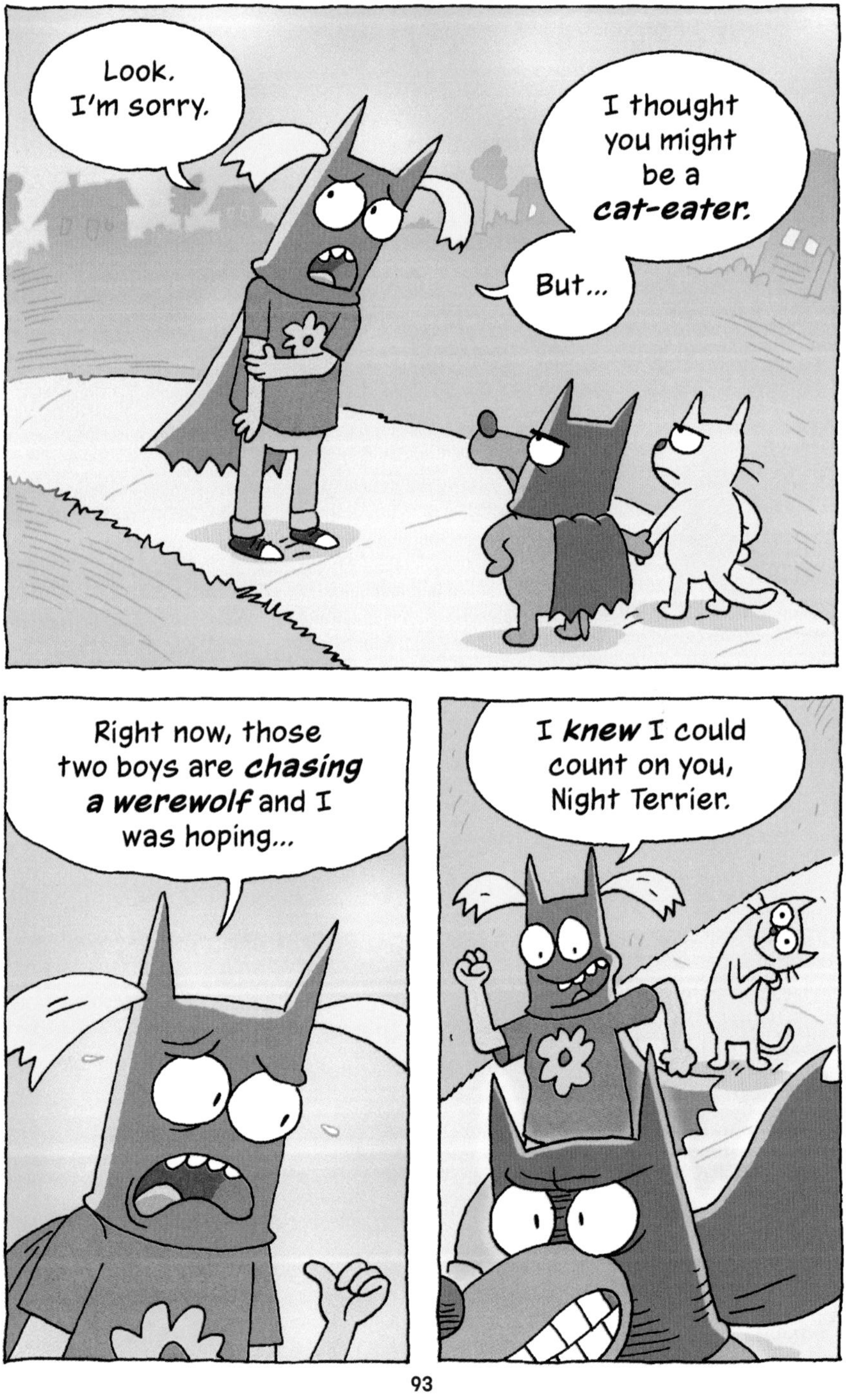
Look. I'm sorry.
I thought you might be a *cat-eater.*
But...
Right now, those two boys are *chasing a werewolf* and I was hoping...
I *knew* I could count on you, Night Terrier.

Yes! Night Terrier has joined the chase!

But where's Eyeshadow?

She's a *genius* at strategy! I'm sure she's going all the way around the block so we can surround him!

EEZE WHEEZE W
EEZE WHEEZE W
EWHEEZE WHEEZ
WHEE
WHEE
EZE

HOW... CAN... THEY...
RUN... SO... FAST... ON
THOSE... STUBBY...
LITTLE... LEGS?

WHEEZE

Would I really be a bad babysitter if I just let a werewolf maul them?

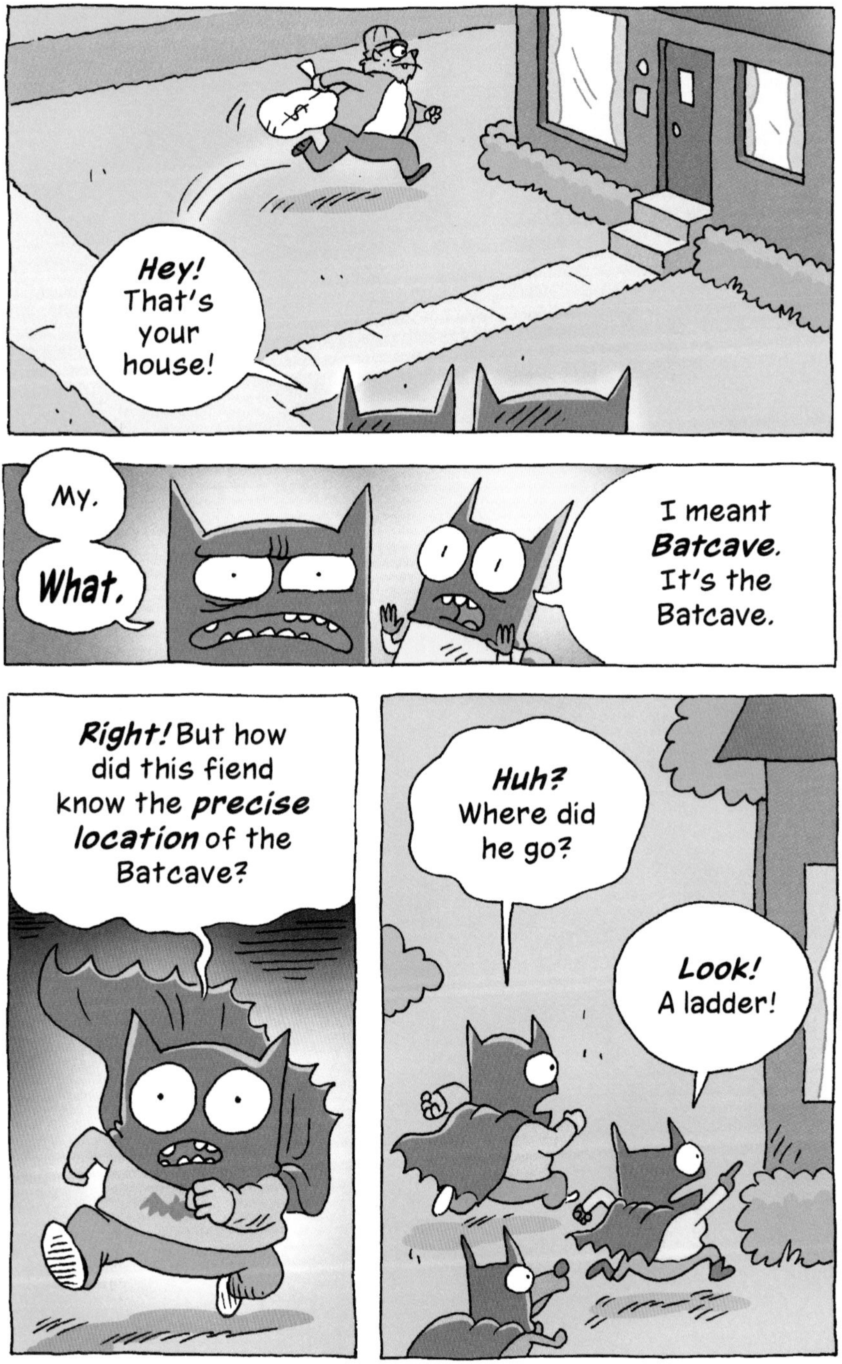

Hey! That's your house!
My.
What.
I meant *Batcave.* It's the Batcave.
Right! But how did this fiend know the *precise location* of the Batcave?
Huh? Where did he go?
Look! A ladder!

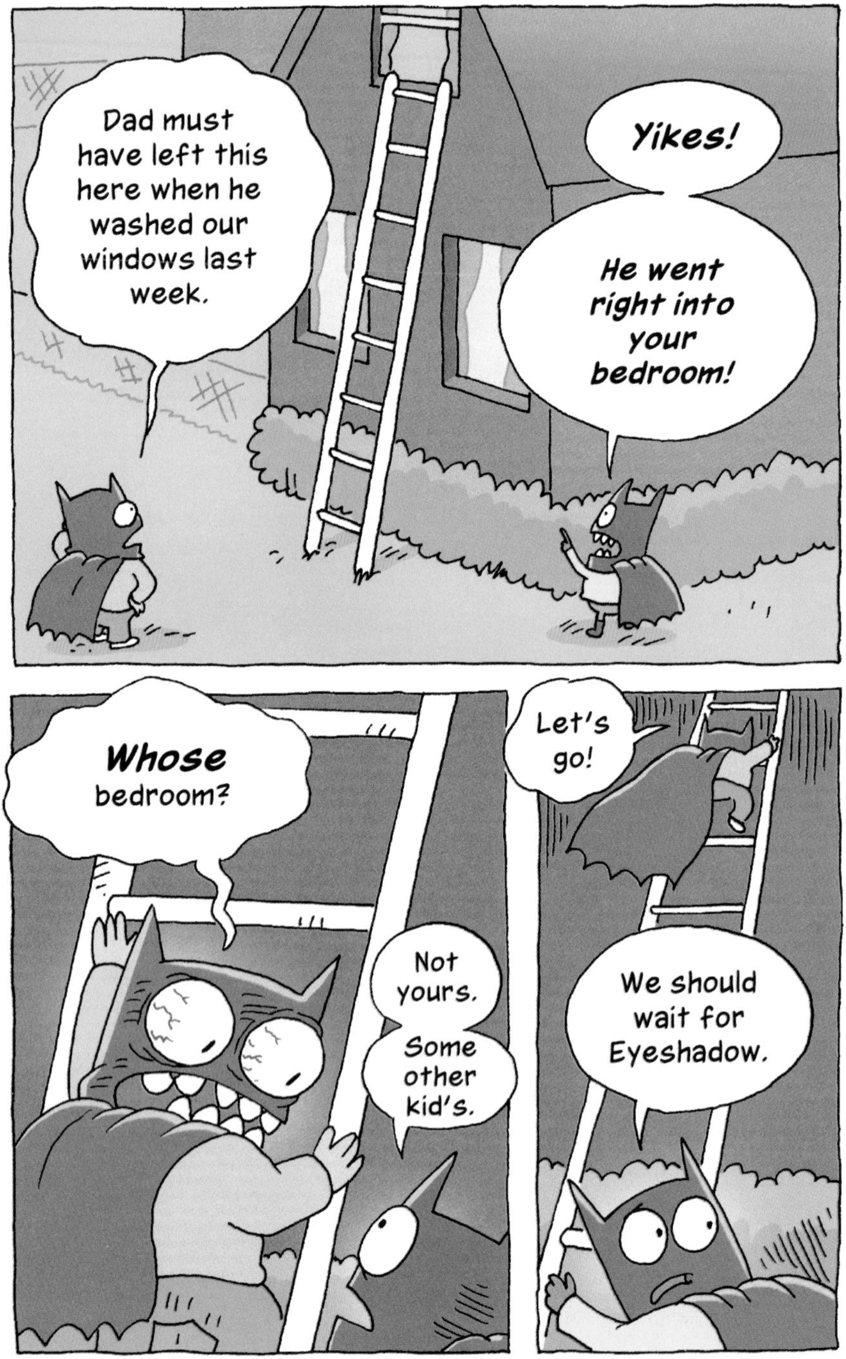
Dad must have left this here when he washed our windows last week.
Yikes!
He went right into your bedroom!
Whose bedroom?
Not yours.
Some other kid's.
Let's go!
We should wait for Eyeshadow.

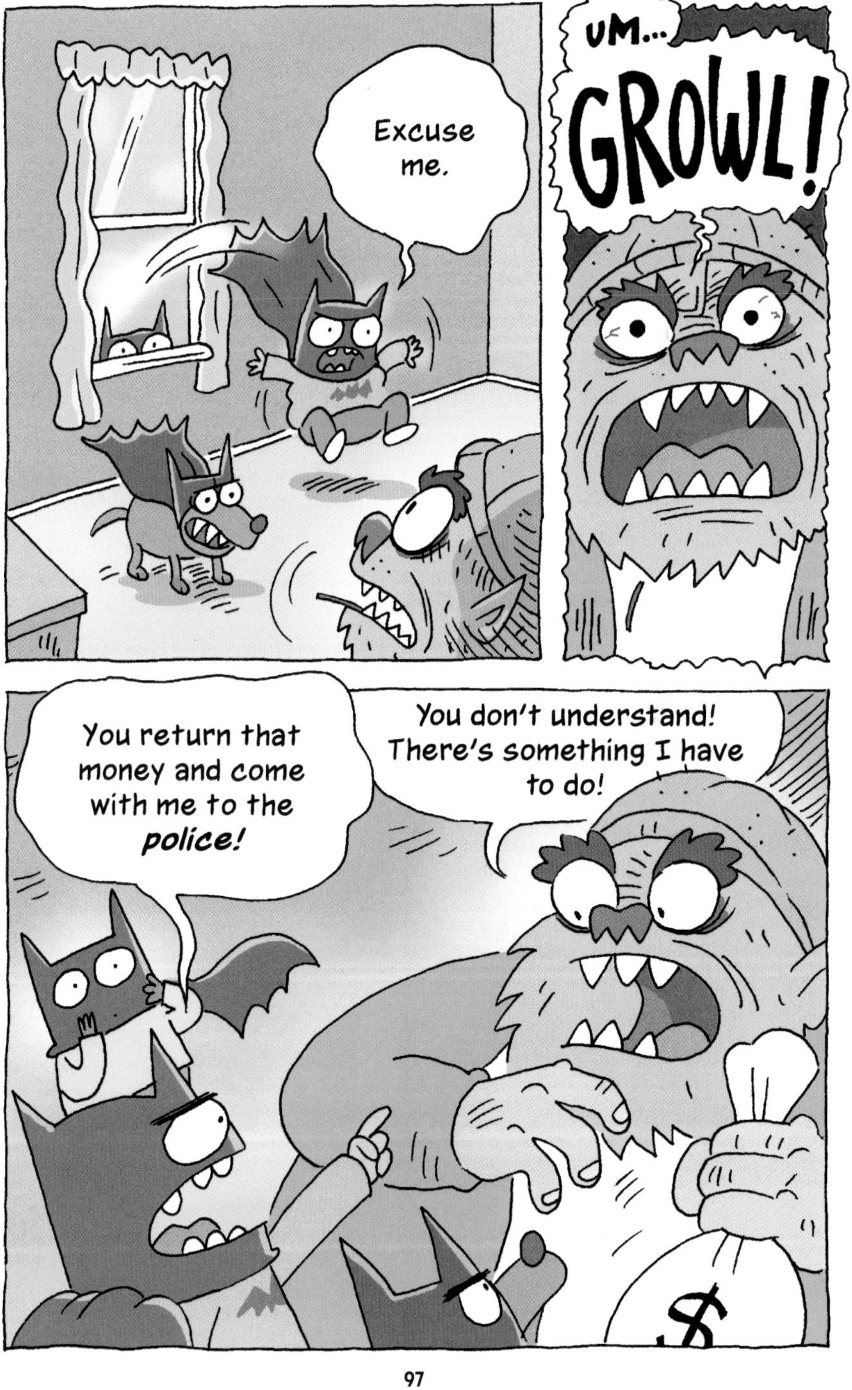
Excuse me.
UM...
GROWL!
You return that money and come with me to the police!
You don't understand! There's something I have to do!

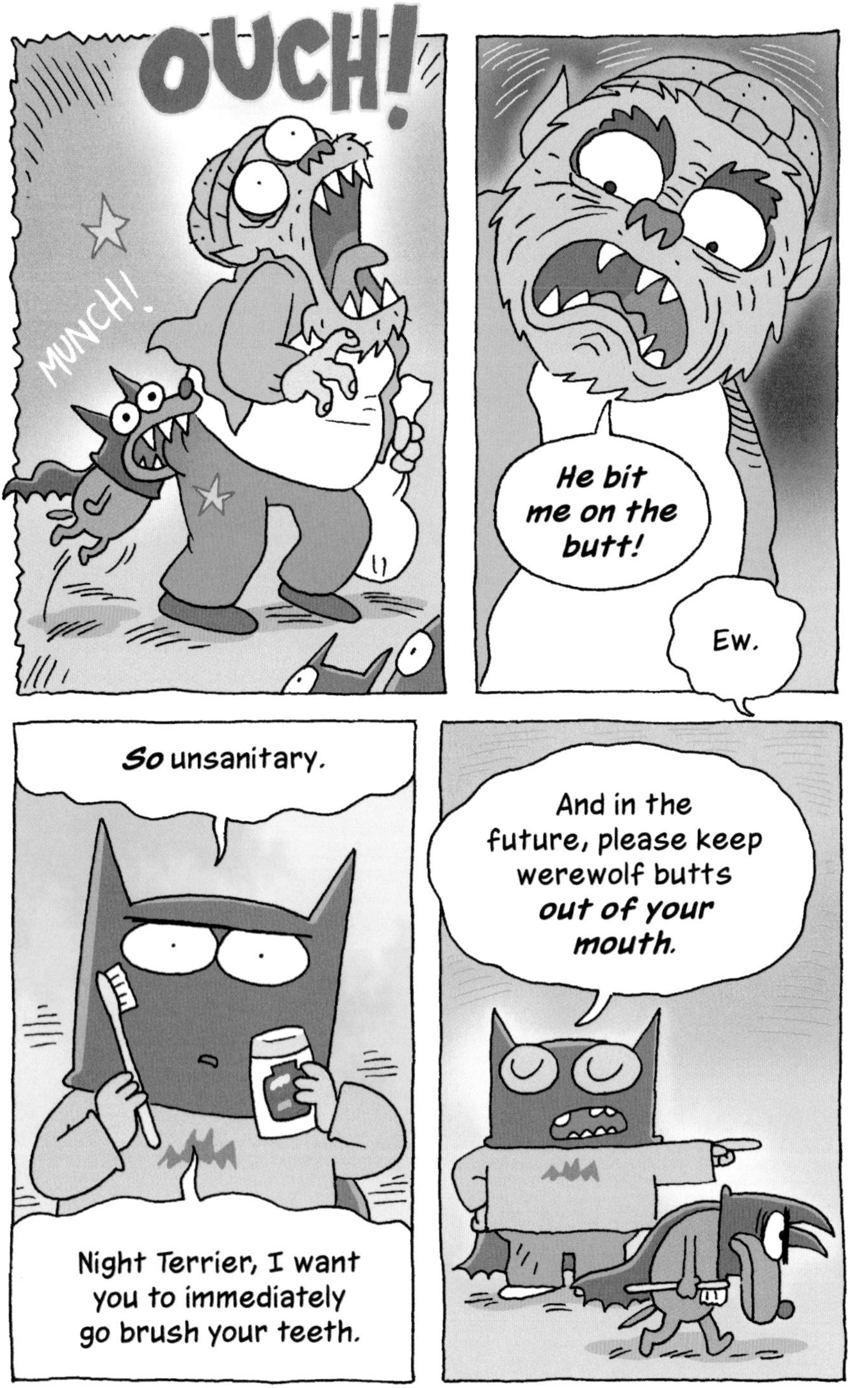
OUCH!
MUNCH!
He bit me on the butt!
Ew.
So unsanitary.
Night Terrier, I want you to immediately go brush your teeth.
And in the future, please keep werewolf butts ***out of your mouth.***

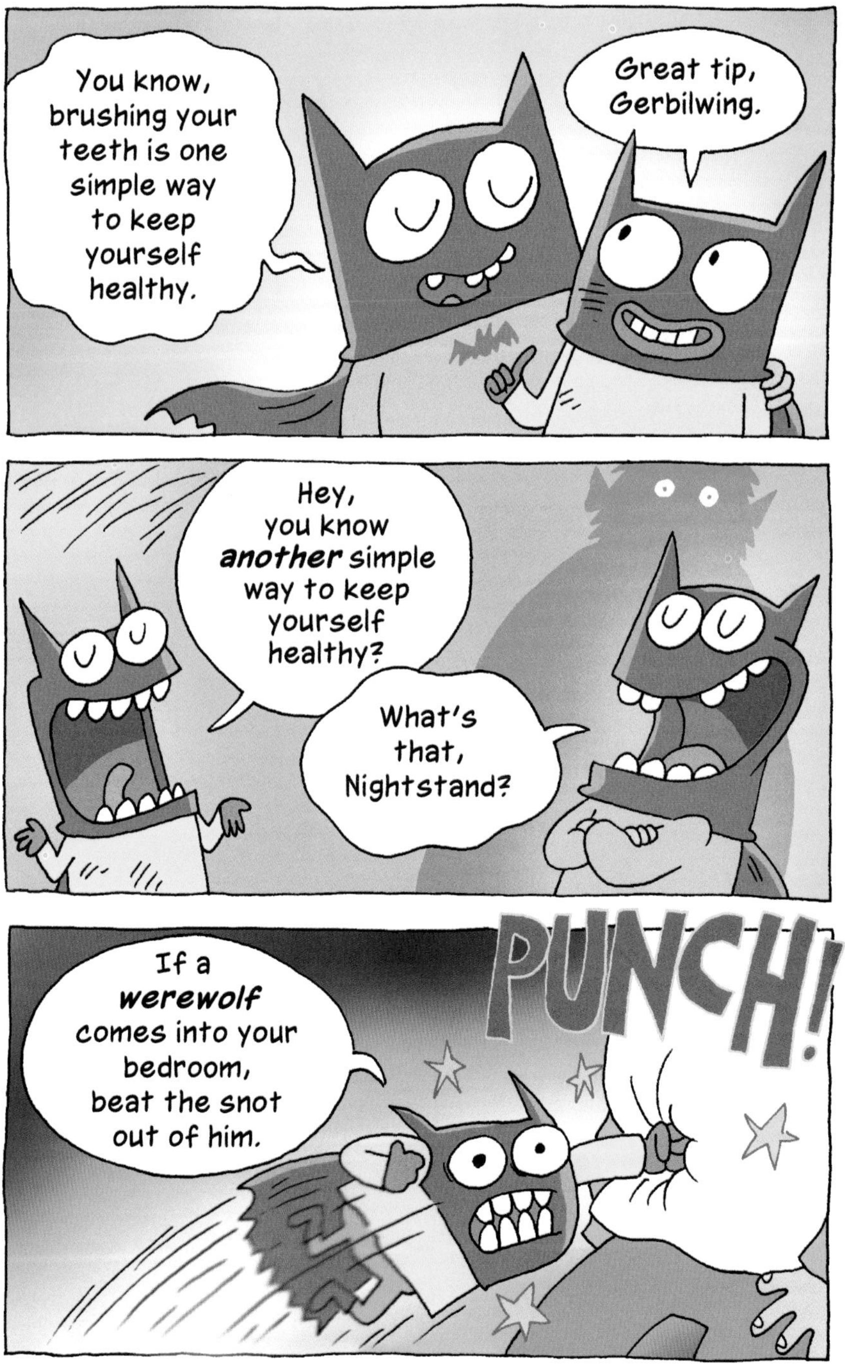
You know, brushing your teeth is one simple way to keep yourself healthy.
Great tip, Gerbilwing.
Hey, you know *another* simple way to keep yourself healthy?
What's that, Nightstand?
If a *werewolf* comes into your bedroom, beat the snot out of him.
PUNCH!

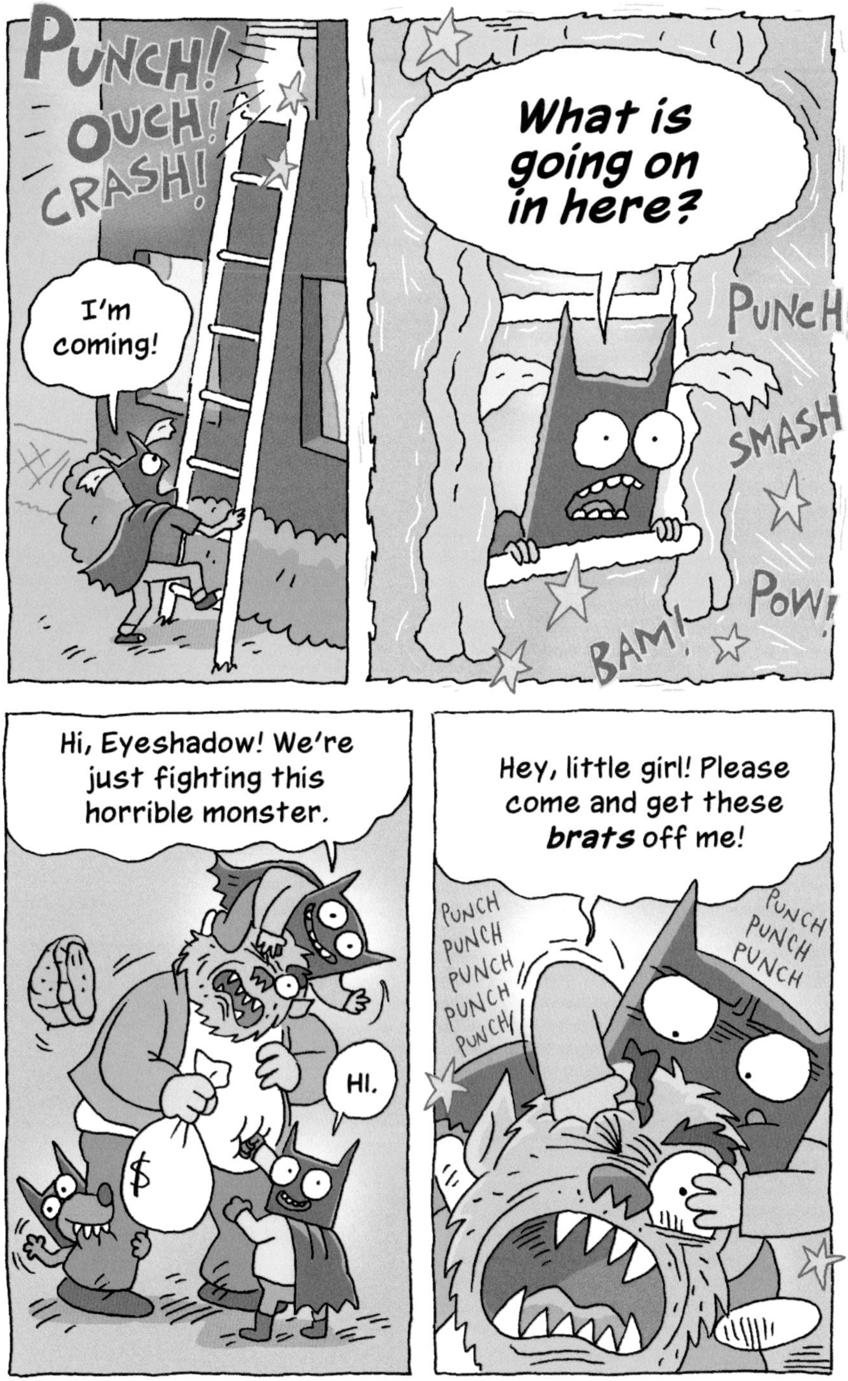
PUNCH!
OUCH!
CRASH!
I'm coming!
What is going on in here?
PUNCH!
SMASH
POW!
BAM!
Hi, Eyeshadow! We're just fighting this horrible monster.
HI.
Hey, little girl! Please come and get these *brats* off me!
PUNCH PUNCH PUNCH PUNCH PUNCH
PUNCH PUNCH PUNCH

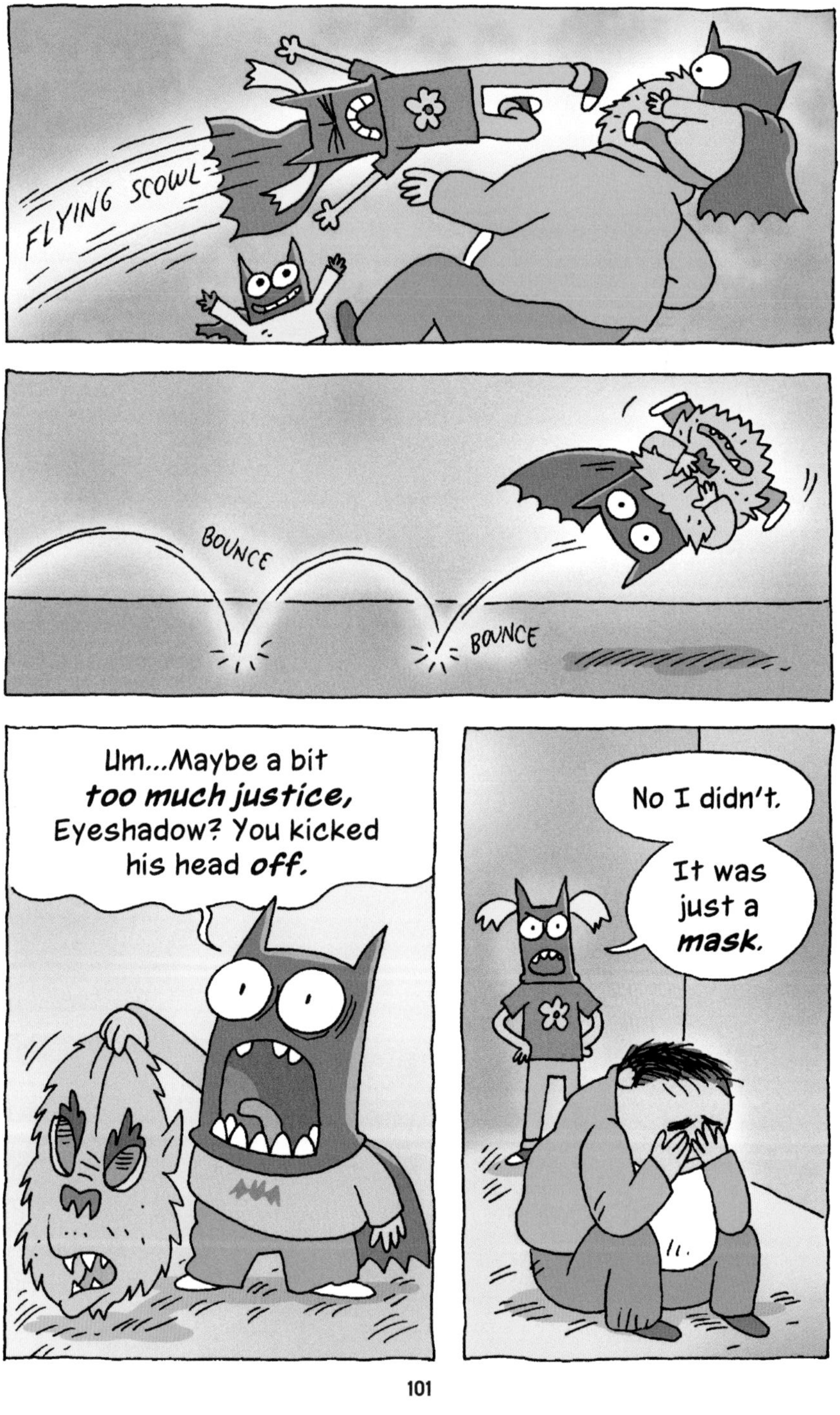
FLYING SCOWL
BOUNCE
BOUNCE
Um...Maybe a bit **too much justice,** Eyeshadow? You kicked his head **off.**
No I didn't.
It was just a **mask.**

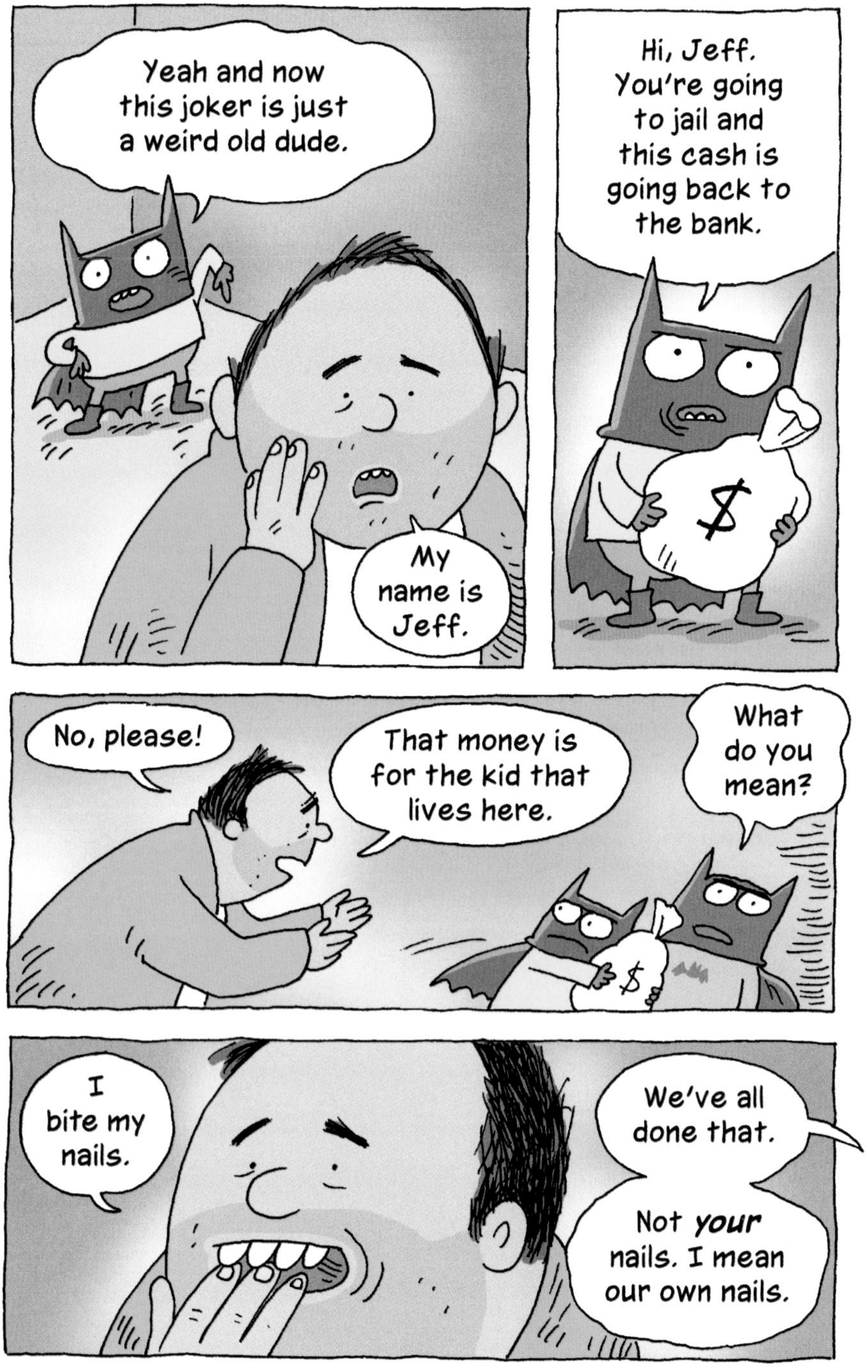

Yeah and now this joker is just a weird old dude.
My name is Jeff.
Hi, Jeff. You're going to jail and this cash is going back to the bank.
$
No, please!
That money is for the kid that lives here.
What do you mean?
$
I bite my nails.
We've all done that.
Not *your* nails. I mean our own nails.

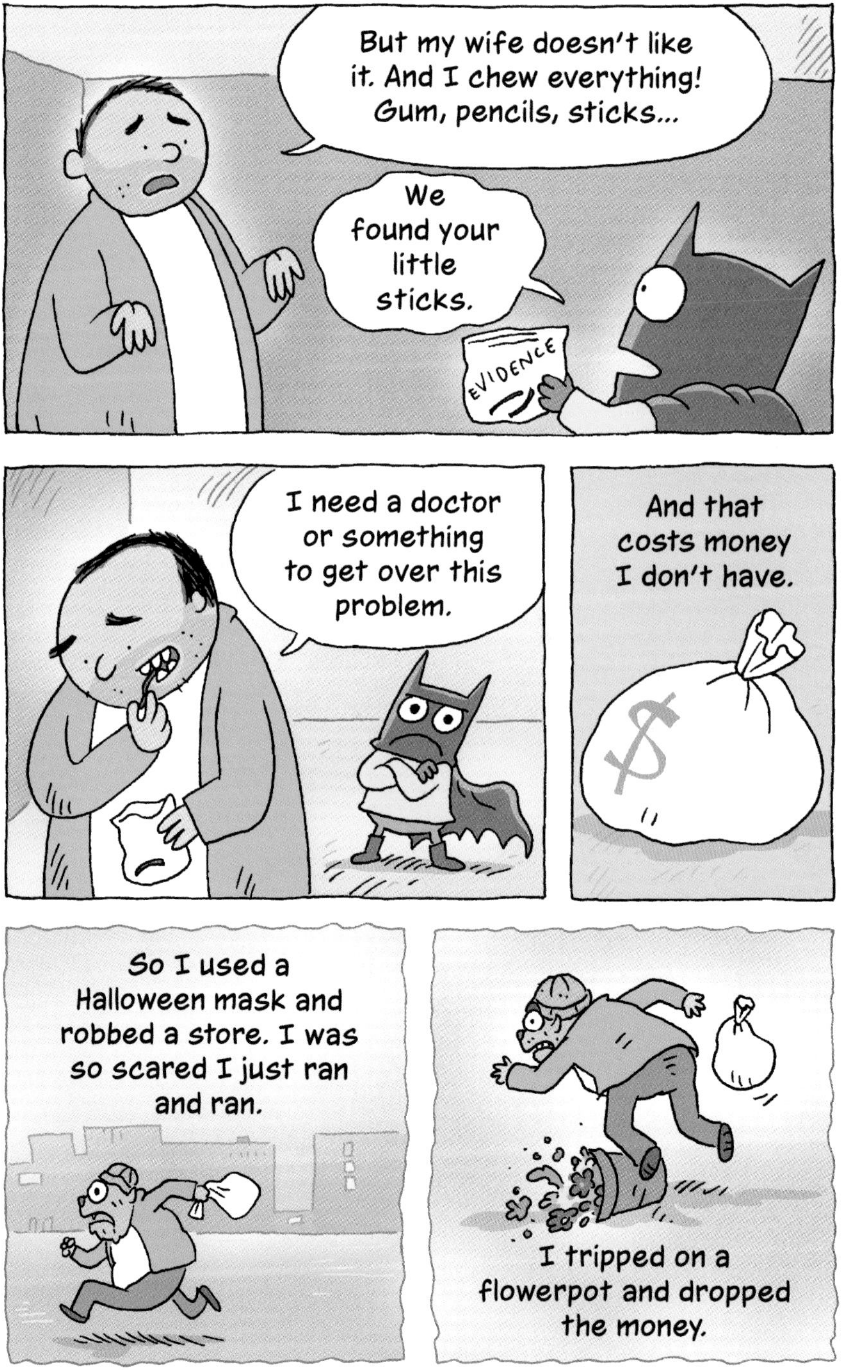
But my wife doesn't like it. And I chew everything! Gum, pencils, sticks...
We found your little sticks.
EVIDENCE
I need a doctor or something to get over this problem.
And that costs money I don't have.
So I used a Halloween mask and robbed a store. I was so scared I just ran and ran.
I tripped on a flowerpot and dropped the money.

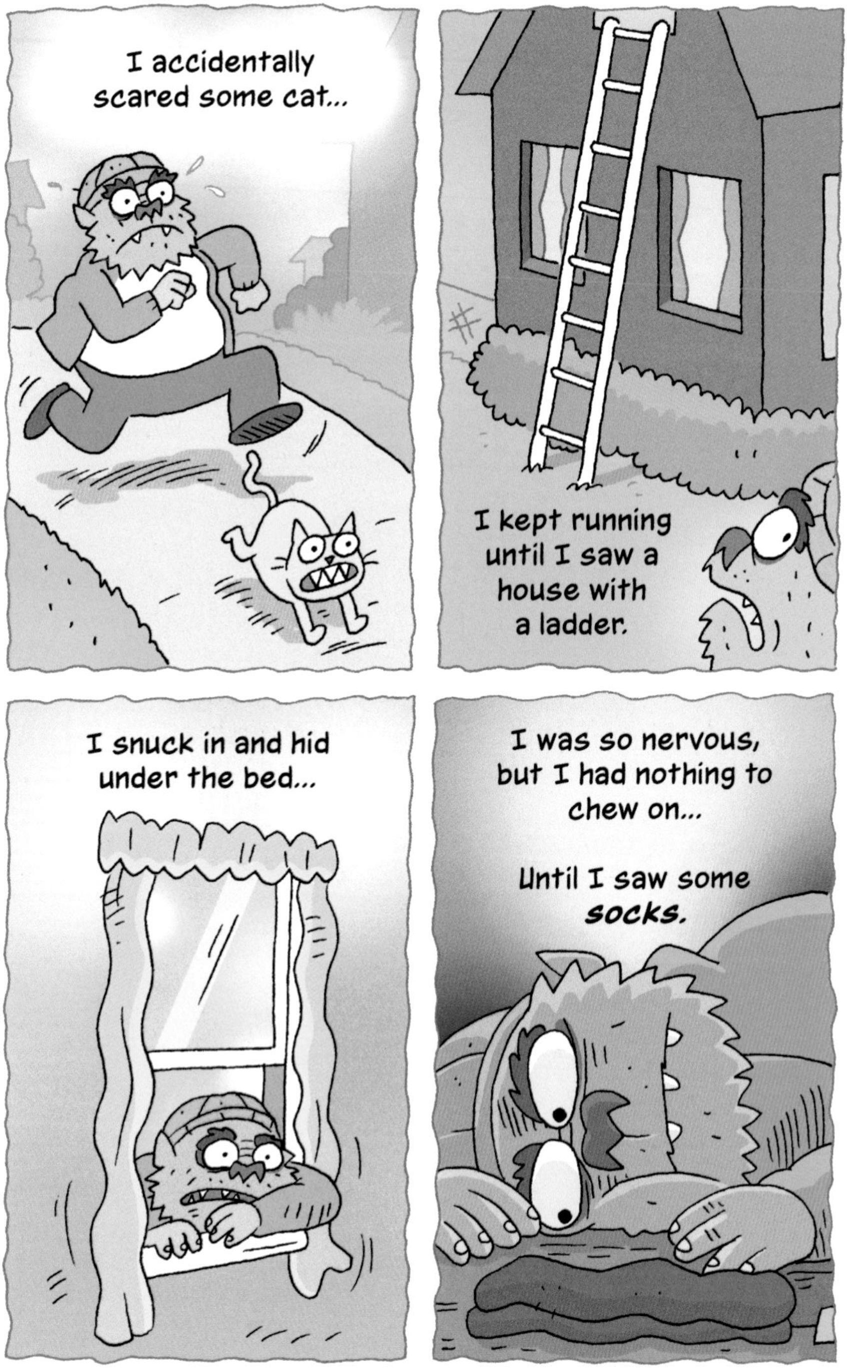
I accidentally scared some cat...
I kept running until I saw a house with a ladder.
I snuck in and hid under the bed...
I was so nervous, but I had nothing to chew on...
Until I saw some *socks.*

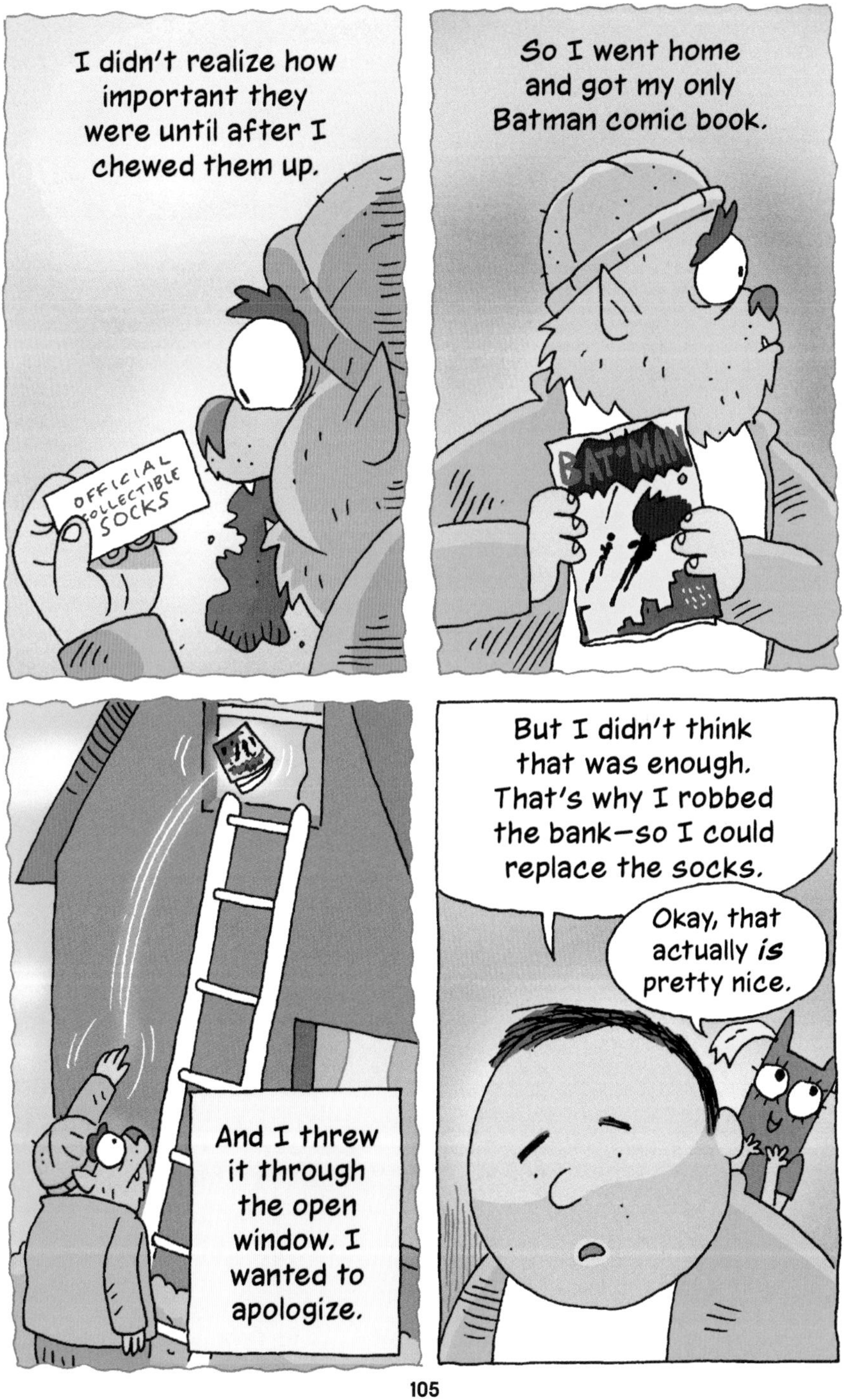
I didn't realize how important they were until after I chewed them up.
OFFICIAL COLLECTIBLE SOCKS
So I went home and got my only Batman comic book.
BAT-MAN
And I threw it through the open window. I wanted to apologize.
But I didn't think that was enough. That's why I robbed the bank—so I could replace the socks.
Okay, that actually *is* pretty nice.

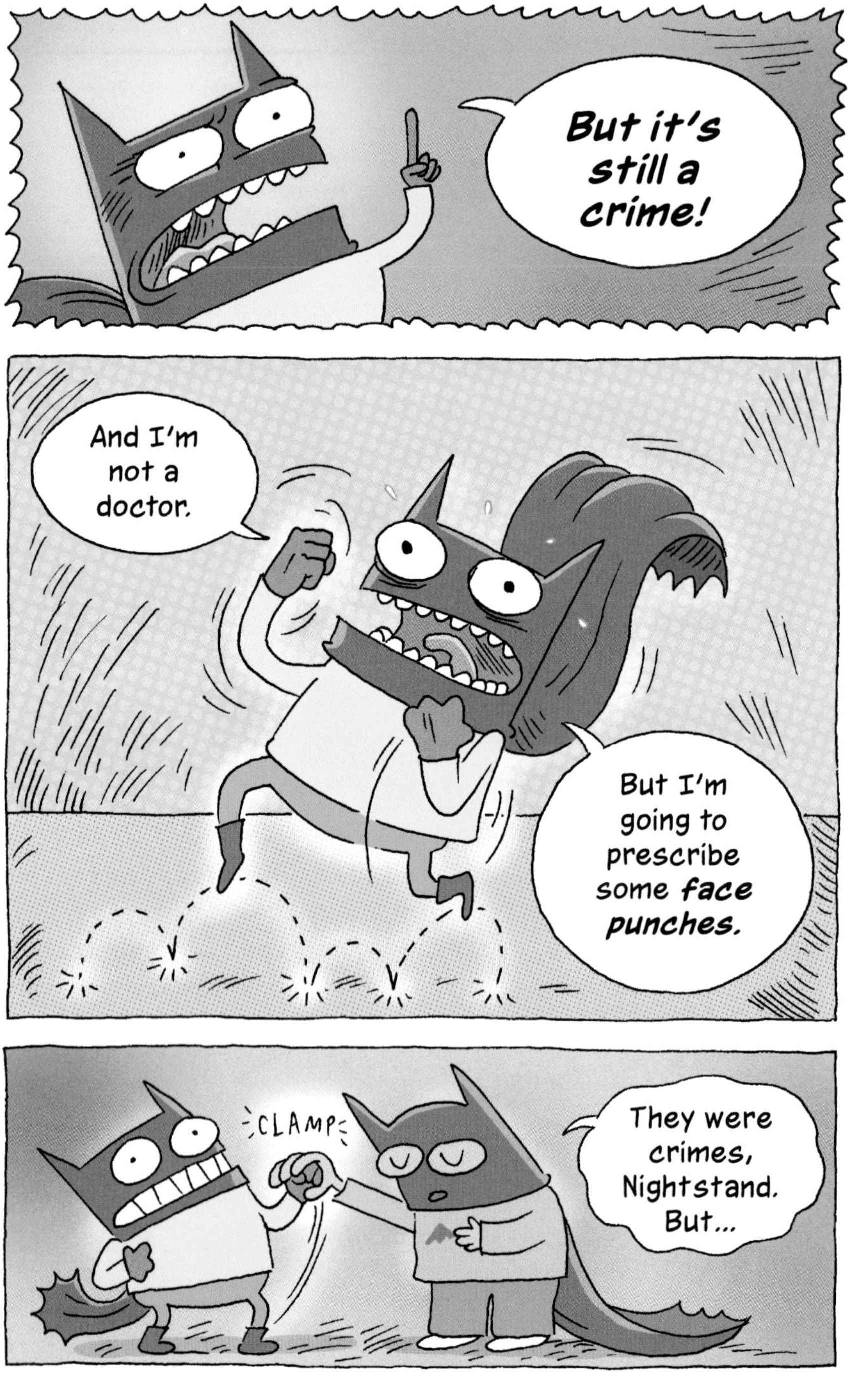
But it's still a crime!
And I'm not a doctor.
But I'm going to prescribe some *face punches.*
CLAMP
They were crimes, Nightstand. But...

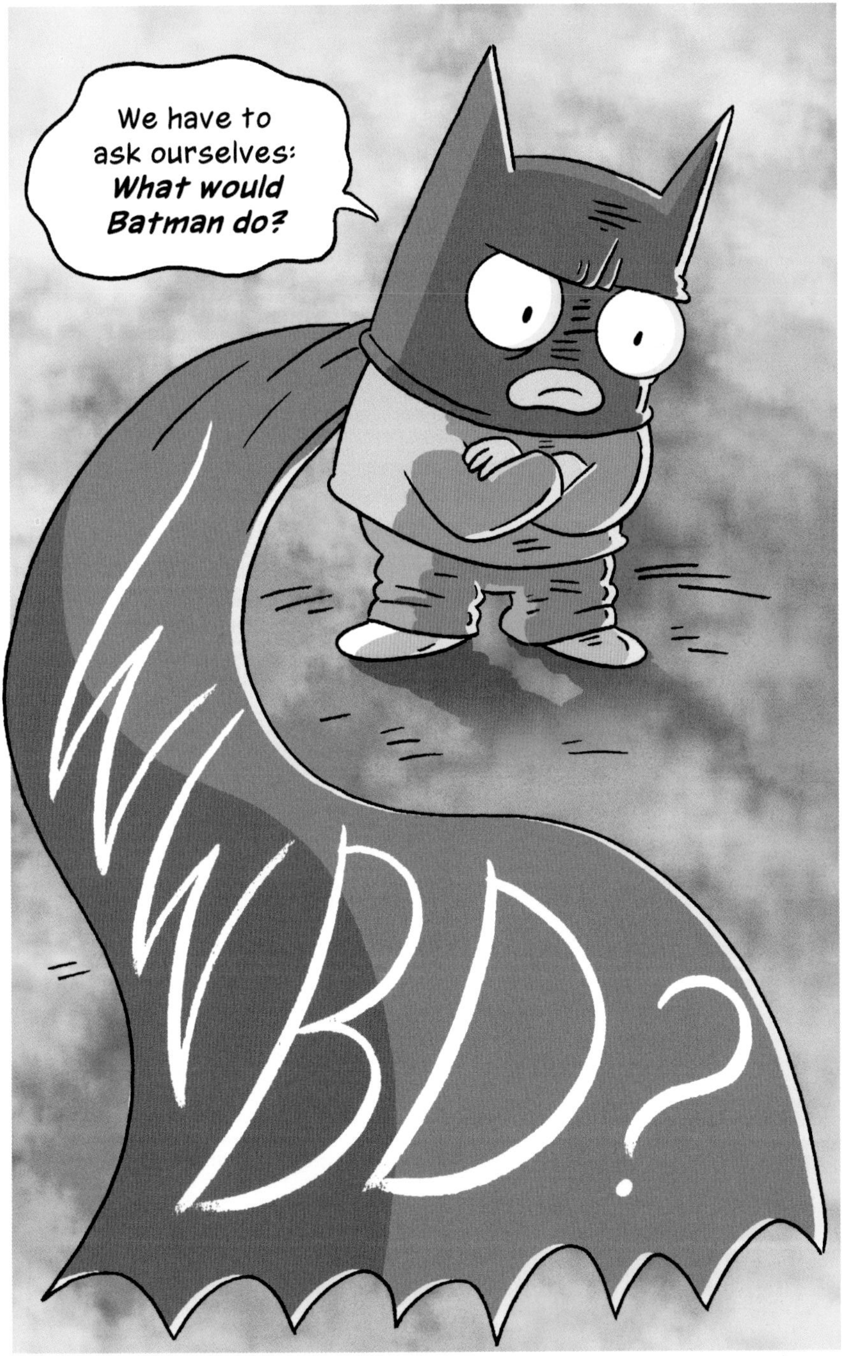
We have to ask ourselves: ***What would Batman do?***
WWBD?

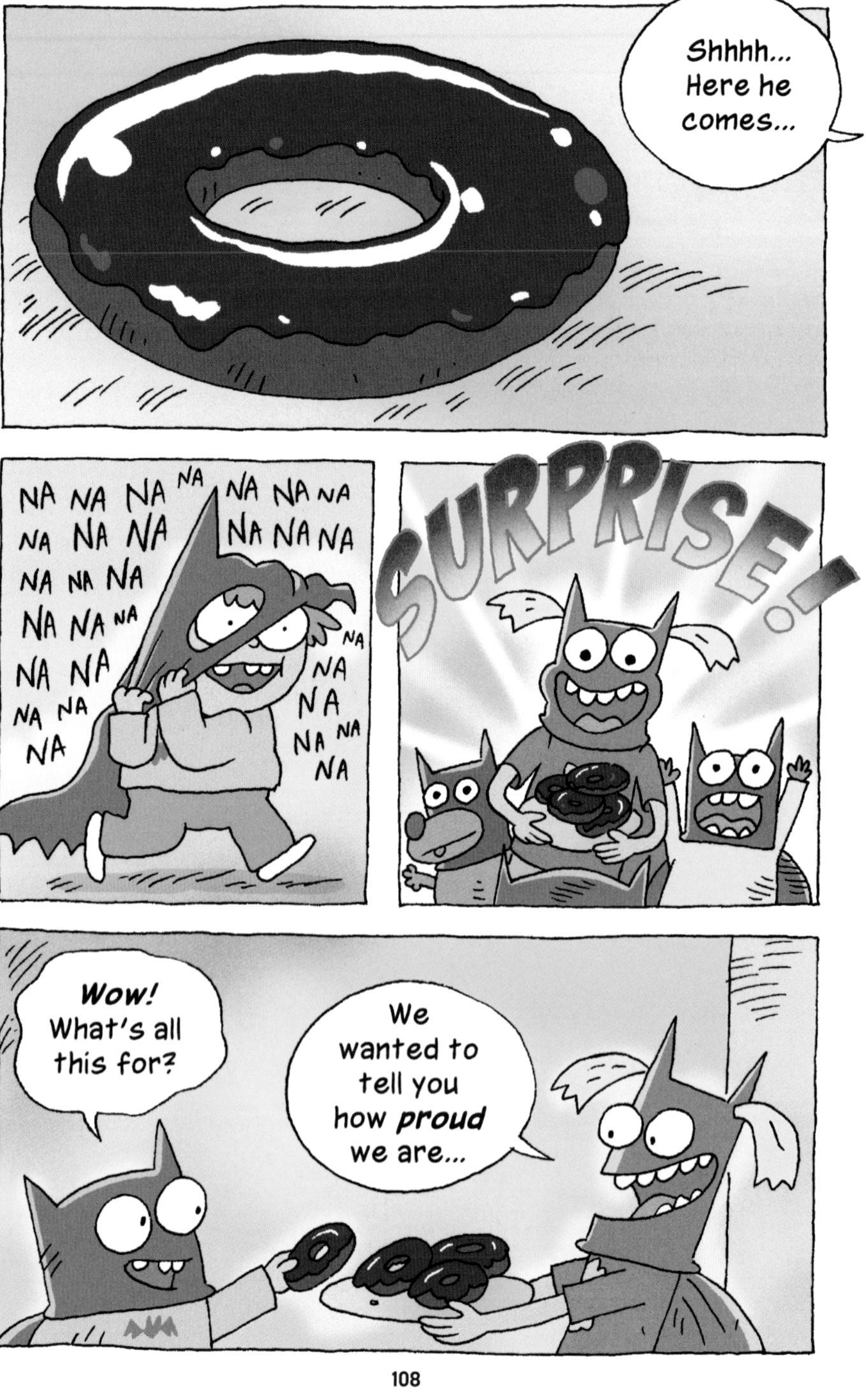
Shhhh... Here he comes...
NA NA NA NA NA NA NA
NA NA NA NA NA NA
NA NA NA
NA NA NA
NA NA
NA NA
NA
NA NA NA NA NA NA NA
SURPRISE!
Wow! What's all this for?
We wanted to tell you how ***proud*** we are...

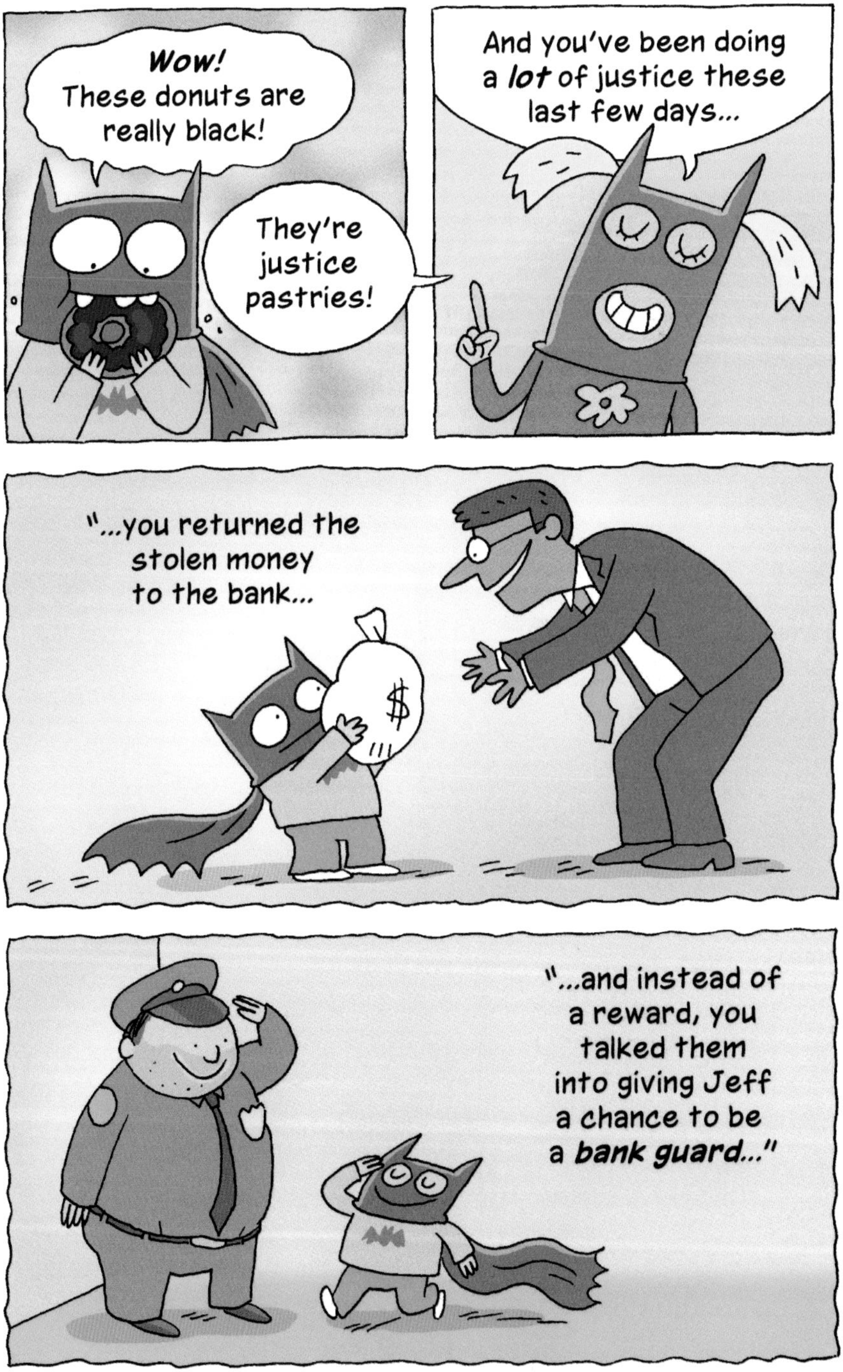
Wow! These donuts are really black!
They're justice pastries!
And you've been doing a lot of justice these last few days...
"...you returned the stolen money to the bank...
$
"...and instead of a reward, you talked them into giving Jeff a chance to be a bank guard..."

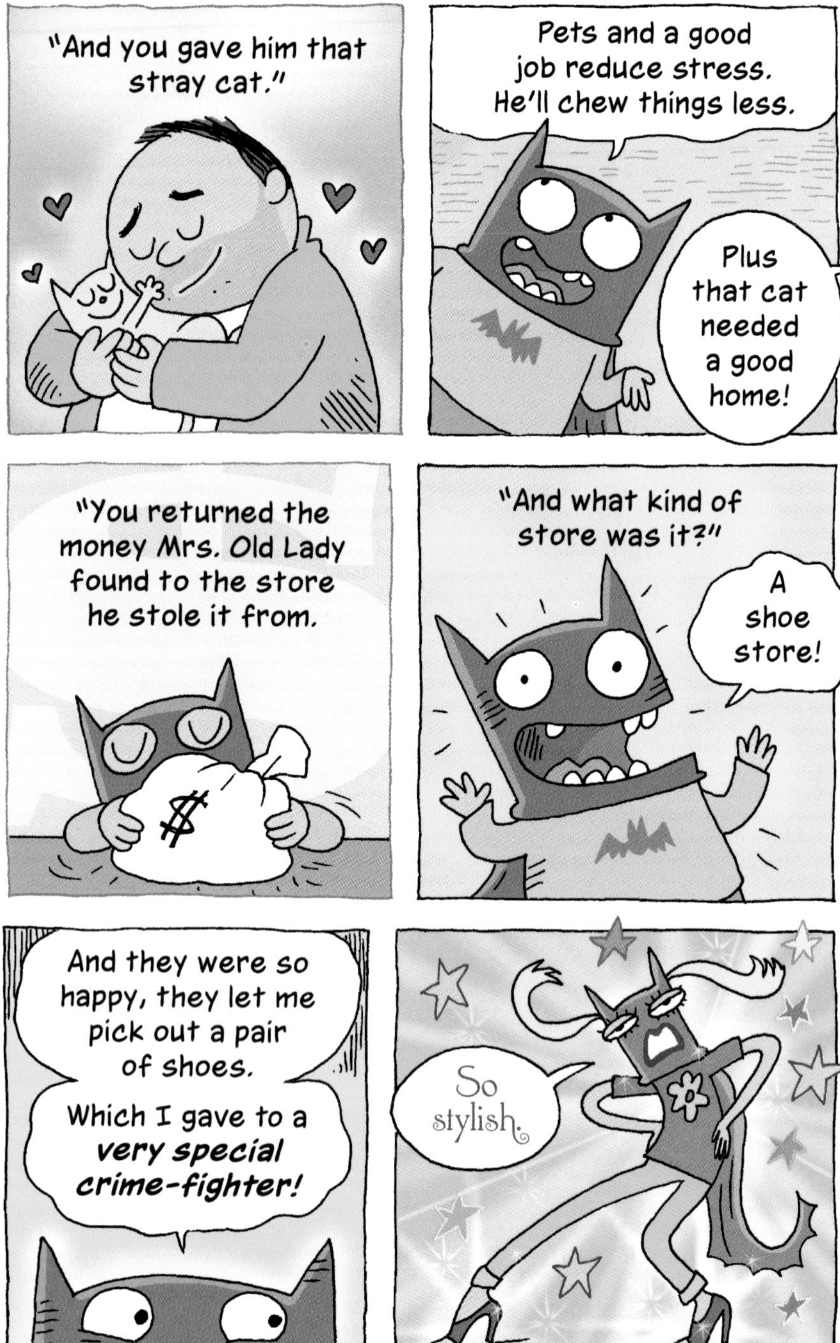
"And you gave him that stray cat."
Pets and a good job reduce stress. He'll chew things less.
Plus that cat needed a good home!
"You returned the money Mrs. Old Lady found to the store he stole it from.
"And what kind of store was it?"
A shoe store!
And they were so happy, they let me pick out a pair of shoes.
Which I gave to a ***very special crime-fighter!***
So stylish.

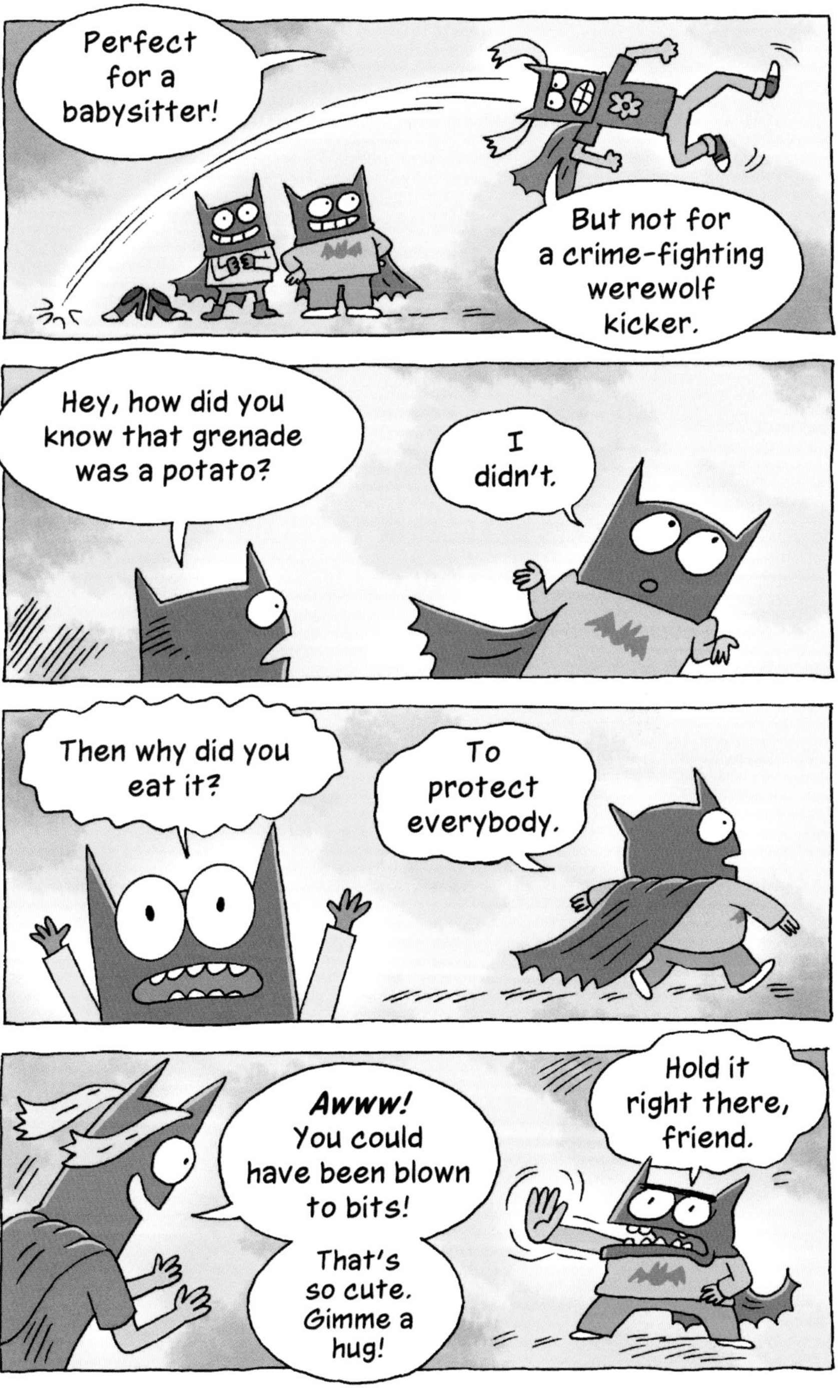

Perfect for a babysitter!
But not for a crime-fighting werewolf kicker.
Hey, how did you know that grenade was a potato?
I didn't.
Then why did you eat it?
To protect everybody.
Awww! You could have been blown to bits!
That's so cute. Gimme a hug!
Hold it right there, friend.

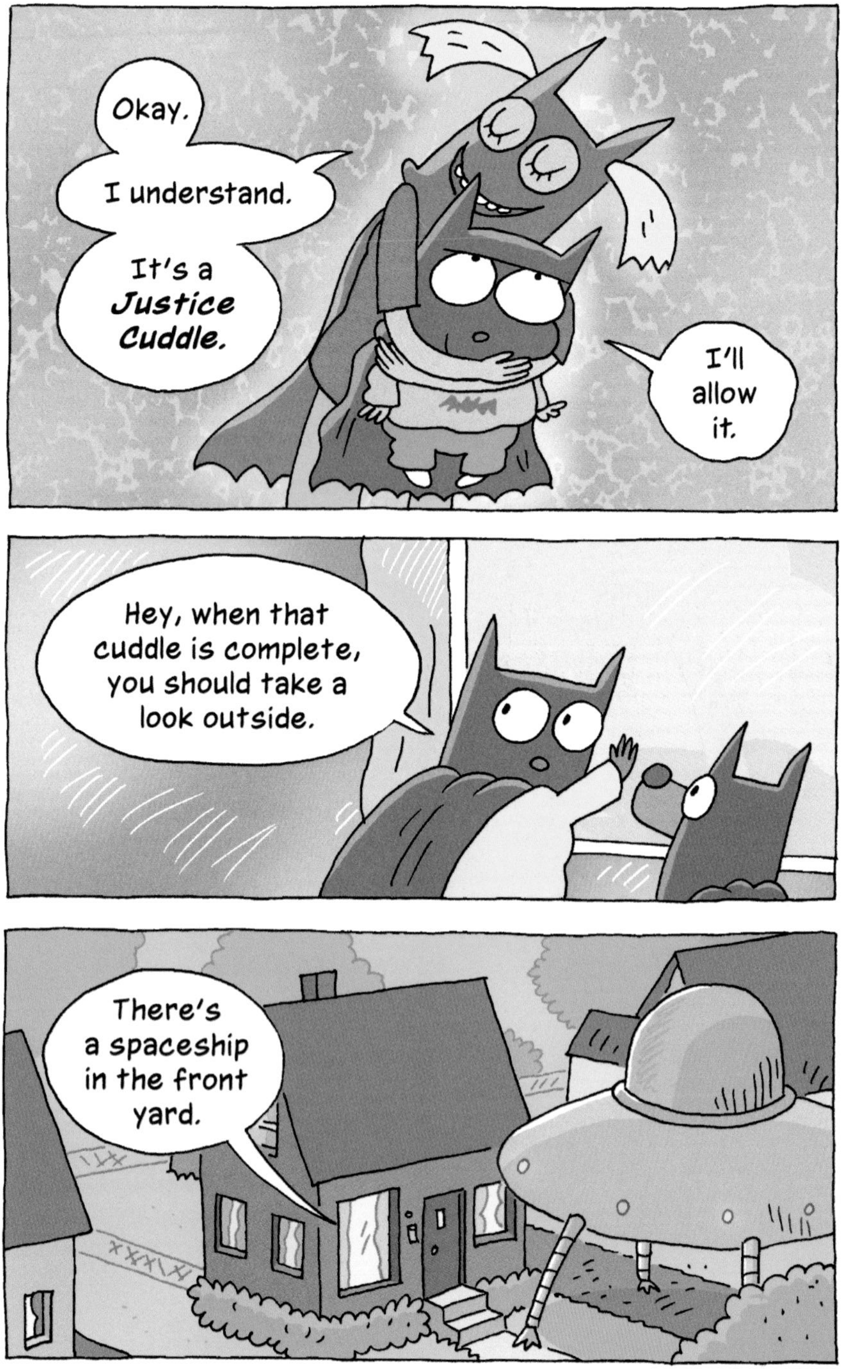
Okay.
I understand.
It's a *Justice Cuddle.*
I'll allow it.
Hey, when that cuddle is complete, you should take a look outside.
There's a spaceship in the front yard.

The end.
Until next time.

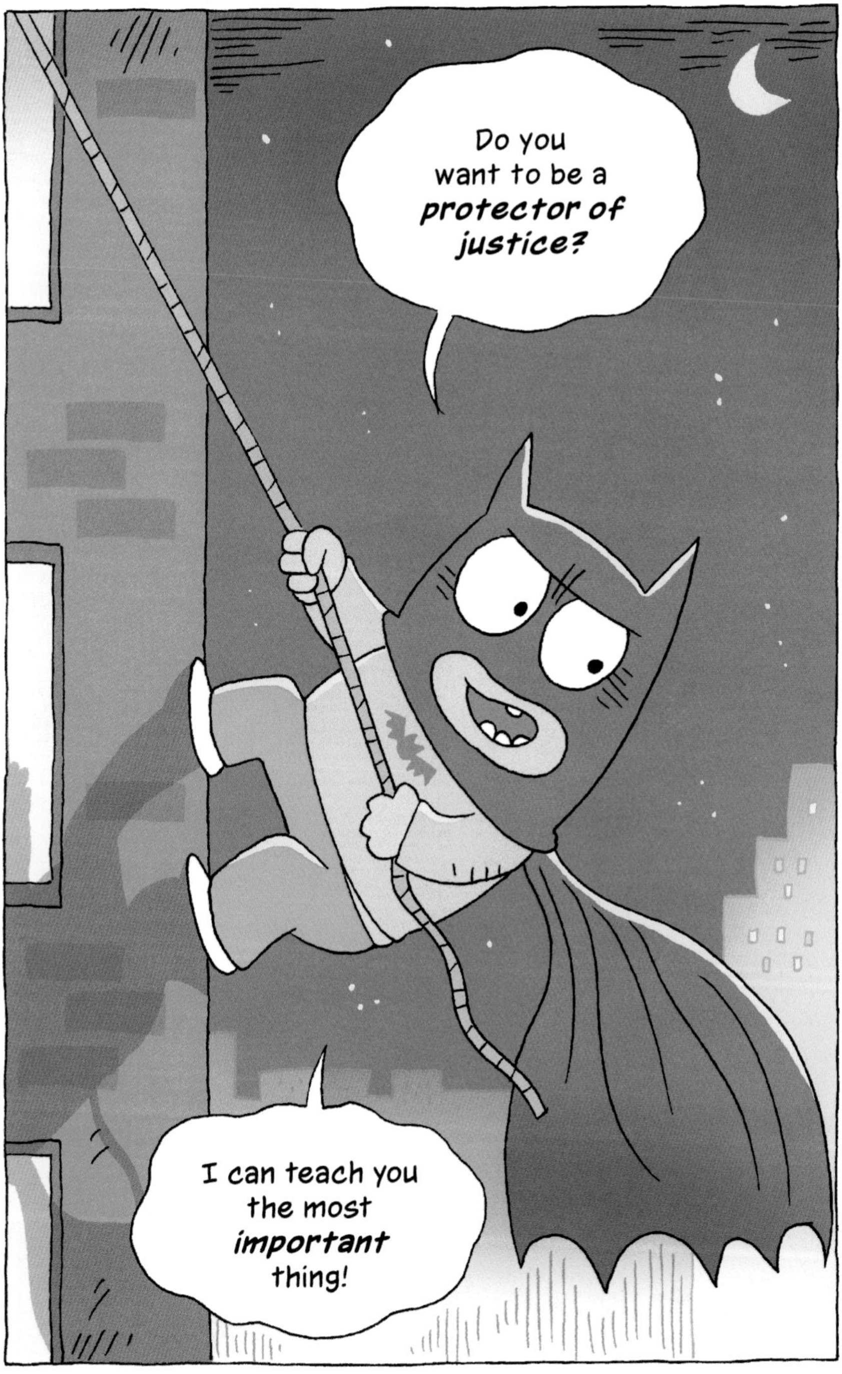
Do you want to be a ***protector of justice?***
I can teach you the most ***important*** thing!

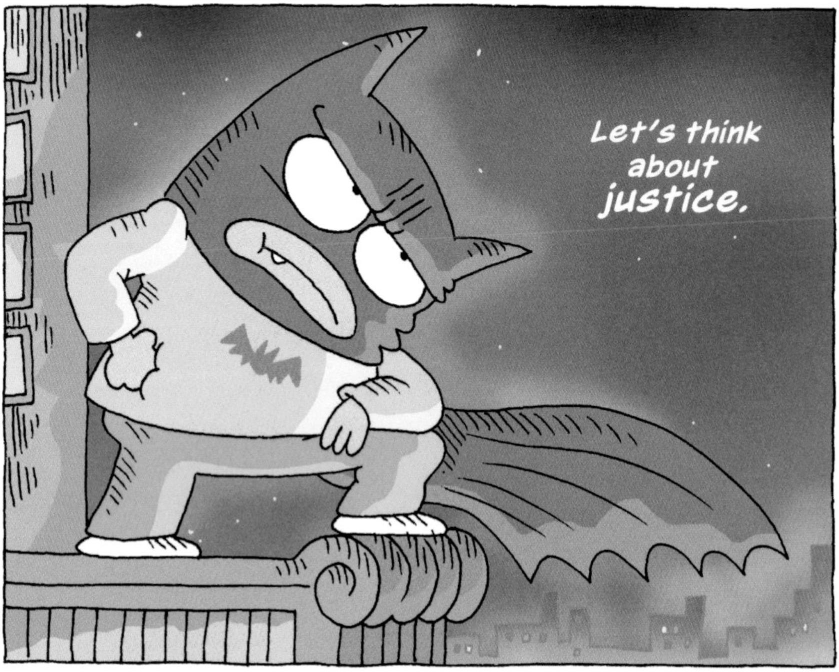
Let's think about justice.

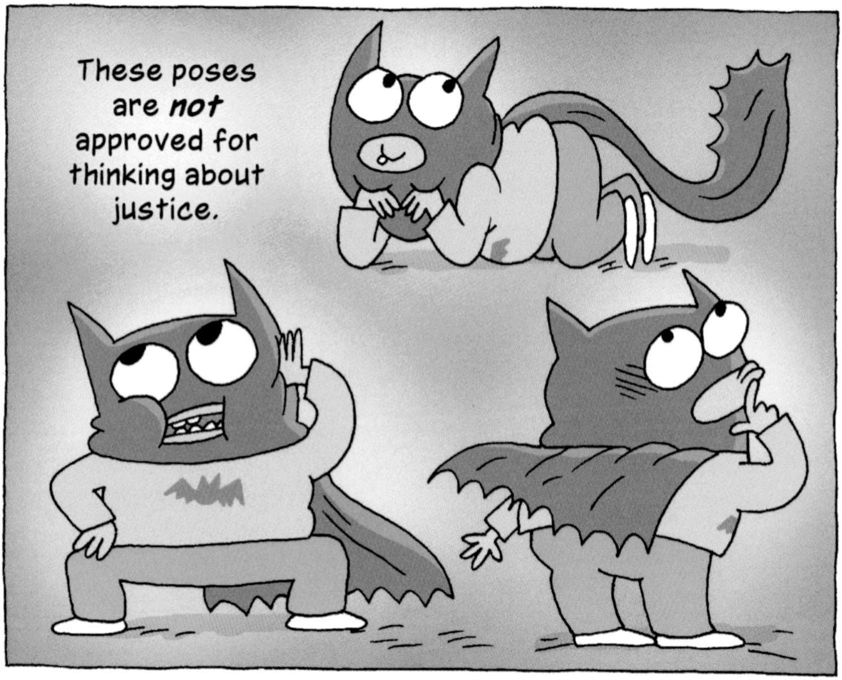
These poses are not approved for thinking about justice.

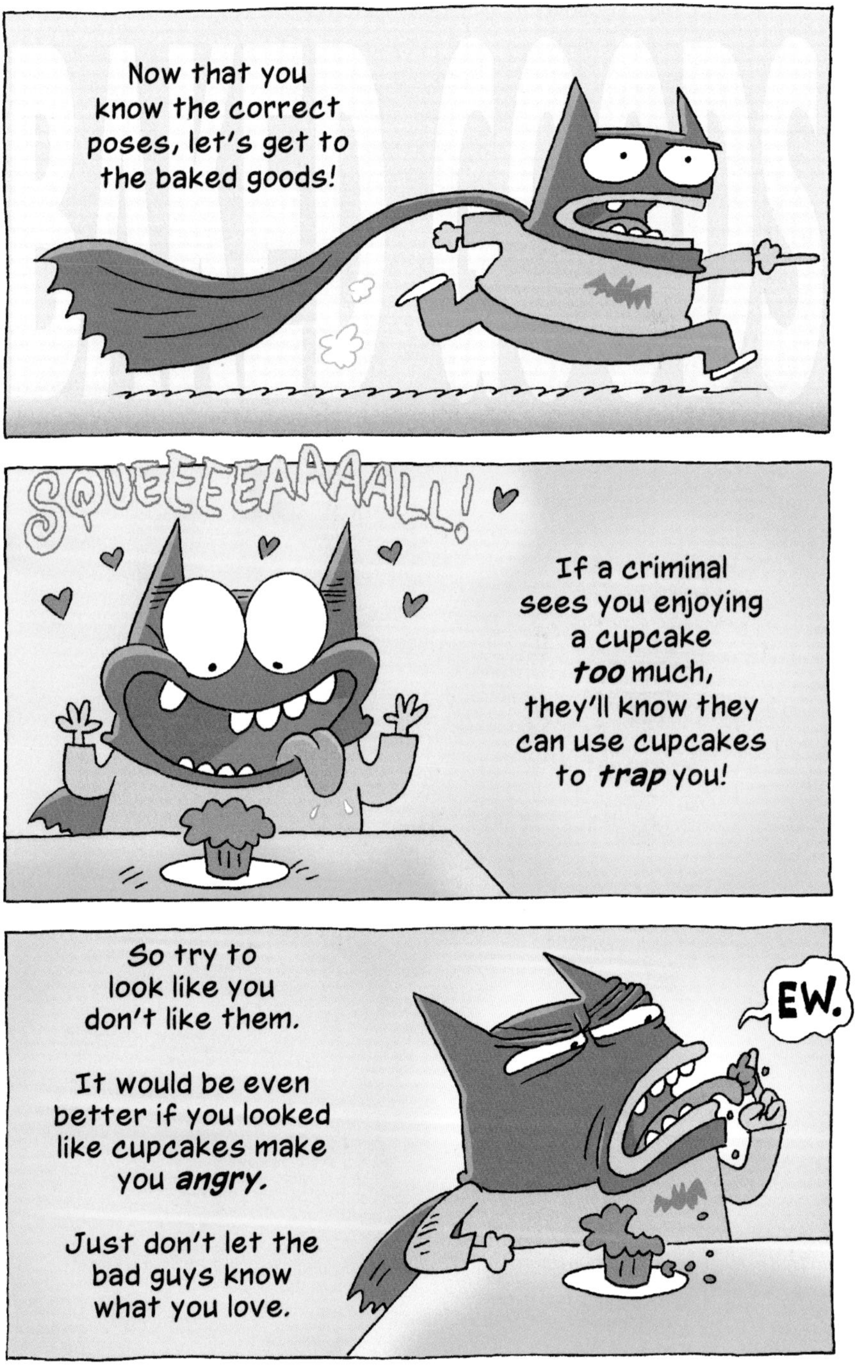
Now that you know the correct poses, let's get to the baked goods!
SQUEEEEAAAALL!
If a criminal sees you enjoying a cupcake *too* much, they'll know they can use cupcakes to *trap* you!
So try to look like you don't like them.
It would be even better if you looked like cupcakes make you *angry.*
Just don't let the bad guys know what you love.
EW.

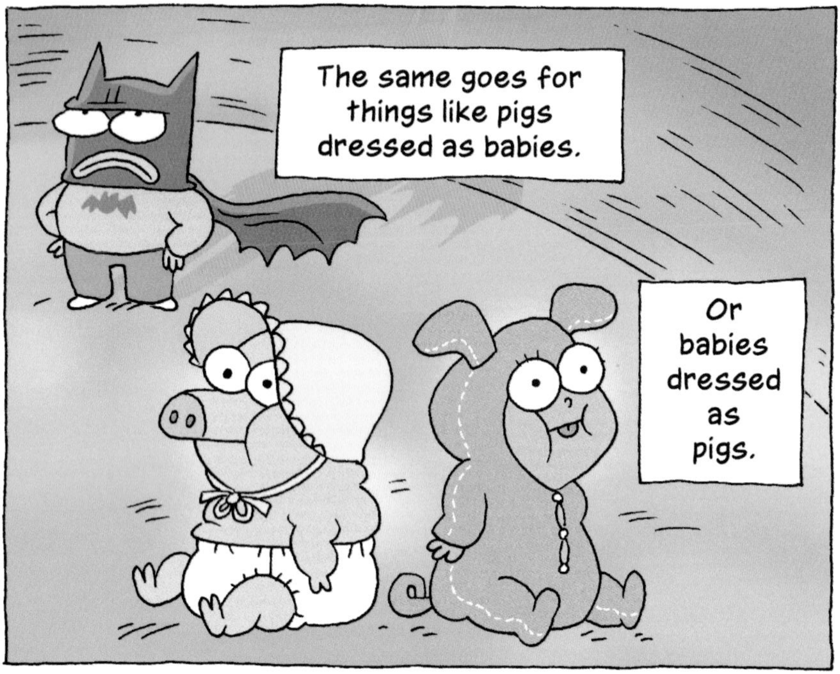
The same goes for things like pigs dressed as babies.
Or babies dressed as pigs.

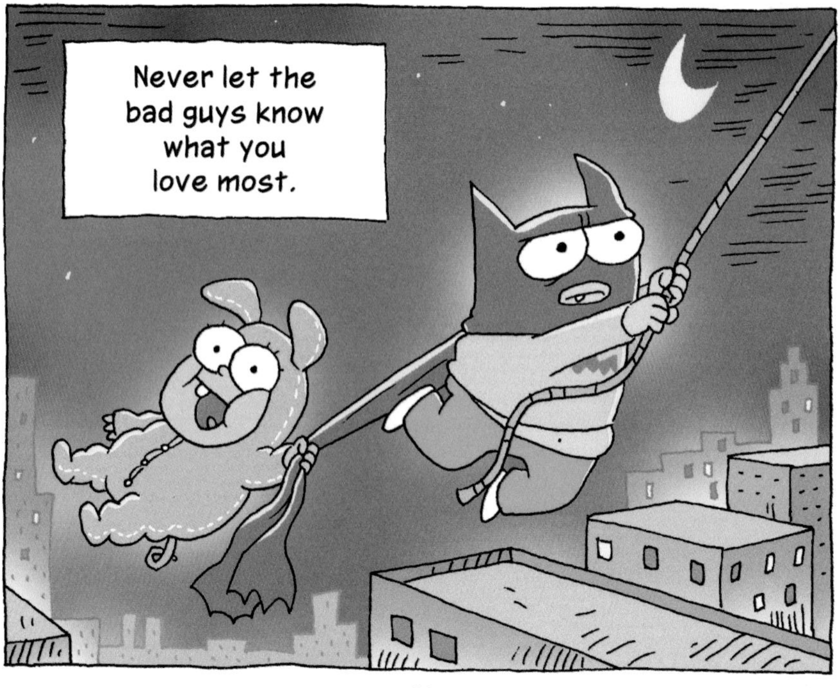
Never let the bad guys know what you love most.

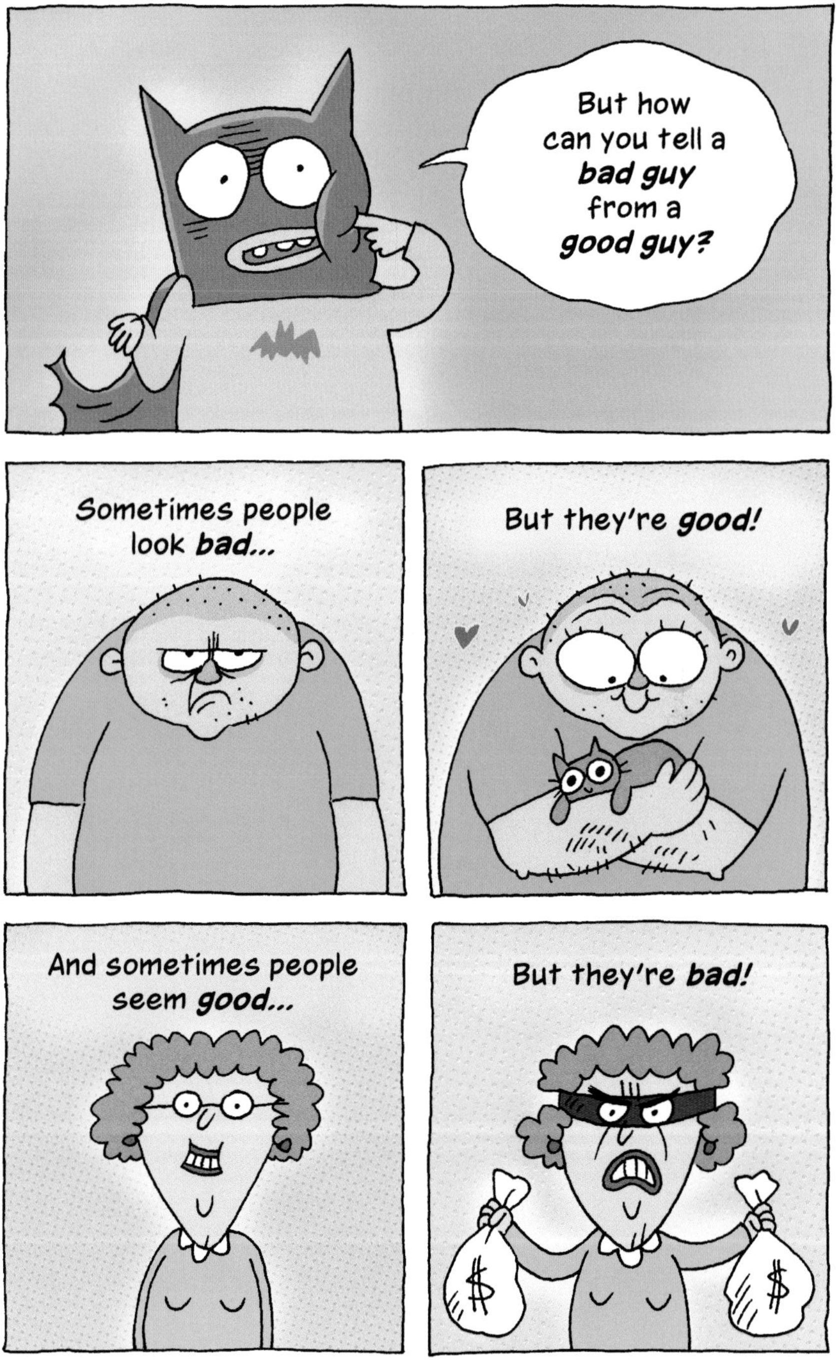
But how can you tell a ***bad guy*** from a ***good guy?***
Sometimes people look ***bad...***
But they're ***good!***
And sometimes people seem ***good...***
But they're ***bad!***

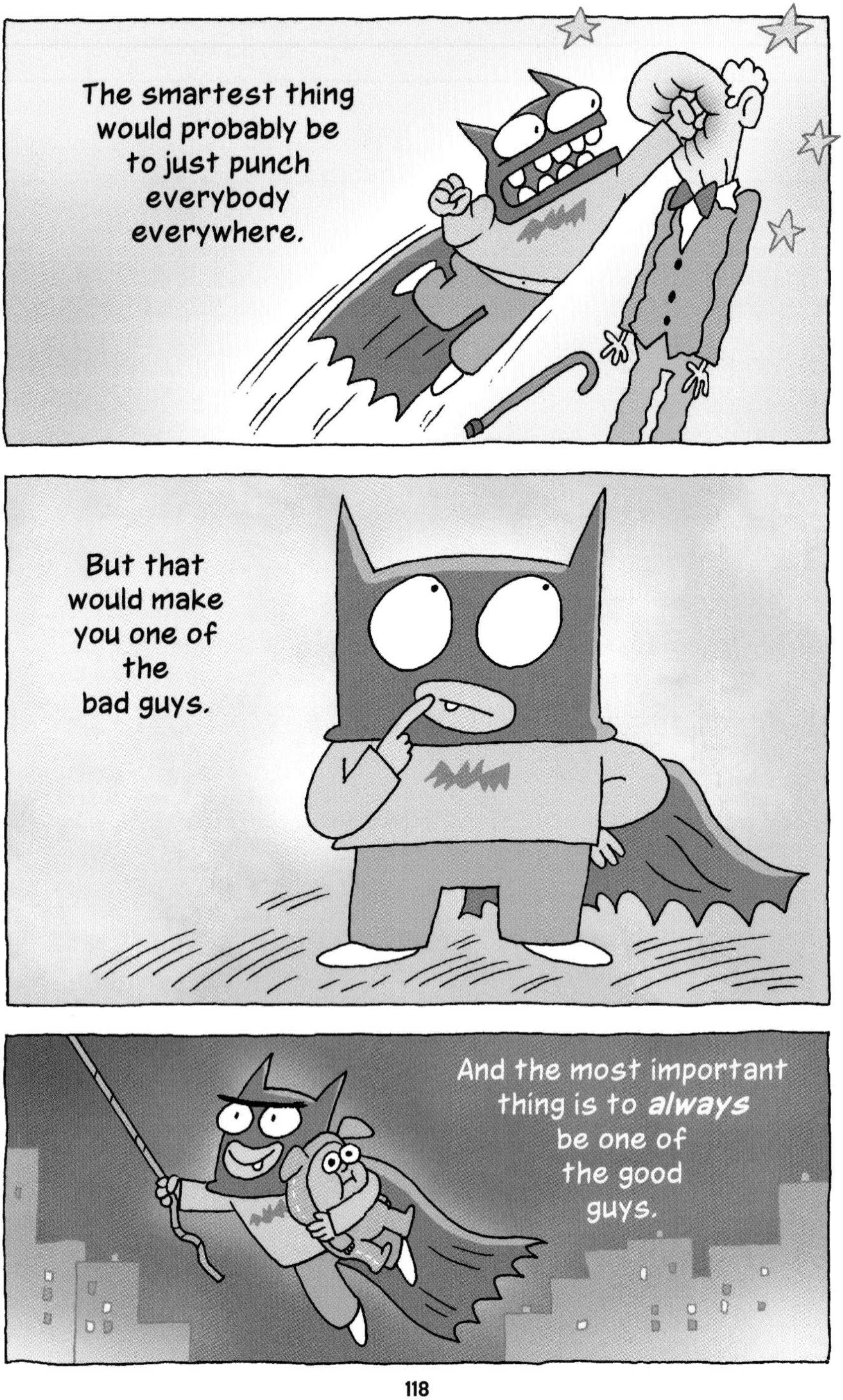
The smartest thing would probably be to just punch everybody everywhere.
But that would make you one of the bad guys.
And the most important thing is to *always* be one of the good guys.

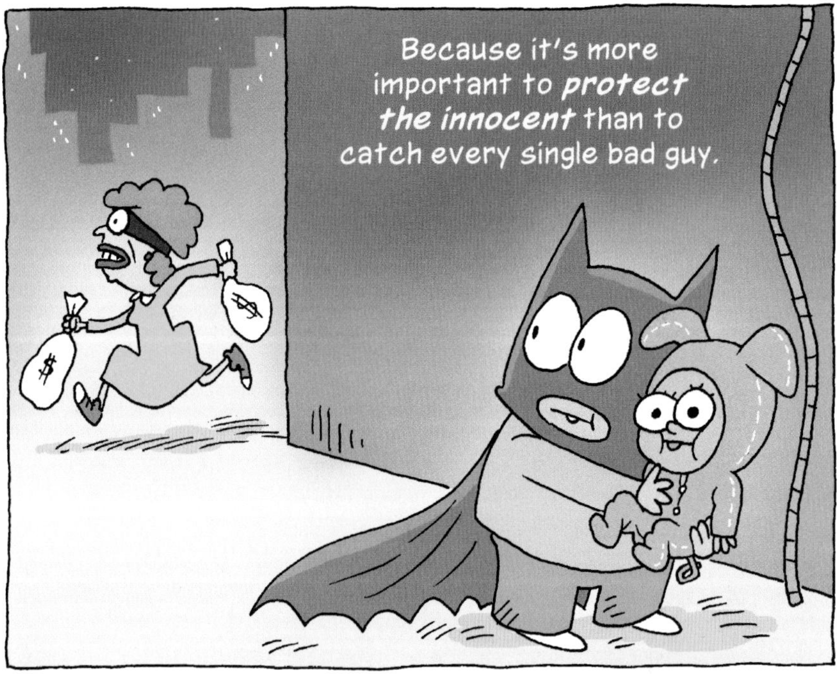
Because it's more important to ***protect the innocent*** than to catch every single bad guy.

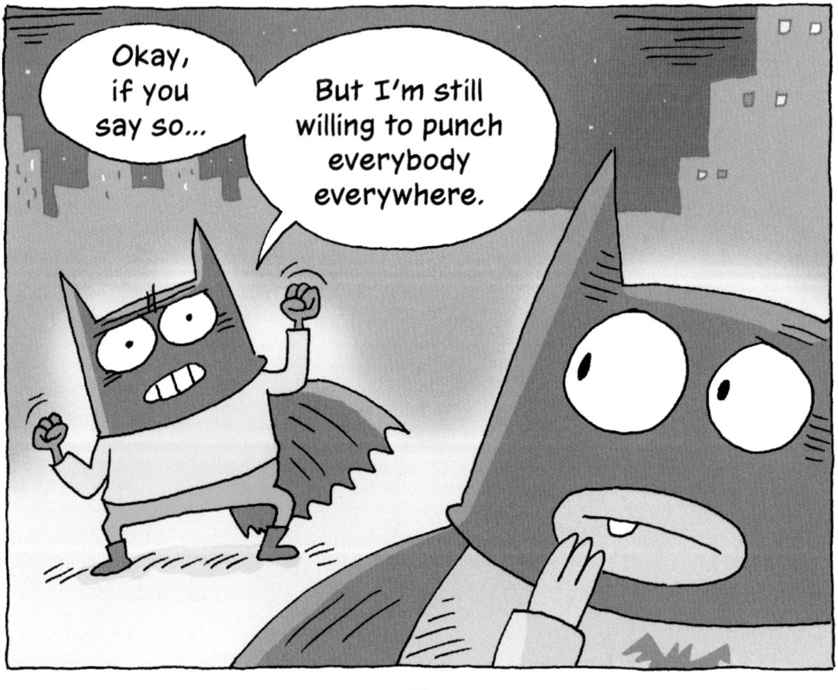
Okay, if you say so...
But I'm still willing to punch everybody everywhere.

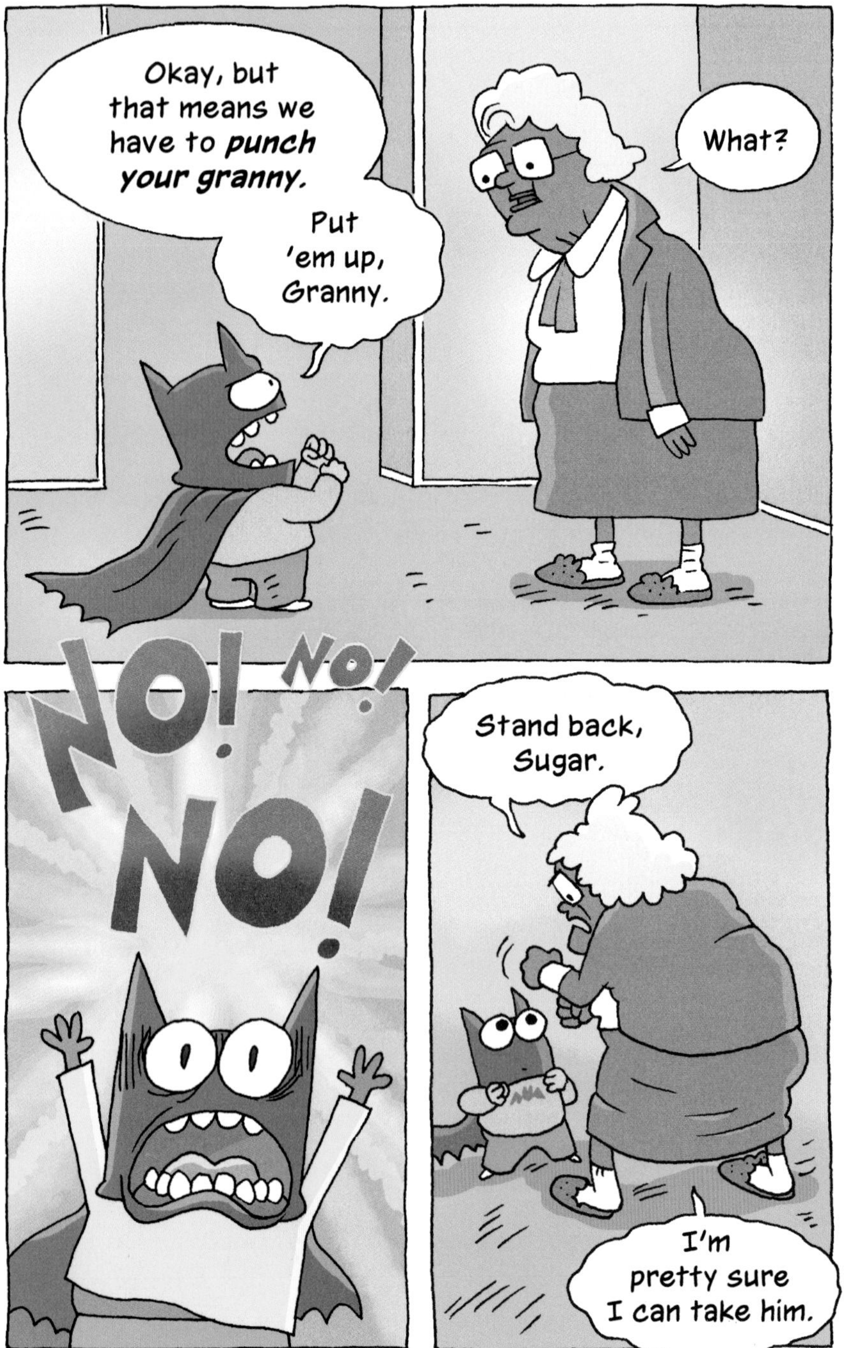
Okay, but that means we have to ***punch your granny.***
Put 'em up, Granny.
What?
NO! NO! NO!
Stand back, Sugar.
I'm pretty sure I can take him.

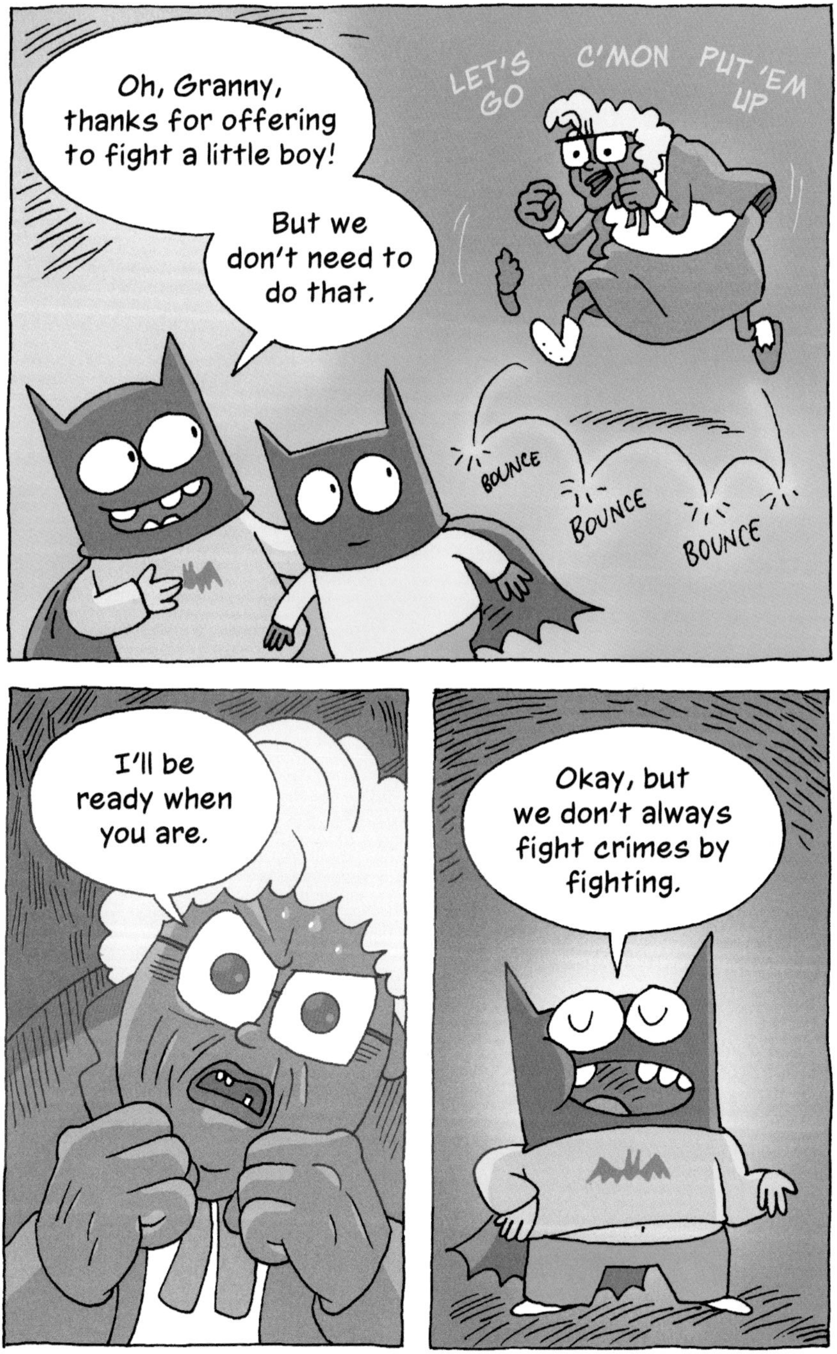
Oh, Granny, thanks for offering to fight a little boy!
But we don't need to do that.
LET'S GO
C'MON
PUT 'EM UP
BOUNCE
BOUNCE
BOUNCE
I'll be ready when you are.
Okay, but we don't always fight crimes by fighting.

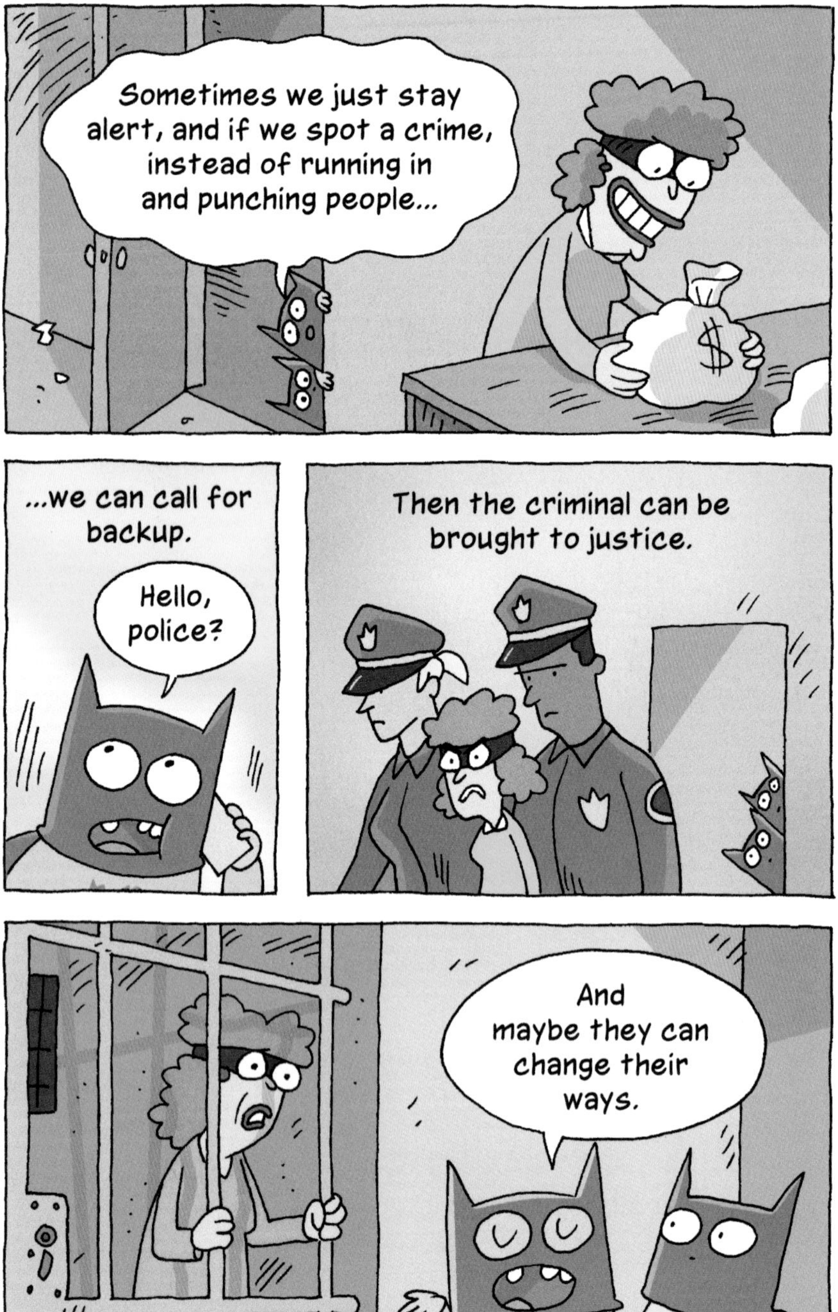
Sometimes we just stay alert, and if we spot a crime, instead of running in and punching people...
...we can call for backup.
Hello, police?
Then the criminal can be brought to justice.
And maybe they can change their ways.

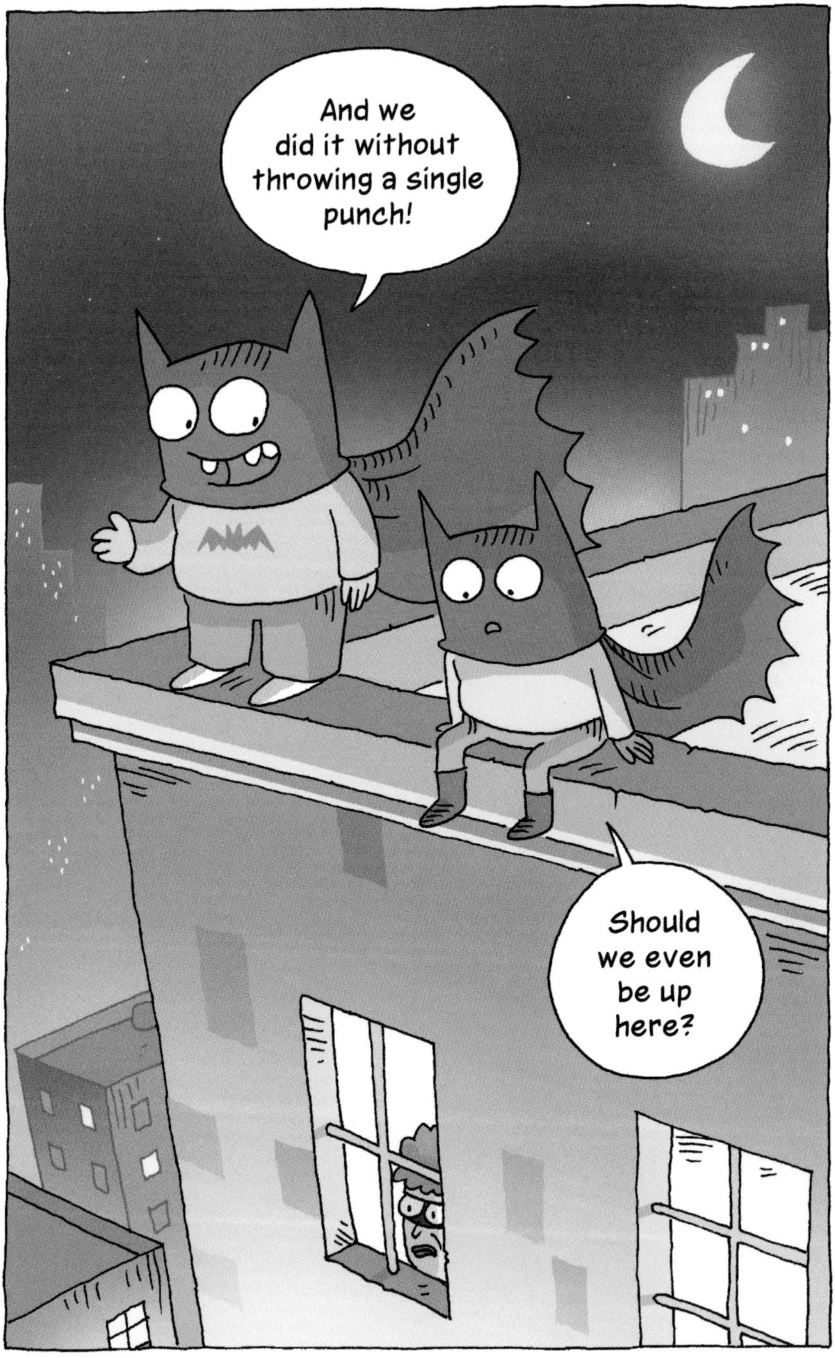
And we did it without throwing a single punch!
Should we even be up here?

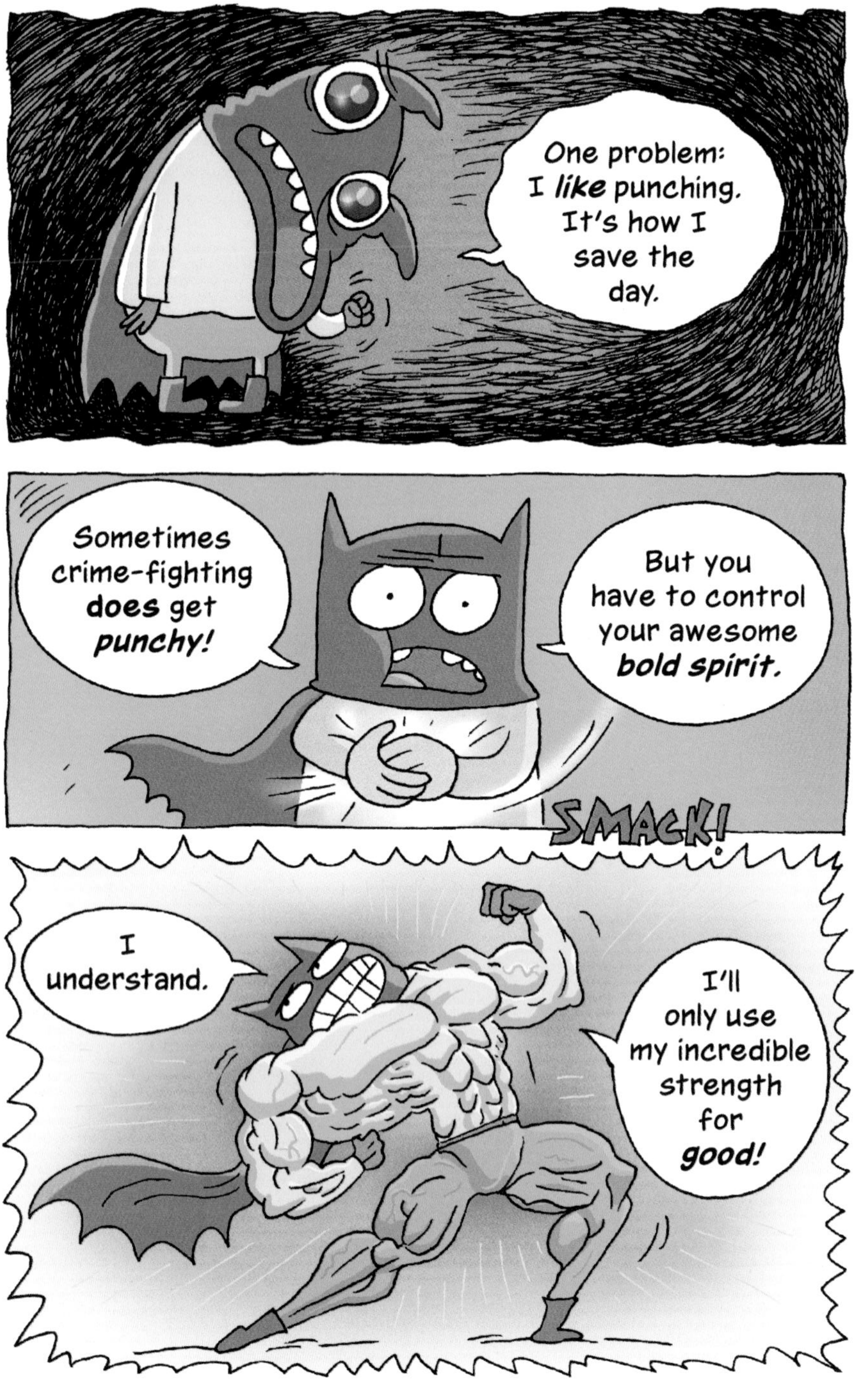
One problem: I *like* punching. It's how I save the day.
Sometimes crime-fighting **does** get ***punchy!***
But you have to control your awesome ***bold spirit.***
SMACK!
I understand.
I'll only use my incredible strength for ***good!***

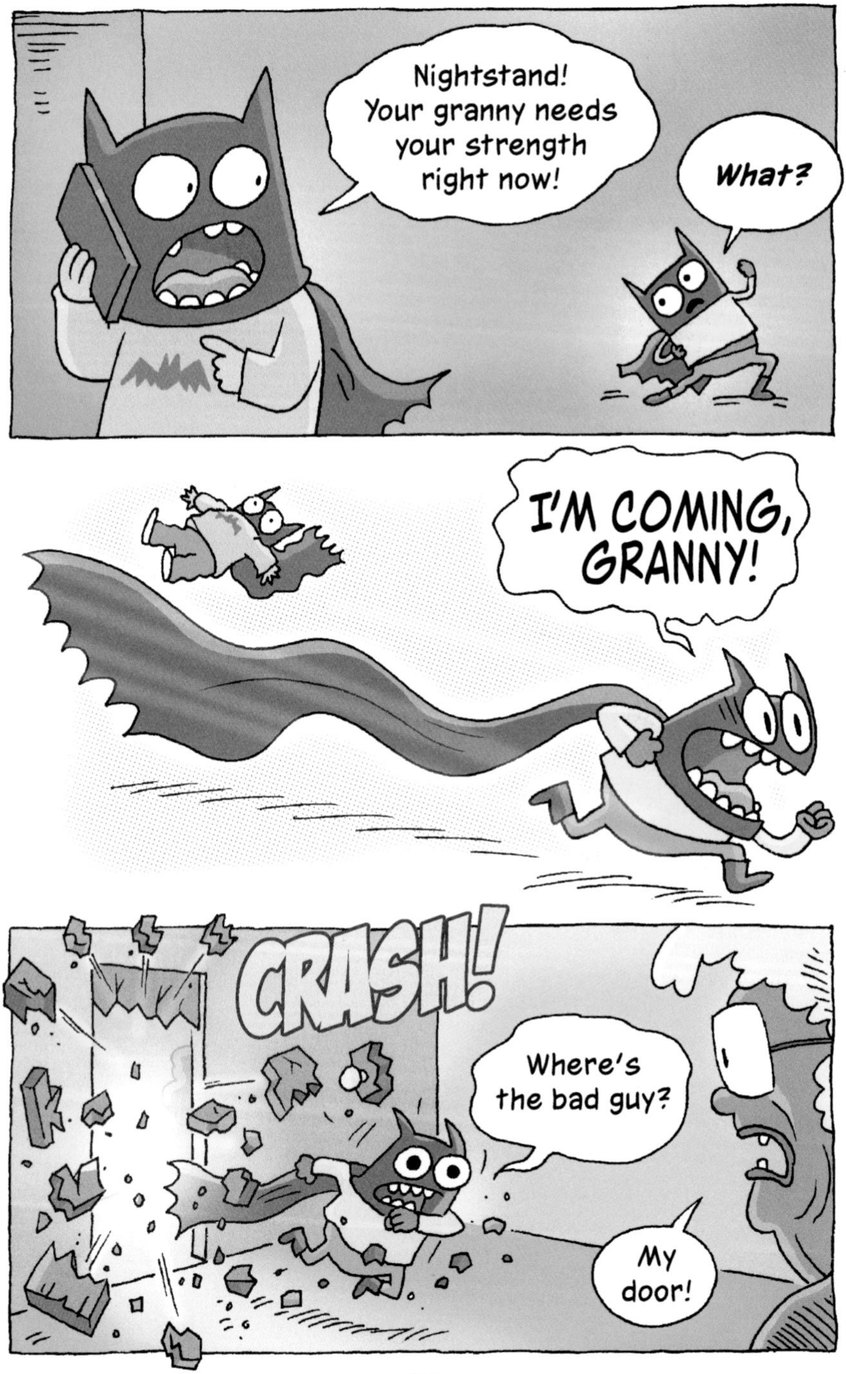
Nightstand! Your granny needs your strength right now!
What?
I'M COMING, GRANNY!
CRASH!
Where's the bad guy?
My door!

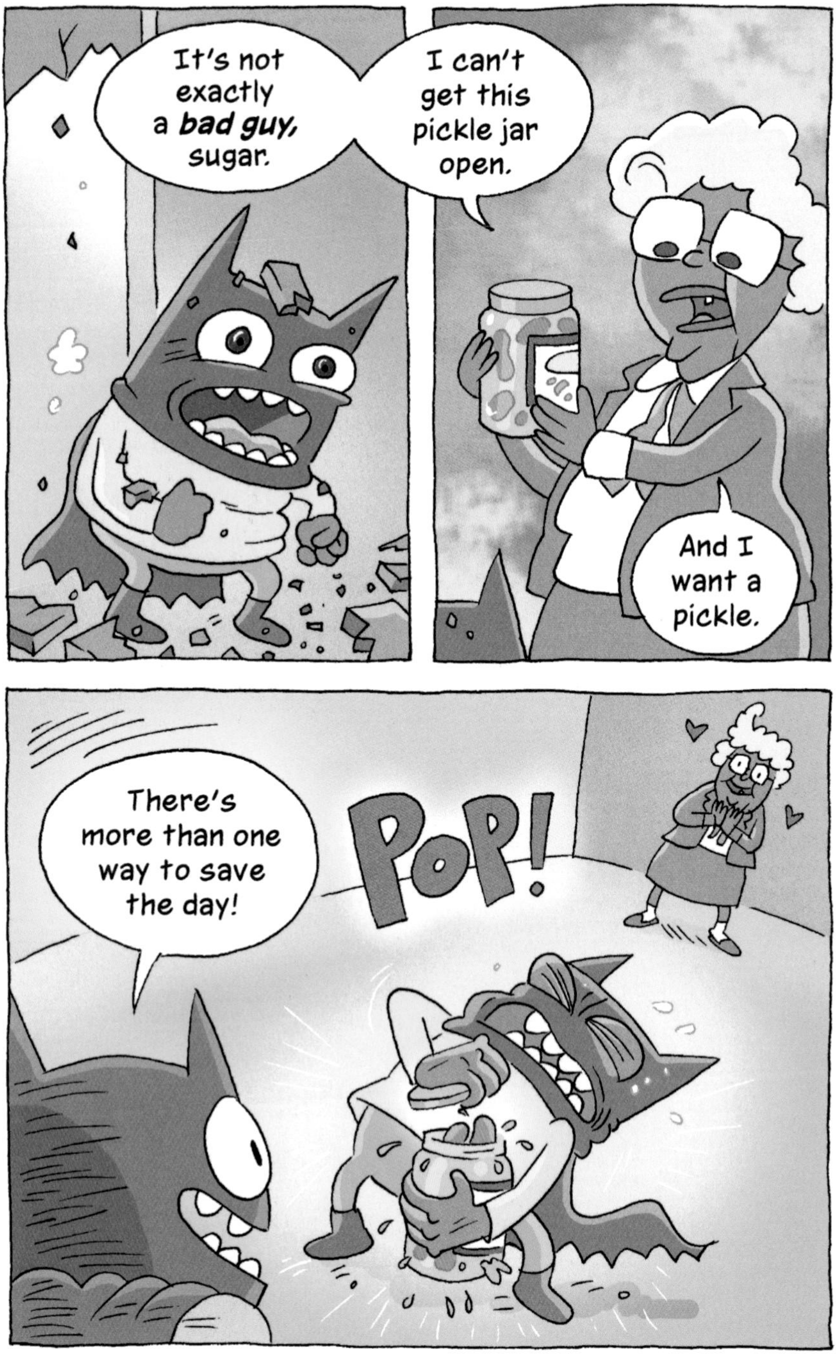
It's not exactly a **bad guy,** sugar.
I can't get this pickle jar open.
And I want a pickle.
There's more than one way to save the day!
POP!

The End

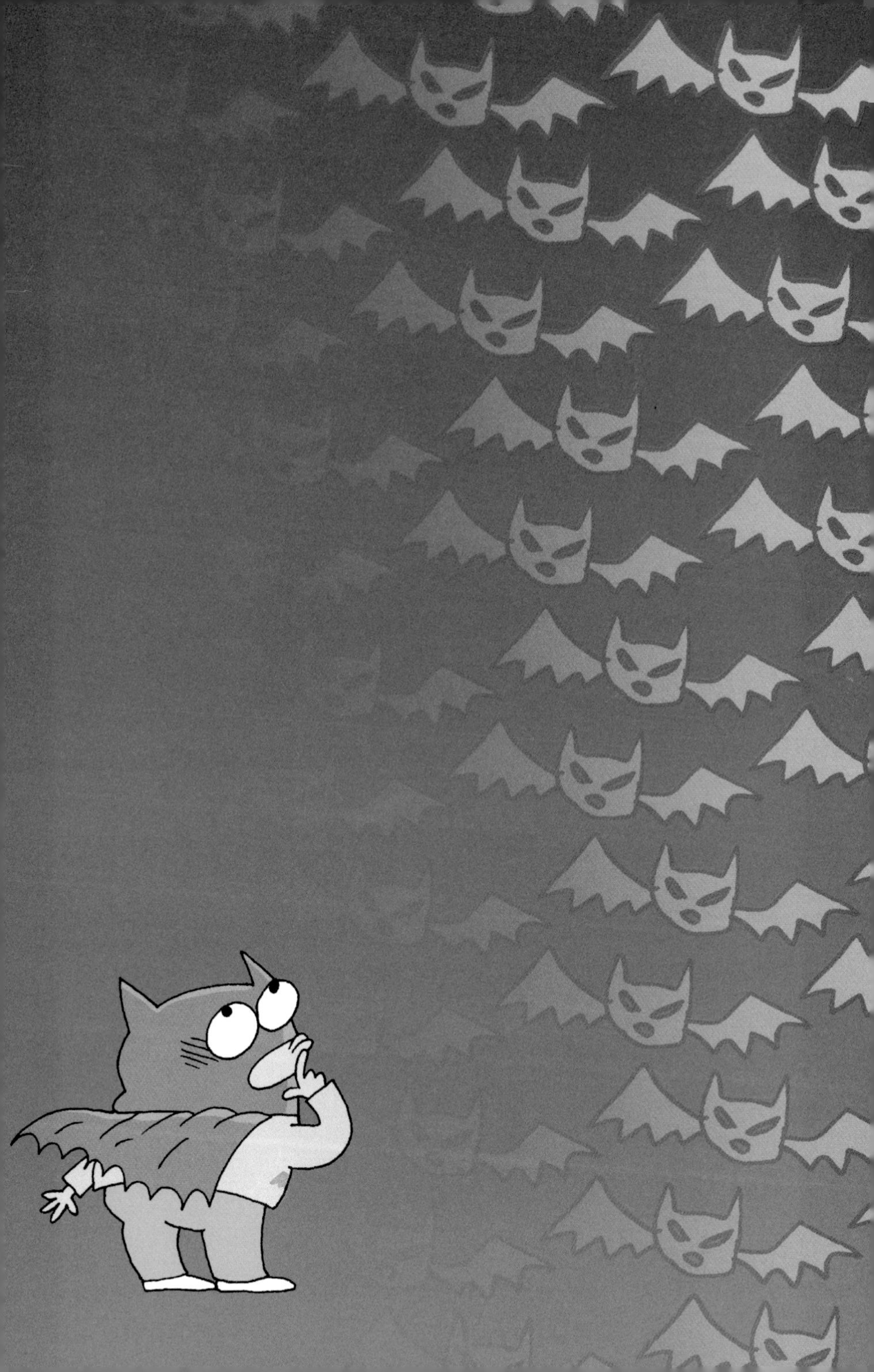

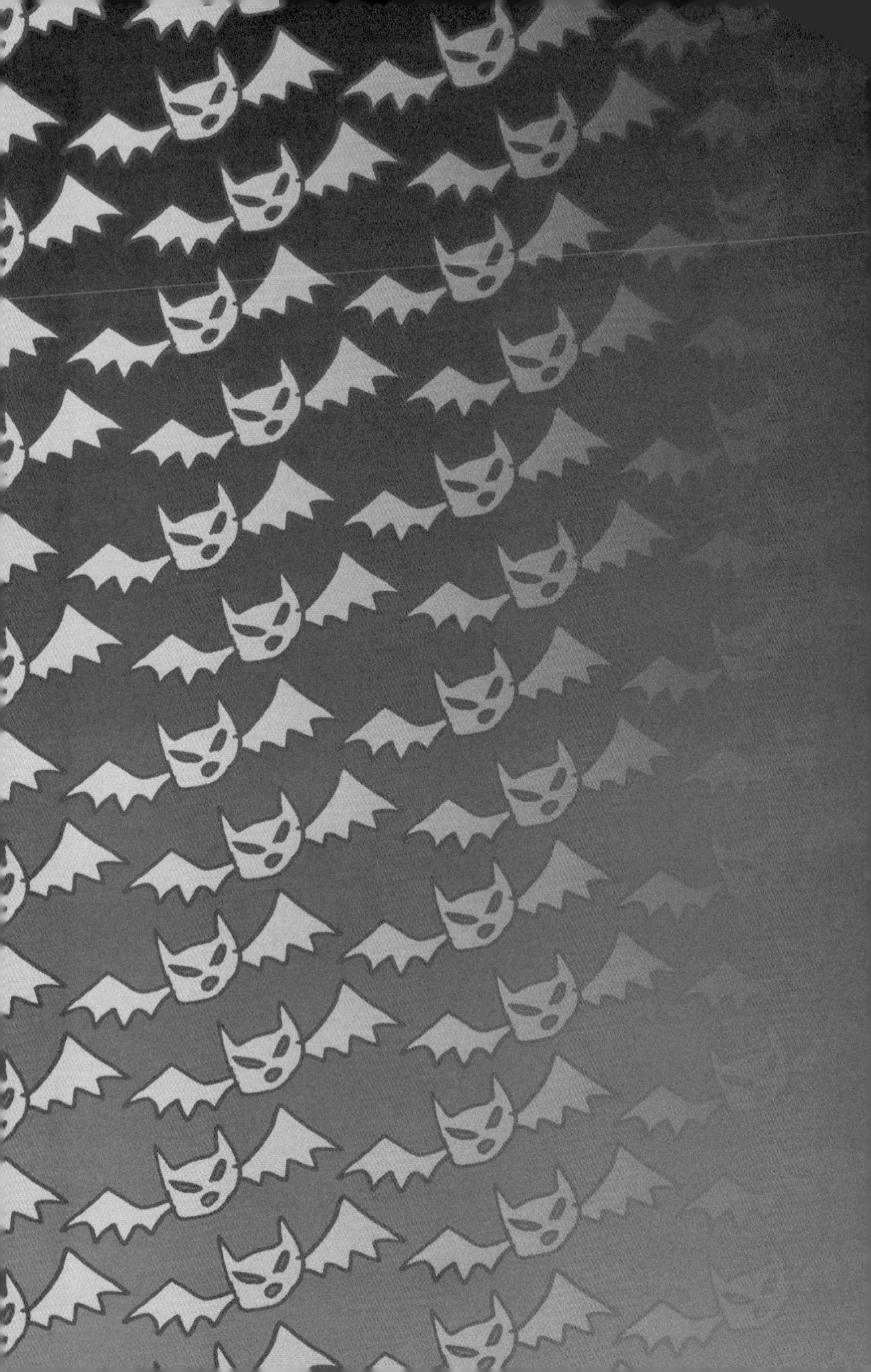

JIM BENTON is the *New York Times* bestselling author-illustrator of *Dear Dumb Diary*, *Franny K. Stein*, *Catwad*, and *It's Happy Bunny*. He is a winner of LIMA and Reuben awards and is an Eisner nominee. Jim is a member of the Writers Guild of America, the Society of Children's Book Writers and Illustrators, the National Cartoonists Society, and the Society of Illustrators. He has also contributed to *The Licensing Book*, *Dark Horse Presents*, *MAD* magazine, and the *New Yorker* magazine and was a joke writer for Illumination's *The Secret Life of Pets 2*.

BONK!

GLURK

WHAP!

Bruce Wayne wouldn't be Batman without his right-hand man, Alfred Pennyworth. But was Alfred born to be the greatest butler in the world? Not exactly...

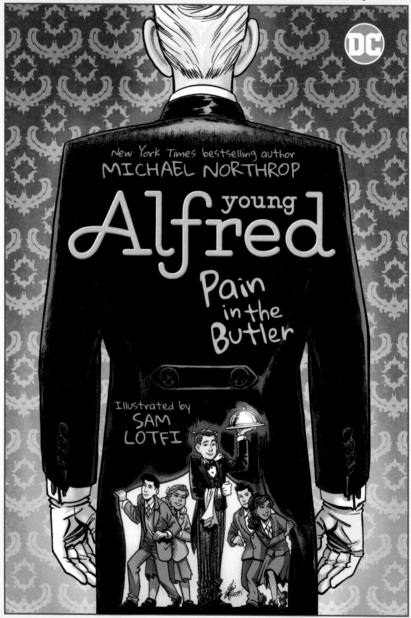

Want to know how the iconic Gotham butler got his start? From *New York Times* best-selling writer **Michael Northrop** (*TombQuest*, *Dear Justice League*), with striking visuals from artist **Sam Lotfi**, comes the story of a scrappy boy destined to become a legend.

In stores August 2023!

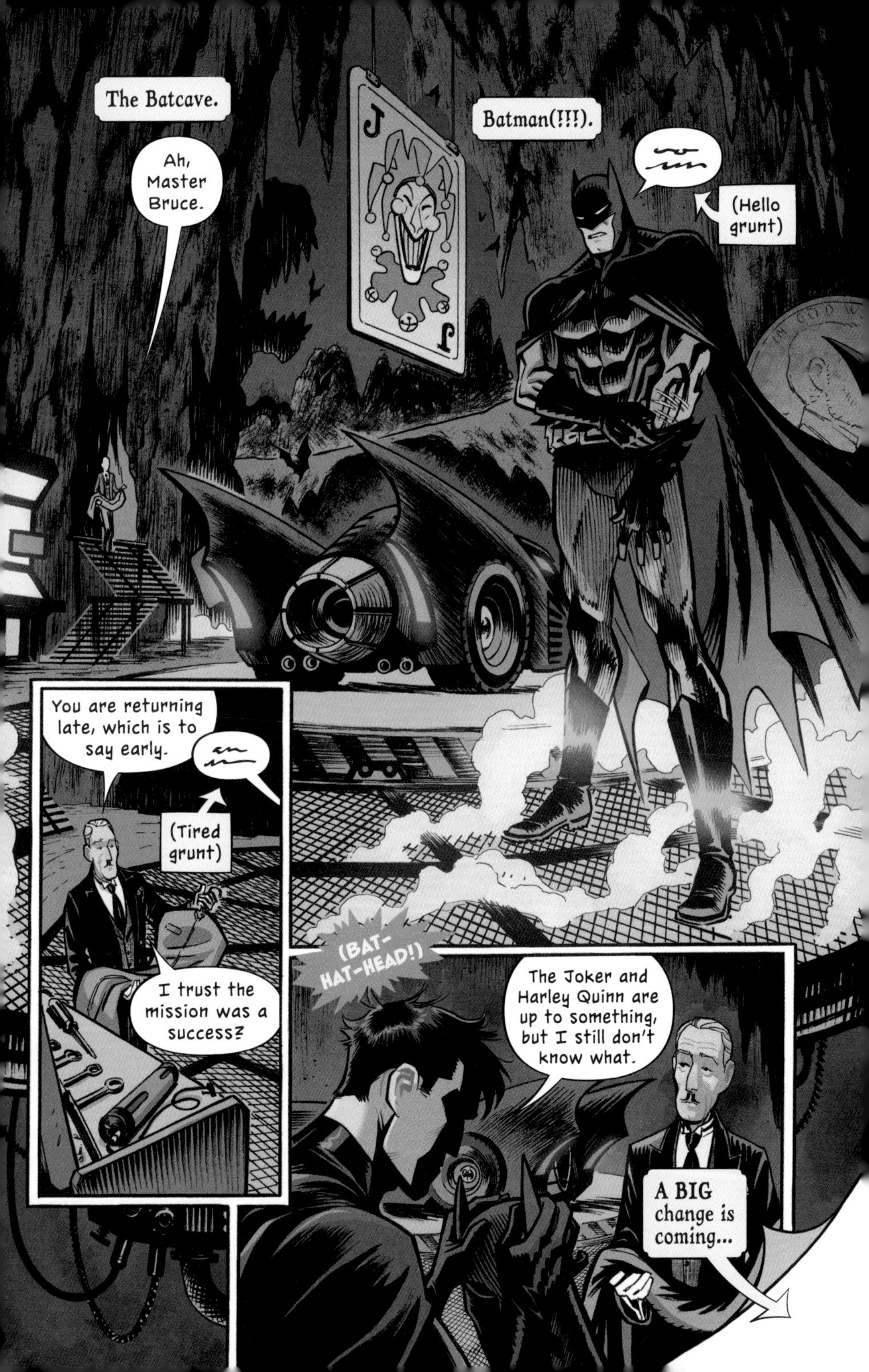

The Batcave.
Ah, Master Bruce.
Batman(!!!).
(Hello grunt)
You are returning late, which is to say early.
(Tired grunt)
I trust the mission was a success?
(BAT-HAT-HEAD!)
The Joker and Harley Quinn are up to something, but I still don't know what.
A BIG change is coming...

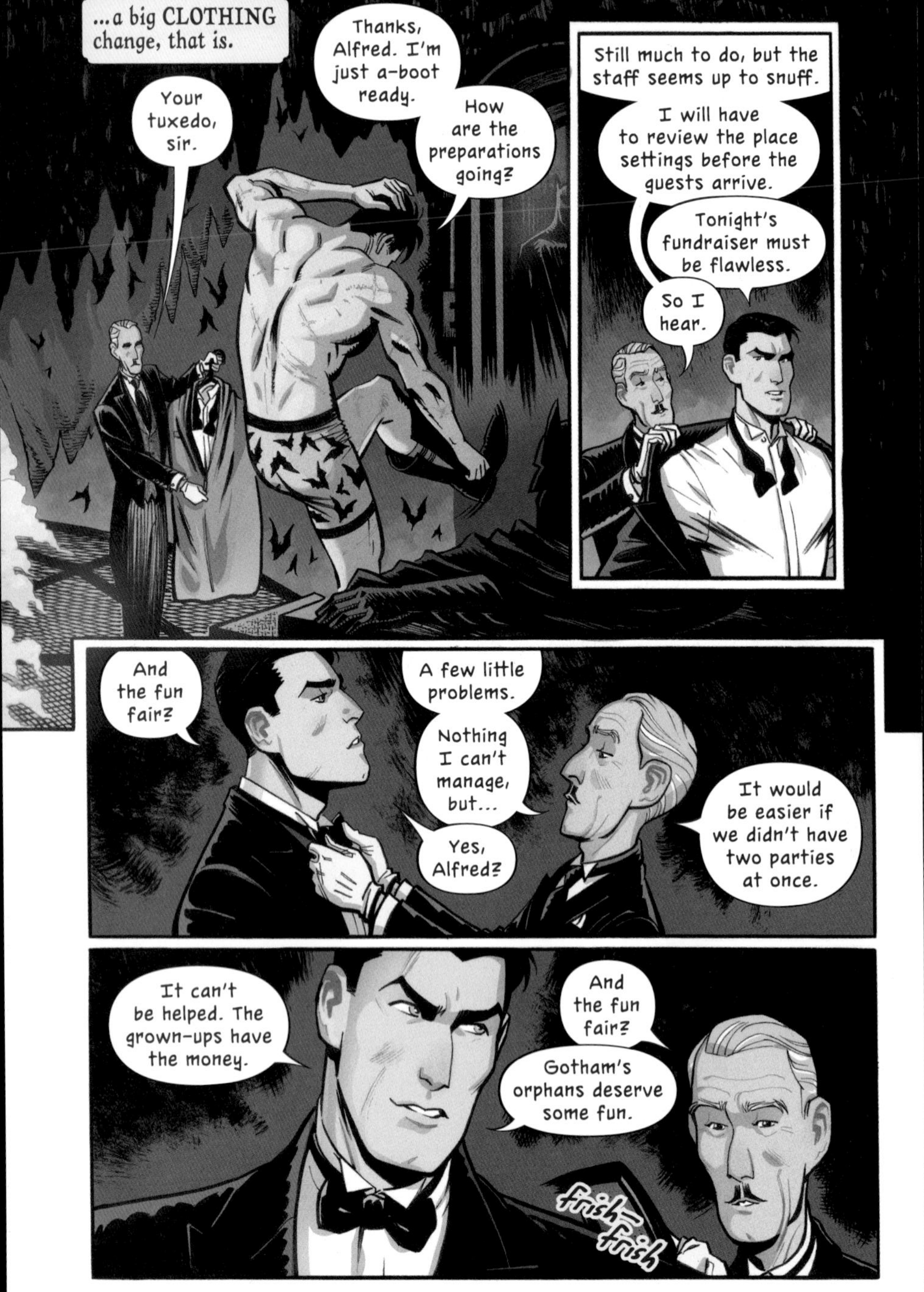
...a big CLOTHING change, that is.
Your tuxedo, sir.
Thanks, Alfred. I'm just a-boot ready.
How are the preparations going?
Still much to do, but the staff seems up to snuff.
I will have to review the place settings before the guests arrive.
Tonight's fundraiser must be flawless.
So I hear.
And the fun fair?
A few little problems.
Nothing I can't manage, but...
Yes, Alfred?
It would be easier if we didn't have two parties at once.
It can't be helped. The grown-ups have the money.
And the fun fair?
Gotham's orphans deserve some fun.
frish frish

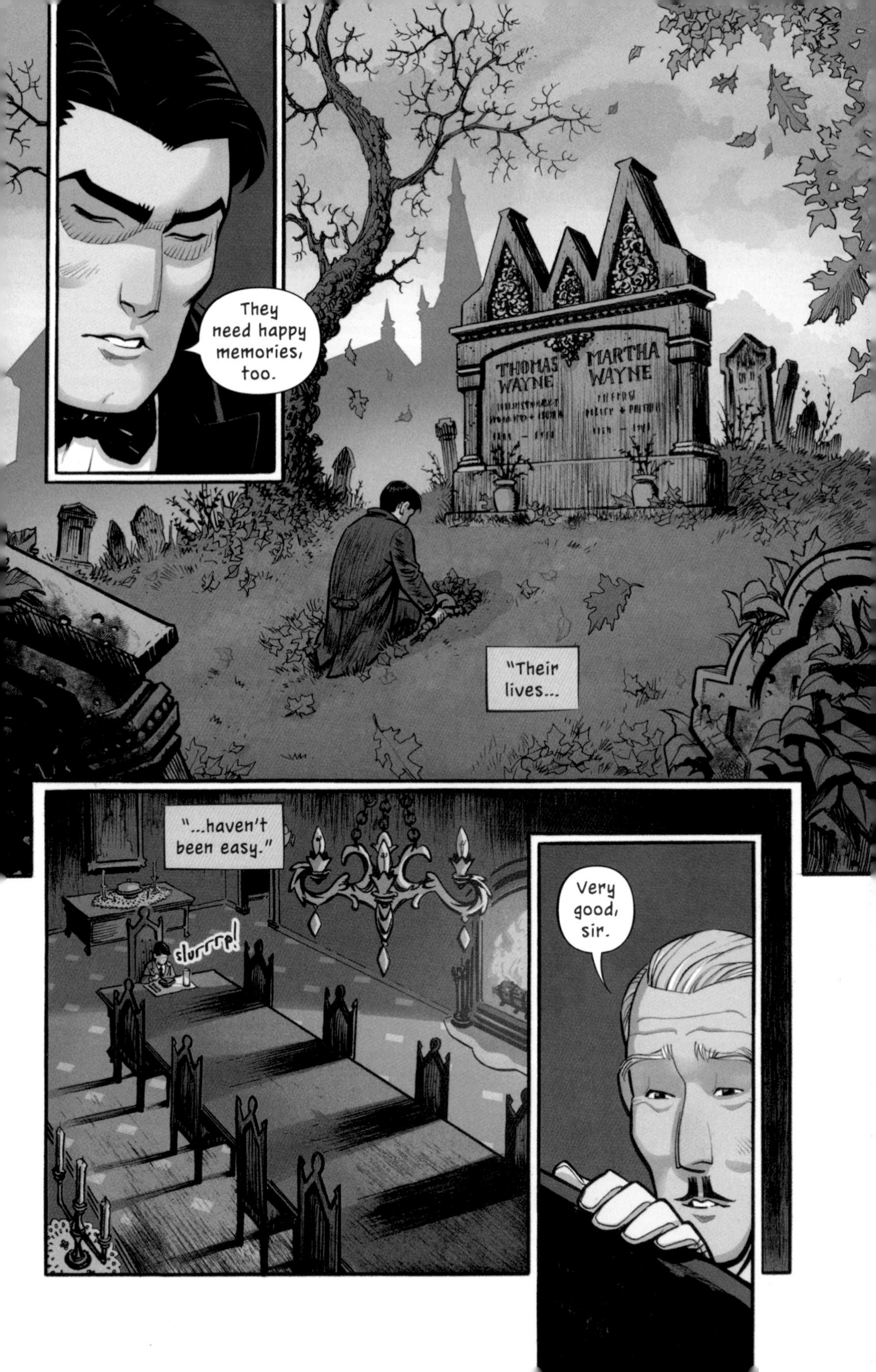
They need happy memories, too.
THOMAS WAYNE
MARTHA WAYNE
"Their lives...
"...haven't been easy."
slurrrp!
Very good, sir.

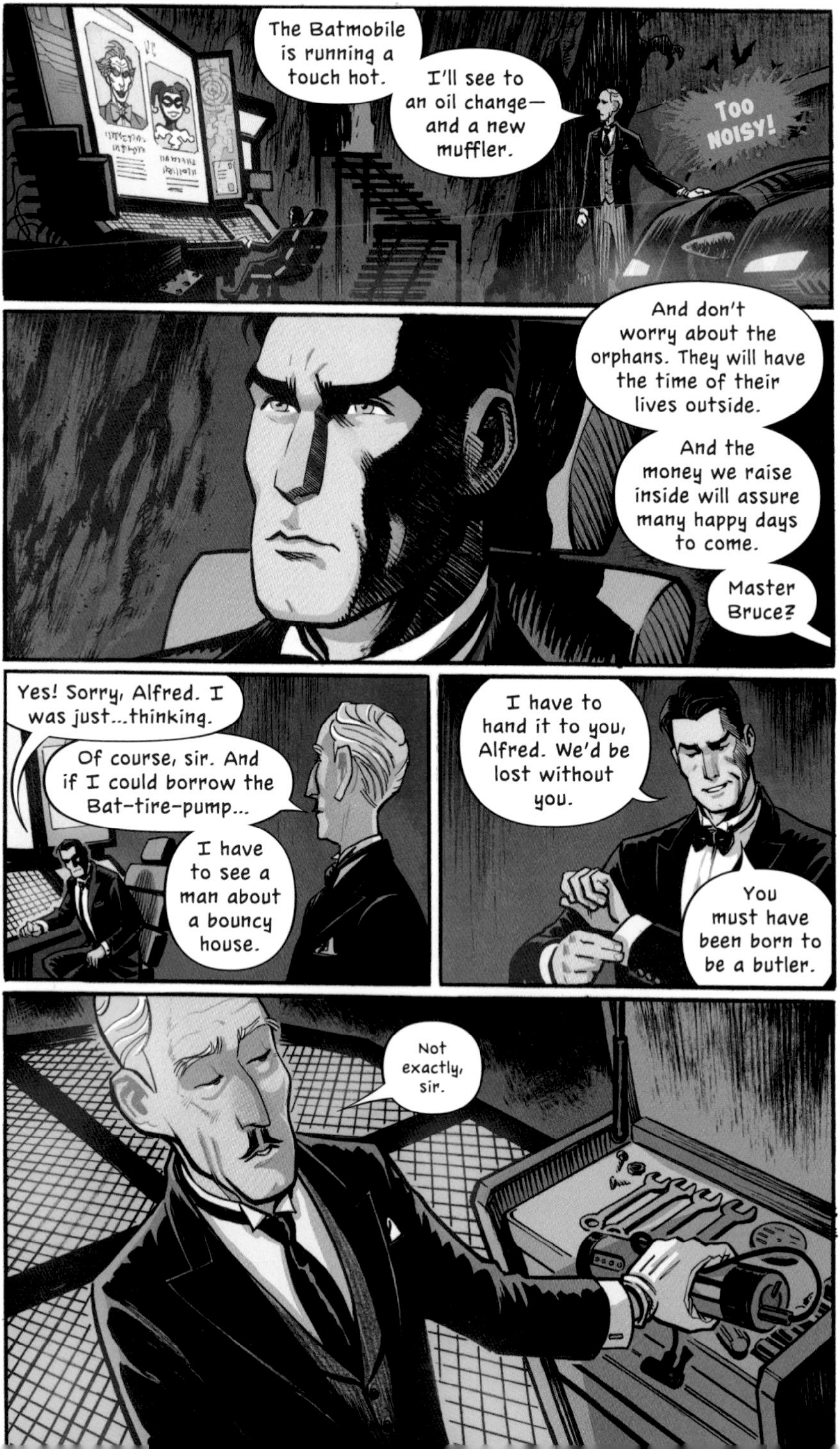
The Batmobile is running a touch hot.
I'll see to an oil change—and a new muffler.
TOO NOISY!
And don't worry about the orphans. They will have the time of their lives outside.
And the money we raise inside will assure many happy days to come.
Master Bruce?
Yes! Sorry, Alfred. I was just...thinking.
Of course, sir. And if I could borrow the Bat-tire-pump...
I have to see a man about a bouncy house.
I have to hand it to you, Alfred. We'd be lost without you.
You must have been born to be a butler.
Not exactly, sir.

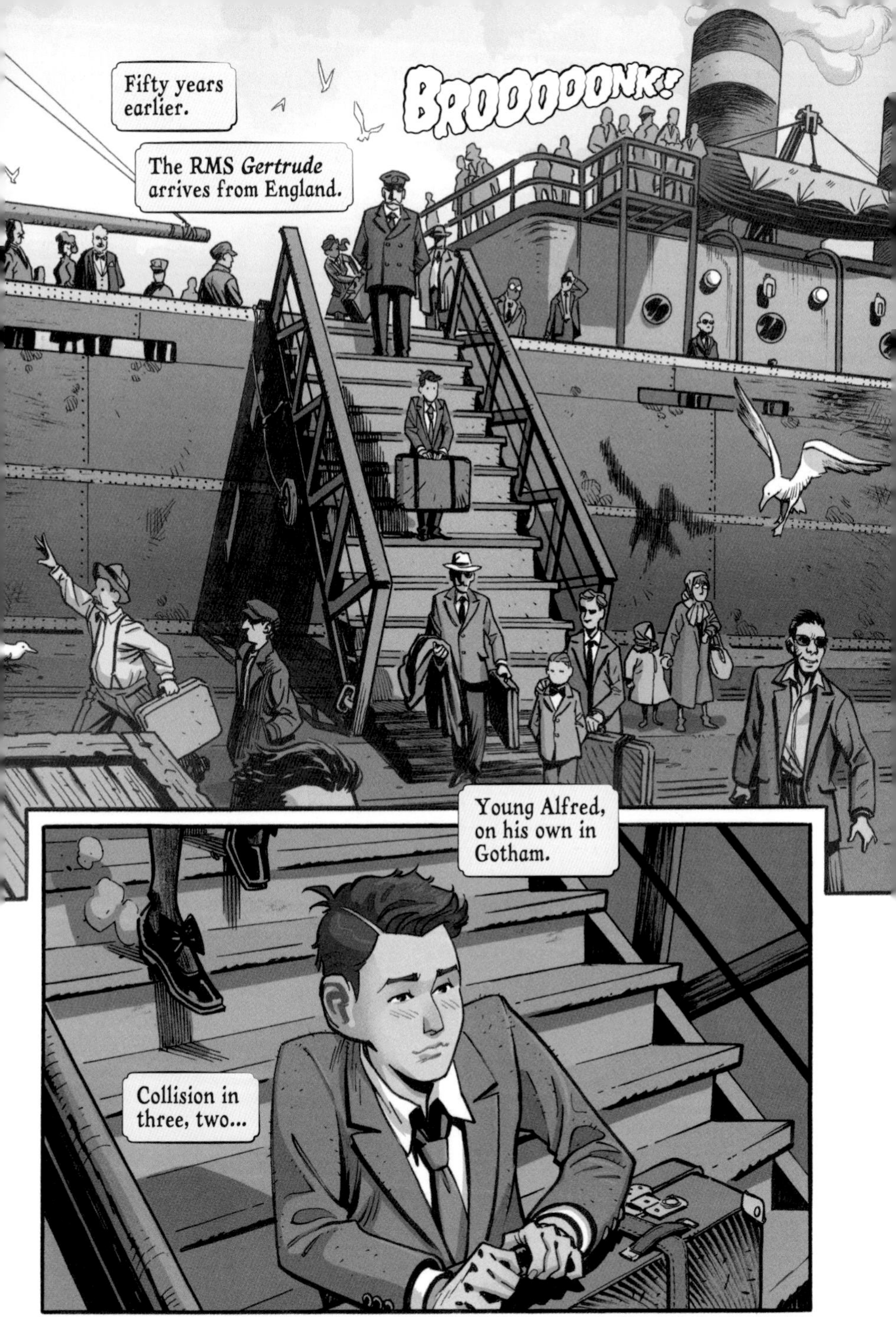

Fifty years earlier.
The RMS *Gertrude* arrives from England.
BROOOOOONK!
Young Alfred, on his own in Gotham.
Collision in three, two...

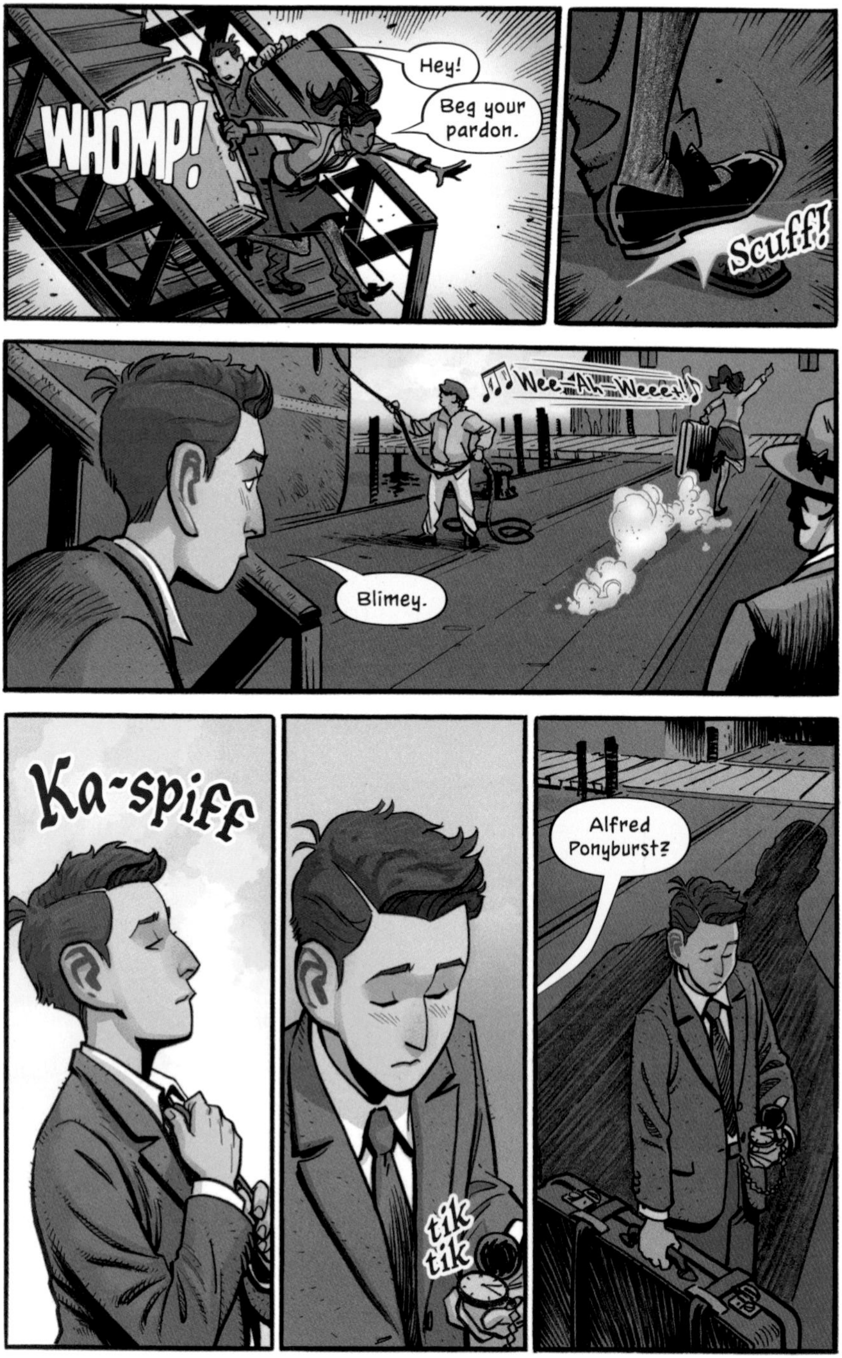
WHOMP!
Hey!
Beg your pardon.
Scuff!
Wee-Ah-Weeee!
Blimey.
Ka-spiff
tik
tik
Alfred Ponyburst?

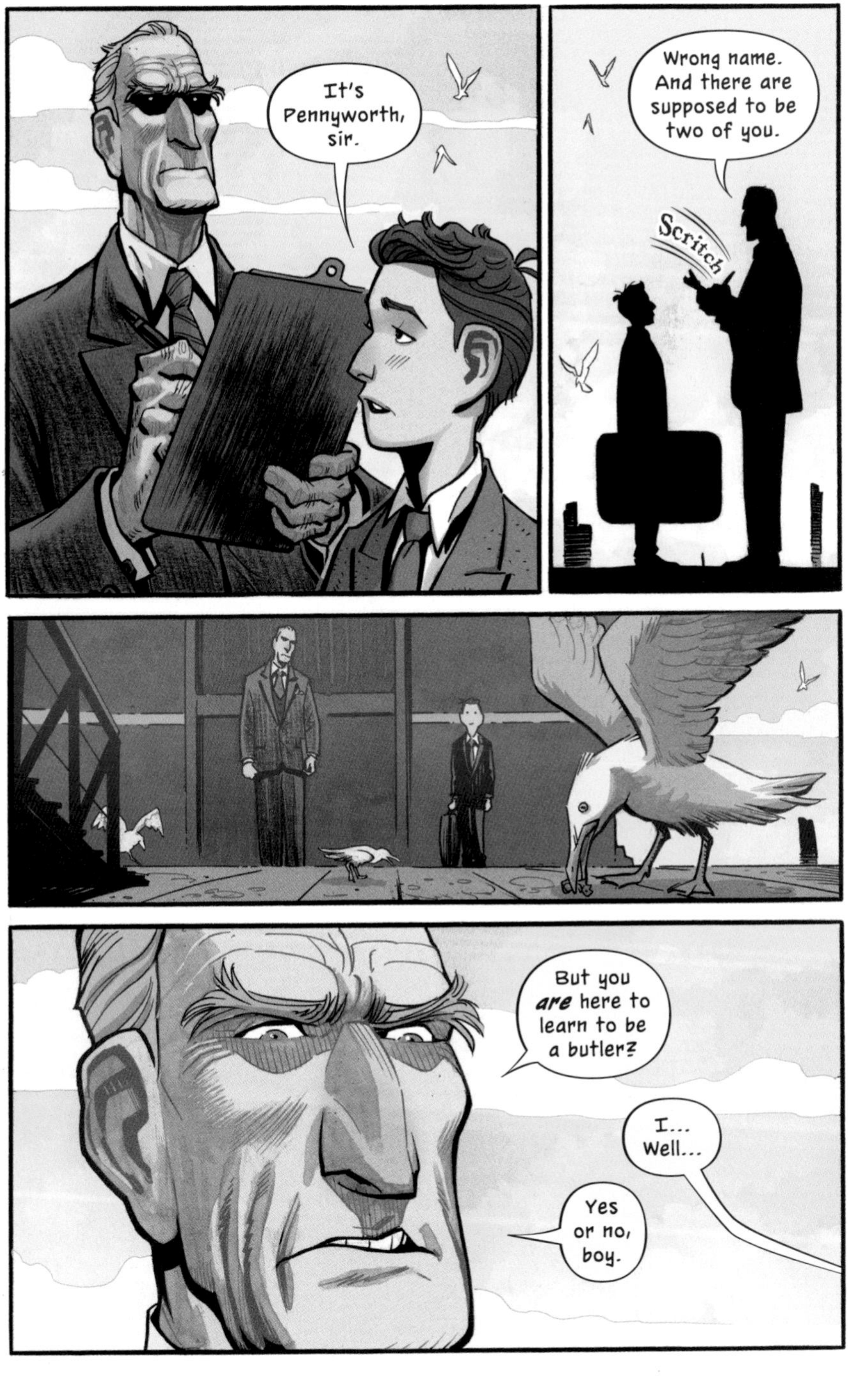
It's Pennyworth, sir.
Wrong name. And there are supposed to be two of you.
Scritch
But you *are* here to learn to be a butler?
I... Well...
Yes or no, boy.

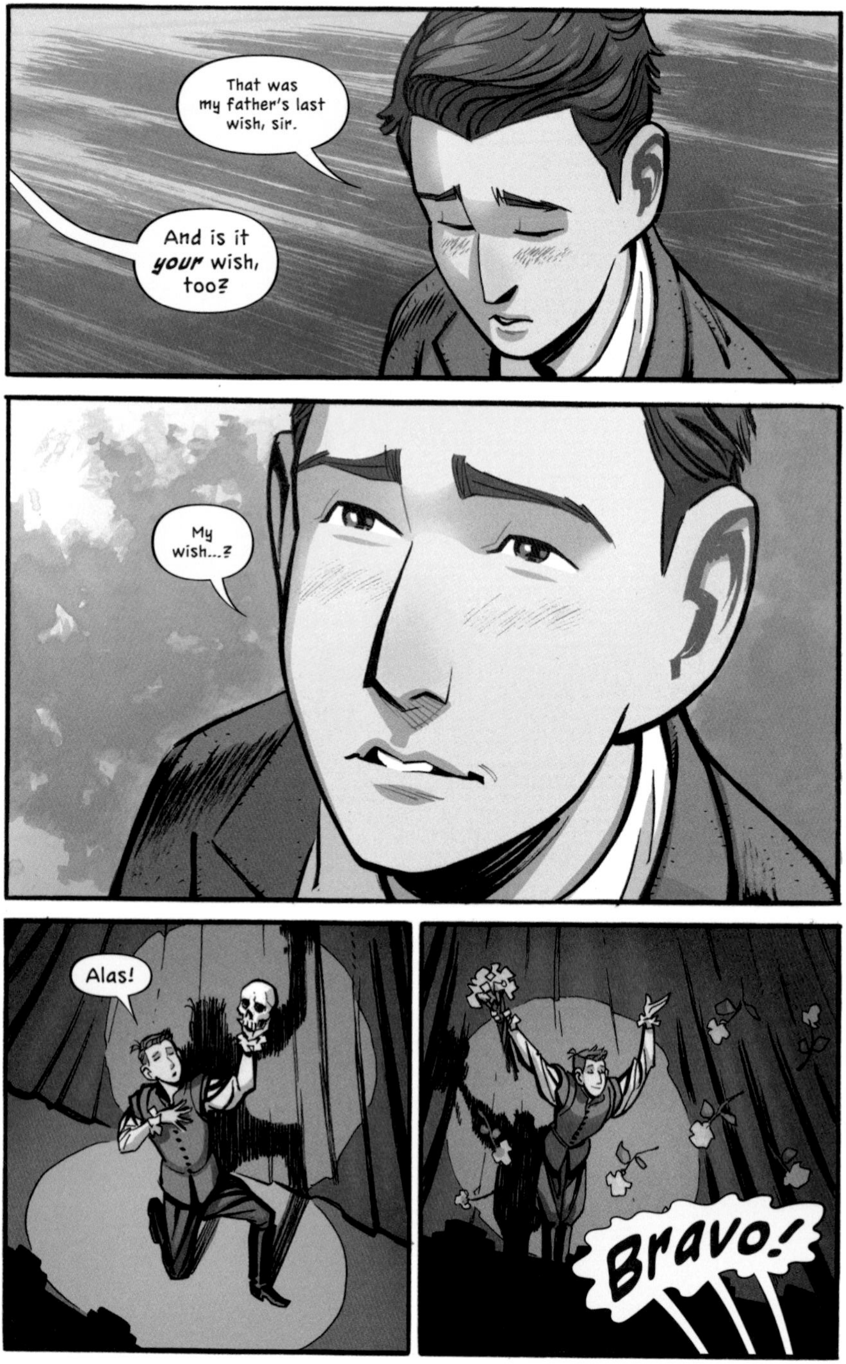
That was my father's last wish, sir.
And is it *your* wish, too?
My wish...?
Alas!
Bravo!

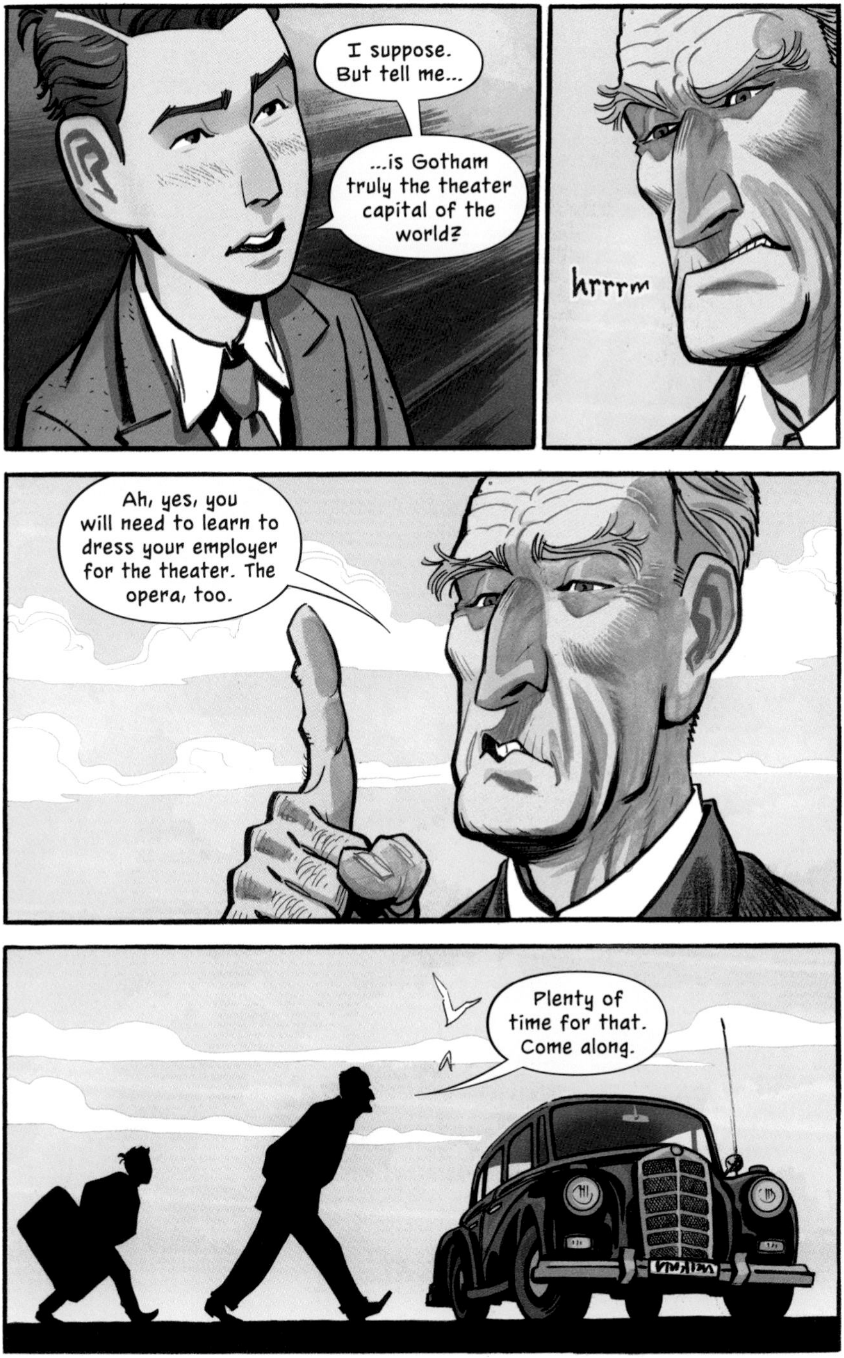
I suppose. But tell me...
...is Gotham truly the theater capital of the world?
hrrrm
Ah, yes, you will need to learn to dress your employer for the theater. The opera, too.
Plenty of time for that. Come along.

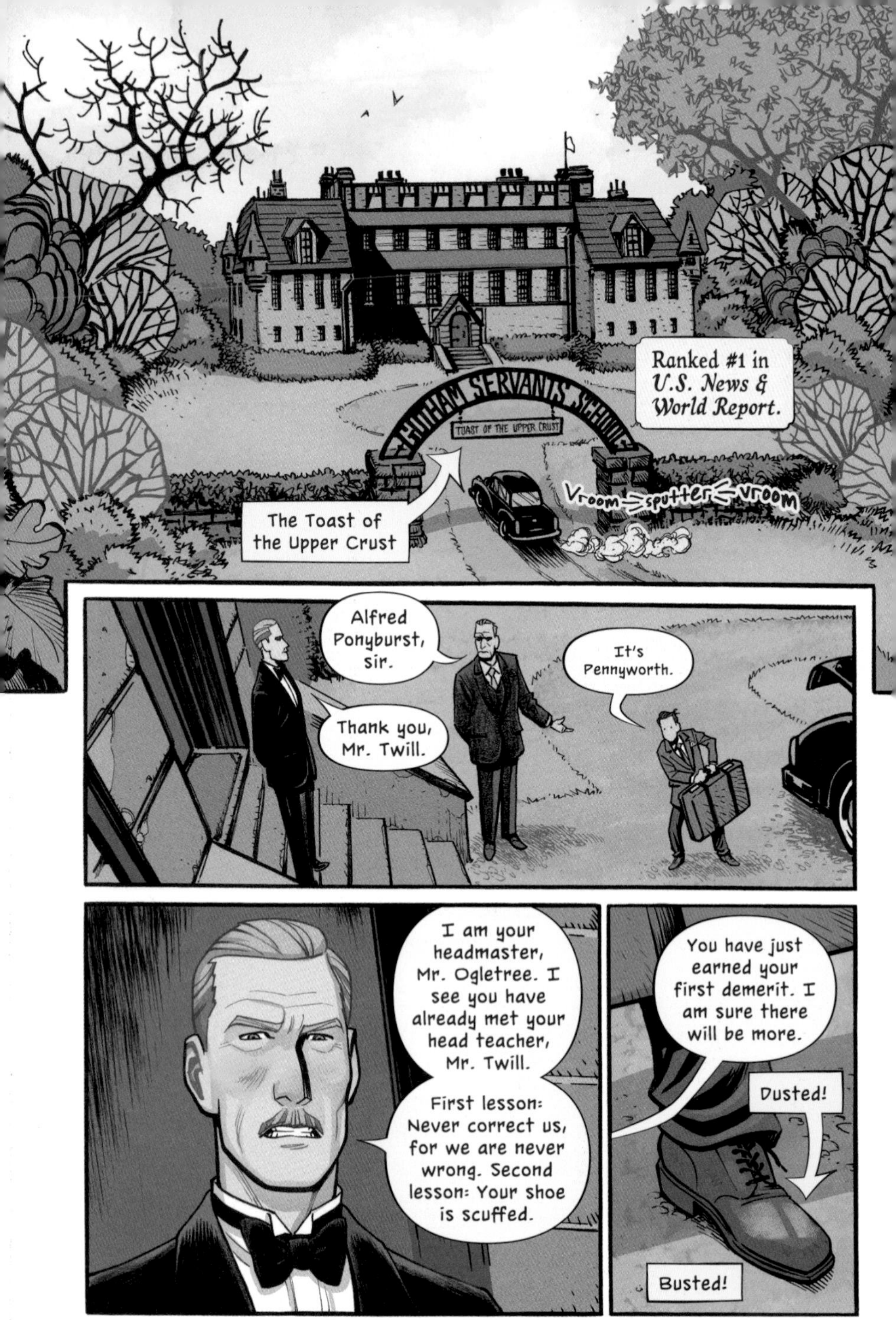
GOTHAM SERVANTS SCHOOL
TOAST OF THE UPPER CRUST
Ranked #1 in U.S. News & World Report.
The Toast of the Upper Crust
Vroom sputter vroom
Alfred Ponyburst, sir.
It's Pennyworth.
Thank you, Mr. Twill.
I am your headmaster, Mr. Ogletree. I see you have already met your head teacher, Mr. Twill.
First lesson: Never correct us, for we are never wrong. Second lesson: Your shoe is scuffed.
You have just earned your first demerit. I am sure there will be more.
Dusted!
Busted!

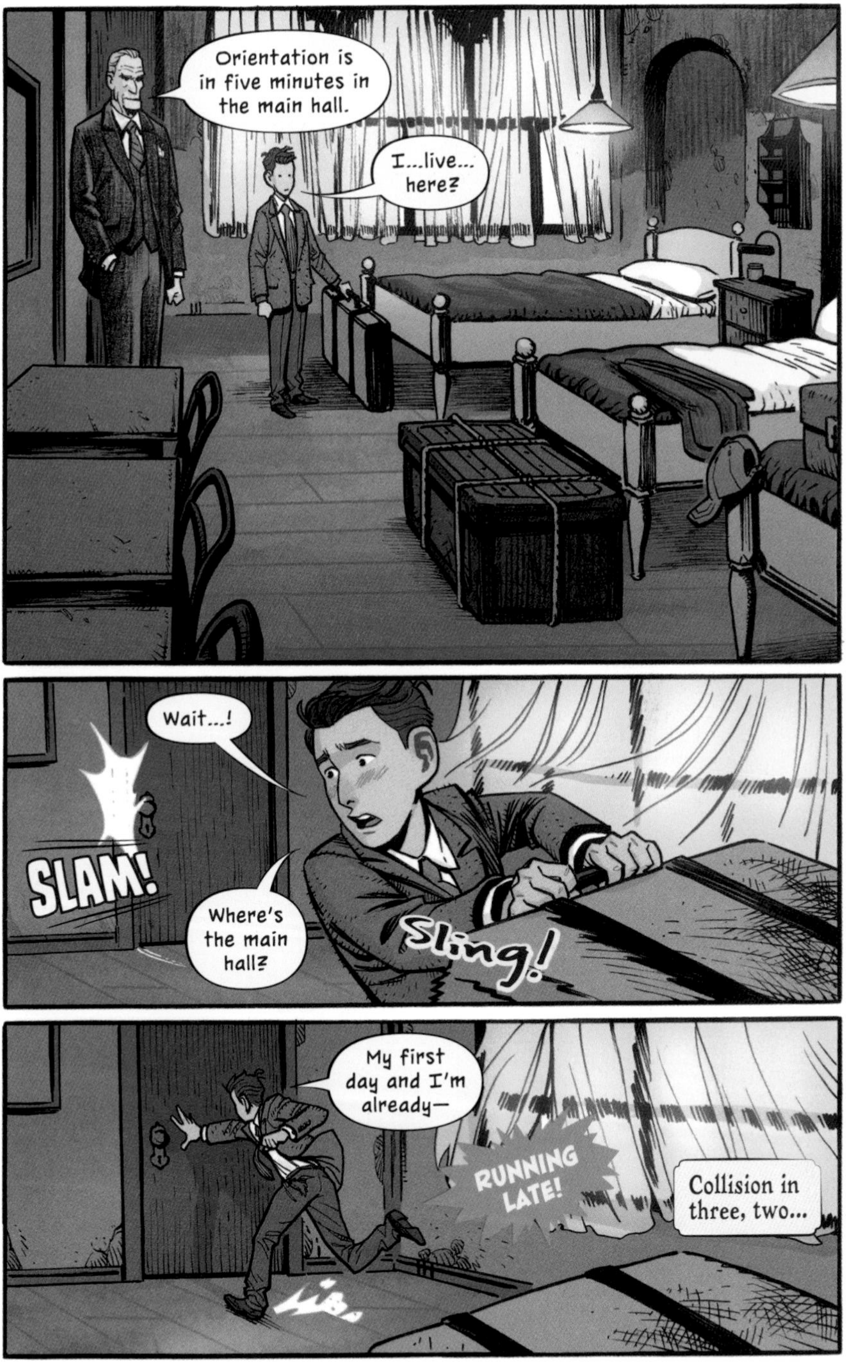
Orientation is in five minutes in the main hall.
I...live... here?
Wait...!
SLAM!
Where's the main hall?
Sling!
My first day and I'm already—
RUNNING LATE!
Collision in three, two...

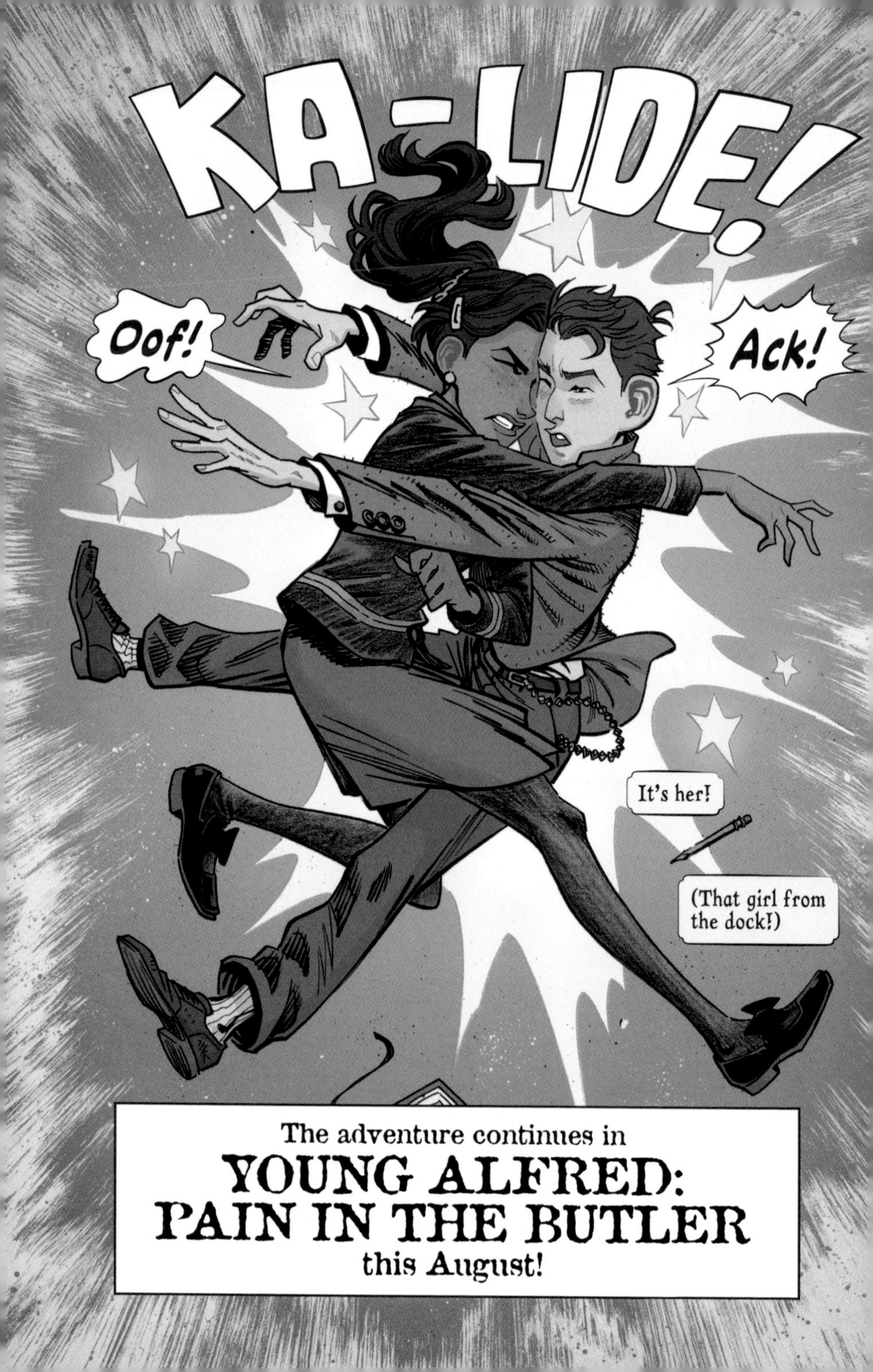
KA-LIDE!
Oof!
Ack!
It's her!
(That girl from the dock!)
The adventure continues in
YOUNG ALFRED: PAIN IN THE BUTLER
this August!

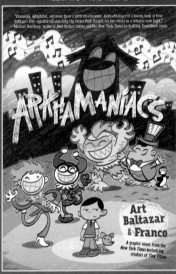
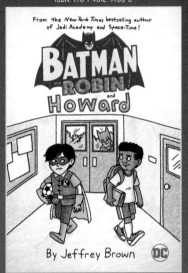
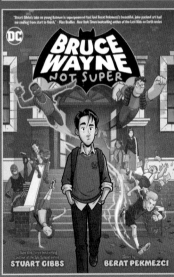

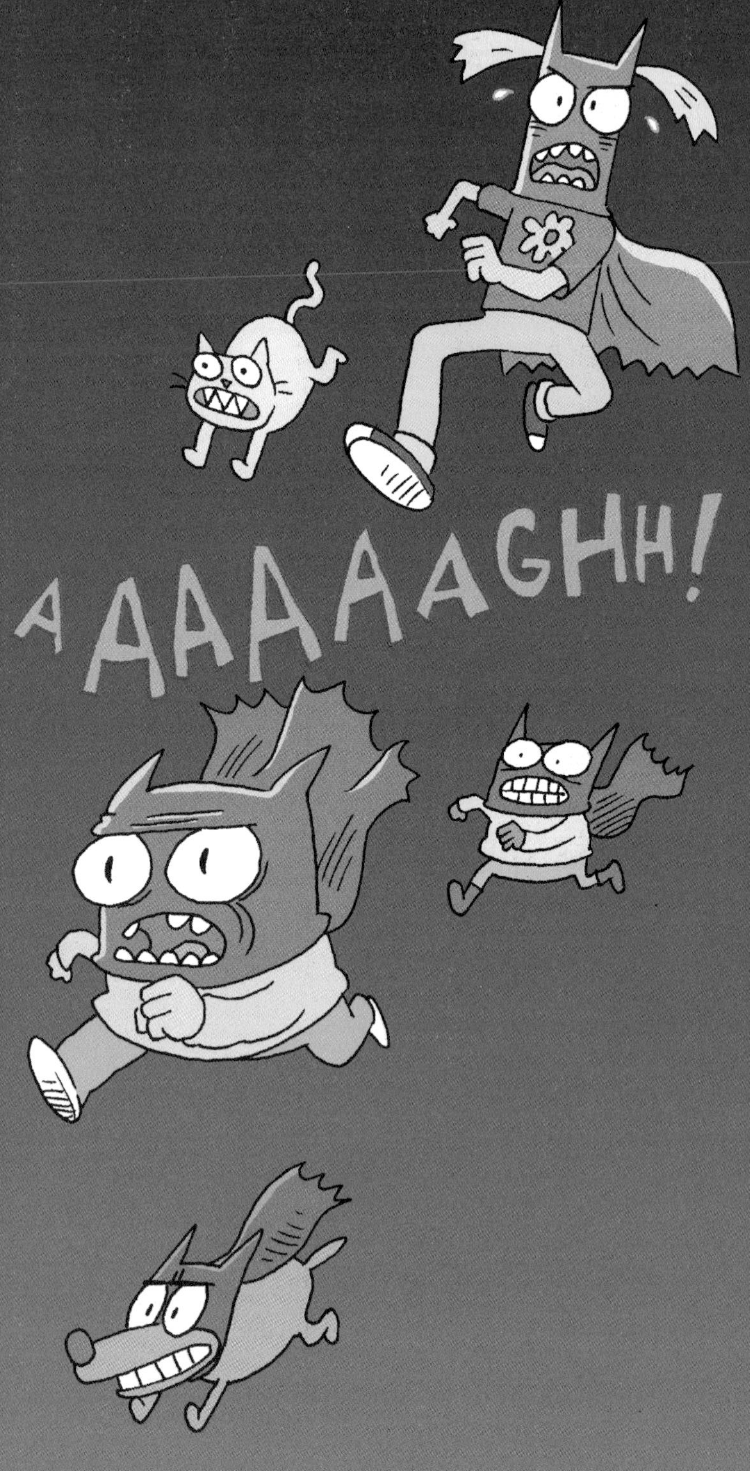
AAAAAAGHH!